THE
SURGEON

by

Francis Roe

A SIGNET BOOK

SIGNET
Published by the Penguin Group
Penguin Books USA Inc., 375 Hudson Street,
New York, New York 10014, U.S.A.
Penguin Books Ltd, 27 Wrights Lane,
London W8 5TZ, England
Penguin Books Australia Ltd, Ringwood,
Victoria, Australia
Penguin Books Canada Ltd, 10 Alcorn Avenue,
Toronto, Ontario, Canada M4V 3B2
Penguin Books (N.Z.) Ltd, 182–190 Wairau Road,
Auckland 10, New Zealand

Penguin Books Ltd, Registered Offices:
Harmondsworth, Middlesex, England

First published by Signet,
an imprint of Dutton Signet,
a division of Penguin Books USA Inc.

First Printing, September, 1994
10 9 8 7 6 5 4 3 2 1

PUBLISHER'S NOTE
This is a work of fiction. Names, characters, places, and incidents either are the
product of the author's imagination or are used fictitiously, and any resemblance to
actual persons, living or dead, events, or locales is entirely coincidental.

THE TENSION IN THE OPERATING ROOM WAS PALPABLE

Dr. Paula Cairns was very aware of the old surgical dictum that surgeons should never operate on their peers. She could feel her heart pounding as she looked at her patient's legs, both of which had turned a mottled blue.

Paula turned to the anesthesiologist. "He's clotted his graft. We'll have to use the arterioscope."

Dr. Pinero's eyes widened in shock. "You can't use that thing! The administration refused to allow you to use it, only a few days ago. It's still experimental, and you think you're going to be allowed to use it on the chief of surgery, of all people?"

"*We have to use it*. There isn't time. Maurice could die."

The tension in the room was so intense it seemed to crackle. People had gathered outside, and Paula felt all their eyes watching her through the windows in the double doors. She pushed the button that activated the arterioscope. A faint hum came from the electric motors, and the green numbers on the digital pressure gauge flicked up.

Paula felt her knees shaking. But she had to carry on—there was no way she could let Maurice Bennett, her friend and boss, die. . . .

THE SURGEON

ACKNOWLEDGMENTS

In this book I have relied on the generous expertise of several people: Paul Cassel, authority on computers and computer fraud; Chris Fuqua, mechanic extraordinaire, who shared his knowledge of various types of automotive mayhem; Carol Cassell (not related to Paul) for her insights into the female condition; Tasha Mackler for her eagle-eyed reading and thoughtful comments; and Linda Ann Smith, M.D., F.A.C.S., who shared her firsthand knowledge of the problems of women in the men's world of surgery.

Working with a really first-class agent is a rare pleasure—thanks, Matt Bialer. And, once again, special thanks to Michaela Hamilton, John Paine, and the rest of the Dutton Signet team for making it all happen.

Chapter One

Paula Cairns watched the Connecticut coastline slide slowly past, courtesy of Amtrak's antiquated Metroliner that was taking her from New York back to New Coventry. She was in the window seat, and the heavyset, red-faced young man sitting next to her kept glancing sideways from his magazine to her, obviously looking for an opportunity to open a conversation. He'd got on at Stamford, looked her over, and taken the adjoining seat, although the train was almost empty.

As he had noticed, Paula Cairns was something to look at: medium to tall, with a discreet but arresting figure, and clear, amused green eyes that seemed interested in everything they looked at. Her hair was thick, dark, with big, springy, occasionally unruly curls. She had a characteristic way of tossing them out of her face that her father once told her reminded him of a fidgety racehorse.

Paula was on her way back from a national surgical research meeting at Columbia-Presbyterian Hospital in New York, where she'd done her surgical training. She'd visited with lots of old friends, including her old boss, and had presented a paper that caused a big stir among the scientists and the medical press. Paula knew that she was on the threshold of something so big that it took her breath away, but she'd worked hard and spent long hours in the lab, and it had taken all of her passion and energy to get it to this point.

"You going up to Boston?" The man beside her leaned over, too close. He'd obviously been drinking, although it was not yet nine in the morning.

"No." She smiled briefly, having no desire to be antagonistic, then looked out of the window to terminate the conversation. The train chugged through the countryside, past the wide expanses of marshy wetlands that had been saved, at least temporarily, from developers. Rattling into Milford, the train slowed, and its whistle sounded mournfully for the level crossings. Paula caught a glimpse of waiting cars and pedestrians, their faces tilted up as the train came by, and heard the strident sound of crossing bells, fading as soon as they passed. She looked at her watch: another half hour and they'd be in New Coventry. Over the gray corrugated roofs of the boatyards she could see the sailboats lined up in a motley parade, still on their winter trestles, most of them covered with tarpaulins but some with people already getting ready for the season. One old sloop had a man kneeling on the deck with an electric sander, another had two parka-clad men caulking between the timbers, and next to them a couple applied a coat of rust–red bottom paint on the keel of their boat. The scene reminded Paula of her childhood, not so many years ago, and how restless her father would get when spring came, anticipating that longed-for day when the boat covers would come off and a new season of sailing would start.

"You a teacher or something?"

Paula turned squarely to face him. "No, I'm not," she said in a firm voice. His face was only a few inches from hers, and she could smell the beer on his breath. "Now listen," she said in a level tone, "I've got a lot of stuff to think about right now and I don't want to talk, okay?"

She turned back to the window and tried to concentrate on what she'd heard at the research meeting, or rather in a couple of confidential conversations, one of which had been in Bob Zimmerman's office. "Your research work's drawing a lot of attention," he had told her. "And not just from your colleagues. There are people out there who want to make big-time money out of it, whether you like it or not. You're going to have to be very careful."

Paula had assured him that her data was encoded in a virtually unbreakable system, and that even her technician didn't have access to it. But still, she took the warning very seriously; spying and theft of data was not unknown in the academic world.

"I like the look of you," said the man, putting his right hand ostentatiously on his crotch. His eyes were small, bloodshot, and hungry. "In fact," he went on, his voice slurred and thick with drunken confidentiality, "I really wanna fuck you."

"Just a second," said Paula calmly, reaching into her purse. With a movement so fast he never saw it, a twelve-inch ice pick appeared in her hand, and she held it in front of his face like a dagger. "Look, asshole," she hissed at him. "I'm a doctor, and I know where to jab this where it'll paralyze you from the neck down. Did you hear me? Paralyze. For the rest of your life, do you hear? Now beat it, get your ass out of here."

He stared at the point of the pick two inches from his face, and all the confident aggression leaked out of his eyes. "Hey, sorry, I didn't mean . . ." With a sudden movement he grabbed the bag at his feet, lurched out of the seat, and half walked, half ran, swaying down the corridor.

Paula sank back in her seat, her heart beating fast, clutching the wooden-handled steel spike until he disappeared into the next carriage. A year before, she'd used the same ploy with a mugger in the doctors' parking lot at Columbia-Presbyterian, and it had worked then too. She gave a little laugh, wondering again if in fact there actually was a place that she could stab someone and cause such paralysis. She didn't think so, and decided to look it up when she got home.

Twenty minutes later, she stepped off the train, took a big breath of cold air, slung her bag over her shoulder, and followed the procession of passengers down the platform. She checked her watch again; for once the train wasn't late, and she had plenty of time before her scheduled meeting with Maurice Bennett, the chief of the Department of Surgery and her new boss. A minute later, just as the train was pulling out, she heard a child scream ahead of her, then a man shouted. She hurried forward and saw a crowd of people gathered near the edge of the platform.

"She got her leg caught by the train," shouted a woman in the knot of people. "Somebody call an ambulance!"

Paula pushed through the onlookers. A young girl was lying on the ground, her jeans pant leg torn, and her right ankle and foot covered with blood. A well-dressed elderly man and woman were on their knees, holding her. Paula squatted down beside them as the last coach went by in a swirl of wind and dust. "Here, let me take a look," she said gently, smiling reassuringly at the girl. She was about twelve years old, with lots of blond hair, and was obviously terrified, biting her knuckles to keep from screaming again.

Paula carefully pulled away the torn material from her pants. "I'll try not to hurt you," she said quietly to the girl. "I just need to take a look. My name's Paula," she went on, talking to keep the girl's mind off what she was doing, "what's yours?"

"Nicky," said the girl almost inaudibly.

"Are you a doctor?" asked the man, taking in her good clothes and youthful, attractive appearance. His voice was shaking, on the verge of panic.

"Yes." She nodded. "Paula Cairns. I work at the Medical Center."

The girl's shinbone was exposed, white against the red of the damaged skin and muscles. At least it didn't look broken. Her shoe and sock had been torn off, and the foot drooped limply to one side. The top of her foot and the toes were already turning blue. The woman looked, gasped, then looked away, putting a handkerchief up to her mouth.

"What happened?" asked Paula.

"We were meeting Nicky at the train . . ." said the woman, barely able to get her words out.

"Somebody bumped into her, and she tripped and fell between the train and the platform," said the man. "Luckily I was holding her arm, so I was able to pull her back." His liver-spotted hand, still holding Nicky's arm, started to shake.

The girl moaned when Paula pulled back the material of her pants. The bleeding was mostly coming from a torn vein, and it stopped when Paula applied a little pressure over it.

"You're going to be just fine," said Paula reassuringly, her smile taking in both the girl and the man. But already she had seen enough to know that it wasn't going to be that simple.

"Nicky's our granddaughter," said the woman, stroking the girl's face with a long, manicured hand. "She was just coming back from New York. And now this. As if she hadn't had enough problems to deal with . . ."

A siren howled, then died, and a minute later two ambulance men arrived, pushing a stretcher.

The first, a slight, blond young man with a small mustache, took one look at Nicky's leg, then turned and said to his colleague, "We'll need to put a tourniquet on this one."

"I don't think so," said Paula, and the man looked at her in surprise.

"Oh, Dr. Cairns," he said, recognizing her. "Sorry, I didn't see you."

"Let's get her on the stretcher, Tom," said Paula. "I'll come in the ambulance with you."

"Thanks," said the young man, relieved. "We'd appreciate your help."

Nicky's grandmother stood up and pulled back a strand of thick white hair that had fallen over her face. She was a good-looking woman, Paula could see, strong, and after her initial shock, seemed to be handling the situation better than her husband.

"We're coming too," she said in a firm voice.

The ambulance man hesitated and glanced at Paula.

"Sure, that's okay," she said. "There's room for all of us. And call the hospital, please, Tom," she went on, "tell them we'll need to take her to the O.R. as soon as we get there."

In the ambulance, the girl seemed to be more composed. Paula saw that she was very pretty, with masses of curly blond hair, now mussed up after lying on the platform, big blue eyes, and a wonderfully smooth complexion.

"Is it all smashed up?" the girl asked. "I mean my foot?"

"We'll fix it," she said. "But you won't be able to play tennis for a while, sorry."

The girl stared. "How did you know I play tennis?" she asked.

"Your windbreaker," replied Paula, grinning. "The crossed rackets."

"She's on her school team," said her grandmother. She and her husband were sitting huddled up on the other side of the cramped rear cabin.

"We'll have to play once you're better," said Paula.

"Dr. Cairns," said the old man, looking hard at Paula. "Didn't I see your photo in the *New Coventry Register* a couple of weeks ago?"

"You could have," said Paula. There had been a rather sensational full-page article in the Sunday paper about her and the research she was doing. She turned to Nicky, whose face was pale, and there was a thin line of sweat at her hairline.

"I'm going to tell you what's going to happen once we get to the hospital," said Paula. The radio in the cab was crackling, and she could hear the harsh noise of a conversation. "We'll come in through the emergency room—"

"And they'll stick an IV into my arm before rushing me to the O.R." said Nicky, trying to grin. "I've seen it on the TV."

"Right. We'll get some X rays, then when we get upstairs, another doctor will put you to sleep, and we'll get on with fixing that leg of yours."

The ambulance negotiated a sharp turn too fast, and as they were all thrown to one side, Nicky screamed with pain. Paula tapped on the window and indicated to the driver to slow down. She turned to the other two. "The operation should take maybe an hour," she said, "so after you've been to the admissions office, have them take you up to the O.R. waiting room. As soon as we're done, I'll come and tell you how it went. Now, does Nicky have any medical problems, like asthma, allergies, anything at all?"

"No way," said Nicky indignantly. "Look at me. I'm as healthy as a horse."

Fifteen minutes later, Paula stood at Nicky's side by the operating table while she was being put to sleep. She talked quietly to her and held her hand. Nicky, shivering with shock and apprehension, was brave, but hung onto Paula's hand like a vise until her eyes rolled up and she went limp. Then Paula went over to the scrub room, and by the time she returned, Nicky's leg had been prepped, the scrub tech was putting the drapes over her foot, and Ken McKinley, the senior resident on her team, had appeared.

"Doesn't look great, does it?" He looked doubtfully down at the foot. Ken was in greens; his thin white arms poked out of the short sleeves, and circles of weariness ringed his eyes.

"I think she's lost her arterial supply," replied Paula. "She doesn't have any ankle pulses."

"Will you have to amputate her foot?"

"I hope not," replied Paula. "I'm going to try to repair the arteries if I can. One of the neuro people is coming to assess the nerve damage. Now go and scrub."

Paula surveyed the foot. It looked worse than she'd thought in the ambulance, even making allowances for the brown Betadine fluid that had been liberally applied to the area. Several tendons had been torn, and the foot looked dead. Maybe Ken was right, and she would have to amputate. . . . Paula tried to put the thought out of her mind, but her anxiety rose. Had the nerves been damaged too? Nerve injuries were harder to diagnose in this kind of situation, and at this stage she couldn't tell.

"You going to start with the tendons?" asked Ken in his quiet, tired voice.

"First things first," replied Paula. "If there's no blood supply to the foot, there's no point repairing the tendons, is there?"

Ken blushed under his mask. He had a great admiration for Paula's professional abilities, and didn't like to look foolish in her eyes.

"I told them to get all the microvascular instruments out," he said to cover his embarrassment. "And I borrowed the operating microscope from the eye people." He nodded at the instrument standing on a pedestal behind her, covered in sterile drapes.

Paula smiled. That particular microscope was jealously guarded by the ophthalmologists. "Thanks, Ken," she said, genuinely grateful. "I don't know what we'd do without you."

Ken blushed again, and it showed over his mask on his high cheekbones.

While they talked, Paula gently pulled back the torn skin above the ankle to expose the structures underneath. "Let's look for the posterior tibial artery first," she said, using a pair of small forceps and a hemostat to probe into the wound. Within a few moments she found the torn ends of the artery, which had retracted away from each other.

"The nerve looks okay," said Ken, trying to find something positive to say.

Paula got a pair of tiny arterial clamps on the torn ends of the blood vessel. "I hope so," she said. "Now let's look for the anterior tibial artery."

"If that's gone too, we're really going to have our work cut out," said Ken anxiously.

"So to speak," murmured Paula, and after a second they all grinned. She had an unerring instinct for defusing tense situations.

Dr. Vic Demarest, the senior neurosurgery resident, joined them, and everything stopped while he tested the nerves going down to the foot.

After about ten minutes, during which he stimulated

the nerves and checked the transmission of impulses into the foot, he put down his testing electrodes and stood back. "They look okay," he said. "The tibial nerve, the deep peroneal both check out. I can't be certain of the others, but I think they're probably intact. We'd like to follow her in recovery, if that's okay with you."

"Thanks, Vic," said Paula, wanting to cheer at this good news. "That's a huge relief. You are a star."

"Yeah, sure, you're welcome, Dr. Cairns," said Vic, heading for the door. Like many of his colleagues, he didn't approve of female surgeons, and felt uncomfortable when he had to work with them.

The next problem was to try to get the ends of the two main arteries joined together, and at least one major vein. There would be no point getting blood into the foot unless it could get out again.

This was going to be the hardest part of the operation, and tension was palpably building in the operating room. Everybody there knew that if Paula wasn't able to repair the arteries, the girl would lose her foot and part of her lower leg, a devastating loss for anyone but, as Paula knew, especially disastrous for an athletic young woman like Nicky.

Paula, at the epicenter of the operating room, made sure that she stayed visibly steadfast and cool; she knew that if she wavered even for a moment, the others would pick up on the tension instantly, and it would spread to them.

"This is just going to be another bit of plumbing," she told Ken, her voice showing more confidence than she felt. "Just a matter of joining a couple of little tubes together . . ."

Ken gave a little snort, the scrub tech giggled, and the tension was off, at least for the moment.

"We'll need the micro instruments in a few minutes,"

she warned the tech. To Ken she said, "How do you think we should do this?"

"I'd start with the posterior tibial artery," said Ken, without too much conviction. He hadn't seen a case quite like this one before. Anticipating Paula's next question, he went on, "Because it's bigger than the anterior tibial and it supplies more structures in the foot. If we can only save one artery, it should be that one."

"Good thinking. The ends are sort of beaten up, aren't they?" she asked, gently bringing the cut ends of the artery into the operative field. "Why don't you free the top end up a bit more, trim the ends so we have clean edges, then we can start sewing them together."

"Right you are, boss," said Ken, glad that Paula was giving him a job to do besides simply assisting. But she was like that; all the residents liked operating with her, and they always got something out of it, an opportunity to do something new, or just learning a new angle, a novel way of doing things.

"Use a knife," she told him when Ken was about to trim the ragged ends of the artery with a pair of angled arterial scissors. "A number thirteen blade. I know it's easier with scissors, but they tend to crush the tissues, and the knife does less damage."

The circulator pulled the sterile covers off the microscope and swung it on its axis so that the eyepiece came around to where Paula could look through it. The electric drive hummed as she pressed the controls to bring the tissues into focus. The tiny arteries were enlarged and looked as big as fire hoses. Paula pressed a button, and the color video screen above the anesthesiology machine lit up to show what she was seeing through the eyepieces.

All eyes were glued to the screen as Paula started to

place the tiny stitches that would bring the ends of the artery together. She could feel her heart beating fast, but her concentration was so intense that the whole place could have exploded around her and she wouldn't have noticed. Ken, whose job it was to hold the guide sutures under tension while she worked, couldn't see too well, but even with an occasional hurried glance at the screen, he could see what a precise and accurate job she was doing. And she worked fast. Within a couple of minutes Paula had put in a dozen stitches, each positioned with exact precision.

"Loosen the guide sutures," she told Ken, and while he did that, she simultaneously opened the clamps on the arteries, just for a moment. The flaccid arteries filled, and in a second blood spurted out between the stitches, just as she had hoped.

"Tighten it up," said Paula, feeling a wave of relief sweep over her. "Then tie the stitches." Carefully judging the moment, she opened the clamps again, and this time there was no leak.

Paula coiled her fingers around the inner back of the ankle. "We have a pulse," she said, struggling to keep her voice calm in spite of the sudden jolt of joy she felt. Ken felt like cheering, and a barely audible murmur of relief spread around the operating room, which now contained several more people, including Maurice Bennett, the chief of surgery.

"Need any help?" he asked.

"We're doing all right so far," replied Paula. She turned to the circulating nurse. "Tell her grandparents that so far things are going just fine," she said. "They're in the waiting room."

It took another hour before the other vessels and tendons were repaired and the skin was closed. Just before putting on the cast that would immobilize Nicky's foot

while the tissues healed, Paula checked the pulses one final time. "They're great," she said happily. "Thanks, everybody."

Maurice Bennett was waiting for her outside. He had
changed, and was now wearing an immaculate white coat
with his name embroidered above the breast pocket in
small blue letters. He was tall, distinguished, and with a
certain ambassadorial presence.

"Do you know who that was?" he asked Paula.

"Who was who?" Paula was heading for the recovery
room where Nicky had just been taken, trying to write the
post-op orders as she walked.

"That girl. Her grandfather, the one who came in with
her, is Sam Millway."

Paula looked at him uncomprehendingly. She was so
preoccupied that for a moment the name Sam Millway
meant nothing to her. Then her eyes widened.

"Wow," she said, awed. "I'm glad I didn't know that before we started."

"You and I had a ten o'clock meeting scheduled this
morning, if you remember," said Maurice.

Paula looked up at the wall clock. It was after eleven.

"How about after lunch?" he asked. "Two o'clock?"

"Yes, sir," she replied.

"I watched you in there," he said. "You do nice work, for
a girl, as Bob Zimmerman once told me."

"I can see why the two of you are friends," replied
Paula, grinning. She watched Maurice stride out of the
operating suite, feeling envious and excluded from the camaraderie of the male-dominated world of surgery. However polite, however pleasant they were to her, and
however competent she might become, it was becoming
clear to her that she could never become a member of
their inner circle.

* * *

In the recovery room, Paula made sure that Nicky was awake, checked that her pain medication had been given, then went across the corridor to the waiting room, peeling off her paper mask and cap as she went. A conscious effort had been made to make the place user-friendly, if not welcoming. There were several chintz-covered easy chairs and a sofa of the same material, with pastoral landscapes on the walls, and in the far corner a wall-mounted television babbled unwatched. There were several people in the room. A young woman with a sleeping child in her arms rose anxiously out of her seat when the door opened, then sank back when she saw Paula rather than the doctor she was waiting to see.

The two older Millways were sitting on a sofa facing the door, and both stood up as soon as they saw Paula. Sitting in the chair opposite them was a large, younger man who turned to watch Paula approach, and after a long moment he got up too.

"How is Nicky?" asked Sam Millway, his voice shaking with anxiety. He was holding tightly onto his wife's hand. "How did the operation go?"

"So far everything looks good," replied Paula. She told them what she'd done, and that Nicky would be in recovery for about an hour before going to her room. She glanced at the man who was with them. She guessed he was in his mid-thirties, very handsome, with big shoulders, beautiful clothes, and curly brown hair around a square-cut face. His blue eyes were gazing steadily at her with an expression that she couldn't fathom, and it made her slightly uncomfortable. Maybe he's Nicky's father, she thought.

"This is our son Seth," said Sam, catching her glance. "He's Nicky's uncle. And I'm Sam Millway, and this is my wife, Charlene." He smiled tremulously. "I'm sorry we didn't have time to get introduced earlier."

"Are Nicky's parents here?" asked Paula, looking around.

Sam's lips quivered, and Charlene tightened her grip on his hand. "They're dead," she said. "An auto accident, almost exactly a year ago. Nicky lives with us."

"She's lucky to have such caring grandparents," said Paula. Seeing Sam's stricken expression, she put a comforting hand on his arm, and he smiled rather shakily back at her. Paula felt a wave of compassion for the old man. "You'll have her back home soon," she said. "It'll be a few weeks before we can take the cast off, but judging from what I've seen of her, it's not going to stop her getting around."

"Thank you, Dr. Cairns." Sam's eyes were fixed on her with a strange, almost hesitant expression. "I've been following your work, and as a pharmaceutical manufacturer, I know about the research you're doing," he went on. "We'd like to be of some help to you. I mean practical help, like . . . that is, if . . ." He hesitated, glancing over at Seth, as if he were receiving some negative vibes from his son. Then he seemed to change his mind. "We can talk about that some other time perhaps," he said rather lamely. "Meanwhile, we thank you for taking such good care of Nicky. We're all most sincerely grateful to you." He held onto her arm, hard put to hold back his tears.

"Do you happen to have a business card, Dr. Cairns?" asked Seth, interrupting the moment. His voice was firm, obviously used to giving orders.

Paula had cards, but didn't carry them around in the hospital. "Not on me," she said. "Sorry."

"No problem," he said, smiling. "I'll find you in the phone book. We'll be in touch."

Paula turned back to the older Millways. "I'll see you all later," she said gently, pressing Sam's hand briefly when he let go of her arm. She headed for the door, and for some reason couldn't help turning her head to glance at

Seth. He was still standing there, watching her with an intensity that momentarily surprised her, but she had other things to think about and promptly put him out of her mind.

Chapter Two

Paula decided to get some fresh air and walk outside to the research building where her lab was situated rather than take the connecting tunnel.

Standing at the main hospital entrance, Paula squinted in the bright sunlight, which still had the pale, luminous lemon-yellow glow of early spring to it. The air was cold and she wrapped her flimsy white coat around herself, walked quickly down the five steps from the hospital entrance, and headed across the street, making her way between a parking lot and one of the few remaining open areas left on the main campus. She left the path and walked directly across the grass, still mostly springy straw from last year, but here and there were encouraging little green patches of bright new blades, and under the slender linden trees, little platoons of crocuses pushed their ellipsoidal buds up through the earth, slender, white, mauve-lined, quivering in the chilly wind.

Ahead of her rose the high tower of the new medical research building; with its ultramodern blue and white design, it seemed to look disdainfully down upon its less spectacular, less well-endowed neighbors. Inside, an exposed elevator overlooked a round central grassy courtyard with an angled waterspout shooting a jet of water high into a raised pool, which then emptied over a wide waterfall into another larger pool. Not everybody liked these hyper-modern garden ornaments. One of the medical center scientists, a researcher with Nobel aspirations, had said, "I don't know if the sound of that waterfall is supposed to provide quiet inspiration for our work, but as far as I'm concerned, all it does is make me want to pee."

It took only a few seconds for the elevator to whisk Paula up to the eighteenth floor, where her lab was situated, down the corridor from the much bigger lab that belonged to Dr. Clifford Abrams, a senior clinical professor.

Just as she was thinking about him, Dr. Abrams came out of his lab, turned, and walked toward her with a portly, fussy stride that would have made her smile if it had been anybody else. He gave her a brief, unfriendly nod as he passed, and Paula remembered vividly the first time she'd met him a couple of months before, when she was being interviewed for the job.

"So you're finishing your residency at Columbia-Presbyterian, huh?" Dr. Abrams had flipped through the folder on the glass-topped desk in front of him as if he hadn't read it, and gave her a quick, appraising glance. "Well, I suppose we can't really hold that against you."

He had a rounded, chubby face with fat pink earlobes and a ring of once blond hair sticking up like a halo all around his bald dome. Paula had a momentary vision of him in monk's garb, sitting down to a big dinner with a white napkin tied around his neck. On the wall behind his desk were several framed awards from the American College of Surgeons, displayed prominently with his medical diplomas. The office was strictly utilitarian, plastic and painted metal, and through the window to the right of his desk Paula had a good view of the city and the Sound beyond it.

"What makes you want to come to work here, Dr.

Cairns?" Dr. Abrams looked at her with sharp, rather unfriendly blue eyes and a tight-lipped expression that seemed out of place in his generally cherubic face, but Paula figured that was probably the way he looked at everybody.

"The Department of Surgery here has a world-class reputation in blood-coagulation research," replied Paula, "and I want to be a part of it."

"Of course," said Abrams with an airy wave. "But so do other competent and capable researchers." His eyes flickered over to another folder on his desk. "What's so special about you, Dr. Cairns, that we should even consider taking you on?"

"Well, I *am* being considered, so somebody must have already made that decision." Paula smiled, but Abrams looked frostier, as if her reply had been merely impertinent.

"My research is recognized as being good, Dr. Abrams," said Paula after a pause. She was now feeling a little on the defensive. "I've had ten papers either published or in print, and all in major journals," she went on. "I got the residents' teaching prize at Presbyterian last year, and—"

"I know that," interrupted Abrams, "it's all here." He pointed a finger at the folder. "But you should be aware that we have another very strong candidate with qualifications at least as good as yours." He paused for a second, watching her. "Dr. Steve Charnley is an M.D./Ph.D. from the Stanford program, and he's already attracting national attention with the instrumentation he's developed. He's also doing fine work on endocrine influences on blood coagulation."

"I'm glad I don't have to make the choice between us," said Paula, still smiling, "but one of the things that attracted me to New Coventry was that the work I'm doing fits in with the overall research direction here in this department."

"Hardly," said Abrams raising one eyebrow. "Your work fits in with one part of our research effort, and that is Dr. Bennett's. Dr. Charnley's work is equally appropriate to what we're doing. Maybe more so."

Paula wasn't sure what to say; she felt that somehow the interview had taken a hostile turn, and she didn't know why, so she temporized, wanting to end that part of the discussion.

"Maybe you should hire both of us," she said lightly, but Dr. Abrams was not amused.

"I'm aware of some of the research work you have done, Dr. Cairns," he said after another pause. "What projects are you working on at the present time?"

"We're working on a way of dissolving blood clots after they've formed in the body," replied Paula. "It appears that—"

"That's already been done, Dr. Cairns," interrupted Abrams sharply. "Streptokinase, Urokinase, and other enzymes belonging to that group. I hope you're not trying to reinvent the wheel."

"I don't think so, Dr. Abrams," said Paula, used to having to explain this even to people engaged in the same type of research. "One of the things that got me interested in the subject was the big problems we've had with these kinases under clinical conditions. As you know, they're dangerous, can cause massive bleeding, and of course they're ineffective unless they're injected into the bloodstream within a short time after the clotting has occurred."

"So you have a better way?" Abrams smiled for the first time in the interview, but it was a smile of disbelief.

"We're working on it," replied Paula, trying to sound more confident than she felt. Her research was based on sound principles and the early tests had been more than encouraging, but it was an entirely new concept and, like all new concepts, had a very good chance of never succeeding.

Abrams put a sheet of paper on the desk in front of him with a little flourish. "Earlier today," he said, "I picked up this . . . *directive* from our personnel department, entitled 'hiring practices.' You're probably familiar with this kind of thing." He tapped the paper dismissively with his finger. "It tells me what questions I can ask you, and those I can't."

His eyes flickered over Paula for a moment. "For instance, I can't ask you your age, but judging from the dates of your schooling and previous jobs, together with my experience in judging ages, I can be fairly confident that you're somewhere between the ages of thirty and thirty-two."

Paula kept her face quite expressionless and said nothing, wondering what this was all leading to.

"Nor, according to this absurdly foolish piece of paper, am I allowed to ask whether you are married or single." Abrams gave a short laugh. "But I *am* allowed to look at your hands, and I see that they are both innocent of rings. Also, were you married, you'd no doubt want your husband to get a job here or in some other part of the medical center, but according to your letter of application, you have made no indication that you have any such desire."

"Maybe he'd want to work at a Pizza Hut," murmured Paula, but he paid no attention.

Then Abrams suddenly seemed to change gears. His voice became confidential. "You see, Dr. Cairns," he said, putting his hands together on the desk, "I am entirely free to tell you that our experience with women faculty in this department has been limited and, I'm sorry to say, bad."

He paused, his eyes on Paula, but she just kept on watching him, without any change of expression that would alert him to the anger that was tightening her whole body. She couldn't help noticing his hands, flat together on the glass desktop. They didn't look like a surgeon's hands; short-fingered and meticulously manicured, they looked like two little pink piggies, cozily delighted to be right there next to each other.

"We had a young lady, a Dr. Barbara LeClerc, in the department two years ago," he went on. "She came well qualified, very personable, and despite the misgivings some of us had, she was appointed to a junior faculty position—actually, the same position you are presently applying for."

Paula didn't move. She had heard rumors but not much more.

"Dr. LeClerc created a minor degree of havoc here," went on Abrams quietly. "She had affairs with certain of our residents, and broke up the marriage of at least one of them. Things came to a head a year after she'd been here when she was caught *in flagrante delicto* having sex with a male patient of hers, right here in the clinic." Abrams face flushed with disgust. "So you see why we might feel reluctant to employ another female faculty member."

Paula crossed her legs and stayed calm. "I remember hearing a story about another faculty member here at New Coventry Medical Center, about a year ago," she said. "A Dr. Carnale, an associate professor of psychiatry, I believe. I remember his name because it seemed so appropriate. Wasn't he found guilty of having illicit sexual relations with several of his patients?"

Abrams' face went from its normal healthy pink to a

dark flush and he opened his mouth to say something, but Paula wasn't finished. "So, using your own criteria, Dr. Abrams, I assume that you are now equally reluctant to employ male faculty members." Paula opened her eyes in a wide, innocent look. "That doesn't leave you a whole lot of choice, does it?"

Abrams pursed his lips, but recovered quickly. "It's not just that, Dr. Cairns," he said in the same infuriatingly confidential tone. "By some biological quirk over which I have no control, women happen to be those members of the human race who've been chosen to bear children. That means repeated maternity leaves, disruption of research schedules, and, much, much worse than that, loss of the total concentration that is so essential to the performance of world-class research. Please don't consider this a criticism," he went on, smiling broadly at Paula, "Far from it. I'm just sharing with you some of the factors we have to consider when we're appointing a new faculty member."

The interview ended soon after, and Paula was about to leave the office when to her astonishment Abrams said, "How would you like to come to work for me? As you probably know, my lab has the best and most modern equipment in the world, and I could make sure your career gets launched properly."

Paula took a deep breath. "I don't think so, Dr. Abrams," she said. "I might get pregnant, or develop chronic PMS, and I'd hate to burden you with that kind of problem. In any case," she went on, her voice hardening again, "my research career is already launched, thank you."

Abrams shrugged and grinned, not at all taken aback, and a moment later Paula was walking back toward the elevators, trying to figure out if Abrams was simply an unpleasant, overly male-oriented person, or whether he was just pushing hard to have Dr. Steve Charnley appointed.

She calmed down quickly; it wasn't the first time she had been subjected to displays of male chauvinism. Far from it—most of the surgical specialties remained jealously guarded male preserves, but still it rankled.

Chapter Three

Paula turned the key of her lab, wondering briefly what
had happened to Charnley. She knew that he had been
the leading contender for her job, but had decided to stay
on in Los Angeles.

Her lab was a spacious enough facility, but at the present time she was using only a part of it. Her technician,
Myra Jennings, was unpacking a UPS case full of chemical reagents and placing them on a shelf above her head.
She looked around when Paula came in.

"A woman called from the *Times*," she said. "To remind
you that you have an interview with her this afternoon.
There's a number on your desk to call her back if there's
a problem." Myra's voice was sullen.

Paula went over to help her unpack. Myra was a skilled
technician, and had mastered many of the intricate procedures involved in Paula's research. She was also obese
enough that even the moderate effort of putting the rea-
gent containers up on a shelf made her grunt with discomfort.

"Did you ever get together with Jean Forrest?" Jean was
a surgical nurse from Myra's hometown of Marblehead,
and Paula had suggested she call Myra.

"Yeah. She came over." Myra's tone suggested that the
visit hadn't been a successful one.

Paula glanced at her. "I thought she was really looking

forward to seeing you," she said, but could already sense what had happened. In addition to her obesity, Myra had an unfortunate, supercilious manner that put many people off.

"We were planning on having lunch together," said Myra, her tone indicating that whatever had happened was at least partially Paula's fault. "Then she changed her mind. Had to go back to the hospital, she said."

"Well, maybe you can reschedule it," said Paula, trying to sound positive.

Myra shrugged, and turned away to hide the anger and jealousy that she felt.

On her desk Paula found a big stack of reprint requests for the paper that had caused such a storm of interest a couple of weeks previously. She flipped through the cards, curious to know who was following her work, then went over to her computer, intending to do some work, and got as far as going through the codes to get into the main program. She sat there, staring at the screen, feeling unaccountably restless and unable to concentrate. She thought about her father. She'd gone up to visit him the week before, and he'd asked what was happening in her life apart from her work, and she'd answered, "Not much, Dad, in fact, nothing." Her father, as always concerned about her, had taken her hands in his and again told her that she needed other things in her life besides work, and wasn't there any young man she was interested in?

Right now she didn't have the time even to think about men. It had been almost a year since she'd broken up with Bob, a rancher from New Mexico who'd wanted her to give up her career for a life on the range. Bob was a wonderful guy, but he couldn't understand that her career was as important to her as his vast ranch near Roswell was to him.

Paula sat at her computer for a while, thinking about

her life, and feeling strange and oddly lonely before she realized she wasn't going to get anything useful done on her computer. She was stalling, she knew it, because two critical aspects of her work had come to a grinding halt, and she couldn't figure a way around the problems. At the back of her mind was the frightening possibility that her research, until recently so promising, might have come to a dead end.

Half an hour later, she was back at the hospital, headed for the elevators. She checked her watch; Maurice didn't like to be kept waiting. Two young male medical students in short white jackets were in the elevator when the doors opened, evidently engaged in a heated discussion. They broke off for a second when Paula stepped in, then started up again as if she weren't there. They had just come from a lecture, and were trying to figure out the difference between thrombophlebitis and phlebothrombosis, two conditions affecting the veins. Paula listened to them for a few moments, then realized that they both had it all wrong. She couldn't resist getting into the conversation, and was still explaining the difference between inflammation of the veins and blood clots forming inside them, when the elevator stopped at Maurice's floor. She told them to come out with her, and finished her explanation by making a diagram on the back of an envelope. They listened, impressed and astonished, then thanked her as she went off down the corridor. She heard one of them say to the other, "Who was *that*?"

Paula spent a couple of minutes in Maurice's outer office chatting with Helen Katz, his secretary, a pleasant, solidly built woman who had worked for him for several years.

A small green light on her desk console lit up. "Go on

in," said Helen. "He's still on the phone, but go in anyway."

Maurice Bennett was sitting at his desk and speaking
on the phone when Paula came in. He smiled up at her
and pointed at the visitor's chair. A craggy man, aloof and
impersonal to many people, Dr. Bennett was an awe-
inspiring leader to the nurses, students, and young surgeons in his residency program. Under that carefully
cultivated exterior was a thoughtful, passionate man, dedicated to his job, and a sworn and outspoken enemy of all
dishonest and unethical elements in the health field.

Paula sat down and looked around; she liked Maurice's
office, which gave an excellent view of New Coventry harbor. He had furnished it in a southwest style that was familiar to her but still seemed slightly out of place here in
New Coventry. A large Wide Ruins Navajo rug lay on the
floor in front of the window, its muted earth colors blend-
ing with the beige decor, and two brooding, sensuous
Georgia O'Keeffe flower prints hung on the wall opposite
the desk.

Paula's eyes went back to Maurice. In the two months
since coming to work at New Coventry Medical Center,
she had developed a great liking for him, although she
knew little about Maurice outside of his professional
work. She did know that he was around fifty, was becoming increasingly involved in the politics of medicine, and
had developed a reputation as a crusader against criminal
elements in the health field. He had never discussed it
with her, but as chairman of a special committee appointed by the president, he was mounting a major attack
against the pharmaceutical industry. He had recently put
them on notice in a televised speech, where he had pillor-
ied them for widespread corrupt practices and warned
that when the detailed report came out in a few months,
congressional action would be demanded. The current ru-

mor was that Dr. Maurice Bennett might well be appointed the nation's next surgeon general.

Maurice put the phone down and paused for a moment to make some notes on a pad in front of him. This man really has such a presence, thought Paula, watching him. It isn't what he says or how he looks. You just feel the strength emanating from him.

"How's your young patient?" asked Maurice, putting his pen down.

"So far, so good," replied Paula. "She seems like a lovely kid," she added.

"Good. Sad story about her parents. But that was before your time." Maurice stared thoughtfully at Paula. "What do you know about the Millways?"

"I know the name. The Millway Foundation—wasn't there something about them in the papers recently? I'm afraid I didn't pay much attention."

"Yes, there was," said Maurice. "There was a piece in the *Wall Street Journal* last week. I cut it out because several of the labs here get funding from the Millway Foundation, although personally I don't." He gave Paula a fleeting, strange look. "Actually, I've been following the fortunes of the Millway organization rather carefully."

"You have shares in it?"

"Not in the usual sense, but every citizen has a share in companies that make products that affect our lives, whether they're pesticides or automobiles or pharmaceuticals."

Maurice got up, went to his filing cabinet, and came back with a thick folder with a half-column clipping attached to the inside cover. He detached the clipping and passed it to Paula.

He smiled as she started to read it, and she looked up, a question in her eyes.

"I was just thinking how nice it was to be able to read the paper without glasses," he said.

She smiled back and settled down to read the piece.

TROUBLES AT MILLWAY was the headline. "The fortunes of ailing Millway Pharmaceuticals took a sharp turn for the worse in the last quarter," she read. "At a special stockholders' meeting yesterday Sam Millway, 70, Chairman and former CEO of the organization, reported a group loss of $18M, which followed a loss of $7M in the previous quarter. Millway stated that the downturn was largely due to the sluggish economy in the area, and that heavy expenditures incurred in opening new stores had not resulted in the expected increase in revenue. Millway went on to say that control of the organization, which he had resumed after the death of his son Hector Millway a year ago, was now being transferred to Seth Millway, 35, his second son. Seth Millway, said his father, has occupied various positions in the organization and is well qualified to lead the group into the next century. Seth Millway then spoke to the group and stated that a major reorganization was underway, that the retail pharmacy operations were being phased out and emphasis focused on the growing and aggressive pharmaceutical division. In response to a shareholder's question, Mr. Seth Millway said that efforts were presently underway to obtain the substantial financing needed to place Millway Pharmaceuticals in a worldwide competitive position, but as yet no decisions had been made.

"Elsa Karash, spokesperson for the pharmaceutical industry, told *WSJ* that they were watching the situation with interest, but felt that the amount of financial backing that Millway would need before it could assume a major position in the industry would be difficult to find, given the present state of the market and Millway's lackluster showing over the past ten years."

Paula closed the folder and put it back on the desk. "That must have been the Seth Millway I saw in the O.R. waiting room," she said, talking mostly to herself. "I'd never heard of him before." She smiled suddenly. "I hope all these problems didn't make them cancel their medical insurance," she said.

Maurice laughed, but there was something about his expression that made Paula think he didn't entirely like the idea that she was getting involved with the Millways. He gazed at her as if he were going to say something more about them, but instead he sat back, tapping his fingers together.

"On another topic entirely," he said, "we have a problem. You remember when you came here, I said I'd arrange interim financing for your research, and I did so."

Paula nodded, watching him carefully, but she felt a tinge of concern, like the first whiff of smoke in an apartment when the building is on fire.

"Well," he went on, "at the university finance committee meeting yesterday, they put a hold on some of these in-house grants, and yours was one of them. And that's effective immediately."

Paula looked at him, aghast. "Why? Damn it, why?" She felt tears of frustration coming to the surface, and she swallowed them down. She'd learned to do that very effectively under Bob Zimmerman's sarcastic tutelage.

"They say that in-house grants were set up to support research that can't otherwise get funded. Your research has a very significant potential, so it is fundable from the usual sources, NIH, the Hartford Foundation, and a dozen others."

"I'm working on that, but it'll take a year and a half before anything comes through. How am I supposed to get money until then? Sell my body?"

"Nobody would want you to barter such a precious resource, I'm sure," murmured Maurice. It was the way he said it that made Paula laugh in spite of herself.

"I've been in this business for some years," he went on in the same calm tone. "And I have access to certain funds that I can use whichever way I want, and these'll keep you going for a while."

He paused, a very faint grin on his face, and Paula blushed, annoyed at herself. Once again she'd forgotten how men like Maurice Bennett operated. He'd used this opportunity to tease her, and she had not only risen to the bait but swallowed it.

"Still," he said, now in a brisk tone, "this does point up the urgency of getting some real money to keep your research on track, and we need to get it fast."

The phone rang, and Maurice picked it up. "It's for you," he said, passing it to Paula.

It was Donna, the secretary Paula shared with another junior faculty member.

"Two things," said Donna. "You have an appointment in fifteen minutes with Ginna Malone from the *Times*."

"Right," said Paula, looking at her watch. "What else?"

"You have a new patient," went on Donna. "A hernia. He wanted to talk to you, but I told him you were in surgery. I made an appointment for him for tomorrow morning."

"I don't see new patients in the mornings, Donna, you know that," said Paula, surprised.

Donna hesitated, then gave a little giggle. "I know," she said, "and I'm sorry, but he was kind of persuasive."

"What's the patient's name?" asked Paula.

"Millway," replied Donna. "Seth Millway."

Chapter Four

Paula went from Maurice's office to check on Nicky Millway in the recovery room. It was almost empty; most of the patients who'd been operated on that morning were back in their rooms. Nicky was in the far corner, her leg in a cast and raised on a pillow. She was groggy from her pain medication and barely able to respond to Paula's greeting. The anesthesiologist had just checked her out, and they were waiting for a transportation orderly to take her up to the surgical floor.

Nicky looked like an angel, with her pink cheeks and honey complexion, her blond hair spread out on the pillow like a halo. For a second Paula felt something biting at her spirit, and wondered if she herself would ever have any children. She shook the thought away. There would be plenty of time to think about that. Wrong, said a little voice at the back of her head. Wrong, and you know the facts as well as anybody That clock is ticking, honey, and you'd better listen.

Very gently Paula checked Nicky's leg. There wasn't much she could see because of the cast, but there was no bleeding, and the toes, poking out through the open lower end, were still nice and pink, and that was a pretty good indicator that the circulation was functioning adequately.

Sam and Charlene Millway were still in the waiting room, sitting close together. Paula chatted with them for a couple of minutes to reassure them about Nicky's condition, and suggested that they spend just a minute with Nicky, long enough to get her settled in her room, then they should go home. "Can you get someone to drive you?" she asked, because the two of them looked exhausted.

"No, we'll be all right, thanks, Dr. Cairns," said Charlene stoutly. "Sam doesn't like to drive much these days, but I'm okay."

When Paula got down to the hospital cafeteria, Ginna Malone, the *Times* reporter, was already there, working on a laptop computer. She was about Paula's age, well dressed in an eye-catching red outfit, and stood up to greet her.

"I'm really happy to be doing this interview, Dr. Cairns," she said, closing her laptop and putting a small tape recorder on top of it. "You're getting to be quite a role model for young women. I saw a tape of your *Oprah* show." A few weeks before, Paula had been on the show with two other young professional women, a trial lawyer and a commercial pilot, and they had discussed the kind of problems they encountered in these predominantly male occupations.

"I got quite a bunch of mail after that show," said Paula, smiling. "Mostly telling me that I should be staying home taking care of the house and kids instead of taking work away from men. The other letters were mostly proposals."

"Proposals?" asked Ginna, grinning. "Marriage?"

"Yeah, some of them," said Paula, and they both laughed and sat down.

"Okay," said Ginna, "let's get on with the show." She opened her notebook. "First, let's talk about your background a bit, then about your research. Where were you brought up?"

"Near Penobscot, up in Maine. Before that, Brookline,

Massachusetts. My dad is a musician, a violinist. He played for the Boston Symphony for years." Paula smiled wryly. One night Norman Cairns had come home late and slightly drunk after a concert. She woke up to hear him telling her mother what had happened. The second part of the concert had been Mahler's Sixth Symphony, and Norman considered himself something of an authority on Mahler; his father had worked with the composer at the New York Philharmonic a couple of years before Mahler's death. Anyway, during the afternoon rehearsal Norman got into an argument with the conductor, and that almost developed into a fist fight. After the evening concert, Norman was called to the manager's office and fired.

After that they'd moved to Maine, where he'd taught music in the high school. He was retired now, but still gave private music lessons.

"I ask you about your background, and you tell me about your father," said Ginna, smiling. "I guess he held a pretty important place in your childhood."

"Like most other kids, I suppose." Paula didn't like to talk about herself; now she felt she'd already overdone it and was backpedaling fast.

"Not me." Ginna's lips tightened momentarily, and Paula wondered what secrets lay in that cheerful-appearing woman's head. "How about your mother?"

Paula's mother had been a slim, tight-lipped, rather humorless woman, a fine amateur cellist whose midlife had been dominated by jealousy, both of her husband's superior musicianship and Paula's happy relationship with her father.

"She taught school," replied Paula. "She was very well respected."

"How about you? What did you do when you weren't at school?"

"Oh, when I wasn't outside climbing trees and picking

fights with the kid next door, I played the piano. We all played a lot together, my folks and I," she went on. "We even cut a record once, but I can't say it ever hit the top twenty."

"With all that music in your background," asked Ginna, "how come you didn't choose music as a career?"

"I did," replied Paula. "I spent a year at Juilliard, but the talent there outclassed me totally, so I went in for medicine instead."

Ginna stared at Paula, sensing that there was more to it than that. She said nothing, just repeated the question with her eyebrows. There was something, an openness about Ginna that inspired confidences.

"I was finishing my first year at Juilliard when something happened to my mother." Paula hesitated; she didn't like to think back to that awful time, but she went on. "She'd always been a quiet woman, strong, very determined," she said. "One evening she called me in New York, and I couldn't believe how she was talking. She was chattering on about our neighbors, things that had happened to them, really weird things, things I knew couldn't actually have occurred . . . then she put the phone down while she was still talking. It was totally out of character." Paula smiled briefly. "Usually when we talked, it would go like this: 'Are you eating properly, Paula? Vegetables?' 'Yes, Mom.' 'You always remember to lock the door of your apartment at night.' 'Yes, Mom.' 'Good. Stay out of trouble. And stay away from those handsome male professors. They're all married, whatever they may tell you.' "

"What had happened? I mean, when she called like that?"

"Well, I was so concerned I called back to ask my father about it. He said it had been going on for two days, almost as if she were drunk, and he'd asked the doctor to stop by and take a look at her. Dr. Cavanaugh thought it was only an accumulation of stress, and said she should take it easy, get more rest, and he gave her a prescription. The very next day she had a little stroke, then another. At the hospital in Bangor they said the blood was clotting inside the arteries in the brain, and there was nothing they could do about it. So I came home and took care of her. She got worse and worse, until she couldn't talk, was incontinent and half paralyzed. She died about eight months later. She was only forty-two."

"That's the real reason you went in to medicine?"

Paula nodded. "I guess. One of them."

"And that's why your research is focused on preventing internal blood clotting?"

"Yes. I had that in my head all the way through medical school."

"I've been reading up on your research," said Ginna, "and it sounds as if you've made a fantastic breakthrough. According to that editorial in the *JAMA*, you're on the brink of something not even the biggest university and pharmaceutical labs have been able to do, with all the resources at their disposal."

"I hope we're on the right track," said Paula, modest as any male in the spotlight, "but we're not there yet, not by any means."

"It's a system of enzymes that you inject into the veins to dissolve the clots?"

"Right," agreed Paula, but in view of the technical problems she was running into, she didn't want to go into details.

Toward the end of the interview, Ginna touched on the commercial aspects of Paula's present work. "From what I can gather, somebody's going to make a whole lot of money if your research succeeds," she said. "The implications are stupendous. If you can really dissolve clots inside the body, and prevent them from forming, you've got a cure for strokes, heart attacks, phlebitis, and a whole bunch of other things. It should save thousands, maybe millions of lives every year, isn't that right? So who's going to get rich? You?"

"Not me," said Paula cautiously, thinking about how her words would be interpreted by her critical colleagues when they read the article. "In any case, even if this research is successful, it certainly won't be a cure-all. And it couldn't have been done without the work of a lot of people who've labored on this problem for years. And as for the money . . ." Paula shrugged. "What I want is the best possible research facilities so I can expand into other important projects. Like getting the body to manufacture different enzymes with specific functions, and cure things as different as liver failure or babies born with deficiency diseases."

"Wow," said Ginna, writing furiously.

Paula looked at her watch. "Five more minutes," she said, thinking about Nicky Millway; she always felt anxious for the first few hours after her patients' surgery, because that was when most post-operative problems occurred. "I'm sorry, but I have to get back upstairs."

"Okay, Paula, actually I think we're done," said Ginna. She stood up, switched off the tape recorder, and put it in her briefcase. "It was a pleasure," she went on, putting her hand out. "I'm not sure when the article'll come out, but it should be some time this month. I'll let you know."

On the way out of the waiting room, Paula saw Ken McKinley, the senior resident, ahead of her, trudging along the corridor. He looked as if he had run out of oxygen on the last lap up Everest.

"What's going on?" she asked, coming up alongside him.

"I'm going up to the O.R. to see what my team's doing," he replied. "Chris Engel's helping the intern do a hernia." Chris Engel was a junior resident. "Wanna come?"

"Sure. Why don't you go get some rest instead? I can check them out."

"Nah. I'm okay."

The operating room suite was on the fourth floor of the main hospital building, linked at the same level to the private wing by a corridor-passage high above Elm Street, the busy thoroughfare separating the buildings.

They went through the doctors' lounge, and there were five or six men there sitting around, reading newspapers or writing in charts. A large TV in the corner had the CNN news on, but the sound was turned off. Paula hadn't met all of them, and Ken introduced them. They were polite, even welcoming, and all of them knew about her, but they were obviously unsure of how to treat a female colleague. Only one of them stood up, a good-looking, smooth-skinned, evenly tanned man of about forty-five who, even in his green scrub suit, had a look of prosperity and success about him.

"This is Dr. Walt Eagleton," said Ken, smiling in his tired way. "One of our leading private surgeons."

"Welcome to the waiting room, Dr. Cairns," said Dr. Eagleton, his sharp eyes taking Paula in at a glance. "As you will find, this is where we spend far too much of our working time, waiting for a room to open up."

"You wait less than anybody," said Dr. Gabriel Pinero, a small, very wrinkled man who was sitting in a leather armchair close by. Paula had already met him; Gabe was one of the senior anesthesiologists. "The nurses go into heat whenever Dr. Eagleton appears, and all of a sudden there's an operating room available. It's the rest of us who have to wait." He grinned at Paula, then blushed, suddenly aware that his comment about the nurses could be interpreted as seriously sexist.

"Dr. Pinero likes to exaggerate," said Eagleton, speaking quickly to cover Pinero's embarrassment, but there was a trace of malicious satisfaction in his voice. "It's his hot Italian blood that makes him do it."

He went on, in a slightly different voice, "Luckily, you'll find that we private surgeons are mostly modest, quiet people, happy to pick up a vacant slot when you academics are kind enough to leave us one."

Everybody laughed, including Paula, but his words reminded her that there was little love lost between the private surgeons and the academics who worked for the university but shared the operating facilities with them.

Walt Eagleton watched Paula as she and Ken headed for the door leading to the changing rooms. He grinned, glanced at Pinero as if about to say something, then changed his mind and picked up his newspaper again.

When Paula had first come to work at the medical center, Ken McKinley had been assigned the task of showing her around the O.R.

The supervisor, a pleasant, gray-haired woman by the name of Karen White, had been apologetic. "I'm sorry," she said, "but you'll have to use the nurses' changing room. We don't have separate facilities for women doctors." She smiled. "Maybe now that you're here, you'll be able to do something about that."

"Fat chance," Ken had said under his breath.

Now Paula opened the door into the changing room, a long, bleak, windowless place with numbered green metal lockers on each side and a wooden bench down the middle. At the far end were a few chairs and a table, and two doors leading to the toilets and showers. A faint odor of cigarette smoke hung in the air.

The scrub tops and bottoms were in bins near the door, labeled large, medium, and small, next to two large laundry hampers full of dirty greens. Paper bootees and head covers were stacked in cardboard boxes on an eye-level shelf above them. Paula picked up a set of medium green scrubs, opened her locker, stripped down to bra and panties, and hung her clothes on the two plain metal hooks inside. She had to remember to bring a few coat hangers, she thought. In her locker at Presbyterian, she'd accumulated all kinds of stuff, a deodorant bottle, a big stack of X-ray and admission forms, a box of tissues, a spare white coat, makeup, pens, reports of various kinds that somehow hadn't found their way into the patient charts.

The operating suite was large and well-appointed, with a corridor that went around the entire suite of fourteen operating rooms, with windows to the outside on the right and doors on the left leading to the various operating rooms, scrub rooms, instrument and sterilizing areas.

Ken was waiting for her outside room four. In greens he looked even paler, with stick-thin arms and lines of tiredness etched deeply into his face.

When Paula reached him, he was looking through the window into the room. Inside was the usual scene, with masked and gowned people around the operating table, a couple of circulating nurses getting supplies, the bright lights reflecting green off the drapes surrounding the invisible patient. Paula's experienced eyes took in the scene. The anesthesiologist was hanging up a small piggyback IV into the existing one on the patient's right arm, and saying something to the surgeon, who was standing back slightly and appeared to have stopped operating. The door was soundproof, so Paula couldn't hear any of the conversation. The anesthesiologist's assistant had pulled back the drapes covering the patient's left arm, had wrapped a tourniquet around the forearm, and was about to start another IV. A tiny red light was blinking on the monitor above the anesthesia machine. To a casual or uninformed observer, all might have looked like the ordinary procedures to be seen in any operating room, but to Paula the sum of it spelled trouble.

"Let's go take a look," she said, but Ken, who had come to the same conclusion, was already on his way into the scrub room.

The noise level was much higher there. The monitor alarm in the adjoining operating room was beeping continuously, and the anesthesiologist was shouting over it to the circulator to go for blood from the blood bank.

"What's up?" Ken asked Chris Engel, who was assisting the intern to do the case. Paula glanced at the intern, who was standing at the table, visibly pale and silent, and felt sorry for him. He was surely thinking that whatever had happened was his fault.

The anesthetist cut in, his voice high with tension. "His pressure just dropped. It's . . ." He glanced at the monitor. ". . . sixty systolic, over zero."

Chris, obviously shaken and very relieved to see Ken, said, "We were going along nicely. Bob here had just cut the sac, and we were putting in the repair sutures."

Ken glanced at Paula, and from his expression she realized that he was too tired to think straight.

"What do you think, Dr. Cairns?" he asked.

"Did you run into any bleeding, Chris?" she asked, making her voice sound as calm and encouraging as she could.

"No. Just the usual little stuff. Just a few cc's, nothing that would cause this."

Paula turned to check the monitor, trying to evaluate the pattern of the patient's heartbeat. "Any changes from his preop EKG?" she asked the anesthesiologist.

"No, I don't think so." The anesthesiologist peered up at the green linear waves traveling slowly across the monitor screen. "His preop EKG was normal. There's nothing to suggest an M.I., but we've drawn enzymes already to be sure."

Paula thought quickly. She didn't want to preempt Ken

or make him look bad in front of his juniors, but on the other hand the patient's life was obviously at risk. She turned her head and spoke very softly to Ken, just loud enough for him to hear.

"He's almost certainly bleeding from an accidental injury to the femoral vessels, don't you think? Why don't you tell Chris to take out all the sutures, apply pressure to the groin, and meanwhile I'll go scrub real quick. If you join me, I'm sure the two of us can take care of this."

Before Ken had time to answer, Paula headed for the scrub room, telling the circulator as she passed, "I'll need size seven gloves, please."

Both Ken and Paula did a "quick scrub," meaning that they scrubbed for only about a minute instead of the regulation four, and hurried out, arms up and dripping soapy water.

As soon as they were gowned and gloved, Chris, still keeping up the pressure on the groin, moved over to allow Paula to take command, and Ken took up his position opposite.

"Ken, you apply pressure above the incision, and, Chris, you do it below. Push down real hard." She smiled through her mask at Chris, who was obviously feeling terrible. Paula knew how that felt; it had happened to her, as it had to most surgical residents at some point in their careers.

With the bleeding controlled, Paula quickly opened up the incision and, after a few minutes of fast dissection, found the artery that was bleeding. It hadn't been cut; one of Chris's deep stitches had gone right through it and torn the artery when he pulled up and tied the stitch.

"Okay, Chris," she said. "You take it from here." She didn't tell him what to do; when she wanted him to cut a suture, she lifted it up for him, in an obvious invitation. When he wasn't sure what kind of stitch to use to repair the artery, she saw his hesitation, and asked if he wanted to use 5–0 proline, or did he usually prefer something else?

Eventually the problem was taken care of, the bleeding stopped, the artery was opened again, and Chris, now in more familiar territory, closed the incision with commendable skill.

Ken wasn't too happy that Paula had allowed Chris to finish the case; it had taken much longer than if he and Paula had done it together.

"It was an investment," said Paula when he mentioned it. "If Chris ever runs into that problem again, he'll know how to take care of it. Now I'm going back to check on Nicky Millway. Do you want to come?"

Chapter Five

The next morning, just before ten, Paula went over to the outpatient clinic to keep her appointment with Seth Millway. The clinic was located in one of the older parts of the New Coventry Medical Center, and according to the monthly hospital newsletter, a major renovation was due to start within the year. As a result, little or no money was being spent on maintenance, and the place had a shabby, peeling, untenanted look, as if it were sullenly waiting for the wrecker's ball. She had been given the temporary use of a small office with an adjoining cubicle, used four times a week by the surgical residents when seeing their clinic patients.

When Seth came in, Paula realized that she hadn't paid much attention to the way he looked when she first saw him in the O.R. waiting room, and felt annoyed at herself. There wasn't much family resemblance; his father was slightly below average height, slender, long-faced and with a rather sallow complexion, but Seth was a shade over six feet, tanned, with the kind of regular features Paula associated with Brooks Brothers catalogue ads. He didn't swagger when the nurse showed him into the tiny office, but there was a kind of smooth, conscious muscularity about his walk. Paula wondered briefly if he was into body building.

"Come on in," she said. She pointed at the orange plastic chair by the desk. "Have a seat."

Seth came in and sat down. He was wearing an open-necked shirt, a thin gold chain around his neck, a gold Rolex, slacks, and brown Italian loafers of the smoothest leather. He certainly didn't look like a businessman who had just assumed control of a major organization. Paula caught a whiff of some elegant fragrance. Overall, there was something very expensive, a kind of costly aura around Seth Millway, but of course she knew how hugely wealthy his family was. Or had been. She remembered the piece in the *Wall Street Journal*.

She talked to him briefly about generalities, asking how he was enjoying being the new boss at Millway. "It must be tough coming in like that as the founder's son," she said.

Seth's eyes flickered and his expression hardened. "So far," he replied, "the toughest part of the job has been unscrewing what's been screwed up daily for the last twenty years." His voice was so cold it shocked Paula. She looked up, surprised, thinking about her own father. She could never had said anything like that about him, whatever he might have done.

He smiled at her expression. "I know I shouldn't have said that," he said. "Dad did his best, and I suppose my brother did too. But they sure made it difficult for me to get the ball rolling again. . . ." He paused, his eyes on Paula. There was something about her that invited confidence, and he was surprised to feel so drawn to her. Mentally he shook himself. He was here with a specific purpose in mind, and mustn't let himself be distracted.

"I don't know if my father told you, but I'm also taking over as chairman of the Millway Foundation," he said. "That's entirely separate, of course, from Millway Pharmaceuticals; Dad set up the foundation years ago as a nonprofit organization to fund medical research. And one of the foundation's major goals," he went on in a different voice, as if he had rehearsed it, "is to make sure that we continue to fund research with the very highest potential. The foundation is what our family is most proud of."

"I've heard good things about it," replied Paula rather vaguely. "Aside from that, I read somewhere that you're going to reorganize the entire business."

"It certainly needs it." Seth's eyes roamed discreetly over Paula's body, although there wasn't much he could see under the white coat. But with the few visual hints and a good imagination, there was enough to construct a very pretty picture indeed. "You're quite right," he went on. "We're concentrating on new products, aiming for worldwide distribution. I figure that's where the real action's going to be in the next couple of decades."

"I wouldn't be surprised," said Paula briskly, suddenly aware of the kind of attention that Seth was focusing on her. "Now why don't we—"

"I've read about the work you're doing," interrupted Seth as if she hadn't spoken. "And I discussed it, after I saw you yesterday, with my top research people, who tell me it could have vast medical importance. To me, it sounds fascinating, with a great potential, just the kind of thing our foundation wants to get involved in. But I assume you already have major funding to support this work?"

"No, I don't," said Paula, surprised. "But let's talk about that another time. You have a hernia? Tell me about it." She looked directly at him; Seth's eyes were a dark, piercing blue, and to Paula they gave a strong sense of a man used to being in command. She had met men like this before: good-looking, confident men who had some grounds to consider themselves irresistible. Paula had to admit, reluctantly, that there was something very attractive about Seth Millway.

"It's probably nothing," he said, waving a dismissive hand. "A week ago, I was lying on my back, lifting some weights and felt something pop in my right groin. When I looked there was a bulge, but it went back in. It comes out when I'm lifting, and when ... well, it comes out when my abdominals are contracting."

"Have you seen anyone else about it?"

"I talked to my family practitioner, and he said I should see a surgeon. So here I am."

"Is it painful?"

"No. Not now. It felt weird when it came out the first time, but it wasn't anything I couldn't stand."

"How's your health otherwise?"

Paula could almost sense his pectorals contracting reflexively in response to the question.

"No problems," he said, sitting back in his chair. "I work out a lot, run, swim. . . . My blood pressure's good and low, and my pulse is about sixty."

"Great," said Paula. She pressed the buzzer on the desk and could hear it faintly down the corridor. "Why don't you go into the examining room? The nurse'll get you a gown." Seth hesitated for a second, then got up and went into the next room while Paula wrote a quick note in the chart.

Seth was really a very fine physical specimen, and Paula was impressed, as was the nurse, who hung in the background, trying unsuccessfully to keep her eyes off him. Paula told him to lie back, and examined his groin, first on his left, then on his right.

"Did you say it was on the right?" she asked.

"Yes. There." He pointed at a spot midway along the groin crease.

"Would you ... contract your abdominals? Maybe

that'll make it pop out," said Paula, but after continuing her examination, she said, "Okay, relax."

"Would you stand up, please, Mr. Millway?"

"Seth," he said, then sat up, without using his hands, and stood by the examining table. The nurse leaned back against the wall, envious of Paula's contact, and wishing she could think of a legitimate reason to come over and touch the flesh of this great hunk.

"Cough," said Paula.

Seth obliged.

"Again, harder this time, please."

After a few more moments of prodding and feeling, Paula straightened up. "I can't feel anything there at all," she said. "From what you told me, it sounds like a hernia, but I certainly can't feel one."

She checked him one more time, but the hernia seemed unwilling to show itself and finally Paula gave up.

"Come back if it reappears," she told him, feeling slightly apprehensive that he might go over to the private side, maybe to see Walt Eagleton, who would of course instantly find the hernia and laugh gently when Seth told him he'd already been to see Dr. Cairns. "Of course, it might have been a lymph gland or inflammation that would make a temporary swelling. Meanwhile, go easy on the exercises. Don't strain any more than you have to, try to avoid coughing, and don't get constipated."

Seth didn't seem at all put out by her inability to find the lump he'd complained about; in fact, he even seemed rather smug about it.

Since she had already given him his instructions, she expected him to get dressed and leave through the changing-room door, but after a few moments he came back through the connecting door into her office and sat down in the orange chair again.

"I never thanked you for saving Nicky's leg," he said. "It

was her good luck that you happened to be there at the railroad station."

"My pleasure," said Paula, looking up for a second before going back to the chart, where she was writing up the results of the physical exam.

"And you were very nice to me in there." Seth nodded in the direction of the examining room. "Very professional. Dr. Cairns, I'd love to take you out for dinner, maybe some evening next week?"

Paula suppressed a sigh, put down her pen, and pushed her chair back. "That's very nice of you, Seth," she said carefully, "but right now I'm really too busy to have any kind of social life. In any case, you're a patient, and I don't go out with patients. Ever."

"I'm not a patient, not anymore," said Seth, smiling. "There's nothing the matter with me and you've discharged me, right?"

"Seth," said Paula, "you weren't listening. I'm too busy, really. But thanks anyway."

Seth got up. He had a swift way of moving, and at this close range Paula felt awed by the sheer size of him.

"Well, that's okay . . . for now," he said, his confidence unshaken. "In any case, I want to get back to you and discuss some possibilities for funding your research. By then things should have settled down and you might have a bit more time, huh?"

"Yeah, right," she said, wishing he would leave. "Meanwhile, take care of yourself, Seth, and let me know if you get that lump back."

Later, Paula felt a growing sense of puzzlement about Seth Millway, and wondered whether the lump he'd complained of was imaginary or real. His initial mention of feeling something "pop" in his groin wasn't the usual way a hernia made its presence known, and he'd pointed at the wrong place on his groin. And if it was imaginary or, even worse, contrived, what had been the real purpose of his visit?

As for funding her research . . . well, she'd be happy to discuss that with him, but in some conference room, not over dinner.

She went back over to do rounds with her team, and they stopped in to see Nicky. She was half asleep, restless, her cast hanging over the edge of the bed, and obviously in some pain. Ken wanted to give her some more pain medication, but instead Paula fluffed her pillows, pulled down her gown, which had ridden up around her thighs, gently repositioned her leg, and with Ken's help straightened the wrinkles out of the sheets. When they came back twenty minutes later, she was asleep and certainly a lot more comfortable. The lesson was not lost on Ken and the rest of the team.

Chapter Six

When Seth Millway drove back to the Millway Building in the business center of New Coventry, he tried to concentrate on the forthcoming meeting with the man from Boston, but Paula's green eyes and something about her physical presence kept intruding on his thoughts, and that annoyed him. Seeing her in the hospital waiting room had aroused his curiosity, but the main reason he'd consulted her was because of his interest in the research she was doing.

He looked at his watch. The meeting was scheduled to start in five minutes, and once again he considered the few options open to him. Things had been going downhill for Millway Industries for years, but matters had suddenly come to a head several months before when Millway had taken out a big emergency loan at exorbitant interest rates just to pay their overdue bills. Walfords, a large national chain, had bought the entire Millway retail pharmacy operation for cash, but there had been a fire-sale atmosphere about the transaction, and the proceeds had barely been enough to pay back the banks and satisfy the secondary lenders, and all of them had refused point-blank even to consider refinancing.

Seth gritted his teeth, and stopped abruptly at a traffic light. For years he'd been telling his father, and then his brother, Hector, that their business practices were leading them to ruin, but they hadn't listened until the creditors started banging on the doors. And now here he was trying to pick up the pieces, reduced to begging for money to set the pharmaceutical division on its feet. And there would have to be huge changes there; the whole direction of the company would have to be turned around. For years Millway had made different kinds of headache pills, had developed techniques for putting medications such as penicillin and various hormones into pill form, and for a long time it had been successful and profitable, but in the past several years they had been overtaken on all fronts by the Swiss, the British, by just about everybody. Seth knew that it was time to get into the nineties and prepare for the new century, and in order to do that, there would have to be some major restructuring of the company.

Meanwhile, to investors Millway was the least interesting pharmaceutical company on the market, although the rest of the industry was flourishing. The company's stock price had sunk to the point they couldn't even consider a new issue, and on the Street, the current thinking was that Millway Pharmaceuticals was a lackluster company that would be swallowed up soon by a bigger, more successful competitor or disappear into oblivion.

The man from Boston was Seth's last hope. His name was Vince Coletti, a man with quite a reputation among the relatively few people who knew about him. He was known to have a great deal of money and had access to a lot more. Vince's money didn't come cheap, and his expectations were high. So although Seth knew that his father would have been appalled, he had contacted the financier. The private and commercial bankers had said no, the big underwriters had shaken their heads, and all the other reputable possibilities that Seth could think of had turned him down. Of course, Coletti was well aware of Seth's increasingly desperate attempts to get financing for his company. Nobody looking for money ever called Vince Coletti first.

Coletti was standing in the waiting room, looking at the David Hockney reproductions on the wall, when Seth came in. There was another man with him, sitting in one of the upright chairs facing the door. When Seth came into the room, Vince turned around. He was older than Seth had expected, with very dark eyes that seemed to be all pupil, and leathery folds of skin that hung from his cheekbones. A thick upper lip overhung his mouth, the kind a vainer man might have covered with a mustache. He was wearing a dark business suit, polished black shoes, white shirt with a button-down collar, and black socks. The only color in his outfit was a thin red stripe in his dark blue silk tie. When Seth had spoken to him on the phone, Vince's deep voice, with its rough-edged Boston accent, made Seth think of a longshoreman or a trucker rather than a very rich, very tough, and, to put it mildly, a very uncompromising financier.

Seth shook hands, aware that Vince was surprised by what he saw. Seth didn't fit the stodgy Millway image, not even a little bit; he didn't even fit the industry image. There wasn't another CEO in the entire pharmaceutical industry who could have been a centerfold in *Playgirl* magazine.

Seth glanced at the other man, who had stood up when Seth came in. "That's Mike Petras," said Vince briefly. "An associate." Mike looked more like a bodyguard than a business associate, with a wary boxer's face and short, bristly, pomaded black hair, a wide neck and a thick-set body encased rather incongruously in a dark business suit. On a nod from Coletti, Mike picked up a black briefcase and followed Seth and Vince into the conference room.

They sat at the end of the long table, Seth on one side, Vince and Mike on the other. A secretary brought in a pile of charts and papers, which she set down in front of Seth.

"We won't need those," Vince told him, waving dismissively at the charts. "What I don't know, I'll ask you."

Seth hadn't expected Vince to be particularly knowledgeable about either Millway's problems or the pharmaceutical industry, but he was wrong. After Seth had made his pitch, Mike respectfully put the briefcase on the table in front of Vince and opened it for him. Vince pulled out a thick folder.

"I don't invest in products, and I don't invest in ideas," he said, as if he'd said it many times before. "People. That's where it's at. If I believe in the people, I go for it."

Seth Millway nodded. "That's exactly how I feel," he said. "I always—"

"Nobody's asking for your opinion," interrupted Vince without changing the tone of his voice. "Right now we're talking about *my* money. Now, you ever heard of Caldwell Investigators?"

Seth, his face red with annoyance, shook his head.

"I got them to check you out," went on Vince, tapping the folder. "They tell me you're a violent man." He paused. "Let's see, when you were eighteen, there was that young black woman you beat up . . . yes, right here in New Coventry. You almost killed her. Cost your folks a bit to get you out of that one, because she didn't see too good afterward, right? But of course you were just young then, a bit frisky, maybe. . . . But it didn't stop there, did it? Two years later you did the same kind of thing up in Hartford . . ." Vince turned a couple of pages, then closed the folder. "The thing that interests me," he said, "is that you were never charged, never tried, never convicted. So it never happened. Like they say, you're better off lucky than smart, right?"

Seth shrugged.

Vince sat back. "None of that bothers me," he said. "It ain't relevant. Now let's talk about money."

He asked some tough questions about Seth's current cash flow, how long Millway was taking to pay its bills, about their long- and short-term debt, dividends, P&L ratios, who the major stockholders were, the company's past and estimated growth rates.

"What do you spend on R and D, percentage-wise?"

"As a percent of gross revenue? About half of one percent. It used to be a whole lot more, closer to five percent, but—"

"Don't bother explaining. I know. R and D's the first thing to get slashed when times are tough. It's the same for everybody."

Finally Vince sat back and stared at Seth for several uncomfortable moments. Then he said, "You're in deep shit, Seth. You don't even have enough cash to pay your bills. Aside from that, the main problem is you don't have a single killer product. Millway Pharmaceuticals doesn't have a damn thing, no new drugs or medical products that your competitors don't have or could have. I know about your research labs, they ain't worth shit. You ain't come up with a worthwhile new product in fifteen years." He held up his hand when he saw that Seth was about to interrupt. "Some guy in *Business Week* called Millway a sleeping giant," he went on, grinning suddenly, showing his long, carnivorous teeth. "Your company ain't asleep, for chrissake, Millway's in a fucking coma, and all the money in the world ain't gonna wake you up. That's what the Wall Street boys are saying, that's what all the others are saying. And I agree."

Seth saw the last set of doors starting to close against

him. He took a deep breath, and made a decision. "We do have a killer product," he said. "It'll be ready by the end of the year. This is something that'll wipe out the competition. Right now it's a top secret, and in different circumstances I wouldn't even mention it to you. I didn't tell the bankers or the other people. So I'm telling you this on the understanding that it's all absolutely and completely confidential, okay?"

Vince nodded, looked at his watch. Seth knew that this was his last chance; whatever he was going to say had better be good.

"I'm talking about a sophisticated enzyme system designed to prevent blood clots from forming inside the body," he said, trying to remember the figures his marketing director had come up with. "We estimate the sale of this product in the first year will be in the region of six million dollars. That figure is low because of the FDA testing requirements in this country, but of course they don't apply in Mexico, South America, or Europe. Within five years the figures goes sky-high, possibly into the billions."

"Billions?" asked Vince, the skepticism loud and clear in his voice. "Seth, you're full of shit. There isn't a single medical product on the market that sells that much."

"Did you know that two out of the three leading causes of death in this country are heart attacks and strokes?" asked Seth, his voice strong. He had done his homework before going to see Paula Cairns, and his enthusiasm was real. "We're talking about a million deaths a year in the U.S. alone. At least four times that number of people are at risk, and what we're talking about is the only viable preventive possibility that would work for all of them. This product is the answer not only for strokes and heart attacks, but for any of the half-dozen diseases that are caused by blood clotting inside the body, like phlebitis, for example." Seth leaned forward, caught up in the excitement of his own semi-fantasies. "Once all the distribution and marketing problems are taken care of, and *as long as we have the money to set up manufacturing and marketing of this product,* it's going to be the biggest pharmaceutical money-spinner anybody could ever imagine, bigger than penicillin, bigger than steroids."

"Oh, yeah?" said Vince disbelievingly. "All this is coming out of the Millway labs?"

"No," said Seth. "Not directly. The Millway Foundation is funding the work. It's being done in one of the most prestigious research institutions in this country, by a top researcher who one day will be a Nobel Prize contender. We have the patent rights on the process. All we need is the money to set up production facilities, increase our international rep network, and be able to service this product properly on a worldwide basis."

"I'll want details," said Vince.

"No problem," replied Seth, already beginning to shake at the magnitude of his lies. But he was desperate. He knew that now he'd have to pull off some kind of deal with Paula Cairns, but he also knew the power he had with women. He had yet to come across one who could resist him when he put his whole mind to it. As for Vince Coletti, although Seth knew he was not a man to fool with, he undoubtedly had the large amount of cash that was needed.

Vince sat back, explored a molar with a toothpick, and looked at Seth for a long time.

"Show me that contract," he said, "and you have a deal. I'll tell you next week how much I'll put in, and what the terms are."

After his two visitors left, Seth walked exultantly back along the carpeted corridor to his private elevator, turned a cylindrical key in the lock, and stepped in. He pushed the top button on the panel and got off at the penthouse floor. He was in the process of redecorating the entire suite, and had ripped out all the old, dark drapes and furniture that had been there since his father first moved in, and let some light in, just like Dickens' Pip tearing down Miss Havisham's curtains in *Great Expectations*. His father had remonstrated mildly about the expenditure, but Seth felt that image was important, and that nobody would take him seriously unless the trappings of wealth were there. Now the nerve center of Millway Pharmaceuticals was being done up with glove-soft beige leather armchairs and sofas, walls with different pastel colors in the various rooms, all of which communicated by high, arched openings which had once held heavy oak double doors. Replacing the enlarged photos of the Millway pharmaceutical plant at various stages of construction, Seth had placed large reproductions of Renaissance paintings on the walls. On the inner wall opposite the high windows, there was a copy of an Annunciation attributed to Piero della Francesca, with an angel on his knees, bringing the news to the Virgin Mary, who was standing with her hands crossed over her stomach, downcast of eye and modest of demeanor.

"That's how I like my women," he had told the decorator, pointing at the picture and grinning. The decorator, an attractive black woman wearing a short skirt, had been at the top of a stepladder hanging the painting. "White, respectful, and with connections in high places."

On this occasion, however, Seth didn't get the best of the exchange. The decorator paused, put one leg up on the next step of the ladder, showing a stunning length of elegant thigh. "Some of us thought you might prefer a repro of Michelangelo's *David*," she said, and when his face darkened, she went on, "as a symbol of Millway Industries defeating the giants, of course."

Marching in, Seth remembered that short encounter with annoyance. He sat at the glass table with its elaborate golden legs and scrollwork, relishing the feel of the silk brocade cushion on the high-backed chair. Dr. Paula Cairns. She had suddenly become central to his plan from a business point of view, but soon his thoughts drifted in a different direction. He stared out of the window, across the harbor, then at the campus buildings and the spires of the churches on the green, outlined in white from a sprinkle of late snow. Right in the middle of his field of view was the tall metallic white and blue tower of the New Coventry Medical Center research building. And in that tower was Dr. Paula Cairns. His eyes didn't close, but an image of her came to him, an image of startling clarity. She was sitting at her computer, wearing a white coat; then she turned in her seat and stood up, her outlines unmistakably spectacular. Seth kept looking at her with an insolent directness that he couldn't have sustained in her real presence, at her straight-backed, confident air, her curly black hair and direct gaze. And now, as he stared, totally absorbed in her, her clothes disappeared slowly, like a mist lifting off a sunny hillside, and she stood there in his imagination, naked. He shook his head, feeling aroused and annoyed. He knew he couldn't do anything in that direction until the contract was signed. Right now Dr. Paula Cairns was just a business proposition.

The phone rang. The company's auditors wished to go over some data with him, and Seth arranged to meet them in a half hour. Seth's mind quickly went back to Paula. He *had* to persuade her to let the Millway Foundation fund her research; the stakes were now higher than anything he'd ever envisioned. And if reasonable methods didn't work, he'd need a backup scheme that would be totally foolproof. To Seth the idea of working with Paula was very attractive, and he was confident that one way or the other he would succeed.

After his meeting with the auditors, which left him angry and aware that he had only weeks to get additional capital, Seth drove home in the gathering dusk to his waterside condo ten miles from New Coventry. He drove past an old brick factory, then the road narrowed, and for a quarter mile led through a marsh as if to a distant Camelot, a clump of super-expensive condos right by the water.

Seth noticed none of his surroundings. He couldn't keep his mind on any one thing for more than a few moments; thoughts about the auditors and the impending financial disaster were interrupted by disturbing images of Vince Coletti and his bodyguard, Mike Petras, but inevitably his thoughts kept coming back to Paula Cairns, like the theme in a set of variations.

Fleur, his live-in girlfriend, was watching television when Seth let himself in. She was dressed in an embroidered red shantung silk housecoat, and nursing her third margarita of the evening.

"Don't you have anything better to do?" he snapped. "Turn that damned thing off."

"It's *Jeopardy!*, sweets," replied Fleur, taking her time before looking away from the screen. She spoke in the husky little-girl voice that had so enchanted Seth four months ago. "I got three of the questions so far. Do you know who the first president of Israel was? Or the name of the deepest lake in Scotland? I didn't get that one, but I remembered about Chaim Weizmann from school. Did you know his name is pronounced 'Hime' like in Hymie? I always thought it was Chaim like in 'chain.' "

Fleur paused to take a sip of her drink, and watched him over the rim of her glass with her big, baby-blue, very perceptive eyes. It wasn't always easy to tell what kind of a mood Seth was in, and usually Fleur would just open her mouth and talk, evaluating his reaction as she chattered on. Sometimes it didn't matter what she said—he would just come in, pick her up in his great, strong arms, and take her through to the bedroom. If she squealed at such times, she had found, he liked that.

Seth wasn't in that kind of mood today, and his first comment gave her a hint. "Just shut the fuck up," he said. "What did you make for dinner?"

"What did I make, sweetheart?" said Fleur, her already nasal tone taking on the slightest of whines. "I made reservations, like you told me to."

Her voice was enough to set Seth's teeth on edge. He found himself comparing Fleur with the classy Paula Cairns, and Fleur was relegated to the basement.

But since she didn't know that, it didn't stop her talking. "At Moretti's. You remember when I made those veal and turkey croquettes yesterday, you remember what you said?"

Seth sighed. Fleur had total recall of every word he'd spoken to her, she remembered every expression, every gesture he'd made from the first time they met at a cocktail party four months before, and by now he knew better than to say anything, let alone argue. She could repeat conversations verbatim, and go on and on until his head reeled.

"What did I say?"

"You said, 'This tastes like shit, honey, and if all you can serve up is shit like that, we're gonna have to eat out.' Remember?" Fleur pouted, and her red lips pursed up. "So tonight I really wanted to please you, and that's why I thought we'd go to Moretti's."

He took a deep breath. For the past couple of weeks the bloom had been off the rose, so to speak, with Fleur, and he had decided to bring their relationship to a close.

But he would have to be very careful. Fleur was a lot tougher and smarter than she looked, and had once made casual mention that one of her best friends was an attorney who'd done some work for Ivana Trump. Fleur stood up, her low-cut housecoat revealing the top half of her sumptuous breasts, and his resolve wavered.

"Okay, we can go out. But that's it for this week. Things are really bad with the business, and it looks as if I might have to sell this condo."

Fleur's crimson-nailed little finger went up to her mouth, and she sucked on it for a moment, her huge eyes on him. There was something so suggestive and sexy about the way she moved it that Seth had to put his left hand deep into his pocket to keep his own situation under control.

Fleur took the finger out of her mouth and inspected it carefully. "Anyway, we're flying to Cannes next week, aren't we?"

Seth's mouth opened slightly. "Cannes? Are you crazy? Of course I can't leave while all this stuff's going on with Millway, and in any case I can't afford a trip like that."

"Oh, Seth, you *promised*."

Seth started to sweat slightly. He shook his head. "No way, sorry."

Fleur pulled her housecoat close around her and sat down again. She took a big sip from her margarita, and licked a grain of salt off her top lip. Her tongue was sharp, pink, long, almost prehensile; under certain circumstances it seemed to have a life of its own, and could get into places that had totally astonished Seth. Her eyes went dreamy, and he knew that she was rewinding the tape of her recent history, and he was about to hear, in as grisly detail as he could stand, the exact circumstances of his promise to take her for a vacation to Cannes.

Her eyes narrowed momentarily. "January the four-teenth," she said. "We were checking in at the Hyatt Regency in Houston, and this big, tall guy with a white Stetson and dark glasses and ostrich-skin boots that musta cost a couple of thousand bucks came in with a bunch of people, and he was obviously their boss. And he kept turning to look at me through his dark glasses, and said something to one of his guys, something like 'Go get me that gal,' or something like that, and that's when you grabbed me, and in the elevator going up to the sixteenth floor, that's when you said we were going to spend a couple of weeks in Cannes, in April. And it's April now. Do you remember, sweetheart?"

"Okay, okay," said Seth, appearing to capitulate but in fact having the germ of an idea. "Yeah, I remember, sort of. I can't go, but why don't you go by yourself to Cannes? I'll try to join you for a weekend, but I'm not sure . . ."

"Deal," said Fleur, smiling. "Now I'll go get dressed, then we're outa here. I'm starving."

Seth cut her off as she made her way toward the door. "I'm hungry too," he said, sliding his hand between the lapels of the housecoat. The firmness and sheer size of her breasts shook him with unexpected excitement, and he slipped the other hand around her legs and picked her up, light as a feather, holding her with one hand under her firm, rounded buttocks. Fleur tucked her legs up so that her knees were under her chin, his thumb slid wetly into her, and she squealed with delight all the way to the bedroom.

Later, Fleur said, okay, they didn't have to go out, and she'd settle for a pizza. He picked up the phone, ordered it, and twenty minutes later the box was lying open on the bed. Seth had got up to open a straw-covered bottle of

Chianti, and when he returned, Fleur was sitting naked on the bed, wolfing down a wedge of pizza, long threads of cheese hanging from each side of her adorable mouth down onto her breasts. Seth picked up the ends with his mouth and followed them up to hers, and she fell over backward on the big bed, still trying to finish the wedge and giggling and pushing with deliberate ineffectiveness at Seth, who landed on top of her. He turned quickly on his back, caught her by the waist, picked her up, and placed her so that she was straddling him, leaning forward over him. The sight of her breasts in that position did something really fierce to him, and he fumbled and found the place and pushed himself into her. Her head went back and she gasped in genuine pain, and that excited him even more. He pulled her down by her hips, impaling her even farther, and she screamed. He bucked upward, while every muscle in her body tightened and shrieked in protest, her nipples erect and hard under his hands, and the pain, a frighteningly pleasurable pain, radiated in throbbing waves up into the rest of her body.

Seth reached over to the beside table, picked up the portable phone, not taking his eyes off Fleur, and dialed a number. "It's a new listing," he told the operator. "I don't have an address."

Fleur closed her eyes and concentrated on her own pleasure, tuning out the faint beeps as Seth dialed the number he'd been given.

When he heard it ringing, he warned Fleur, "Don't you make a single sound, or I'll ram my cock right through you."

When Paula answered, Seth started to move again, and Fleur put her hand firmly over her mouth to cut off any sounds she might inadvertently make. He turned his head slightly to hold the phone against his shoulder to free up both his hands. He rolled her nipples gently between his thumbs and forefingers, feeling them swell and harden. She'd once told him that when he did that, electric impulses passed straight from the nipples down between her legs, and set her whole body on fire.

"Dr. Cairns?" He pushed up hard when he said her name, and Fleur had to bit her lip to prevent herself from moaning. "I'm sorry to bother you at home," he said into the phone, watching Fleur. A little rivulet of sweat made an irregular track along her neck and ran down between her breasts. "But I've been thinking about you . . . and your research project. I would like to fund your work, through the Millway Foundation, and I'd like my people to come over and discuss it with you. Yes, tomorrow. Somebody will call you first thing, okay? Good, thanks." Seth put the phone back, and simultaneously rammed up with all his strength, holding her down on him with one hand on her shoulder.

Fleur really screamed, and with the pain felt a fear of him that wasn't entirely related to his penis.

Paula put the phone down very thoughtfully, surprised by the call, although some instinct at the back of her head told her that it wasn't so unexpected. And she had to admit to herself that she'd been quite happy to hear his voice; Seth Millway had certainly crossed her mind a few times since his visit to the clinic. Then she wondered again if he'd arranged to come to the clinic just to check her out. If he had, it would seem a strange way for the new head of an important corporation to be behaving, but again, if he was serious about getting the Millway Foundation to fund her research, how important were his little peculiarities to her? When Paula went to bed that night, it wasn't his eccentricities, his wealth, or his status that she thought about. Instead she fell asleep with a very physical picture of Seth in her mind, an image that included his broad shoulders and hard muscles, and the smooth, athletic way he moved.

Chapter Seven

Paula woke up at six the next morning, and her mind turned to Nicky Millway. The cold truth of it was that Nicky had only about a fifty-fifty chance of regaining the full use of her foot, even considering her youth and access to the best rehabilitation facilities. In her mind, Paula saw Nicky limping painfully around with a useless, dangling foot instead of dashing full tilt across a tennis court to retrieve a drop shot, and the thought made her shiver. Still wearing her thin white nightgown, Paula went over to close the bedroom window; it was cold and gray out there in the early light. A thin haze of white ice lay on the ground and on the car windshields below her in the parking lot. Patches of tarmac with black tire marks leading away showed where early workers had already left.

The bathroom was like the inside of a deep-freeze, and she switched on the ceiling infrared lamp. As she did so, she could hear her father's gruff voice, just as she had years ago when they went camping: "Don't be such a fluff, child. It's not cold until your breath solidifies, falls on the ground, and breaks." She'd giggled at the idea, and remembered it ever since.

After a shower she felt warmer, and cleared an area on the big, steamy mirror with a soapy hand, another of her dad's cold-weather tips. She leaned forward and for a long moment stared at herself, looking for her mother in the shape of the cheekbones, fitting into her own face the sunken, mindless eyes that had flickered from side to side, the sharp jaw, the thin, hollow cheeks that would unexpectedly puff out like a trumpeter's, just for a moment, in those few weeks before her death.

Feeling the sobering weight of mortality, Paula turned away, wondered briefly how her own death would occur, and hoped that it wouldn't be like that.

She dressed carefully and took her time putting on her makeup, but took no pleasure from her last-minute reflection in the bedroom mirror.

When she arrived at the surgical floor, Nicky was sitting up in bed, both legs straight out in front of her, and unsmilingly watched Paula approach.

"It's hurting," she said when Paula asked.

"Let's take a look."

The toes were still pink but puffy, and looked crammed together in the sausage-shaped opening of the cast.

"We need to elevate your foot," she said. "I'll go get a couple of pillows."

She came back a few moments later holding two pillows under her arm, and again Nicky watched her, with her big, serious blue eyes.

"Okay, lie back, Nicky, and raise up your right foot . . ."

Nicky gave a sudden, mischievous grin, and did as she was asked, and said very quickly. ". . . and swear to tell the truth, the whole truth, and nothing but the truth, so help me God." Then she put her encased leg down firmly on the pillows. They both laughed.

"How does that feel?"

Nicky thought about it. "Better," she said. "Do you know the story of the pig with three legs?" she asked Paula.

Paula braced herself. "No," she replied cautiously.

"Well," said Nicky, folding her hands rather primly on

her lap, "there was this man walking down the street, and he met another man leading a pig with only three legs. 'Excuse me,' said the first man, 'but why does your pig only have three legs?' 'Oh,' said the other man, 'this is the most wonderful pig in the world. Once I was fishing in the river and fell in, and this pig swam out and helped me get back. Another time, there were burglars at our house, and he squealed until we woke up and chased them away. He's a wonderful pig,' 'That's great,' said the first man, 'but you didn't tell me why he had only three legs.' 'Well,' said the first man, getting huffy, 'a wonderful pig like this, you can't eat him all at once.' " Nicky grinned proudly at Paula, relieved that she'd got the story right first time around. "My friend Mary told me that story last night on the phone."

Paula sat down on the chair by Nicky's bed, feeling slightly breathless.

"Mary says that if you cut off my leg, she'll take me around town like that on a lead."

"Well, you can tell Mary we're going to do no such thing," replied Paula. "We're going to have you back on that tennis court, but it's going to take a while."

"How long?"

"It depends," said Paula, and went on when she saw that Nicky wasn't going to be satisfied with that answer, "on how quickly you heal, and if there's any damage we couldn't see while we were putting you back together."

"I was almost killed," said Nicky, staring straight ahead. She shook her head to get rid of the thought and turned to face Paula. "The nurses say you're a really cool person," she said, looking intently at her.

"I pay them to say things like that," said Paula, smiling, feeling very close to the cheerful Nicky and remembering how she herself had been at that age. She'd been much quieter with adults, for one thing, less outgoing, less willing to converse with strangers. In Nicky's position, she probably would have been too shy to say anything when the doctor came around.

"Did you meet my uncle Seth?"

"Yes, I did." For some reason Paula didn't want to say anything about him to his niece.

"Did you like him?" Again Nicky stared at her with that disarming and slightly unnerving honesty.

"He seems very nice."

"Well, I don't like him." Nicky lay back and closed her eyes. "And now I'm going to sleep."

Walt Eagleton, the private surgeon, was at the nurses' station, standing with a pile of metal-covered charts on the desk in front of him, his tan as even as ever. There was a lean, competent look about the man; no wonder female nurses got restless when he was around, she thought, passing behind him to replace Nicky's chart in the rack.

"I see you have one of the Millways as a patient," he said, looking around. "Not bad going for a newcomer, and an academic at that."

"Word travels fast," said Paula, smiling. She always had a sense of crossing swords when she spoke with Walt, and she'd found that modesty was wasted on him. "And people know class when they see it, even in an academic."

Walt leaned forward, speaking softly so that the nurse sitting a few feet away wouldn't hear. "Listen, Paula, if you feel the case is getting too complex, or you get out of your depth, let me know. I'll be happy to help you out."

"Thanks," replied Paula, momentarily at a loss for a cutting reply. By the time she thought of one, Walt had given her an amused look and was on his way down the corridor, swinging his stethoscope in a nonchalant, jaunty way.

Damn that man, thought Paula, annoyed. Every time we talk, he makes me feel like an idiot.

* * *

Back at her office, she found a message from Seth Millway's secretary. The Millway Foundation team was coming in to see her that morning, and if eleven o'clock wasn't suitable, she should call and set up a different time. The meeting would be in the office of Dr. Franz Lockyer, dean of the medical school, and would she please bring an up-to-date research budget with her. Surprised by the short notice, Paula tried to reach Maurice to discuss the situation with him, but he'd taken an early morning shuttle flight to Washington, where he was to testify at a congressional hearing on health fraud, and he wasn't expected back until that evening.

Promptly at eleven, feeling excited but a little apprehensive, and wondering what all the hurry was about, Paula arrived at the dean's office, located in the original administrative building in the oldest part of the medical school. The secretary's office was larger than Paula's lab, with high plaster ceilings and elaborate cornices, an old-fashioned wooden desk with a side extension, and polished floors covered with worn rugs. The most modern thing in the room, aside from the telephone console, was a green IBM Selectric typewriter.

"Dr. Cairns? The gentlemen from Millway are already here," the secretary said. "They're talking with the dean and Mr. Susskind, the university attorney, but they should be out any second." She looked up at the old round regulator clock on the wall opposite her.

The polished brass handle of the door turned, Paula heard the sound of conversation and laughter, and Dean Lockyer ushered four men in business suits out of his office. Seth Millway was there, with his father, Sam, who was looking frailer than ever; he came over and held her hand in both of his for a moment.

"My father insisted on coming," said Seth, smiling. "He's still on the board, of course, and for some reason he seems to have taken a shine to you. And this is Desmond Connor," he went on. "Des is our research director at Millway Pharmaceuticals, and also on the board of the foundation." Connor came forward to meet Paula. He was in his late fifties, grizzled, sturdy-looking, with a square Irish face and dark eyes, small feet with shiny black pointed shoes. He wore a rumpled light olive green suit and a dark green tie.

Dean Lockyer, still beaming at Paula as if that were his one programmed expression for the day, pulled forward a portly middle-aged man with a tired smile and a lock of long, graying hair hanging over one eye.

"Dr. Cairns, I want you to meet Geoffrey Susskind, from our legal department," Susskind nodded amiably and put out a limp hand. His left shoulder drooped, weighed down by the large black briefcase he was carrying. "Geoff is here to make sure these fellows don't do anything illegal."

Seth laughed, and the lines of Mr. Susskind's tired smile deepened for a moment, and they all followed the dean across the corridor to the conference room.

"Why don't you gentlemen sit over here?" said the dean, indicating the far side of the rosewood table. There was more than enough room for the three men on the Millway team, and they sat down. Sam Millway was at the end, next to Desmond Connor, the head of the Millway research labs. Paula figured he would be asking most of the scientific questions. Old Sam was looking very weary, Paula thought, and not at ease with his son.

"There's plenty of coffee and doughnuts over on that table," the dean went on. "I won't be staying for your meeting, but if there's anything you need, don't hesitate to ask my secretary. As you know, she's right there across the corridor."

Before leaving, he smiled encouragingly at Paula, who

sat in a chair on the opposite side of the table, facing the four men. Suddenly she felt that she was being placed on trial, and wondered why there never were any women at the top levels of the organizations she had to deal with.

Sam, who had stayed quiet until now, told Connor and Susskind about the incident in the railway station with his granddaughter Nicky. Paula listened and watched. The rumpled-looking Desmond Connor appeared neither as expensive or as businesslike as the others, and somehow didn't seem to belong with them. His face had a rakish, worn look about it, and Paula wondered if he drank a lot.

"Des is a doctor," said Seth, seeing Paula's glance. He put his hand for a second on Des's shoulder and smiled paternally at the older man. "We kid him that he's not a real doctor, not like you, Dr. Cairns, but he got his master's at Harvard and his Ph.D. at Berkeley. It'll be his corner where all the hard scientific questions are going to come from."

All four men had yellow legal pads and pens in front of them; Seth unfolded a small cellular phone and put it next to his legal pad. Sam pushed his chair back as if he were in some way distancing himself from the proceedings.

"Well, Dr. Cairns," said Seth when everyone was settled. "We don't want to take up too much of your time, so let's get down to business. Maybe you could start by telling us something about the research you're proposing to do."

He was watching Paula very carefully, memorizing her appearance, the dark blue gabardine suit, the white silk blouse that half hid the outlines of her figure, the fine-denier black hose on her long legs. There was no question; she looked stunning.

"Sure," replied Paula, looking straight back at him with her cool green eyes. "The work I'm doing is to prevent heart attacks and strokes. Together these account for forty percent of all deaths in the United States. We're talking here about close to a million deaths a year."

The men watched her, all of them paying strict attention as she talked, sizing her up. She noticed that Desmond Connor had placed a two-inch pile of reprints of her scientific publications next to his pad, and wondered if he had read them.

Seth put his hands together, palms down, in front of him, and smiled in an enigmatic way. "We're all familiar with these statistics, Dr. Cairns," he said, remembering that he'd used a very similar pitch with Vince Coletti. "We're anxious to hear what you can do to improve them." Seth was watching her attentively, and there was something in his look that made her wonder if his mind was entirely focused on scientific matters.

"Our main project," she said, "is to find a way to dissolve blood clots that form inside the vessels, and allow the circulation to be restored. The way we're approaching that problem is to attach a set of enzymes to a transport system—"

"A *set* of enzymes?" asked Connor. Paula noted how sharp and acute his eyes were.

"Yes. A single enzyme isn't adequate," she said. "Fresh clot that's less than a couple of hours old can be dissolved without too much difficulty. That's been the basis for the work on streptokinase and urokinase, current treatment for recent myocardial occlusions. That form of treatment has it's own risks, of course . . ." She paused for a second, looking to see if they knew what she was talking about.

"You mean the risks of hemorrhage?" asked Seth. "I had an old neighbor who had a heart attack a couple of months ago, and was treated with streptokinase. A day later he had a brain hemorrhage, and unfortunately that killed him. The doctors said that hemorrhage was one of the dangerous side effects of streptokinase treatment."

Paula was trying to keep her mind on what Seth was saying, but she could feel a mild but growing interest in this obviously smart and certainly wonderful-looking man. Cut it out, she told herself. This is business, pay attention.

"Exactly," she replied. "The problem is that the streptokinase doesn't just dissolve the blood clot, it inactivates the entire normal blood-clotting mechanism, which exists partly to prevent internal hemorrhages. What we're working on is a powerful enzyme system that attacks clots only after they've already formed, but doesn't interfere with normal blood-clotting mechanisms."

"I was asking you why you need a *set* of enzymes," said Connor. "Isn't one enough to do the job?"

"Sometimes, but usually not," replied Paula. "The kind of clot that travels through the system often starts sometimes days or even weeks before it gets dislodged. So by the time it travels up to get jammed in a main lung artery or the brain, the oldest part of the clot, the core part, has already become thick and fibrous, and needs a different type of enzyme to dissolve it."

Connor was taking notes and looked up, obviously very interested. "Can you tell us the names of these different enzymes?" he asked.

"Actually, we're testing a whole range of them," Paula replied, not wishing to disclose anything that wasn't essential for the Millway people to know. "And that's a good part of the reason I need this funding."

Paula noticed how acutely Seth was following the exchange, and got the feeling that he understood a whole lot more about her research than he was letting on.

"That's all most interesting, Dr. Cairns," said Connor. His soft voice had Irish overtones. "But how do you pro-

pose to get the enzymes in contact with the clot? I understand that the type of clot we're talking about can be up
to several inches long, and if there's no blood circulating
past it, merely injecting your enzymes into the bloodstream won't do the trick. Or did I miss something in your
presentation?"

"No, Dr. Connor, you didn't," replied Paula, looking him
straight in the eye. "The enzymes are delivered through a
catheter that is put into the artery or vein under X-ray
control, up to the site of the blockage." Paula took a deep
breath. "Actually, the delivery part of the project still
needs a major amount of work before we can start to use
it clinically."

They discussed the overall research project for about a
half hour, then got down to what Seth called "brass tacks,"
which was a discussion of line items in the budget that
Paula had hurriedly put together.

It became clear that they weren't impressed with her
overall assessment of the costs of the project, and after a
while Seth spoke up. "I'm sorry, Dr. Cairns," he said, "but
we don't think you have asked for nearly enough money to
get this job done properly." He tapped the papers in front
of him. "We often see this with young and inexperienced
researchers, and it's part of our job to straighten that out."
He smiled, taking any sting there might have been out of
his words. "For instance," he went on, when he saw that
Paula was surprised, "we don't believe you can do all this
work with a single assistant. And you need a great deal
more specialized help in the enzyme-isolation area, probably a Ph.D in enzymology, maybe two. When you're a little
further along, there's no question that you're going to need
a much more sophisticated computer system, a scanning
electron microscope, and a sequential analyzer—"

"Actually, I was just asking for enough to keep the work

going, Mr. Millway," said Paula. "I didn't expect you to even consider this as a request for major funding."

"Where and when do you expect to get that major funding, Dr. Cairns?" asked Seth.

"Well, I'm in the process of applying to the NIH, the Ford Foundation—"

"Tell her, Des," said Seth, glancing at Connor.

Connor sighed and put his hands flat together. "I don't know if you've ever put in for a NIH grant before, Dr. Cairns," he said. "But you probably know how long the process takes, even if the application is approved and funded."

Paula raised her eyebrows.

"For a start," went on Connor briskly, "there are only two times in the year when you can apply, and the next application deadline is five months from now. Then there is the initial selection process, and as I'm sure you know, that takes several months. If you pass that hurdle, the next is the site visit, when specialists in your field come and inspect your lab and see whether they feel the work is worthwhile. Then—"

"Mr. Connor," said Paula, "I'm quite aware of all that. My estimate is that NIH funding should become available some time between a year and eighteen months from now. That's why I'd like funds from your foundation, but only to carry me over until then. And if you remember, I'm doing it at Mr. Seth Millway's suggestion."

There was a long pause, and Paula had an odd feeling that a kind of silent conversation was going on among the four men opposite her.

"Dr. Cairns," said Connor very quietly, "I was merely outlining some of the problems researchers have with the National Institutes of Health and the other big granting agencies and foundations." He paused, his dark eyes fixed on Paula, and sighed when he saw that she wasn't convinced. "Look, Dr. Cairns," he said, "we really didn't want to get into this, but we've done our homework too." He tapped the small pile of research papers with a tobacco-stained finger. "You don't have a track record with the funding agencies. The money's already allocated to professors and senior researchers who have spent their entire careers getting into the system. Let's be serious, Dr. Cairns. You may be in that position one day, but it'll take years. Meanwhile, the best you can expect from the big agencies is ABNF, Approved But Not Funded."

After his speech Connor sat back, and there was a brief silence, broken by Seth.

"Dr. Cairns," he said in a gentle voice, "all of that brings us back to the Millway Foundation. One of our great strengths is that we don't have to work under these kinds of constraints. We can react quickly and effectively to the needs of researchers who meet our criteria. . . ." He gave a small smile and leaned forward, a curious gleam in his eye. "I don't know if you've had time to do your own research on our foundation," he said, addressing her in a quiet, measured voice. "We don't make small grants anymore. We don't fill in spaces, or provide carry-over funds. When we truly believe in a project, or in an individual investigator, we back them to the hilt, to the point where they neither want nor need any other form of outside backing."

Now the three men were smiling at her, Seth in a satisfied kind of way and Connor as if he'd just had the pleasure of telling her she'd inherited a fortune.

"I'm going to send one of our staffers up here first thing next week to help you rewrite your application," Seth went on. "Then we can get on with processing it, writing up a contract, and have all the signatures on it by the end of the month. We can do that, right, Des?"

"I guess we can rush it through, sir," replied Connor.

He was still smiling, the corners of his mouth stretching as if he didn't do that too often.

"While you're here, Mr. Susskind," said Seth, "would you mind going over our pro forma contract with Dr. Cairns? Otherwise, we're done, I think." He looked at Connor and for a second at his father.

The three of them got up, shook hands with Paula and Susskind, and left them to it.

Susskind stood up, took his large old briefcase, and came around the table to sit next to Paula. There was something large and ponderous and tired about him, as if he'd come to the Friday evening of his life, worn out by a week of uninspiring work. He put the case on the floor beside him and pulled out several files and loose papers and placed them carefully in front of him, taking care to line up the papers with the edge of the table. He took a thick contract out of a folder; each page had the word SAMPLE stamped on it in thick red letters. Susskind then proceeded to go over the entire form with her, in excruciating detail. By the time an hour had passed, all the legal jargon and unfamiliar terms were making her feel slightly dizzy, even though Susskind did his best to explain what it was all about.

Paula pointed at a small-print footnote, and Susskind peered shortsightedly at it through his glasses.

"It says here that any patent or other proprietary rights to any process or invention developed under the grant would become the property of the Millway Foundation," she read aloud. "Doesn't that mean I'd lose the rights to my own work?"

"No, no," replied Susskind, smiling. "It's a standard rider to present-day contracts of this type. It's there because a number of recent Internal Revenue and other statutory regulations governing nonprofit foundations and agencies, promulgated at both the federal and state levels to prevent certain excesses and abuses of the nonprofit system. You don't have to worry about it."

Paula shook her head, and he went back to his line-by-line explanation of the contract. By the time he was done, Paula felt as if she were escaping from some kind of Chinese water torture. She also felt a sympathy for Geoffrey Susskind, who had to deal with this kind of stuff day in, day out. No wonder the poor man looked so tired of life.

Aside from her excitement at the possibility of major funding for her projects, Paula had been very impressed with Seth Millway. He had been professional, knowledgeable, and seemed in complete command of the situation. She thought about him all the way back to the hospital.

Chapter Eight

Maurice returned from Washington late that afternoon. When he picked up his voice mail and got Paula's message, he paged her, figuring that she'd be somewhere around the hospital.

Paula was alone in the lab, getting the bugs out of a new 3-D computer simulation, when her pager beeped. She called Maurice's office; in his typically courteous way he said he didn't want to interrupt her work and would come up to the lab.

Five minutes later, she heard the door buzzer. She got up, walked over to the door, and, working on old habits learned in New York, asked who was there before opening it.

"How's it going?" asked Maurice after he came in. He looked fit and full of energy, although he'd spent the day testifying before a tough congressional committee.

"Not great," replied Paula rather somberly.

He pulled a chair up next to hers, facing the computer, and sat down. The three-dimensional color graphics fascinated him, and he watched in silence while Paula manipulated the images, trying to get them to fuse together and simultaneously shed a segment which would activate the next sequence. After a few minutes she put the program on hold and turned around to face Maurice. Her face was drawn.

"I've run into a big problem here," she said. "A real big problem."

Maurice waited, watching her face.

"It has to do with the carrier solutions," she said. "Each enzyme has to be in a carrier solution that keeps it from breaking down. When it hits the fresh outside part of the clot, it liquefies it, and the breakdown products activate the next enzyme that attacks the next layer, and so on."

"I know. The cascade effect. Tod Wilson at Ciba Labs spent ten years trying to figure it out, and finally they closed down his operation."

"Well, we've licked most of the problems he had, I think," said Paula. "The cascade effect now works perfectly in the lab. That's what everybody's calling the big breakthrough, and that's why the work is getting so much attention. But we can't do it with humans because the carrier solutions are simply too toxic. We'd destroy the clot, but we'd also kill the patient."

"I don't suppose you expected to solve every technical problem overnight," said Maurice, smiling at her frustration. "That's why we're going to need major long-term financing for your lab. These things can take years. Ask Tod Wilson."

"It's not just that," went on Paula, flicking a lock of hair out of her face, "I don't have a delivery system to get the enzymes to the clot, not when it's in a vessel deep inside the body. If I just inject them through an IV, even using a catheter, they'll be too diluted to work by the time they get to the clot." Paula tried to keep her voice calm and reasonable, just the way she'd been taught. "Dissociate yourself and your feelings from your problem," Bob Zimmerman had once admonished her. "Tell it as if it were happening to someone else. In this business, nobody listens to a whiner."

But still, Maurice could detect a note of desperation in her voice. "So what are you doing about it?" he asked.

"I'm really scared," she confessed. "If I can't solve those problems, the whole concept goes up in the air, like it did for Tod Wilson and lots of others."

"So what are you doing about it?" he repeated.

"I've been trying different combinations, using new preparations and carrier solutions, and setting up different computer simulations." She pointed at the still-lit screen. "Every time, though, all I'm left with is a mess of inactivated enzymes. I'm afraid this is just going to turn into another fiasco, wasting my time and everybody else's money."

Maurice stood up and went over to the window. When he spoke, his voice was a shade brusque. Oh God, thought Paula, Bob Zimmerman was right. Nobody likes a whiner, and that goes for Maurice too.

"So what else happened today?" he asked, changing the subject abruptly. "You were looking for me this morning."

Paula switched off the computer, then told Maurice about the interview with the Millway group.

"Who was there?" he asked. Paula told him.

"Seth Millway," said Maurice slowly, coming back to his chair and sitting down. "The new broom. Tell me what he looks like, and what you thought of him."

Paula kept her description bland, but felt Maurice's quizzical gaze on her.

"I've been hearing disturbing rumors about Millway," he said, pushing his chair back so that he could look at her. "You probably know that my HHS committee's been taking a hard look at the entire pharmaceutical industry. There's a lot of stuff beginning to surface, from all kinds of sources, including some from insiders at Millway Pharmaceuticals."

Paula watched him, feeling the force of the man, his

strength and tenacity. Maurice was not a man who just talked; on the contrary, he was willing to take the time and energy—and risks—to shake and rattle rotten systems until the rats fell out.

"Anyway," he said, "I think you should consider very carefully before getting involved with the Millways. When old Sam Millway was in charge, all was well. He's a man of great honor and integrity; the foundation funded lots of promising projects that couldn't get money elsewhere, some quite small, and really provided a great service to the scientific community. His older son, Hector, was the same, old-fashioned but honest, but of course he wasn't in charge there very long. But there are indications that Seth isn't cut from the same cloth, and we know that Millway Pharmaceuticals is strapped for money."

Maurice moved in his chair. "There's also a suspicion that he's trying to divert some of the foundation money back as loans to the pharmaceutical division, but I don't suppose he'd be foolish enough to do anything like that. All the same, you might be wise to steer clear of the Millways. I do realize, though, that if you turn them down it will almost certainly slow your research by maybe a year."

"A year!" said Paula. "I can't afford that." She stared at Maurice with astonishment. "You know I can't let my research fall behind for that length of time." She shook her head. "In any case, the Millway Foundation is quite separate from Millway Pharmaceuticals, right? The foundation's nonprofit, it has different funding, so I don't see why I shouldn't accept their money." Paula's voice took on a stubborn note, remembering the intelligent and thoughtful way Seth had acted during the meeting. She was sure that Maurice had entirely the wrong idea about him. "In fact, in a lot of ways the Millway thing seems like a golden opportunity to me. They're really interested, they want to give me more money than I'd asked for, and of course they're right about how much I need. If this work is to go on at the speed it should, it'll cost a lot, and I'm just about out of funds right now."

Maurice's eyes seemed to be focused on a point above Paula's head, and when she stopped talking, it took him a moment to refocus on her.

"Yes," he said. "Of course. I'm working on it, but you know that research money's hard to come by these days."

Maurice stood up a few moments later and left, and Paula's anxiety rose, because he hadn't come up with any satisfactory alternative to Millway. She looked at her watch—it was almost six o'clock, and she felt a sudden tiredness come over her. It often happened around this time of day; it lasted for an hour or so, then her energy returned.

The phone rang, and it took her a second to recognize the voice. It was Seth Millway. "You were great today at the interview," he said. "And everybody's very enthusiastic about your work. I have a couple of additional questions I'd like to ask you, but I'd rather do it over dinner, okay?"

"I'm really busy just now, Mr. Millway," replied Paula.

"That's all right," said Seth. "It's six o'clock, and I'll pick you up at eight at the front entrance of the hospital. That'll give you two more hours of work. Will that be okay?"

Paula struggled with it for a moment. "Okay," she said.

From then on, she tried to concentrate on her task, but whenever she wasn't doing something that required her undivided attention, a vision of Seth Millway kept intruding into her mind. It wasn't even a vision but a feeling, an aura made up of impressions of size, quickness, the power that she could sense he wielded over people, the unmistakable interest he was showing in her. The fact that he was a big-time corporate tycoon, head of a foundation that had sufficient financial clout to distribute millions of dollars worth in research money, also gave him a certain status, but Paula had seen plenty of very wealthy people in the Harkness Pavilion of her old hospital, and mere wealth didn't impress her anymore.

At ten minutes before eight, Paula closed the program, copied the coded material onto the backup tape, shut the system down, and left the lab. She was locking the door when she heard a voice close behind her. "Working late?"

She jumped and whirled around. It was Cliff Abrams, grinning sarcastically at her.

"I'd have thought you'd be out dancing, or doing whatever you young women do these days in your spare time."

"No," replied Paula, annoyed, and feeling certain that he'd surprised her on purpose. "Actually, I was just finishing up a research paper for the *Annals of Surgery.*" She paused, gathering her strength to strike. "You used to publish quite a few papers in the *Annals,* didn't you, Dr. Abrams?"

Cliff took a sudden breath, and went a furious red. He *had* published several times in that prestigious journal, but as Paula was pointing out with deadly politeness, not recently, not for some years. And publications in journals of that caliber were what determined the standing of a researcher. Beet red with anger, and unable to think of a suitable reply, he turned abruptly on his heel and strutted angrily back toward his lab.

Paula was instantly sorry that she'd reacted so savagely, but he'd given her a hard time ever since she'd come on the scene at NCMC. Abrams had desperately wanted Steve Charnley, the California surgeon, to get her job, and had never let her forget it. If Charnley had come, he'd have been working with Abrams, and would no doubt have infused some urgently needed new life into his lab. No wonder Abrams was bitter about her. Paula made a mental note to ask Maurice why Charnley had turned the job down.

On the way out of the hospital, she stopped in briefly to see Nicky, then, as she went along the quiet corridor toward the hospital's main entrance, she could feel a strange anticipatory feeling that tingled through her entire body.

It was exactly eight o'clock when Paula stepped out into Elm Street. Cars passed, their tires hissing on the wet, rain-slicked surface. A light mist hung over the city, blurring the streetlights, blotting out the tops of the taller buildings. A large black BMW shone and sparkled at the curb, and when Paula walked down the steps, Seth emerged and opened the door for her. The car was a recent model, still full of the aggressive smell of new leather. The motor was on, but after her door closed with a heavy, Teutonic thud, and before Seth came around to the driver's side, an expensive, cossetted silence reigned in the car. Paula found the comfort of the luxurious, padded upholstery admirable but somehow oppressive; even the click of the seat belt was precise and rich. She thought with affection of her old MGB, with its sagging seats, bumpy ride, and noisy motor.

"We're going to Chez Jacques up in Centerbrook," said Seth as the car pulled silently away from the curb. "It'll take us about twenty minutes."

Paula nodded. She would just as soon have eaten in some simple place closer to home, and Seth's evident liking for the trappings of wealth made her want to tease him.

"Have you been there?" he asked, slowing for the lights at the end of Elm Street. "I mean, to Chez Jacques?"

"No, but I hear it's not bad," said Paula in an offhand way. She knew it was an expensive and exclusive French restaurant near the Connecticut River.

Seth laughed. "What do I have to do to impress you?" he asked. "Hire a Concorde to fly us to Paris and eat at the Tour D'Argent or Lasserre?"

"No. Actually, any old place would have done just fine," she replied, smiling. "I'm not that difficult to impress."

Seth said nothing while he negotiated the ramp leading to I-95, then joined the heavy traffic on the motorway. It had been raining lightly when they left the hospital, but now the rain was heavier, and even with the windshield wipers working at maximum speed, it was difficult to see more than about ten yards ahead. The other traffic filled the air with a haze of greasy water droplets, and once when he passed a semi, the deluge from its wheels blotted everything out, and for a few nerve-racking moments all Paula could see was torrents of water sluicing down the windshield.

As he drove, Seth watched her out of the corner of his eye, feeling caught between two conflicting urges. If he'd been merely going out on a date, there would have been no problem; he knew exactly what he would have said and done. But right now she was a person he needed to do business with, and that required an entirely different strategy. When he glanced at her again, he could feel a place, tight with sexual tension, right in the middle of his gut.

"I'm not that difficult to impress." What had she meant? Seth didn't like that kind of cryptic comment; was it a criticism? Did she mean that he was trying too hard?

Meanwhile Paula was beginning to enjoy the ride. It was taking her away from the anxieties of her work. And after her long, self-imposed drought, it was exciting to be out with a man like Seth Millway, even for a business dinner. But she too could feel the tension rising within the car, and it made her uncomfortable. Aside from business, she hadn't had much to do with men for a long time, and she wondered if that was why she felt that way.

"I saw Nicky before I left," she said. "She's a sweet kid, and so far she seems to be doing very nicely."

"Good," he said rather vaguely, and Paula, looking at his shadowy profile, could see that she had interrupted his train of thought. Maybe that was a good thing.

The rain was slackening, and Seth was able to take his eyes off the road for a moment and glance over at her. Even though Paula hadn't had time to change after working all day, she looked fresh and laundered and cool; something about her reminded him of a certain nineteenth-century Meissen figure, a ballerina, decked in exquisite china lace, that had once belonged to his mother. He also remembered one snowy winter's day when he was six years old, going to his mother's room, where she kept that little figurine in the center of her dressing table, on a little shelf in front of the mirror. He'd sat, alone, on his mother's satin-covered stool for maybe ten minutes, maybe more, staring at the ballerina's graceful shape, at the incredibly delicate lacework around the hem, at her reflection in the mirror. She seemed to get larger, until she reached life-size, smiled coyly at him, and pirouetted slowly on one pointed, white, shiny toe. And then suddenly, for no reason that he or anyone else could ever figure, he snatched her up and flung her to the ground, hard enough to smash her into tiny fragments.

Shaken by the memory, Seth turned the automatic CD player on, and instantly the sound of Elgar's cello concerto filled the vehicle with quadraphonic sound.

"That's André Navarra," said Seth. "With Barbirolli and the Hallé Orchestra. I love that disc."

Paula listened.

"I know that recording," she said, not wishing to let Seth get away with anything, not at this stage, anyway.

"But it's an EMI remastering of a 33rpm disc, and even though it is digital, it's not technically quite as good as, say, the Jacqueline DuPré recording, do you think?"

Seth's mouth opened slightly. He liked good music, but all he knew about it was what he read on the CD inserts, and Paula's comment had taken him completely off guard.

"Are you a classical buff?" he asked. "You seem to know a lot about it." His normally confident voice seemed to have lost some of its timbre.

"Yes, I do," replied Paula, who still played her piano when she could, and even occasionally regretted Juilliard. "Aside from running a business, what are *you* interested in?"

"Fast cars and faster women," said Seth without thinking. He was used to an answering giggle to that comment, but none came from Paula, and he knew instantly that it had been a stupid thing to say to her.

He was acutely aware that the evening wasn't starting off very well, and did his best to warm the situation up. "Talk about *them*," his mother had told him as a teenager when he complained of never knowing what to say to his dates.

"You made a terrific impression on my group today," he said. "My father was saying really nice things about you and how competent and sympathetic you were with Nicky."

"I'm glad," said Paula simply. "I really like your father. Dr. Bennett, my boss, says he is a man of true integrity and honesty."

Again there was a brief silence, while Seth wondered if Paula's praise was a subtle dig at him, but her face showed no sign of such an intent. She was really quite beautiful, decided Seth suddenly, glancing at her profile in brief moments stolen from watching the slippery road ahead. But the strength of his reactions disturbed him.

He was beginning to feel the power of an attraction that was quite unfamiliar to him.

By the time they reached Old Saybrook, the rain was diminishing, and Paula had found that Seth had played football in college and was interested in hunting.

"What I love best is stalking deer," he told her as they turned north toward Centerbrook. "I used to go to Scotland every year during the season. You could find a buck, an eight- or a ten-pointer if you were lucky, then spend sometimes a whole day stalking him on foot through the moors, up on the hillsides. It's the most exciting kind of hunting."

"Did you use a local gamekeeper or a tracker?"

"Only the first time. It's something . . . well, being alone is where it's at, really. It's just you and him."

"I went hunting for woodcock a couple of times with my dad," reminisced Paula, happy to have found a topic of common interest. "Up in Maine. I love the excitement of walking through the woods and not knowing when a bird would suddenly explode out of the brush. Dad used to tell me to aim for their kneecaps."

Seth laughed. "Your dad sounds like a great guy," he said. "I'd love to meet him sometime."

"Who knows?" replied Paula, not at all sure whether he would like Seth. He certainly hadn't cared much for Bob, whom he had called "that cowboy."

Seth was feeling a growing contact with Paula, as if some invisible cosmic tentacles were joining them, then shrinking to pull them together. There was something about her that rang some deep chord inside him, some previously unrecognized longing; looking back at when he had first walked into her office, maybe it had happened instantaneously. He could see the way she had been sitting, the clothes she had worn, the shape, the movements, even the texture of her body beneath. But Paula's intellect was making him uncomfortable. Seth normally depended on a safe margin of intellectual superiority over his women. And he couldn't figure out what she was thinking about him, whether she was well disposed toward him or not.

Seth drove down Centerbrook's Main Street, past the well-lit restaurant, and found a parking space fifty yards farther down, just short of the boat marinas. The air was still stirring in the wake of the rain when they got out, and the halyards and shrouds rattled and tinkled from the nearby boatyards. The rain had stopped, and a light breeze brought wafts of humid, chill spring air as they walked together back along the empty road to the restaurant. Most of the street was dark, with long black puddles left by the recent rain, and Paula took his arm, feeling a sense of security from his presence beside her. Seth, very aware of her touch, was feeling increasingly tense. The lit windows of Chez Jacques glowed welcomingly as they approached, and they could see shadowy diners on each side of the candlelit window tables.

Chez Jacques was about half full, and pleasantly decorated in a French provincial style, with heavy, varnished square tables covered with stiff linen tablecloths. Near the swing doors to the kitchen, a huge old oak sideboard bore its burden of fruit, cream-topped desserts, and mille-feuille pastries. At each end, on Normandy lace doilies, were set heavy silver candlesticks, lit with long, tapered white candles that flickered every time a waiter bustled through the doors. At the unoccupied tables, napkins were serenely folded, and sparkling silver and glasses winked in the light of a candle in a glass holder.

Seth didn't like the table the hostess led them to, and rather abruptly asked for a table by a window. They waited for few moments while a window table was bussed; Seth watched the busboy with an expression that must have made him nervous, because he knocked over a pepper mill which rolled off the table and fell at Seth's feet. Paula expected Seth to bend down and pick it up for him, as she would have, but he did no such thing, and watched while the busboy groveled around his feet, hunting for the elusive mill.

By the time they were finally seated, and each had been presented with a handwritten menu, Seth was feeling so tense that his hands were balled up into fists and his palms were sweating. He made an effort to ease up.

"The white *aspèrges* sound delicious," he told Paula. "And when I was here a year ago, I had the *duckling à l'orange*, and it was just, Mmmm!" He kissed his fingertips in Gallic fashion, with a flourish.

"I'll just have a hot dog with double mustard and lots of ketchup and relish, I think," said Paula, teasing. She closed the menu firmly and put it down on the table.

Startled, Seth glanced quickly at his menu to see if he'd missed that item, but of course no hot dogs, not even as *chiens chauds*, figured there. He stared at her, and she grinned impishly back at him. Slowly his face relaxed, but he didn't seem particularly amused.

"Actually, I think I'll try the grilled salmon," said Paula.

The wine waiter came over. He was a young man, slim, with short black spiky hair, and spoke with a strong French accent. Seth spoke back in French to him, and the young man seemed embarrassed, and obviously didn't understand a word Seth had said. Finally the boy confessed that he was from Hartford, and although he knew quite a bit about wines, he only knew a few words of French, enough to get by with the average customer.

Seth's face went red and his pent-up tension erupted. "Then why the fake accent?" he asked angrily. "Do you think it's smart to pretend you're something you're not?"

The boy stepped back. "No, sir. It's just—"

"Maybe you're just learning the tricks," went on Seth as if the boy hadn't spoken. "Are you going to appear next in New Coventry Medical Center masquerading as a doctor?" He glanced at Paula. She shook her head slightly, as if to say, lay off the kid, leave him alone.

"No, sir," whispered the boy, looking anxiously between the tables toward the front desk. "Would you care to order some wine?"

"Not from you," said Seth. "Go get the owner, the manager, whoever's in charge, and bring him or her right here. We're not here to take this kind of pseudo shit from you."

"Just a second," said Paula, sitting up very straight. "Seth, if you don't want to order the wine, I will." She turned to the boy and grinned at him. "How eez your numbaire seexteen? Le chardonnay de la Napa Valley de la California?"

The boy gave her a weak, grateful smile. "Sure, ma'am," he said in his native Hartford tongue. "A good choice, thank you. I'll be right back."

Seth was already feeling that he'd overdone it, and mumbled something to that effect.

"We're here to have dinner," said Paula, annoyed with him. She opened the linen napkin with a flick of her wrist. "And even if it's on business, we can still make it a pleasant occasion. We're not here just to show the help how well educated and important we are, right?"

The boy came back, nervously holding a bottle of chilled wine wrapped in a white towel. "We're out of the Napa chardonnay, sir, I'm sorry," he told Seth. "But this is a Hafner 1991, one of our most excellent chardonnays, not from the Napa Valley, sir, but it's at least as good."

Seth took a deep breath. "Alexander Valley, huh?" he said, examining the label.

"Yes, sir." Anxious to please, the boy went on, "It's a

small winery, near Healdsburg, sir, along the Russian River, if you know that area."

"I don't," he said, returning the bottle. "But I'm impressed with your knowledge."

The boy beamed, and his hand shook a little as he cut off the top of the lead seal, then drew the cork, unscrewed it, and placed it on the tablecloth in front of Seth. Seth sniffed it, put it on his bread plate, then after tasting the wine and rolling it around his mouth for several moments, with a brisk nod he pronounced it good.

Paula, used to this rather silly ceremonial, which she suspected had something to do with male bonding, waited while the boy filled her glass the regulation two-thirds full. Seth watched the boy give the towel-covered bottle a half twist so that there would be no drips and nodded approvingly. All in the space of a few moments, Seth had changed from bad-tempered to benign. Paula hoped the conversion would last through the meal.

"I think you enjoy stirring things up," she said, smiling after the wine waiter had left. She was determined not to let that episode spoil her meal. "You seem to like being a bad boy."

Seth grinned at her, feeling that he'd redeemed himself and she had forgiven him. "It's only now that I'm grown up that I can truly express myself," he said jokingly. "I had a very difficult childhood."

"It doesn't sound as if your childhood's quite over yet," said Paula. "If it was difficult for you, I can imagine what it must have been like for your parents."

Seth's grin weakened. He tried but couldn't think of a suitable repartee; Paula's quickness had once again been too much for him, and once again he had this strange, confusing reaction to being outgunned by a woman, and particularly this woman.

Seth quickly returned to safer topics of discussion, and

between courses they talked mostly about the grant. Seth did his best to convince Paula to accept it; he had a very persuasive case and knew how to present it. And at the back of his mind was the fact that he'd told Coletti that her contract was already in the bag, and that gave added urgency to his appeal.

"Does the foundation fund many projects in New Coventry?" asked Paula.

"Several," he replied. "I'm sure you know Dr. Clifford Abrams, for instance. He's out of our grantees. At this point he gets all of his funding from us, I believe." Seth was feeling the tension grow. He wanted to talk to Paula about other things. He ached to reach out and take her hand, touch her, start to develop an intimacy with her, but right now he had to keep the discussion on a business basis. But next time, he promised himself, oh, next time it'll be different.

Paula was feeling indecisive, an unusual situation for her. It wasn't easy to separate Seth the head of the Millway Foundation from Seth the impatient hothead, but her annoyance hadn't lasted, and she felt a pull, a strong physical attraction to him that surprised her.

She still hadn't made up her mind about the grant when they finished dinner, and they decided to continue their conversation on the way home. When the waiter brought the check, Seth didn't even look at it and slapped down a platinum American Express card. As they were leaving, he left the wine waiter a more than generous cash tip, and gave Paula a little apologetic glance as he did so.

Outside, the street was still wet, and Seth took her elbow and steered her between the puddles back to the car. Encouraged perhaps by two-thirds of a bottle of excellent chardonnay, he felt that things were going his way. Paula seemed to be easing up, smiling and chatting with him, not in an intimate way, not yet, but in a way that could lead to intimacy. He made an effort to keep his mind on the job, but in the dark car, sitting next to her, his fantasies swelled.

"I'll be perfectly frank with you, Seth," she was saying. "My boss, Dr. Bennett, is against my accepting a grant from Millway. He says . . . well, it doesn't matter what he says. He's agin it, and you can see that it would make things tough for me if I went ahead and accepted it."

"Do you think there's maybe a personal angle to that?" asked Seth, coming off I-95 at the first New Coventry exit.

Paula didn't answer. He was going fast, and the tires squealed most of the way around the ramp. The accurate way he steered and controlled the big vehicle gave her a kind of excitement, a feeling of safety and risk at the same time. This guy is a really good driver, thought Paula, held securely in her contoured seat. He's fast, but he knows exactly what he's doing.

Seth had a sense that she was making up her mind, that everything was coming to a head with her; she was going to decide about the grant, she was going to accept it, and she'd be so happy about the decision that after they celebrated it with champagne, she would spend the night with him.

He drove slowly now. "Where is it that you live?" he asked, savoring her presence beside him.

"My car's at the hospital," she reminded him. As they drove through downtown New Coventry, where the quiet streets were still wet around the edges from the rain, Seth felt a strong need to touch her, to put a hand on her thigh, hold her hand, make any kind of physical contact.

Paula could feel the tension and was relieved that the trip was coming to and end. She didn't feel ready for anything more with him just yet.

"Could we do this again?" he asked. "I mean, not on business, just for fun."

"Maybe," she said. "Look, Seth, about the grant, I'm sorry, but there's still a lot of things I have to consider. Anyway, thanks for the evening. I had a good time."

He watched her walk across the street to the doctors' parking lot, then drove slowly and thoughtfully home.

Chapter Nine

The next day, a little over three thousand miles from New Coventry, Steve Charnley sat in a darkened room in the X-ray department of the Los Angeles Memorial Hospital, next to Deke Farmer, the chief of radiology, and his senior associate, Dr. Ted Brown. The three men sat in complete silence, watching the large, flat screen of a color video monitor. The tension was so palpable that one of the other doctors working on the other side of the room at a bank of viewing boxes got up, hesitated, curious to know what was happening, then decided that this was too heavy for him and tiptoed out of the room.

"Could we run through that last section again, Deke?" Steve's voice sounded unnaturally loud.

Deke nodded, Ted partially rewound the tape, and a moment later the image reappeared. It showed a three-dimensional transparency of a woman's head and neck, with the blood vessels pulsating in rhythm with the heartbeat.

"Can you center it, Ted? We need to see both carotids in the same plane."

Ted made an adjustment to the control on the panel in front of him, and the image rotated slightly.

"Beautiful." Steve watched the lower part of the neck, and when he saw the contrast medium start to come up the carotids, he said, "Slow it . . . now."

When the contrast medium had been injected into the bloodstream forty minutes before, real-time visualization had showed the fluid shooting up through the head arteries in a fraction of a second. That had been filmed at a hundred and fifty frames per second, but now that the video was running at a slow fifteen frames per second, the medium seemed to creep slowly up the inside of both carotid arteries, like the mercury in the stem of a thermometer.

"Can you hold it when the contrast gets just past the bulb?" asked Steve.

When Ted pressed the stop button, it was precisely at the point where the contrast medium showed the carotid arteries in the neck as they divided into two branches. On the left side, the medium showed a severe constriction in the artery, as if it had been partially pinched off.

"How much narrowing, would you say, Deke?" Steve's face was tense in the fluorescent glow from the viewing boxes.

"I'd guess about eighty percent, just looking at it," replied Deke. He was a big man, with a gruff voice and a gray, bristly crew cut. "If you can wait a second, I'll do the flow calculations." He pressed some numbers on the console.

The door opened a crack, and the head and shoulders of Steve's intern appeared. He was already in his greens. "We're all set, Steve," he said. "She's prepped and ready to go."

"Three minutes," said Steve, not taking his eyes away from the screen. "I think we'll be using the scope on this one."

"It's ready."

"Ninety-four percent blockage," said Deke when the door closed. His voice expressed surprise, and he stared, annoyed at the glowing green numbers in the corner of his screen that were contradicting his intuition. From where Steve sat, the bristles on Deke's crew-cut head glowed like a halo in the reflected light.

"I'd never have guessed it was that tight," Deke went on, a hint of apprehension in his voice. "This woman's looks ready to shut down any minute." He shook his head. "I'd never have guessed it," he repeated.

"She's had four small strokes already," said Steve.

"It said three in the chart," commented Deke, glancing around and thinking he'd caught Steve out on this minor matter.

"She had another about two hours ago," replied Steve. "That's why we're here."

They stared at the images in silence.

"Let's turn the head slowly all the way around, Ted," said Steve. "It looked as if the blockage was mostly on the back wall."

The image started to rotate slowly, and the details of the partial blockage became clearer. Two minutes later, Steve stood up. "Thanks, guys," he said, "that was just fantastic."

"Our pleasure," said Deke. He paused for a second before going on, and the tone of his voice surprised Ted. His boss sounded more like a kid asking for a favor than the head of a major department talking to a mere senior resident.

"Do you mind if we watch you doing the arterioscopy?"

"Sure," said Steve. "We've set up a slave monitor in the small O.R. lounge. There's a whole bunch of people who want to watch this, and I'm not letting anybody into the O.R. who isn't directly involved in the operation."

"Okay," said Deke mildly. "We'll go on over."

Steve left the room, and Ted switched the equipment so that the tapes could be viewed and remotely controlled from the operating room. He addressed Deke. "Quite a guy, our Steve, isn't he?" he said.

"He sure is," replied Deke with a hint of envy in his voice. "Invents and develops instruments for his own medical equipment company, does good research ... I don't know how the guy manages to squeeze in a surgical residency when he's doing all that."

"Somebody said he's going to New Coventry when he finishes the program here," said Ted.

"He'd be better off staying here," replied Deke, shrugging. "He's got everything in place right in this hospital. But I guess that's his decision."

When Steve Charnley came into the operating room, the atmosphere was electric. This was the first time that his arterioscope was to be used on a human patient, and everybody in the huge hospital knew it. Although various kinds of scopes had been available for years to look inside lungs, bladders, stomachs, and intestines, until now no one had been able to master the technical difficulties of looking inside arteries and veins. The problem that had defeated all previous efforts was that the blood inside the vessels was opaque and prevented any kind of visualization. Attempts had been made to overcome this by blocking segments of the artery and clearing it of blood to give a view of the inside of the vessel, but that caused a stoppage of the circulation, and the tissues beyond the feeding artery risked being irreparably damaged.

Since Steve was technically still a resident and not yet a fully qualified surgeon, Dr. Armand Nessler, one of the senior vascular attendings, was in the operating room with him. Steve had selected Armand to assist because he was one of the most competent vascular surgeons at the hospital. Some weeks before, in preparation for this day, Armand had spent several hours in the lab with Steve, learning how the equipment worked. Then they had gone to the animal lab and worked there until Armand felt comfortable with all the complicated controls and tricks of using the arterioscope.

Nessler was very interested but nevertheless a little apprehensive. A capable, careful, methodical man, he preferred to use well-tested equipment that he was totally familiar with, and innovations of this kind made him nervous.

"You did tell the patient this was an experimental procedure?" he asked Steve as they scrubbed.

"Sure. I explained it in detail to her and also to her husband and daughter. I got them all to sign the release forms, and I explained the possible dangers and risks to them. We also have the FDA one-time approval letter and the hospital administrator's official permission to use the equipment. We're one hundred percent legal."

Under the bright lights of the operating room, the prepared area on the left side of the patient's neck glowed orange-yellow. The overhead video camera was on but would remain immobile until the operating team operated the directional controls from the operating table. To the left of the anesthesia machine stood the high TV monitor which would show the view from the tiny, flexible fiberoptic probe within the arterioscope as it transmitted a video picture from inside the pencil-thick artery.

Deke Farmer picked up his pager, clipped it to his belt, and, with Ted, left the X-ray department and went off to the small O.R. lounge to see the show.

"I don't understand how they can ever see anything inside an artery," said Ted in a quiet voice. "You'd think all they could see would be blood."

"He injects a stream of oxygenated saline ahead of the tip," replied Deke, who'd already asked that question of Steve and was pleased to be able to answer the question. "So when the blood's cleared, they can see the inside of the artery long enough to make a diagnosis and do whatever procedure they need to do."

They stood just inside the door of the small lounge. It was already packed with about twenty other people jammed into a space designed for about ten occupants, and all the chairs had been taken. Two ceiling-mounted color monitors at the front of the room glowed. One showed the operative field; the other, attached to the arterioscope, was blank.

Steve followed Armand Nessler as he backed into the operating room, hands raised, and the scrub nurse turned toward them, then hesitated. The correct protocol was to give the senior surgeon the first sterile towel to dry his hands, then do the same for his assistant, but she knew Steve was doing the case and it was his show. She gave the towel to him and put the second towel in Armand's hands a moment later. Armand grinned at her, not at all put out, but she blushed with embarrassment under her mask.

Once they were gowned and gloved, Steve went over to the patient's left side, and Armand stood opposite him. Steve took a green towel off the small console and pressed a button. A beam of intense light came from the tip of the arterioscope, and the image on the second monitor came to life.

In the small lounge, the murmur of conversation stopped when the screen lit up. Steve put a hand in front of the scope, and the hugely magnified brown-gloved image appeared on the screens for a second.

"Shows pretty good detail," said Ted approvingly. Deke nodded, then the screen went dark when Steve shut the light off.

They watched on the other monitor as Steve made a two-inch incision in the neck, an inch above the left collarbone. The wall-mounted speaker clicked, and Steve's voice came through. He sounded calm and matter-of-fact, as if this were just a routine case, although he could feel his heart beating hard inside his chest. "I don't need to make the usual long incision here," he explained. "I just need enough length to expose the artery and get the scope in."

With Armand's expert help, it didn't take long to have the carotid artery exposed and visible. It showed up on the screen as a whitish cord about the thickness of a pencil, next to the floppy blue jugular vein. Steve isolated the artery and picked up a pair of small arterial clamps. "We're about to occlude the artery," he told the anesthesiologist, then addressed the people in the lounge again. "I'm going to check the forward and back flow first," he said, "then I'll put in the scope. When I do that, all you'll see on the screen for a few seconds is a lot of red." The surgeons in the audience grinned in anticipation. They knew the big moment was approaching.

The image on the monitor went wild for a few seconds as Steve switched on the light and picked up the scope. Then they saw the tiny incision in the artery get rapidly bigger as the tip of the scope approached it; then, just as Steve had warned them, the entire screen went red the moment the probe entered the artery. About three seconds later, long enough for Steve to push the end of the scope up to where the blockage was, he injected clear saline into the artery and the screen cleared as if by magic. A gasp went through the audience; for the first time in a living patient, they could see the artery from the inside, magnified to the point where it looked like a road tunnel with curving, irregular yellowish walls.

"There's the blockage," said Steve, unable to keep a quaver of excitement out of his voice. "Dead ahead. It's about a centimeter beyond the tip of the probe."

The screen went red again for a while, and then Steve

injected a fresh dose of saline to clear the blood from the vessel. When the picture cleared, they could see that the probe was now right up against a hard, calcified mass that projected into the artery, narrowing it almost to the point of closure.

"That little black hole is all the opening she has left for the blood supply to that side of her brain." Steve's voice reflected the urgency of the situation. They all knew he had only a very short time to open up the artery.

"Now we'll use the roto-rooter," said Steve. The "roto-rooter," was a tiny, motor-driven drill with a hard steel bit. When it was switched on, it was automatically advanced from the tip of the instrument and started to rotate. By adjusting its position and speed, Steve could grind away at the hard material blocking the artery. It had taken a lot of practice to get it right, and Steve had spent hundreds of hours perfecting his technique. "You won't be able to see too much for the next few minutes," he told his audience. "While we're drilling, we'll suction out the debris before it can get loose and travel up into the brain."

For the next two minutes, the spectators saw the drill biting into the blocking material, and fragments accelerating, then disappearing from the screen as suction carried them away.

"We have to go real carefully at this point," said Steve's voice. "It's hard to tell how thick this calcified stuff is, and we don't want to drill through the wall of the artery."

There was absolute silence in the lounge as the spectators considered the implications of what he'd just said. Drilling a hole through the wall of the artery would be a catastrophic and possibly fatal complication.

"I'm glad it's Steve doing that in there, not me," whispered Ted, just loud for the others to hear. There was a faint murmur, a stirring, and a couple of people looked around and grinned. Ted could see that he wasn't the only one who felt that way.

"You're looking good," said Armand from his side of the table, watching the operating room monitor. And in fact, a major part of the blockage had been drilled away, and the exit opening was now enlarged to about half its normal diameter.

From time to time there was a pause in the action and the screen went red when Steve allowed the normal circulation to proceed. Each time before he did that, he searched meticulously around for debris floating around. The magnification made even the smallest loose particle in the artery look like a boulder on the screen. Then, using the video monitor, he would point the suction tip at a fragment. It instantly vanished, sucked up into the scope and thence into a small, saline-filled glass reservoir on the table.

It seemed like a long time to the audience, and even longer to Steve and Armand, but after less than six minutes, the blockage had been completely removed. The artery wall was rough and irregular where the material had been excavated, but when Steve gave the final saline flush, everybody could see that the opening had been transformed from a pinhole to almost a normal diameter. Ted, standing on tiptoe with excitement, felt like cheering.

Steve was having a last look, checking for loose fragments, when suddenly the screen filled with dark, red-black material.

The watchers thought this was a normal occurrence, something part of the show, until they heard Steve's voice with an edge to it. "What's that?" he said.

"Looks like clot," said Armand. "Jesus. Yes, isn't that what it is, Steve?"

"I guess. It's not . . . Where the hell did it come from?" Steve's voice sounded close to panic.

The dark red material seemed to be moving up inside the artery in a jerky, irregular fashion.

"Take the scope out, Steve." Armand's calm voice reflected his years of experience in dealing with life-threatening emergencies. "Now clamp the artery, up high, as far as you can reach." That was followed by a faint blur of voices, and Ted and Deke figured Armand had turned to talk to the scrub nurse.

"Give me a small DeBakey . . . Steve, can you retract the vein a bit more?"

"Armand's taken over," muttered Deke to no one in particular. "He should have been doing this case in the first place."

They all heard the anesthesiologist's voice. "Her pressure's way down, Dr. Nessler," he said. "What's going on up there?"

"We're in some trouble, and I'm going to open the artery," said Armand in a tight voice. "Somehow a clot got in there, we don't know how. We have to try to get it out."

Steve, trying hard to keep control of himself, knew that wherever that huge clot had come from, the tiny suction tube on his scope could never handle it.

"Eleven blade," said Armand. He made a longitudinal incision in the axis of the artery and opened it wide with forceps. The artery was full of what looked to both Steve and Armand like old, stringy blood clot. For ten minutes, they worked at removing it, but each time they removed a segment of clot, more appeared from below. On the eleventh minute after the clot first appeared, the patient's heart rate became briefly irregular, then it stopped. They were able to restart it the first time by thumping on her chest, and the second time with the defibrillator. The third time, they tried everything they could do to restart the heart, but nothing worked, and none of the medications the anesthesiologist gave made any difference. By the time they gave up a half hour later and the patient was pronounced dead, the lounge was empty except for Ted and Deke. Slowly Deke stood up from the seat he'd taken at the back, walked up the narrow aisle, then reached up to switch off the monitors. On the way back to their department, the two men didn't say anything to each other.

At the autopsy conducted the next day, the pathologist found a clot extending from the left carotid artery all the way up into the brain. "It started in her heart," he explained to Steve, who hadn't slept the night before and looked haggard and tired. "There was an old clot lodged in the top of the left atrium. Here, can you see where it broke off?" He held up the partially dissected heart. An irregular fragment of clot was still attached to the thin wall of one of its chambers. "There was no way you could have told it was there, or how long it had been there. It dislodged and traveled up into her head at just the wrong moment. Sorry." He put a hand on Steve's arm and smiled. "Hey," he said. "Cheer up. You can't win 'em all."

A week after the catastrophe, Steve Charnley went to see Deke Farmer, the head of radiology, in his office.

Deke didn't look happy to see him. In fact, he looked decidedly uncomfortable. "Come on in," he said, but there was no warmth in his tone. "What's up?"

"Nothing good."

To Deke's eyes, a remarkable change had come over Steve in the past few days. Even in the throes of the last few weeks of his residency, when he was so busy that three hours of sleep a night was all he was getting, he had always managed to be alert, quick-witted, and generally on the ball. Now he seemed to be moving more slowly, there was little in the way of expression in his face, and a generalized gray depression seemed to have settled on him.

"The investigation?"

Steve nodded. "Yeah. You know what happened. They crucified me. I appreciate that you stood up for me, though. That made me feel better, although I'm sure it didn't make you too popular with the guys who wanted to make it unanimous."

Deke shrugged. "Witch-hunting is a great American pastime," he said. "And in this particular institution they've brought it to a fine art."

Steve's shoulders sagged. "You know I was going to stay on here as an attending? Well, yesterday my boss called to tell me there are no openings at this time, and I'll have to find a job somewhere else."

"What about New Coventry? I thought for a while you might go there."

"That was a couple of months ago. They've already appointed somebody there. A woman."

"Well, there are plenty of other medical centers," said Deke, looking surreptitiously at the clock on his desk.

"I've been calling around everywhere, and I'm hearing the same story everywhere. No openings, sorry."

"News travels fast, huh?" Deke felt sorry for Steve and wished he could do something to help. "Everybody seems to have got the idea that the arterioscope didn't work," he went on. "I suppose that's what you risk when you try something new."

"Right. They're saying it hadn't been properly tested, that we shouldn't have tried it on such a sick patient, that I was just trying to get publicity for myself, that I was taking an unnecessary risk with the patient's life." Steve's expression hardened. "I guess everybody's just trying to protect their own ass, and don't want to be associated with something that didn't work."

Deke sat there, wishing that Steve would go away.

Steve took a deep breath. "Deke, I'm really stuck. I don't seem to be able to get a job at any of the major centers, but that's where I need to be to keep up the level of work I'm doing here."

Deke moved in his chair. "Steve, the real reason you ran into problems is that you're a high flier," he said. "When you're up, everybody's on your side, because it brings them up too, but when you're down, those same people have no mercy. If you were just a run-of-the-mill surgical resident, nothing like this would have happened. But there's so much jealousy, so much competitiveness in this institution, so much fear of top-notch people, that once they get you down, they make damn sure you don't get a second chance to get up again."

"Thanks for the encouragement." Steve grinned. "What do you suggest I do?"

"You have more options than most," said Deke, picking up a pencil and bouncing it, eraser down, on the desk. The repeated slight sound started to get on Steve's nerves. "How about going into private practice? That's what most of your colleagues are doing."

"And take care of hemorrhoids and varicose veins, and fight with the insurance companies to get paid, for the rest of my professional life? No, thanks. In any case, it would be throwing away all the research training I've done for years and years. It would be a really dumb waste."

"How about one of the surgical instrument companies that make different kinds of scopes, like Olympus? You'd get a high-paying job with them in a second. Or one of the pharmaceutical companies?" suggested Deke. "There are plenty to choose from, and the big ones, like Pfizer and Merck, all have top-notch research facilities, and they'd just love you. They just don't get people of your caliber, and you'd go straight to the top."

"Well, maybe," said Steve, standing up. He was feeling desperate, and it showed in his eyes. "Can you imagine working in one of those pharmaceutical sweat shops? Spending twenty years testing fifteen thousand substances to see if any one of them can make a strip of smooth muscle contract? Thank you, but no, thank you. That isn't the kind of research that turns me on. But I do appreciate your suggestions, anyway."

Deke stood up too, and his embarrassment was almost palpable. "Well then, Steve," he said, holding out his hand, "I hope it all works out for you. Good luck."

Chapter Ten

Two days later, Seth sat in his office, feeling tense and increasingly anxious. He was still waiting to hear from Paula, and time was running out. The image of Vince Coletti was looming in his head; Seth had seriously misled him, and that thought made him suck in his lips with apprehension. Part of Vince's money was already gone to support cash flow, to restore the plundered pension fund, and to retire some major overdue short-term debt. But it wasn't just a case of returning money; because of the size of the investment, Vince had told him, he had gathered a group of people to put the financial package together.

Seth stood up and walked around his office, his head down, hands behind his back. If it ever came out that Seth had defrauded them, Vince would not only look foolish but also incompetent to his backers, and Vince could never tolerate that. Seth felt a cold sweat coming out all over when he thought of the certain consequences to him. There would be a wait, but sooner or later a car bomb would go off under him, or a drive-by shooting would occur. He'd known the risks when he showed Coletti the forged contract with Paula Cairns, the one in which all patent rights from her work were assigned to Millway Pharmaceuticals. Most of all, Seth had known exactly the risks he was taking when he accepted their money.

There had to be some way of getting around this situation. . . . Seth sat down again and banged both sides of his head with his fists, but nothing came of it, except the image of Paula Cairns, a three-dimensional hologram of her that he had carried with him every moment since he watched her walk back to her car that rainy evening.

Seth went over to the lab to talk about Paula's research with Desmond Connor. It gave him a strange kind of relief even to say her name out loud.

"It's not even a new idea," Connor told him as they sat by one of the long teak benches in his lab. "Merck, Glaxo, Ciba, a lot of the big guys have had their eyes on such a system for years, and they've spent millions of dollars trying to make it work. To my knowledge, though, they've all given up."

"So how did Dr. Cairns figure out how to solve it, for God's sake, when with all their resources, even those big guys weren't able to do it?"

"She hasn't got the final sequence yet, I don't believe, not completely. And we know she's still got some other major problems, like the delivery system."

"Yes," said Seth irritably, "I understand that, but what I'm asking you is how in the hell did she manage to figure out the sequence when the big corporations with all their fancy equipment and scientific talent couldn't do it? And why can't you do it? That's the key question, isn't it?"

"I'll tell you why, sir," said Connor, looking hard at Seth, trying not to show his exasperation. "It's because she's one of those people who just appear out of nowhere from time to time in the science field, maybe once very few years. It's because she's a fucking genius, that's why."

Seth pulled a folded piece of perforated computer paper from an inside pocket. It was an alphabetical listing of all the institutions and researchers who received funds from the Millway Foundation. Surely, with all the money they were spending, one of them could find a solution.

At the top of the list was Dr. Clifford Abrams; Seth knew that Dr. Abrams' research was dead in the water, so there probably wasn't much that he could do to help.

But the sight of Abrams' name sparked the germ of an idea inside Seth's head. "Des," he said, "tell me what you know about Dr. Clifford Abrams' work. We're paying him enough so he should be coming up with something pretty damn good."

"He used to be pretty good," replied Connor. "He's done some work on blood clotting but nothing worthwhile for years."

"Okay," said Seth. "So Abrams is on our payroll. Why can't we get him in here, tell him to hire whoever he wants, get whatever experts and fancy equipment he needs to duplicate the work Dr. Cairns is doing? It might take a while, but surely we'd come up with the process eventually, right?"

"Wrong," said Connor.

Seth flushed.

Connor sat back, weary at having to explain all this again. "You remember I said that Merck, Ciba, and all those guys had tried and failed? Well, if we went out hiring, we'd get these same guys working here, getting nowhere just like they did before. My guess is that by the time we got set up, Dr. Cairns will have come up with her final answers. So I think we'd be wasting our time and money."

Seth smacked a fist into his other hand, tense with frustration. "So she's it?" he asked. "Paula Cairns is the only answer?"

"Unless somebody shows up with that kind of expertise," replied Connor. "And I don't know of anyone who has it."

"So somehow we have to get her working for us," said Seth, reflexively scratching the inside of his thigh.

"I don't know how we'd do that," said Connor. "She'll have a long wait getting her first grant, but once she has it, she'll be set. When her process is completed, the granting agency will most likely put it in the public domain, and that'll be that. Or else the university'll pull some kind of multimillion deal with a consortium of pharmaceutical companies."

Seth shook his head. "We cannot allow that to happen," he said, emphasizing each word, thinking apprehensively about his upcoming meeting with Vince Coletti. He had to come with something, and fast. "Somehow I have a feeling that Clifford Abrams has the key to all this. Let me think about it."

Several times later that day he put his hand on the phone to call Paula, but each time he decided not to. He knew that if he tried to push her it wouldn't help, and might even make her go in the other direction.

Meanwhile, Paula was concerned and apprehensive about how she should proceed. If she went ahead and took the grant, she knew that her relationship with Maurice would take a very severe blow, and that was the last thing she wanted to happen.

And Seth himself was adding to the confusion. Her feelings about him varied almost from moment to moment; he was charming, quick-tempered, sexy, devious. . . . Paula hadn't forgotten about his visit to the clinic, and still couldn't figure it out. What she did know was that she wouldn't at all mind seeing him again.

Nicky Millway was Paula's only private patient in the hospital. When she first had come to New Coventry, Maurice had warned her not to count on developing a private practice overnight. The competition for patients with insurance was fierce, he told her, and the "city doctors" like Walt Eagleton and his internist colleagues referred all insured patients to one another, leaving the academics to take care of the poor and the uninsured. So as the private surgeons drove to their luxurious suburban homes in their Jaguars and Mercedeses, they'd check the emergency room from their car phones. And occasionally an insured patient would show up, causing the surgeon to make a fast U-turn on Route 9 and hightail it back to the hospital to claim the patient before he or she was snatched up by one of the academic teams. All it cost them was an occasional lavish pool-side party, and a few well-chosen birthday and Christmas presents to the key people in the emergency room.

Paula had taken to looking in on Nicky Millway three or four times a day, mostly because she enjoyed her so much. And Paula got a refresher course in contemporary early adolescent thinking; she found that things had changed a lot in the twenty-odd years since she was at that stage.

"What are you listening to?" she asked Nicky, who was moving her shoulders in time with the music in her headphones. Nicky didn't hear her, because the music was turned up high. She grinned at Paula, and knew she was talking to her, but wasn't about to turn her music off.

Every square millimeter of Nicky's cast was covered by signatures and messages from her school friends, scrawled in every color imaginable. Some even glowed in the dark, Nicky proudly told her. So Paula examined her foot, noting the broken edges of the cast. It looked as if it had done six months in the trenches.

"She just won't go on the bedpan," the frustrated nurses had told Paula. "All the time we're catching her hopping over to the bathroom, or else she's standing at the door waving goodbye to her friends."

"I think I can feel my toes," said Nicky, holding one earphone against her ear. "Listen to this song," she went on, pointing at the other earphone. Paula rather gingerly held it a few inches away from her ear, and even then it was too loud. "I need you, I want you . . ." Nicky sang along. "That's how I feel about my boyfriend," she said, glancing at Paula with her huge blue eyes. "God, I want his body close to me . . ."

Using the end of a ballpoint pen, Paula tried to determine which of Nicky's toes, if any, had recovered sensation, but Nicky had her earphones on again and couldn't hear her questions.

Chapter Eleven

When Geoff Susskind, the university lawyer, called, Seth, sitting in his office, said "I can't talk right now. I'll get back to you." He replaced the phone and looked up at his visitors who had just come in and were now standing over him from the other side of his desk. They were Vince Coletti and Mike Petras.

"No phone calls for a little while, okay?" Coletti's request to Seth sounded like an order, and his expression was not friendly.

Seth, feeling a chill descend on him, pushed the intercom button and told his secretary to hold all calls until further notice.

"You look as if you have a problem," he said to Coletti, trying to ignore Petras. "Why don't you sit down?"

"You're the one who has the problem," said Coletti in a regretful voice. "Seth, you lied to me. You sold me a line of bullshit, and you backed that up with forged documents. You took a lot of money from me and my associates."

Seth braced himself. He wasn't physically afraid of either Coletti or even Petras, but that wasn't the point. How had Coletti found out? It had to be Susskind; nobody else knew that Paula hadn't signed any contract.

Petras moved over to the door and stayed there, facing them.

"You're quite right, Vince," said Seth. "And I feel bad about misleading you, although it was just a minor thing. All I did was jump the gun a bit. Everything I told you about the project was correct. It's going to make us hundreds of millions of dollars, there's no question about that."

"Maybe," said Coletti. "The problem is that those millions ain't going to be coming to us, not the way I see it." Coletti's Boston accent was now very noticeable. "Those patent rights you told me about, they don't belong to you, Seth, or to the foundation. You should have told the truth." Coletti's voice was quiet, but Seth didn't like the way he'd positioned himself, too close, standing over him, although the desk was between them. He felt at a physical disadvantage, and there was an implicit threat of sudden violence in the air.

Seth took the safest course and told him exactly what had happened, and only skewed the facts a little.

"So you see," he said, "everything I did was in good faith. In any case, we haven't had a definite answer from her, one way or the other, about the grant. I've spent hours telling her that it would be the smartest move she could possibly make—"

"Maybe you should have shut up and let her figure it out herself," said Vince roughly. "What if she says no?"

"Then we'll have to figure out another way of legally getting the rights to her process," said Seth.

"Legally?" said Coletti. "Are you kidding? Is 'legally' what you worry about when something needs to be done?"

"Well, you do have to take that into consideration, don't you?" said Seth, but even to him it sounded lame.

"The only reason I'm here," said Coletti in a conversational tone, "and the only reason you're not decomposing at the bottom of the Thames River, is that I have a lot of pride, and don't want to be embarrassed in front of the other people in my group. Seth, they trust me. They look to me for their profits. And I have to protect their investment, and mine."

"They'll get their profits," said Seth. "And so will you. We just need to iron out a few details."

"Start ironing," said Coletti. He sat down and put his long, shiny shoes up on Seth's desk. "You were talking about staying legal. Well, as far as we're concerned, the law is just another business risk. The guy who figures the risks correctly wins, not the guy who worries if it's legal. Now let's get back to your project. You tried legal, and it didn't work." Vince surveyed Seth coldly. "Now what?"

"If she decides not to accept a grant from Millway? Geoffrey Susskind says he can convince her, for sure. That was him on the phone just now. He doesn't come cheap, but if it works, it'll be worth a hundred thousand times what we pay him. One way or another, we have to get her in under the Millway umbrella."

Seth explained what he had in mind.

"You haven't thought it through, Seth," said Coletti when Seth had finished. "What if she sidesteps all of that and sells the process on her own to Schering or Merck? Or to a foreign company like Glaxo or Farmacia?"

"I *have* thought it through," replied Seth, regaining some of his confidence. "First, she's going to be working for us, one way or the other. Second, she doesn't have a viable product yet. And if she did try to sell it when she's working with Millway money, it would be illegal and we'd have legal recourse."

"Bullshit," said Coletti, out of patience. "That is just pure bullshit." He gave a short, disbelieving laugh. "Legal recourse . . . Are you kidding? All she'd have to do is publish the complete process in one of the scientific journals. That puts it instantly in the public domain, and everybody and his mother would be free to go ahead and manufacture it. And don't tell me the patent laws would protect us. The big pharmaceutical labs would just make a few minor changes to get around them. Jesus Christ, man, those people have dozens of scientists and some of the smartest lawyers in the world, hired to run rings around assholes like you."

"So do you have any suggestions?" asked Seth, his voice insolent. "All you've done so far to help is to knock down the ideas I've come up with."

Coletti stared at Seth for a moment, and the look in his eye made Seth think he might have gone too far. "Seth," he said very quietly, "I don't think you really understand what's happening. You're so close to being dead, your temperature's probably dropping already."

Mike Petras seemed to take this as a signal and started to move forward, but Coletti waved him back.

"Yes, I do have some suggestions," he went on. "As of right now, I'm personally going to take over this operation, and try to pull your fucking chestnuts out of the fire. That's because they'll burn to a cinder with your lah-di-dah methods. Direct action, that's what we need. We need the process, so we take the whole thing out of her computer. While you're trying to get her to sign your contract, my guys are going to get the info right out of her computer programs."

"That won't work," said Seth.

"Why not?"

"Because the process isn't complete, that's why. Why the fuck do you think I'm putting up this money and going to all this trouble? Anyway, you won't need your computer people. When the time comes, when we're ready, I have access to her computer entry code. No need for break-ins or any of that kind of stuff. You've been watching too many movies."

Coletti put his feet on the floor again and sat up

straight in the comfortable visitor's chair. "By the way," he said, "did you know that you're being investigated?"

"No, I didn't," said Seth, startled. "Who by?"

"I'm not sure. It's not one of the official agencies, I can tell you that. It has to be somebody with a fair amount of clout, I'd guess, because they've been talking to the FBI and the IRS. Did you remember to file a corporate tax return last year? Got anything to hide?"

Seth shrugged. "You, for a start, I suppose."

"Yeah," said Coletti. "Right. You keep that hid, okay?"

"Is that all, Vince? Is it okay with you if I get on with my work now?"

"When I tell you. One last thing. What are your plans for the researcher woman once we own the process?"

"I guess she'll go on to get herself a Nobel Prize or whatever. Why? That's not my problem."

"Yes, it is," replied Coletti. "Once we've got the process, *we* know how to keep it a secret. But she doesn't have to. That's why I asked, what are your plans for her? Are you going to take her to a desert island, one that doesn't have a phone?"

"That's an idea," said Seth, grinning. "Smartest thought you've had all morning."

"Yeah, but it won't do, Seth. Not really permanent enough. But don't worry," he went on when Seth opened his mouth to say something. "When the time comes, we'll take care of her."

Chapter Twelve

Two days later, Clifford Abrams strode importantly into the foyer of the Millway Building in downtown New Coventry, doing his best to look like a man in charge of his own destiny. In fact, he was very apprehensive about the urgent summons he'd received to meet with the senior representatives of the Millway Foundation.

Sure, acknowledged Abrams as he waited, answering their as yet unspoken criticisms, in the past couple of years the pile of research papers on the table had been smaller, but you can't measure the value of research on an avoirdupois basis. Abrams figured that the Millway people probably wouldn't realize that this year's few reports had been published in less prestigious journals, although he himself was acutely aware of that.

But this time things were starkly different. Budget cutbacks—that's what the Millway secretary had mumbled. Abrams knew about those. He'd been hearing that song, like a recurrent, monotonous mantra from the Ford Foundation, the National Institutes of Health, the Johnson Foundation, the Army. But until now Millway had stood firm, though alone, each time pumping in close to the amount of money he asked for, and each time thanking him for accepting their humble contribution to his invaluable work.

Things were changing fast, thought Abrams, waiting

impatiently outside the conference room. He dried his palms on the outside of his gray pinstriped pants, high up so that it wouldn't show.

"Dr. Abrams?" The secretary, slim, black-haired, dressed in a dark business suit, as exquisite as any account executive, put his head around the door and beckoned with an elegant, manicured hand.

Abrams jumped up, too quickly, and came forward. He knew the room well; it was long, heavily paneled in dark oak, dark despite the three tall windows on the left side that overlooked the city. Instead of the usual ten or so smiling execs from the Millway organization, there were only three sitting at the far end of the long table. As Abrams walked up, his smile of greeting already fixed on his face, he recognized Seth Millway sitting next to Sam, who was at the head of the table, looking tired and anxious. Next to him was Desmond Connor, head of the Millway research labs.

Sam stood up, thin, aging, in an almost black suit with a white shirt and tie so dark blue that it looked black also. Three points of a white handkerchief emerged from his breast pocket.

"Dr. Abrams," he said, sounding very formal, "thank you for coming on such short notice. You remember Desmond Connor from previous meetings, I'm sure. And you know Seth, my son. He's sat in on many of our discussions in the past."

After shaking Sam's hand, Abrams went first around the table to Seth, who shook his hand in a reluctant, offhand way and nodded, although he didn't bother to look Abrams in the eye. Slightly shaken, Abrams came back to Connor, whose handshake seemed normal enough.

"If you'd like to sit next to Seth," said his father, his voice sounding frailer than Abrams remembered, "then we can get down to business."

To Abrams' sensitivities, heightened by the tension of the moment, there was something almost sinister about the way the old man spoke, but he shrugged that feeling off and sat down, still smiling his most confident smile.

Seth moved back in his seat, spread his legs, and his eyes moved in a leisurely, almost insolent way to survey Abrams. There was a complete lack of the respectful, smiling attention Abrams was used to, not only from Sam Millway but from all of them.

"Well, it's sure nice to be back here with you all," said Abrams. "I have to take the shuttle to Washington tomorrow to talk to the secretary of HHS, and I dread the heat down there."

"Yeah," said Seth unexpectedly. He smiled over at Connor. "I guess it'll be hot, all right."

Abrams' pale eyebrows went up. "I meant the weather," he said. "Did you?"

Seth ignored the question. He pointed at a tiny stack of three reprints by Sam's right hand. "Is that your research output for the last year, Dr. Abrams?"

Abrams stretched out a pudgy hand. "Let me see," he said.

Seth silently passed the three reprints over to him.

Abrams checked each one. "We have a number of papers in press at the present time," he said. "Anyway, you can't judge the work of a lab simply by the number of papers that comes out of it."

Sam was looking at him with what seemed an apologetic look, and Abrams took strength from it. "Look at Einstein," he went on. "His reputation was made with a single paper on the general theory of relativity, in Switzerland—"

"Einstein was a genius," interrupted Seth. "And in any case, just to get the story straight, his original 1905 papers on relativity appeared in *Annalen der Physik,* a German publication. Isn't that right, Des?"

Connor nodded.

Seth put his left hand on his crotch and scratched it for a few moments. His father looked away. "Also, unlike *your* research grant, Dr. Abrams," he went on, "Einstein's funding request was merely for one blackboard and a box of chalk." He grinned over at Connor, who grinned back. Putting his hands flat on the table, Seth said, "Anyway, we're not here to discuss Einstein."

"Not by any means," said Connor softly, not taking his eyes off Abrams.

After a second's silence Seth laughed, loud and appreciatively. "Right on, Des," he said. "Point well made." He turned to Abrams again. "Now, Dr. Abrams, to get back to your research. You were telling us about these papers." He indicated the three reprints spread out in front of him.

"These papers represent a great deal of work by me and my staff," said Abrams, beginning to sound blustery. "We're doing ground-breaking research on the changes in the blood chemistry that precede clot formation inside the body."

Seth had picked up the reprints. "*Southwest Journal of Medicine and Surgery, Belgian Annals of Research, Mississippi Medical Memoranda,*" he read from the top. He glanced across the table at Connor and pushed the reprints over to him. "Des, would you consider these topclass research publications?"

"Never heard of any of them," said Connor, shrugging. He looked questioningly across the table at Abrams. "I assume you offered each of these papers to the leading research journals first, surely, Dr. Abrams?"

Rattled, Abrams answered, "Yes, of course," before realizing his mistake. He hurried to correct the error. "Of course, the top journals are limited to the material they can accept, and in any case they have a backlog and can't publish everything that's sent to them. Everybody knows they have to turn down even excellent articles. . . ."

Sam moved in his chair, an expression of acute discomfort on his face. "Dr. Abrams," he said, speaking for the first time, sounding conciliatory and apologetic. "We realize how difficult it is for anyone to keep on producing first-class research year after year, the kind we've been so proud to see coming from your lab for as long as we've been funding your efforts—"

"Dad, just let me deal with this," interrupted Seth, without looking at his father. There was something in his tone that chilled Abrams, and Sam seemed to shrink visibly within his suit.

"Sure, of course, excuse me," he said, leaning back and unconsciously crossing his hands in front of his chest in a protective gesture.

"Right," said Seth, again looking straight in front of him but addressing Abrams. "Dr. Abrams, last year the foundation paid you 1.3 million dollars, about the same as we've been paying you for the last five years. We've got no returns on this money. We're in business, Dr. Abrams. We can't afford to keep pouring money down the sewer."

"No returns?" asked Abrams loudly, finally goaded into action. He thumped his fist on the table. "What are you talking about, returns? Your foundation is supposed to be a nonprofit organization, interested in funding pure research, not looking for returns on your dollar. Isn't that right, Sam? Isn't that what you told me, not once but many times?"

Sam looked at Abrams, then at Seth, opened his mouth as if to say something, then shut it and stared at his feet, his pain clear for all to see.

"Well then, what the hell's going on here?" went on Abrams in a belligerent tone, hoping that he could get

Sam to take command again. "Who's in charge of this organization? Sam, are you letting your boy take over, destroy all that you've built up here?" Abrams waved his hand to include the conference room, the entire building. "Are you going to allow all the good work your foundation's done over the years to go up in smoke like this?"

There was a silence, then Sam said hesitantly, "Seth's the foundation chairman now, Dr. Abrams, and as he says, one hand should feed the other."

"So you want to use the foundation to do your corporate research for you?" asked Abrams sarcastically. "Does that mean Dr. Connor's out of a job? Don't you know that if you do that, the Millway Foundation loses its nonprofit status? Immediately? Then within days you'll have a whole pack of investigators from the IRS poring over your books, sniffing around to see how much back taxes you owe them."

Abrams looked around at the men. Seth was unmoved, but it seemed he might have scored with Des Connor. Two red spots had suddenly shown on his cheekbones. "We do all of our own research in our New Coventry labs," he said stiffly. "Occasionally we'll subcontract part of a project. But certainly nothing of any real value has ever come to us from the money the foundation pours into university research." The corner of Connor's left lip went up with barely disguised scorn. "And certainly nothing from your department."

"Yeah, I know the kind of work you do," said Abrams. "You test a million different combinations of aspirin, phenacetin, and all that other garbage to come up with yet another cure for rheumatism or insomnia or whatever. Brilliant. Really brilliant. A succession of intellectual triumphs. And you were the one who knew all about Einstein, right?"

He stood up, full of righteous indignation, and faced

Sam. "Sam," he said, "I'm truly disappointed that you've let this happen to your fine organization. But I want you"—he turned to Seth with an expression of contempt on his face—"to know that I don't need you. I can get funding from any one of a dozen sources, institutions far-sighted enough to see the potential—"

"Please sit down, Dr. Abrams," said Seth calmly. "There's no need to lose your temper. And anyway, I haven't finished talking to you."

Panting with his exertion, Abrams looked at Seth with aggressive satisfaction. When push came to shove, he had known Seth Millway would fold. Abrams had plenty of experience in browbeating funding agencies, most of whom knew little or nothing about medical research but were filled with respect for it. He had learned at the feet of his old boss, Dr. Frank Moore. "It's like selling shoes," he once had confided to Abrams, "the customer needs what you've got, and you need what he's got. You just gotta find what he wants, figure the price, and make a deal."

Abrams slowly subsided into his chair, expecting that Seth would now get down to business. He was merely flushed with his new power and position, Abrams figured, and wanted to make everybody know who was boss.

"Do you know Terry Knight?" asked Seth. "And Paul Benicewitz? And Bob Ramo? And Joan Pincus?"

Abrams stared at Seth. The names were all of site-visit team leaders, Knight at NIH, Benicewitz at the Heart Foundation, Ramo at Ford, and Joan Pincus was in charge of the Mellon Foundation team. All were people Abrams had dealt with in the past, and who had given his lab funding at one time or another.

"Yes, I do," he said slowly. "But what . . .?"

"I've talked with each one of them, and others, within the last week," said Seth. "You know, in the foundation business we all talk to each other."

"So?"

"They all agree with me," said Seth. "You're over the hill, Dr. Abrams. There's been nothing coming out of your lab for years that's worth shit. At this time, not one of them is prepared to recommend giving you one more red cent in the upcoming round of applications. And you can be sure that goes for every single institution that funds research in this country, Britain, and Japan. As I said, they all talk to each other. The word is out on you, Dr. Abrams, and you might as well consider that as final."

Cliff Abrams said nothing. There was nothing to say. The jowls on his round face sagged; he knew that what Seth had said was true, because he knew it himself already. Slowly he stood up, and there was a kind of defeated dignity about him that made old Sam Millway feel terrible, as it was designed to.

"Thank you, gentlemen," said Abrams, "for your support in the past. Now I'll be getting on my way."

As if on cue, the door opened and a secretary came in, holding a folded message slip. "This was sent over from your office, Dr. Abrams. The girl said it just came in from Washington."

Abrams opened the note. The secretary of HHS had cancelled their meeting and had not suggested a new date.

"Not bad news, I hope," said Seth, grinning.

Abrams didn't answer, but folded the paper and put it in his pocket. He pushed his chair back and was about to leave when Seth spoke again in a quiet, reflective voice.

"There may be one way out of this, Dr. Abrams. I've given the matter a lot of thought, and there is a possibility that Millway could resume funding for your laboratory. If what I have in mind works out, it would restore your reputation as an avant-garde researcher and in addition bring a breath of new life into your laboratory."

A gleam of irrational hope lit up somewhere in Abrams' chest, and he sat down again, eager to listen to anything they might suggest.

A half hour later, exhausted by the unpleasant interview, Abrams drove back to the hospital, thinking about the final part of their discussion.

"Why don't you simply fund her research directly yourself?" he'd bluntly asked Seth, whose answering smile was about as warm as an eel's blood.

"We've chosen not to take that route, Dr. Abrams," he said curtly, preempting any further discussion. "This is what we want you to do. You will start a crash program in the same area of research as Dr. Cairns . . ." He glowered at Abrams, who seemed about to interrupt. ". . . so that your lab will be in position to take over her research if for any reason she can't get funding. That way you will get the credit when her work is completed, and that will put you back in the mainstream of research, making you re-eligible for further funding."

Seth stared at Abrams, who thought he'd never seen such chilly eyes, and continued. "A scientific success of this magnitude will make you politically unassailable; if you want a dean's job, transfer to another major medical center, or obtain whatever power position you want, you'll be set up for it."

Abrams licked his pink lips.

"In addition," Seth went on, "when the project is demonstrably underway, we will transfer to your brokerage account a substantial number of stock options in Millway Pharmaceuticals. When we announce that we are starting to market a system that will abolish spontaneous blood clotting inside the body, you will be free to convert, sell, or save them for later. Either way this project can earn you a fortune."

"I can't do it," said Abrams doggedly. "I don't have a researcher on my staff who would be credible in this area, and I can't just start writing papers on that topic. No, I'm sorry, it simply wouldn't work. If at this stage in my career I presented a paper on how to destroy blood clots, it would raise a lot of eyebrows and simply wouldn't be taken seriously by the scientific community."

"Then hire somebody who would be taken seriously," said Seth sharply.

"I don't know a single . . ." Abrams voice faded. Suddenly he did know. That fellow from California, Steve Charnley. Although some of his research had to do with developing surgical instrumentation, he had published a number of good papers related to the coagulation mechanism. Charnley was smart, ambitious, and known in the field. And Abrams had heard about the screw-up in Los Angeles, and knew Charnley had not found a suitable job.

"Pay him or her whatever you have to to get him," Seth was saying. "Buy whatever equipment you need. We'll pay for it. Just do it. Now."

Chapter Thirteen

Steve Charnley walked down to the beach at Santa Monica with his board under his arm, concentrating on the look of the surf and trying to put everything else out of his mind. He had a temporary job in the emergency room at Memorial because he hadn't been able to get the kind of job he wanted, and was getting more and more depressed. Everywhere he'd applied, they'd heard about his disastrous case with the arterioscope, and none of the major medical centers wanted any part of him. Today he'd felt an irresistible urge to get out and spend some time by himself, so he strapped his board to the roof of his old Toyota and headed west to the beaches.

The surf was high, and ragged gray clouds were hurrying across the sky, pushing to the northeast. A strong, steady onshore wind whipped the tops off the crests, and sets of five or six waves were coming in tight and fast, curving in to the rocky headland and exploding against the steel pillars of the pier that stuck far out into the water to his right.

This was more dangerous surfing than he would have chosen, and he also recognized that he was seriously out of practice. He'd been at it long enough to know how crucial that was in difficult surf; even being away for a day or two took the edge off his reflexes and increased the risk of getting into trouble.

A whole new crop of long-stemmed, rubbery, tough brown and green *laminaria* kelp had washed up at the high-water mark, and Steve subconsciously noted this further indication of stormy conditions out there. He paused to attach his wrist strap, and looked up and down the beach. It was almost deserted; a few walkers plodded along the sand. A couple of hundred yards out, two or three intrepid surfers appeared as black dots from time to time, but mostly they were obscured by spray. Steve noted that they were keeping well clear of the west end of the beach, where the surf could curve them onto the rocks or into the steel supports of the pier.

Steve tried to concentrate on the surf. He'd heard the sound of it from a long way off, and now that he was on the beach, it was a continuous roaring from the crazy, disordered sea. Between the breakers the water was white with foam, and the interval between waves was shorter than he'd ever remembered it. And they rolled in fast, one after another, crashing in a confused welter of water. A gust of spray blew onshore hard enough to sting his body and legs, and again he thought about giving up and going home. For the first time in his life he was breaking one of the safety rules; surf where other surfers are or, better still, go with a buddy.

He walked into the foamy, frothy shallow water, felt the bubbles rising and bursting against his legs, and even before he was knee deep he became aware of the power of the undertow pulling at his legs and scooping the sand out from under his feet.

Nothing was going right for him. He'd stopped calling the major medical centers because their answer was always the same. "Sure, send us your résumé, Dr. Charnley, but we don't have anything in your field right now."

The water was now waist high, and he pushed the board out in front of him and started to paddle. There was so much foam in the water that his progress was slow and sluggish from the loss of buoyancy. He waited to get out between the breakers, but the sets were coming in fast and close together, and a couple of times he just escaped being dumped on by a few hundred tons of flying water. He retreated for a while, trying to keep his mind on the surf, checking with his experience to judge a pause or a change in the rate as the waves came in.

In desperation Steve had even called an old friend of his who worked in the medical affairs department of Johnson and Johnson in New Jersey, and for whom he'd done a number of major favors. Jerry enthusiastically promised to set up some interviews, and said he'd call back, but never did. Steve heard later that Jerry had called around, heard the story about the arterioscope, and decided he didn't want to get involved.

"Now!" said a voice in his head, and he raised himself on the board and paddled out as fast as he could, helped by the retreating water from the last wave. Then up he went, up, up, but the front of the wave went higher still and towered over him, the hard green wall almost vertical, and Steve felt sure that it was going to break right over him and slam him into the sandy bottom, but it held long enough to pass him by and broke with a thunderous roar just a couple of yards behind him. Normally the next phase would have been relatively calm; he'd have paddled out to where the breakers were starting to rise, picked a good wave, and come in on it, but today the water was rough and choppy, the stinging spray was in his nose and eyes all the time, the noise was deafening, and he was starting to get chilled in spite of his wet suit. The sun was covered by mile-thick clouds, and he had real trouble keeping his bearings. Every so often, bobbing on top of a wave, he got a glimpse of the pier, once with solid water and spray crashing over the end of it. Paddling hard, working to produce body heat, Steve continued to head out. Even now, when he should have been concentrating with every ounce of energy on what he was doing, his thoughts kept turning back to that last meeting at his hospital, when he'd been criticized for the way he had handled the case. All the people who'd previously been so enthusiastic about the arterioscope had suddenly become stony-faced and accusatory.

After all the shouting was over, the board had let Steve off with an unofficial censure, but, Armand told him later, only because a formal reprimand would increase the risk of finding themselves up to the neck in lawsuits.

The current was rapidly pulling Steve to his left, toward the rocky end of the beach. He tried to paddle in the opposite direction, but the current was running too fast. With a shock he realized that if he was to get out of this in one piece, he'd have to take the next wave and ride it in, hoping that it wouldn't dump him on the rocks or, worse still, into the concrete and steel supports of the pier. The wind was howling around him now, and he was getting disoriented and stiff with cold. He managed to get up on an incoming wave, but he soon found it was curving wickedly to the north, so he got down, hung onto his board for dear life, and tried to angle back, using the momentum of the wave to help him. The water was so rough that his mouth and nose filled, and he choked on the cold salty water, almost unable to see or figure out where he was. All he could hear was the sound of the surf screaming, and getting louder. Something made him look up, and he saw a huge vertical wall of water looming above him, high as a four-story building, long veins of foam crisscrossing the green surface. He barely had time to take a breath when the top of the wall broke, and the entire mass came crashing down on him like the end of the world, smashing him hard and flat against the sandy bottom. He couldn't get up, his lungs were bursting, and he knew that this was his last ride. The next wave flung him high up onto the rocks, just to the right of the pier, and the only reason he wasn't washed out to sea again in the undertow was that his body remained jammed between two rocks. A solitary fisherman, walking back along the pier because the wind was so strong he couldn't even cast his line, saw him and clambered over the rocks to reach him. By some coincidence Steve's broken board was washed up by the next wave, about twenty feet away.

Chapter Fourteen

The fisherman found that Steve was still breathing, called an ambulance, which arrived quickly and took him to the nearest hospital. He partially woke up on the way in, coughing, wheezing, and shivering, and by the time they pulled up outside the E.R. entrance, the medics figured he might survive. After being wrapped in warm blankets and undergoing X rays and a number of other tests, both Steve and his doctors were astonished to find that although he was bruised, battered, and concussed, he didn't seem to have suffered any major injuries.

Because of his concussion and the exposure, the doctors decided to keep him in the hospital.

"You're a lucky son of a gun just to have survived," said one of the E.R. docs, who knew him. "We're keeping you here until the morning. I don't want to hear next week that you died from a subdural in some other hospital."

Thus it was two days before Steve picked up his voice mail, which included an urgent message from Clifford Abrams, asking him to get in touch immediately. Steve's muscles were so stiff he could barely move, and although he felt lucky to be alive, he was very shaken and disinclined to talk to anyone, certainly not Clifford Abrams; he'd never particularly liked the man.

When he got back to his apartment, he made arrangements for a friend to pick up his Toyota at the Santa Monica beach, and thought about Abrams some more. At this point he needed all the help he could find to get his career rolling again. He had no idea what Abrams wanted, but Steve knew that the man was a force to be reckoned with in the surgical research world, and that was where he hoped his own future lay.

So about noon he called. It was three in the afternoon when Abrams came to the phone in his lab in New Coventry.

"Steve! Thank you for calling back!" He tried to control the excitement in his voice. He was talking to the biggest potential meal ticket he'd ever encountered, and he'd met a few. "Listen," he said, his voice dropping to a confidential purr, "I've been thinking about you, because I'm still certain that New Coventry is where you should be working. I've been working on getting additional funds, and I can now put a very attractive package together for you."

Steve's fingers were so stiff he had trouble holding the phone, so he held it between his shoulder and his chin, but that wasn't much better. Every muscle in his body was hurting.

"So at this point in time," said Abrams, unable to keep the triumph out of his voice, "I'm all set. I can offer you the post of senior research fellow in my lab, and since the funding for this is private, that means no more interviews, no committees."

Steve could hardly believe his ears. "I don't know," he said, deliberately hesitant. "How about the lab equipment and supplies I'd need? You may already have some of it, but you know how expensive that stuff comes."

"Steve, that'll be no problem. We'll get you whatever you need, within reason, of course."

"What about surgical privileges at the hospital?" asked Steve.

"We'll get them for you," said Abrams confidently. "You'll just have to be a bit patient on that score. As you well know, there's a lot of bureaucracy and politicking when it comes to hospital privileges. However," he hastened on, "meanwhile we'll give you moving expenses, and your salary will be substantially higher than what went with the job you'd originally applied for."

"How much higher?" asked Steve, smiling at the thought of moving expenses. Everything he needed to move from his furnished apartment could be put into two suitcases.

"Eighty," said Abrams with total recklessness. After all, Seth had told him to pay whatever it took, and he might as well have a guy who worked with a will on whatever he was asked to do. "Eighty thousand. Plus health insurance and the other usual benefits. We're starting a program to combat intravascular clotting, and you're going to be in charge of it."

Steve's mouth opened slowly. "When do you want me to start?"

"Immediately." Abrams was almost dancing with joy, but he didn't want to give Charnley time to change his mind. "Like now."

Steve said, "I can fly out tomorrow. I don't have much stuff to bring with me, and I can stay with friends in Mystic until I get an apartment."

Seth couldn't wait any longer and called Paula at her office at four o'clock that afternoon. He was feeling so tense that he had trouble keeping his voice at its natural pitch. She wasn't in the office, said Paula's secretary, who transferred the call to the lab, where Myra took it.

"She's in a research meeting, Mr. Millway," she told him. "Is there anything I can help you with?" She knew about the Millways, about Nicky, and thought what a wonderful voice this Seth had. A familiar spasm of jealousy hit her hard. Here was yet another man sniffing around the bitch. . . .

"When do you expect her back?"

Myra looked at the clock. "In about an hour," she said. "Shall I have her return your call?"

"No," he said, "I'll call later."

He put down the phone and cracked his knuckles, one after the other. He knew that his interest in Paula Cairns was fast becoming an obsession; he'd thought about her so much that he was quite certain that she was feeling the same way, and fantasizing about him. And now he was fighting a fierce desire to see her, to go wherever she was, to talk to her. . . . He got up and paced to and fro around his office, stopping at the window to look over at the medical research tower a mile away, looming over its lesser neighbors and, for once, etched into the cloudless sky with beacon-like clarity.

"In about an hour," the girl had said. An hour! It seemed like a lifetime away. Impulsively Seth left the office and ran down the back stairs to the underground car park. He went to his BMW and, without quite knowing where he was going, drove out of the building. He headed west and after driving fast for a few miles, parked his car at the edge of the Crownview golf course, a favorite spot for joggers, and started to run around the perimeter path. Soon his feet reminded him that he was wearing loafers unsuited to this kind of exertion, but he didn't care. The pain distracted him, and he almost enjoyed it as he ran on.

After a complete circuit of the course, about a mile and a half, he felt just as restless and tense as when he'd started. But it was now ten minutes to five. He sat in the car, his feet throbbing, for another five minutes, then drove off. The research tower was straight ahead of him, and a few minutes later he was there, parked his car, and ran up the steps. Lots of people were leaving for the day, and he pushed past them. In the lobby a large indicator with the names and locations of the various research doctors told him what he wanted to know, and soon he was striding along the corridor of the eighteenth floor toward Paula's lab. But for some reason he didn't stop, but kept walking after he reached her door, continuing on the circular corridor until he came back to the elevator. Then he returned to his car, and ten minutes later he was back in his office, having accomplished nothing and feeling, if possible, even more tense than before.

He picked up the phone, and this time he was able to reach Paula.

"I need to talk to you," he said.

"Is that Seth? I'm sorry I didn't get back to you sooner," she said, flustered, not recognizing the urgency in his voice. "I'm still having trouble making up my mind about the grant."

"Let's go out this evening, just for a quick drink," he said. His lips were dry, and he licked them. He could feel his whole body shaking as if with a chill. She had recognized his voice, and she was glad to hear it; he could *feel* that. "We can talk about it then."

Paula hesitated for a second. It was the least she could do, she told herself; she'd been discourteous by keeping him waiting all this time. And in any case she would be glad to see him again.

"Okay. You want to pick me up at home?" She gave him the address.

Seth put the phone down, his heart beating like a hammer. He put his head between his hands. What was going on? What was happening to him?

An hour later, just before leaving the office, he went to the small refrigerator at the base of one of his file cabinets, took out two red-striped bottles of champagne, and put them in his briefcase, which he then placed in the back of his car. A surge of strength and anticipation flowed through him. This was going to be a landmark evening.

She was waiting at the door of her apartment building, and he drove to the new high-rise Garrison Hotel downtown. There was a bar at the penthouse level, expensive but very popular, and thought by many to be the best place in town. When they got there, it was noisy and crowded, mostly with young businessmen and women. All the tables were taken, but two people left the bar as they came in and they grabbed the bar stools and sat down. Paula too was feeling tense, partly because his physical presence did that to her. It had been the same the time they went to Centerbrook, but in the interim she'd forgotten about it. She asked for a margarita, and Seth ordered a double Macallan single malt for himself, hoping that it would ease the tightness he could feel invading his whole body. Being close to Paula made it worse, not better, and when she happened to touch him it really felt like an electric shock going through him. There was no doubt in his mind now; how he felt about her had nothing whatever to do with the foundation grant, Vince Coletti, Millway Pharmaceuticals, or anything else that wasn't Paula Cairns.

Paula didn't want to talk about the grant, because she still hadn't made up her mind. "I was thinking about you last night," she told Seth, and he stiffened. "My dad gets me a subscription to *Gray's Journal*," she went on. "There's a great article on deer stalking in Scotland in this month's edition. I'll mail it to you if you like."

At that moment a large young man in a bright sports jacket and a loosened tie pushed past them, heading toward the door and evidently in a hurry. He accidentally bumped hard into Seth, knocking his drink over Paula's dress, then kept going without pausing to apologize. Seth grabbed a couple of paper napkins, gave them to her, then put down his glass and in an instant was off his stool and pushing his way through the crowd after the man. Seth caught up with him down a side corridor just outside the mens' room, and now all the pent-up tension in him was ready to explode. He caught the man by the shoulder and spun him around.

"Whassamatter?" The young man, half drunk, sounded aggressive but was obviously startled by Seth's expression.

"You spilled my drink over a lady's dress," said Seth through clenched teeth. A bright fire was crackling inside him and spreading fast. He gave the guy a hard push in the chest with the heel of his hand, hard enough to make him stagger against the door.

"Fuck you," mumbled the young man. He was having trouble regaining his balance, and didn't know how to deal with the level of aggression he was facing. At his words, everything peaked in Seth's mind and his right hand swung out, balling into a fist as it went, and he hit the man with all his strength, just below the breastbone, catapulting him through the door into the men's room and onto the floor. As he turned, Seth, his eyes rimmed with red fury, could hear the man throwing up, and hoped it was blood.

He went back to the bar, straightening his jacket, and sat down again next to Paula, who looked at him with sudden apprehension.

"I'm sure that was an accident," she said. "And no damage was done." She indicated the little spot on her dress. "See? It's almost dry."

"Yeah," said Seth. "Good."

"Where did you go?" asked Paula, wondering if he'd had an argument with the man.

"The men's room," replied Seth tersely, rubbing his knuckles with the other hand.

Seth was clearly on edge, and a few minutes later rather abruptly suggested they leave, which they did just as two New Coventry police officers came out of the elevator. Paula wondered if there was any connection between their appearance and Seth's taking off after the man who'd bumped into him.

In the car, Seth tried to calm down, but he couldn't do it. He drove slowly, acutely aware of her presence beside him, and feeling the sexual tension growing with every moment that passed. He was hoping that Paula would invite him back to her apartment for a drink, they'd talk for a while about the grant, she'd accept it, then they'd celebrate with the champagne he'd brought, and of course he'd spend the night there with her.

But Paula had different ideas. She could feel an aura of violence about Seth, and it made her nervous. Initially it had crossed her mind to invite him back, but now there was too much tension between them; she wanted to decide about the grant without that kind of pressure, and in any case she had a lot of work to do before going to sleep.

Seth pulled up about ten yards from the well-lit front entrance to her apartment building.

"Thanks, Seth," said Paula, undoing her seat belt the moment the vehicle stopped. Her hand was already on the door handle. "That was fun. I'm sorry I don't have a decision yet, but I promise to let you know by the end of the week."

Seth understood that he wasn't going to be invited in, and couldn't bear the thought of her just slipping away like the last time. He put a finger on the switch that locked the car doors. "I'm sorry, but I need to know about the grant *now*," he said. "There are other demands on our money, and we have to make a decision. Why don't we go in and discuss it, and come to a conclusion?"

There was something about Seth's voice that caused a flicker, a sixth sense of danger, to light up in her mind, and she tensed, feeling suddenly claustrophobic in this closed space, so restricted that she could feel the body heat of the man next to her.

"I don't think so," said Paula. "Thanks, but it's late and I have work to do. Sorry . . ." She reached again for the door handle. It was locked, and the flicker of danger turned into a Roman candle.

Seth sensed her fear, and felt a predator's response, a surge of adrenaline that hit every fiber of his body.

"C'mon, Paula, let's stop pretending . . ." His voice was unrecognizable. He reached for her in the darkened car. Away from the entrance there was little light, and she wasn't able to distinguish his features, just the swift movements of his body. She felt his hand on her thigh, and it moved swiftly, all the way up.

"Stop! Seth! God damn it, I said stop it!" Paula tried to pull his hand away from her, but she was no match for his strength. He was right up against her now, and she could feel his breathing and his face close to her, searching for her lips. He was trying to put his other arm around her shoulders when she put her hand up to his face, found his cheek with her fingers, and gouged with her thumb hard into his left eye. He yelled with pain and let go her leg. Instantly Paula turned to pull up the latch of the locked door, grabbed the handle, and was out of the car. Without looking back, she ran to the entrance and let herself in, tears of anger and fear running down her face.

Chapter Fifteen

A few days later, Paula, still shaken by her encounter with Seth, was coming back from her student teaching assignment when she met Maurice Bennett in the corridor.

"I'm on my way to lunch," he said, "and I need to talk to you. Would you like to join me?"

The cafeteria was crowded, and after they'd filled their trays, Maurice looked around for an empty table. He saw Clifford Abrams sitting with someone at a table over on the far side. All the other tables were full. Maurice hesitated for a second, then headed toward them, with Paula in his wake.

"Mind if we sit here?"

"Please." Both Abrams and the man with him moved their trays to make room, and Maurice and Paula sat down.

"You remember Steve Charnley?" said Abrams.

"Yes, of course." Maurice nodded at Steve.

"Sure," said Paula, smiling. She stuck out her hand, and Steve took it rather stiffly, without looking at her. "We met at the Surgical Association meeting in Denver last year. Steve gave a great paper on platelet aggregations after traumatic injuries."

Abrams looked pleased. "We've just appointed Dr. Charnley to be senior research fellow in my lab," he said, then leaned toward Paula, his voice dropping so that only she was able to hear. "If he lost anything by not taking your assistant professorship, he'll make up for it by making twice as much in salary."

"Congratulations," said Paula to Steve, smiling. He was tall, with long streaky blond hair that fell over the right side of his face. A big, recent bluish bruise and an abrasion over his cheekbone made Paula wonder if he'd been involved in an auto accident. He had a California surfer's tan and a wonderfully smooth, golden skin. According to what Paula had heard, Charnley was very smart too; it wasn't fair when some people seemed to have everything.

But Steve didn't appear interested in making conversation; he put his head down and went back to his chicken à la king, muttering a brief reply when Paula addressed a comment to him.

Maurice and Clifford Abrams were soon deep in a discussion of departmental matters, and although they appeared superficially cordial, Paula felt an undercurrent of tension between the two men.

Abrams and Steve left soon after. Steve nodded to Paula, but his eyes met hers only for a second as he got very stiffly out of his chair. She noticed that he had a noticeable limp as he walked away, as if he had an injury to his leg.

"Dr. Charnley didn't seem too forthcoming, did he?" asked Maurice when they had gone.

"I suppose he has a lot on his mind," replied Paula, "and he looks as if he'd recently fallen off a cliff." But she did think that Steve Charnley might have made a little effort to be pleasant. After all, they were the two newest members of the department, and that should have made some sort of bond between them.

"He'll be a good addition to their unit," went on Maurice. "They need someone to perk up the action there, and maybe he's the guy to do it." He sat still for a second. "But there are a couple of odd aspects to his appointment at this particular time, don't you think?"

Paula was having similar thoughts. "Myra told me that Abrams is starting a crash program to catch up with us, and that Steve Charnley's been hired to lead it."

"Can they do it?"

"No way," said Paula decisively, but deep down she wasn't so sure.

They left the cafeteria soon after. Back in Maurice's office, Paula sat down in the visitor's chair and Maurice watched her approvingly, thinking what a pleasure it was to have such a capable and imaginative colleague.

"I've decided to turn down the Millway offer," she told him. She had mailed the letter the morning after her last encounter with Seth.

He nodded as if he'd expected her to say that. "I'm glad," he said. "That was a wise move, although you won't know how wise it was, not for some time, anyway."

"But it still leaves me without any real funds," said Paula, feeling rather desperate.

"You're right," said Maurice. "And it's getting urgent, especially in view of Steve Charnley's arrival on the scene. This morning I talked to a couple of people I know at NIH and the Army. I told them how important your work is, and hopefully they'll be able to bend some rules and lay their hands on some unassigned funds for you."

"That would be great," said Paula. "I really appreciate your help. I know you have plenty of other things to worry about besides my problems. Maybe one day I'll be able to help someone as much as you've helped me."

Maurice smiled at her. "Paula," he said, "I don't know if you fully appreciate the magnitude of the work you're doing. If it succeeds, and I believe it will, you'll be in a position to do anything you want, and help ten times as many people as I ever could." He looked at the clock. "I'm leaving in about five minutes," he said. "I have a plane to catch."

Maurice was on his way to Chicago for a council meeting of the American College of Surgeons, he told Paula. He grinned. "They want me to stand as the official candidate for president of the college."

"Wow," said Paula, impressed. "Are you going to?"

"No," he said. "That organization has gone downhill to the point where now it's just an elitist social club. The office holders have lavish parties for themselves, paid for by the membership, they invite each other to be visiting professors at their institutions, but don't do anything of any real substance for their own foot soldiers."

"Aren't they active up on the Hill?" asked Paula, who had just paid several hundred dollars for her annual membership to the college and was still wondering what she was getting in return.

"No." Maurice's voice showed his disgust with his own professional society. "They don't have any voice in medical politics, even though they know that Rome is already burning. They just hope it won't come crashing down on their heads during their shift."

"Couldn't you change it, turn it into a useful organization? If anybody could, surely you could."

Maurice shook his head. "It's a matter of critical mass," he said. "The top members love their perks, and don't want any big or painful changes, so nothing's going to happen. Not till the entire structure is visibly crumbling, and by then it'll be too late." He grinned wryly at her. "And as you probably know by now, Paula," he went on, "I prefer to be a builder rather than an archaeologist scrabbling among the ruins." Maurice stood up and put on his overcoat, picked up his briefcase and was gone.

* * *

"I think you can probably go home tomorrow," said Paula after checking Nicky's leg and foot. "I talked to the rehab people yesterday. Have they been to see you yet?"

Nicky shook her head. "When can I go back to school?" she asked.

"I didn't know you liked school that much." Paula smiled at her, thinking she'd miss Nicky's lively presence.

"I don't. We all decided a couple of weeks ago that the only reason we go is because it's a good place to meet your friends." Nicky gave Paula a sideways look, and Paula wondered if Nicky was teasing her.

"Don't you also enjoy learning stuff? Finding out about all the things that this world is all about? Like biology, or history?" Paula was puzzled. Nicky was obviously a curious and intelligent girl, on the brink of life, but as different from Paula at that age as chalk from cheese.

Nicky shrugged. "Not specially," she said. What's really important to me is my friends. In fact, they're the most important thing in my life. Having a boyfriend, that's important too, but mostly because all the other kids have one."

"What do you talk about?"

"Oh, I don't know. Boys. Sex. Music. Clothes. We talk about clothes a lot. We hang out in the mall and go around all the stores, seeing what's new, what's cool."

Paula left soon after, feeling very old. She wondered whether nowadays all twelve-year-olds were like that. Nicky had so much going for her; she was beautiful, courageous, funny, clever, and had every advantage—money, social position, friends—and went to a very good private school . . . she had everything any twelve-year-old girl could desire, everything except parents. The elder Millways were very nice people, but Paula couldn't imagine the kind of conversations that would take place between them and Nicky.

Later, doing her rounds, it occurred to her that the things that had most struck her about Nicky was her like-ability, her honesty, her ability to be at ease with everyone, with the nurses, the therapists, herself. But there were also things that worried her about Nicky. Didn't she think about anything except herself and her friends? Did she have any concerns about her future? The environment? Or was she just another insouciant rich kid like the ones described by F. Scott Fitzgerald and anticipated by Aldous Huxley?

After Paula left the floor, it took a few moments for her to realize that the bruised and suntanned image of the gorgeous but ungracious Steve Charnley had somehow found its way into her mind.

Chapter Sixteen

Paula had managed to put Seth and the Millway Foundation right out of her thoughts, and her interest in her new neighbor down the hall could have had something to do with it. That interest was mainly about what he was doing in the lab; apparently Abrams had been boasting that his new hotshot, Steve Charnley, was going to blow Paula's research out of the water, and naturally enough, Paula was curious to find out how he was planning to go about it.

In the course of the next few weeks, Steve and Paula crossed each other's paths from time to time, in the cafeteria, at staff meetings, more often in the curving corridors of the research building.

When she and Steve happened to meet, Paula was always the one who stopped. Steve's body language indicated: "I'm going to nod, smile, and walk on," but Paula would stop a couple of yards in front of him, and it would have been difficult and discourteous for him to walk around her. His bruises were disappearing fast, but Paula was still curious about who or what had caused them.

Late one afternoon Steve came out of his lab, carrying a canvas bag with the leather-wound handle of a racquetball bat sticking out of it. Paula happened to be passing and stopped.

"I didn't know there was anywhere to play racquetball around her," she said, indicating the bag.

"Sure." Steve patted the handle of his racquet. "Across the street in the athletic building. The Racquet Club's better, though, and the courts are in better shape."

He looked at Paula and heard himself say, "Why? Do you play?"

Paula put one leg slightly forward and stuck her thumbs into the waistband of her skirt, taking up a rather comical, macho stance. "Yes. But you wouldn't want to play with me. I got thrown out of my last club because I was wrecking the courts. Hitting too hard, and making too many holes in the wall."

Steve stared for a second, taking in her expression. "Yeah? We'll see. How about tomorrow after work?"

"I don't have 'after work,'" said Paula. "How about seven tomorrow morning? To get the day started right."

"I'll book the court," said Steve, pleased, although he certainly had no wish to be.

"The Racquet Club," said Paula. "See you then." She walked airily on toward her lab, feeling ridiculously cheerful and sensing the prickle of Steve's eyes on her back before he turned to walk in the opposite direction. Tomorrow, she told herself, I'll find out what he's up to.

Desmond Connor, the head of Millway's research lab, had visibly aged in the past few weeks. Now his hair looked straggly and unkempt, and lack of sleep had put thin, watery red rings around his eyes. Seth Millway was making impossible demands on him, and the anxiety was wearing him out. New ideas, that was what Seth wanted. Get us ready for the next century, he kept saying. Let's get into genetic research, immune mechanisms, all that stuff Seth read about in *Today's Health* or *Newsweek* or wherever. As if you could suddenly get into one of these fields from one day to the next.

"We can't do it," he kept telling Seth. "We don't have

that kind of expertise, and we don't have the staff to do that kind of work. Look at our research budget. That's not the field we're in, sir. We sell more oral antibiotics, steroids, and over-the-counter non-prescription drugs than anyone else in the industry."

But Seth was not satisfied; as he complained to Connor, the only new products that Millway Pharmaceuticals had come up with were merely variations on an old theme. Even when his father was still in charge, Seth had realized that Desmond Connor was another of those senior people in the pharmaceutical industry who bristled with fine academic degrees but when placed in responsible positions regrettably had no original ideas of their own.

After Seth had got over the first flush of rage and disappointment after his last encounter with Paula, it occurred to him that if he could prevent her from obtaining research funds elsewhere, she would either be forced to come back to Millway, hat in hand, or else abandon her independence and do her work in another lab. Seth had a couple of ideas about how to block her access to research funds, but he needed more information about the ways of the scientific community, and that he could get from Des Connor.

"And how's Nora doing?" he asked, coming into Connor's office one evening. It was late, and most of the scientists and lab techs had gone home. Only Connor remained, as usual. He did work hard, Seth had to admit, but Seth was interested in results, not how many hours the man put in.

"Better," replied Connor, closing a thick three-ring binder full of handwritten material and looking up at his boss. "She came back from the hospital yesterday, a bit weak after the surgery, but overall the doctors are pleased, and said that although she's progressing as well as—"

"Good," interrupted Seth. He didn't want details about Connor's wife. He was here to get information and insights into the workings of the scientific mind.

"Des, I was reading an article about that research scandal at Yale—you know, the one where some junior doc published a fraudulent paper that his boss hadn't checked, although his name was on it as a co-author. Do you remember it?"

"Sure, I remember." Des grinned tiredly. "Did you know that that same boss later joined one of the big pharmaceutical firms as a senior researcher?"

"Yes, I heard that," Seth replied. "It figures. But why do you think he skipped out of academia?"

Des stared at him. "Well, he was totally discredited," he said. "Not only at Yale, but in his entire research field. Nobody wanted anything to do with him after that."

"He was fired?"

"No. I believe he had tenure. But in the scientific world, a public exposure like that is the kiss of death. He was a pariah, and he'd never have been able to get himself another grant, and anything he published after that would have been laughed at behind his back. In any case, no reputable journal would want to publish anything of his."

Seth nodded, his mind working overtime. "The kiss of death, huh? But isn't that kind of thing common enough, really? Doesn't the scientific community accept the fact that honest mistakes can be made without crucifying the scientist who makes them?"

"No," said Connor. "Every scientist knows that a good percentage of all scientific papers have major flaws in them, but nobody really has the time or the desire to check them. But if somebody does blow the whistle, then ultimately there's no mercy. Like with that guy at Yale. He was right inside the system, you'd think he'd be protected up to the hilt, but they got him. They were forced to, because there was this obsessed woman scientist who kept getting up at meetings and denouncing him."

"Very interesting," said Seth, but he wasn't listening anymore. He was now busy formulating and extending the idea that had come to him earlier.

Seth went on to his other preoccupation, which was to change the basic task of the Millway Laboratories and turn it into a true research facility, with state-of-the-art equipment and people.

"That would get us away from ringing the changes on aspirin, phenacetin, and all that other junk," said Seth, his voice rising with excitement. "We'd work on genetic mutations, on mouse antibodies to transport heart medicine to the heart, kidney medicine to the kidneys, things like that. That's where the action and the money's going to be in the next decade."

Connor shook his head. "That's not for us," he said. "No, sir. Companies like Schering, Wellcome, the biggies, sure, that's fine for them. But they've been at it a long time, and we could never catch up. We're better off doing what we do best. It's not exciting, but it makes money—"

"Not enough," interrupted Seth. "Not by a long way. Don't you read the annual reports?"

Connor shrugged. "We do our job, sir," he said. "It's the marketing division that isn't doing theirs."

Seth had been holding a magazine in his hand when he came in, and he put it on Connor's desk. A paper clip marked one of the articles. "Have you read this?" he asked.

Connor picked it up, sighing inwardly, and opened it at the paper clip.

"It's about Alzheimer's disease," said Seth. "Do you know that four million Americans have it? Well, it seems that late-onset Alzheimer's may be caused by a protein called apolipoprotein E-4, manufactured by a defective gene on chromosome 19." Seth leaned forward and tapped the magazine in Connor's hands. "This is exactly the kind of thing I'm talking about," he said. "Somebody's going to make millions by figuring out a way of neutralizing that apolipoprotein. We're in the business, why shouldn't it be us?"

"Because we're *not* in that part of the business, Seth," said Connor, running his hand through his hair. "If anybody's going to cash in on that, it's going to be some combination between a big university lab and a high-powered pharmaceutical company with a background in this kind of work, scientists who've specialized for years in genetics and biochemistry. We don't have anything or anybody to compete with that, it would take years to set up the lab to work on that, and by then somebody would have already figured out how to do it."

Seth got up, containing his anger with difficulty. Connor's stubborn refusal even to consider entering the modern era was so frustrating that he wanted to pick him up, slam him against the wall, and pound him until he was tired. Connor, watching him, felt a sick apprehension seep through his entire being. But he was only doing his job, he told himself rather desperately. Encouraging Seth to go off half cocked and try to set up a bunch of high-tech projects would be dishonest and ultimately destructive.

Then Seth's face lightened, to Connor's relief, as if he had come to the same conclusion.

Seth said goodbye, and seemed about to leave when he turned back. "Oh, by the way, Des, do you have a key for this lab?"

"Of course." Connor fished around in his pocket and came out with a small bunch of keys.

"May I see it?"

Puzzled, Connor slipped the key off the ring and

handed it to Seth, who looked at it, then flipped it carelessly in the air before putting it in his pocket and turning
again to leave. Connor was about to ask for it back when
Seth stopped and snapped his fingers with annoyance.

"Damn it, I knew there was something I forgot to tell
you." He took a step back toward Connor, put a hand on
his shoulder, and stared at him, eyeball to eyeball. "Des,
you're fired."

Connor tried to move back, but Seth's hand held him
close. Connor smiled uncertainly. "Good joke," he said.
"Can I have my key back now, please?"

"No joke," said Seth, watching him with narrowed eyes,
carefully noting and enjoying the sequence of changes
that followed one another across Connor's face when he
realized that Seth was serious. "I'm telling you to get the
fuck out of this lab, right now. Don't even think of taking
anything with you except your coat."

Driving home a few minutes later, Seth remembered
with grim pleasure the different expressions that had
passed over Desmond Connor's face after he'd fired him.
They had gone from anxiety to disbelief to fear, and finally
to anger when Seth virtually marched him out of the lab,
telling the two guards at the door never to let Connor in
again under any circumstances.

Seth pushed a button, and the music from a CD of *Ex-
cerpts from Classical Favorites* flooded the car. As Seth's
post-conflict adrenaline level came back down to normal,
he thought about Connor's comments on the repercussions of the Yale research scandal. Seth had a strong
hunch that maybe he could get at Paula Cairns that way.
What was it Connor had said? Many scientific papers
have flaws, but usually no one pays much attention unless
somebody blows the whistle, and then they're merciless.

Seth followed that train of thought to its ultimate conclusion, and felt pleased. If getting Abrams to set up a competing project didn't work, he might be able to discredit Paula, which would cut her off from all sources of funding, and ultimately force her to work for Abrams, which would be the same thing as having her work for Millway. That would provide a relatively painless and legal way of getting access to Paula's research. He grinned, thinking about Coletti, who'd said that dealing with the law was just another business problem.

The key to all this was of course Clifford Abrams, so he decided that before the evening was over, he would call and instruct him how to proceed.

Almost of its own volition, Seth's BMW turned off the highway and steered itself to the apartment building where Paula lived, pulling up in the parking lot that faced the front of the building. He turned off the music just as Ravel's *Bolero* was reaching its rhythmic climax, and sat in silence for a while, looking at the five-story facade, bright in the orange glow of the parking lot lights. All the anger of his last date with Paula came back to him, and he rubbed his left eye; she'd almost blinded him that night, for no valid reason, and his bloodshot eye had attracted comments for days. Many of the apartments were lit, but he couldn't see into any of them, and of course he had no idea which one was Paula's.

He got out of the car and walked over to the front entrance, jumping over the puddles from the recent rain. That reminded him of their short walk from Chez Jacques back to his car, the feel of her arm where he'd held it. Now the air was chilly, nobody was around, and the entire area was silent and would have seemed deserted if it hadn't been for the lights in the windows. The main door was locked, of course, but on the right side was a panel bearing the names of the tenants, each with a doorbell beside it, and some of them had the number of the apart-

ment. Seth was about to press one at random, hoping that
he could talk the occupant into letting him in, when he
saw the small TV camera fixed above the door, its eye-like
lens pointing at him. He turned away from it and stared
hard at the small card halfway down the panel. It bore the
name PAULA S. CAIRNS, next to APT. 5L, in small, neat,
hand-written lettering.

Then he turned and went back to his car. "S," he said,
out loud as he sat facing the building. "What does that
stand for? Samantha, Sheila? Sandra?"

He stayed there for ten minutes, watching, hoping that
Paula would either come in or leave, but without any real
expectation of such an event. Nor did he know what he
would do if she did appear. Then, assuming that she was
home, he drove slowly between the cars, trying to guess
which one was hers.

On the way back, it occurred to Seth that although
there was a TV camera at the entrance, he hadn't seen
any security guards. He found that he had memorized
Paula's telephone number from the time he'd called the
phone company for it, and now he repeated it like a mantra, over and over again, as if by doing so he was in some
way able to communicate his anger to her.

When he got home, he called Abrams. His wife answered rather testily and said Clifford was asleep. "Then
wake him up," said Seth. "Tell him it's Seth Millway."

When Abrams came on the line, Seth explained to him
what he had to do. Go over every one of Dr. Cairns' published papers, he told him, check out every detail. Make
friends with her technician; she'll know better than anyone if Cairns has ever done any slipshod work, try to find
anything at all that isn't one hundred percent kosher.

"Okay," replied Abrams, fully awake. "Yes, sir. I'll get
busy on it tomorrow."

Later, after Fleur was asleep, Seth called Paula's

number, as he'd done a few times before. He listened to her saying, "Hello? Hello? Who is this?", then he quietly hung up. He woke up about four in the morning for no reason that he could identify, but he was thinking about her and called her again, wanting to scare her, but again he felt no need to say anything. He could visualize Paula sitting up in the darkened bedroom, wearing a white nightie with a little pink silk ribbon interwoven around the neckline, feeling afraid of the mystery caller, holding the phone in one hand and with the other pulling the bedclothes up around her. At that moment Seth felt very, very close to her. After putting the phone down, he shook Fleur until she woke up, pulled her warm legs apart, and pushed up into her with a huge hard-on that was not intended for her at all.

Chapter Seventeen

Next morning, promptly at seven o'clock, Paula, dressed in short white shorts, a green-and-white-striped shirt, and new Reeboks, came out of the women's dressing rooms with her bag, feeling clear-headed, tense, and ready for battle.

Since they had booked late, their assigned court was in the back, and Paula felt grateful. If she was going to get hammered, and of course she expected to, she might as well be hammered away from the glass-windowed show courts facing the main desk, where there would be an appreciative audience to witness her defeat.

Steve was already inside the court, which resounded with the repeated, regular whack of the ball as he practiced. She watched him for a moment through the peephole in the door. He was strong, fast, with smooth, muscular legs evenly fuzzed with blond hair, and powerful forearms and hands. She always looked at people's hands, and Steve's were forceful, long-fingered, and there was something about them, a kind of precision, even in the way he held his racquet. Now he was reaching, slashing at the ball with a whiplike action that was so fast it was hard for her to follow, leaping for high balls, stretching even for the ones he could never reach, doubling back for the low bouncers, and finally a desperate grab, racquet outstretched, overreaching. He missed it, lost his balance and landed flat-out on his belly, and slid to a stop, spread-eagled.

Paula chose this moment to push the spring-loaded door and came in, clapping for the performance. Steve pulled himself up on all fours, stayed like that for a moment, grinned at her, then bounced up to his feet. He looked wonderful in his racquetball gear, glowing with physical health, a hard body, not built up and worked at to look good, but one that looked good because of the work he did with it.

"You caught me at a typical moment," he said. "Missed the ball, fell flat on my face, just when I was hoping to impress you. You want to practice for a couple of minutes?"

He picked up the ball and gave it a gentle pat against the far wall. It came back, landing a few feet in front of Paula, who tapped it back to the wall just as sedately.

After a few rounds of this Edwardian country-house pat-a-cake, Paula, standing in the right court, got bored and whacked a return low into the left front corner. It wasn't quite as hard as she wanted it to be, but had enough zing so he had to leap to get it. Still, he put enough control into the return so that it bounced off the wall to land inoffensively three feet in front of her, just as the others had done.

He grinned at her.

Paula caught the ball with her hand. "Ready to play?" she asked. Her smile had a little edge to it. She didn't mind getting beaten, her smile said, if that was what was going to happen, but she wasn't going to be patronized.

They played for service, and Paula won, although she suspected that he let her have the point. Well, she thought, there's only one way I can make this guy play hard, and that's by playing as hard as I can myself.

She stood at the service line, keeping him in the corner

of her vision. He was crouched forward, racquet pointing forward, behind her and to the left. Paula grinned to herself; she knew exactly what to do to distract his attention away from the game, just long enough to win the point. Left-handed, she stood so that when her arm came back in her service stance, he got a momentary glimpse of her breast through the wide opening of her sleeveless shirt, then Pow! The ball smacked the line and came back, landing very fast at his feet and he jumped at it but missed. It wasn't really a killer serve, he was perfectly aware of that, but Paula was very fit and had moved deceptively fast. It had caught him by surprise, and he knew that he had to shape up and pay more attention to the game. But she'd got him flustered, and went on to win the first five points in quick succession, more by her unexpected angle and spin shots than by sheer power or speed. Also, she had pulled her shirt in and now stood in a position that, to his disappointment, revealed nothing at all, and that put him off too.

Steve took a big breath and settled down. He rarely played with women, and when he did, his tactic was to make them play his kind of game, and from then on it didn't usually take too long, because he was strong and able to overpower them. But now he was in danger of getting beaten, and he couldn't stand even the thought of that. Pushing himself into high gear, he got the next four points, but try as he might, he couldn't catch up. Paula managed to catch him off guard again and again with her service, and although he'd win the next point, he was getting rattled.

In spite of that he could feel some kind of electric charge building up between them as they played. They were both increasingly aware that they were alone, together in this flat-walled, closed space, this court that resonated with their attempts to defeat each other. There was no antagonism in that struggle, only a feeling of excitement and competition which increased as the game progressed. The electric charge built up, soared, and went off the scale when they came physically close, and that didn't help Steve. On a couple of occasions he felt she might even be taking advantage of that fact, because she'd come real close to him, close enough so he could feel the sparks crackling between them, then she'd let off some devastating shot and he'd lose the point.

Paula won the first game, but he won the next two, and that was all they had time for. Steve was a powerful and smart player, but he'd had to work hard for his wins, and they were both panting and exhilarated by the time the match was over.

He couldn't prevent himself from putting his hand around her waist and giving her a brief little hug while they were leaving the court, and she didn't stop him. The sensation of touching her body, even through a sweaty shirt, gave him goose bumps.

The cafeteria was being renovated, and since they both had a little time, Steve suggested they go and have a cup of coffee somewhere, by common unspoken consent anywhere but the hospital.

They went to the Coffee Klatch, a small, busy coffee house situated between the Raquet Club and the hospital.

It was crowded, but they found a small table by the window.

"So how's it going in the lab?" asked Paula with a grin. "I hear that you and I are now in competition."

Steve reddened for a second. "I guess that was Dr. Abrams' idea," he replied, "so I'm working on it." He hesitated, smiling rather awkwardly at Paula. "I don't really understand why he's trying to do this," he went on. "He must know that you're way out ahead."

"Well, as he doesn't have any valid projects of his own," said Paula tartly, "I suppose the best he can do is latch on to someone else's"

Steve quickly changed the subject, and before they knew it an hour had passed. They found they had acquaintances in common, in Connecticut and California, that Steve was interested in music, and used to play the classical guitar pretty well. Also, by the time Paula noticed she was ten minutes late for her students, she realized that the sexual tension between them had built up to an alarming level.

Steve had paid for the hour on the court, so she paid for the coffee.

"Let's play again," said Steve on the way out.

"How about tomorrow?" replied Paula quickly. "Same time, same place?"

Myra Jennings couldn't believe how nice Dr. Abrams was, and thought she was maybe even falling in love with him. Myra was chronically lonely, and had always found it difficult to make friends, even when she was less obese. And now, out of the blue, Dr. Clifford Abrams, who everybody said was such a big shot, stopped by the lab, just to chat with her and make her feel more at home. He even invited her back to his own lab, introduced her to a couple of his techs, and took her into his private area at the far end of the lab, and sat her down with a cup of coffee and a plate of cookies and assorted doughnuts in front of her.

"I really shouldn't," she said, looking guilty, her hand hovering over the plate.

"Go ahead," he urged. "You only live once, so enjoy them. They're fresh from the Donut Shop over on Green Street, and they're the best you can get in New Coventry."

Myra, encouraged by his words and also by a sense of

camaraderie that exuded from his own chubby appearance, started in on them, feeling a familiar, almost orgasmic, angry pleasure of biting into a succulent chocolate-covered doughnut and wolfing it down almost unchewed.

He watched her, sitting back in his chair, and she could see his expression change gradually from a cheerful "mine host" look to a thoughtful frown. Myra thought he was concerned about the way she was eating, and slowed her chomping jaws, but after a few moments he said in a quiet and confidential voice, "Myra, I'm so glad I've got to know you, because I'm going to need your help."

"Sure," mumbled Myra, her mouth full. "Whatever."

Abrams pulled an official-looking folder on the desk so that it lay directly in front of him. "You see this?" he said, tapping the top of the folder with a pudgy index finger. "This is an official request from the National Institutes of Health to me, concerning your boss, Dr. Paula Cairns."

Myra said nothing, but kept her eyes fixed on his. Her expression didn't change.

"Apparently there have been some questions about some of her published research," he went on, a frown creasing his forehead into horizontal pink folds. "And because I work in the same institution as she does, and because of course the NIH people know me pretty well, they've asked me to do some *very discreet* looking into the matter."

"Nothing I did," said Myra sullenly. "I just do what I'm told. I don't write the papers, she does."

"Of course, my dear, I know that," said Abrams, his voice vibrant with sincerity. "I've already checked you out, and everybody, *without exception,* says what a conscientious and capable technician you are. If you weren't such an outstanding person, Myra"— Abrams leaned forward over his desk—"I certainly wouldn't be asking you to cooperate with me in this matter."

"What did she do?" asked Myra, reaching unobtrusively for the last cookie. A guilty thought struck her. "Was it that paper about thrombolysins, that one she did in New York?" She looked at him for a clue, then smiled. "It was, wasn't it?"

Abrams smiled sadly. "Yes, Myra, I'm sorry to say it, but that paper was certainly one of the problems mentioned by the NIH team. How incredible that you figured that out."

Myra shrugged, and without meaning to, looked at the empty plate. Abrams noticed and immediately pressed the intercom button on his console and asked the receptionist to bring in some more doughnuts and cookies.

"I'm sorry," he said to Myra, smiling apologetically. "I'd hate you to think we were stingy."

Myra said something to the effect that she'd had plenty, but her eyes said different.

A moment later, the receptionist came in with a fresh plate loaded with cookies and doughnuts and set it in front of Myra, but avoided looking at her. Myra didn't have to be told what the woman was thinking. But she didn't care either.

"You were telling me about that thrombolysin paper of Dr. Cairns'," prompted Abrams, pressing his fingertips together, his elbows and forearms flat on the desk in front of him.

"That was the first research paper she'd ever published," said Myra. "And it was three years ago, just a few months after I started working for her and Dr. Zimmerman. When they were working on that technique, there was some trouble with the chemical reagents, and she wasn't happy with the results."

"Then why did she submit the paper, do you think?"

"Dr. Zimmerman was anxious to get it in before some deadline. I think it was the annual Surgical Society meeting; I don't really remember. Anyway, he just about told her to go ahead and do it, and so she did. But I knew that sooner or later she'd hear more about it."

Myra's round face broke into a wide, satisfied smile. She was feeling really good right now, although she knew that it wouldn't last. The bloating and that awful feeling of food guilt would hit her in ten to fifteen minutes.

Abrams shook his head in admiration of her shrewdness and intuition. "Dr. Cairns wasn't happy with the results, isn't that what you're saying? But on that paper her name was first in the list of authors, wasn't it? She must have known then that that implies full responsibility for everything in it, right? The methods, the materials, the conclusions, everything?" Abrams spoke in a low voice, heavy with sadness and concern for Paula Cairns, whose ambition had evidently led her to make such a serious error.

"Actually, while they were writing up the paper, Dr. Cairns insisted that they do a complete independent check of all the reagents they used," said Myra. "Dr. Zimmerman finally agreed, but that meant sending them to a commercial testing lab, and by the time the results came back, the paper had already been published."

"And what were the results of those independent tests, Myra?" Abrams waited for her answer, his pen poised over a yellow legal-sized pad.

"They reported that the batch of reagents was outdated," replied Myra. She moved in her chair, trying to release her sphincters gradually, and hoping that Dr. Abrams wouldn't hear the wind escaping. "Nobody thought of it at the time. You see the bottles up there on the shelf, you use them every day, and you never think about them going out of date. Anyway, two of the reagents we used were unstable, so nobody could be sure the overall results were correct." Myra pointed at the thick file in front of Abrams. "I suppose you know all that already."

"Indeed I do," he said smoothly, tapping on the "NIH file," which in fact contained nothing more incriminating than one of his old grant applications. "All the main facts are here, of course, but you can understand how very important it was to me personally to have those regrettable facts confirmed by a person who was there, someone who really knew what was going on and who had your expert knowledge and integrity."

Myra smiled, still on her doughnut high, but she could feel the skin on her cheeks getting red, and her stomach was already beginning to itch. "Is there anything else?" she asked. "Because Dr. Cairns should be coming out of the O.R. pretty soon, and I don't want to be out of the lab when she comes in."

"I don't think she'll be done for another hour or so," said Abrams, who had checked the O.R. schedule before going to see Myra. "She's helping the residents do an aneurysm, and that usually takes around three hours. But I won't take up any more of your time, Myra, aside from one last question I have for you." Abrams' troubled smile was so sincere that Myra wished she could do something to make him feel better. It must be terrible for him, she thought, having to investigate one of his own colleagues in this way.

"You don't happen to know if the findings in that paper were ever retracted? I mean officially? With a letter to the editor of the journal that they printed?"

Myra shook her head. "She said something about doing that when the test results came in from the lab, and Dr. Zimmerman said he'd take care of it, but I guess with all the other things going on they forgot about it."

Abrams stood up, delighted that his intuition had landed him such a rich strike. The funny thing was, of course, that Paula had probably never even seen the outdated reagents, since that would have been the technician's task. How ironic, thought Abrams, that this pathetic creature Myra, who had given him the key to the problem, had herself been responsible for those reagents, but had obviously failed to check them properly.

He came around the desk and took Myra's hand in both of his. "Myra, I can't thank you enough for your help in this miserable business. And of course I don't need to tell you how important it is that this remains completely confidential."

"Of course," she said.

"Stop in any time," said Abrams, taking Myra's elbow and walking her toward the door. "And thanks again."

After Myra had gone, Abrams went over to the main library and asked for a computer check of all the papers that Paula had published, either as the lead author or as part of a team. Later, holding a reprint of Paula's first paper, the one on thrombolysins that Myra had alerted him to, he went into Steve Charnley's office.

"Steve," he said, putting the reprint down on the desk, "I want you to read this paper, and I'd like your opinion on whether we could duplicate these results."

Steve picked it up and glanced at the title and the list of authors, then looked up at Abrams, surprised. He turned the page to the section headed MATERIALS AND METHODS. "Sure," he said after a few moments. "We can repeat them. But why? It'll take a while to set the experiment up, and they're describing a technique that nobody else has ever used, to my knowledge. We can do it, I suppose, but it's three years old and outdated. It seems like a waste of time to me." Steve, already disenchanted with the few weeks of working with Abrams, felt that this was yet another unnecessary diversion.

Abrams leaned back against the door post, and told Steve that they might need to use this technique, and he wanted to be sure it worked in every detail. "It's rather a complicated process," said Abrams. "Normally I'd give it to the senior tech, but I want to be absolutely certain it works exactly as advertised. How long do you think it'll take?"

"We have all the reagents," said Steve. "If we follow the techniques they describe, we don't have to figure anything out ourselves. If you want me to shelve everything else, I suppose I could do it in about a week." He looked at Abrams. "But why don't we just ask Dr. Cairns? She's right down the corridor," he added unnecessarily. "If she's still set up, she or her tech would probably do any testing you want, and it would save us a lot of time and effort."

Abrams pretended to consider the matter.

"No," he said finally. "In a sense, they're in competition with us, and I don't want them to be aware of everything that we're doing. And I'd like to have that information ready if we need to use it, so if you're sure it's only going to take a week, why don't we just go ahead and do it?"

"Okay," said Steve. "Whatever you say. I'll start on it tomorrow."

When Abrams had gone, Steve looked again at the front of the reprint. It was from a minor journal, the kind that researchers use early in their careers or after their careers are over, or when they want to let off a trial balloon. *A Simple Technique for Measuring Thrombolysins and Their Degradation Products in Frozen Blood Derivatives*, by Paula S. Cairns, M.D. There were a couple of other names in the authors' column that Steve hadn't heard of, both with B.S. degrees, and therefore probably technicians, and at the end, in the usual position for the head of the lab, Robert W. Zimmerman, M.D., Paula's old boss in New York, whom Steve had met.

What did Abrams want with this? Was he really going to use this measuring technique? Unless he was going off in a different research direction, it wasn't the kind of test he would ever use. Abrams was no fool, and there had to be a very powerful reason before he would transfer his new researcher to such a task.

Steve shrugged, and wondered if Paula knew of Abrams' sudden interest in her old work. He stared at Paula's printed name again, thought about how she'd looked on the raquetball court, and about how she'd look the next time he saw her. Those thoughts made him very restless, so he put them out of his head and got back to work.

The restlessness kept coming back, however, and when it got too bad, he got up and took a walk along the corridor, past Paula's lab, hoping to bump into her. He did that several times, but the only person he saw during those sallies was Paula's tech, Myra, going back into her lab. Steve felt sorry for her, and wondered what it would feel like to carry all that extra weight around.

Chapter Eighteen

"Maurice, I'm not at all sure whether I should be mentioning this to you, but I've been hearing a persistent rumor about your Dr. Cairns." Abrams held tightly onto the phone; he didn't particularly enjoy doing this, and fooling around with Maurice Bennett might be a dangerous thing to do, but it was part of the deal he'd been bullied into by Seth Millway. *She has to be totally discredited, to the point where her professional reputation is in tatters.*

"She's not *my* Dr. Cairns," said Maurice curtly, and Abrams grinned to himself at his tone and thought, "Don't you just wish . . . !" "And I haven't heard any rumors either," went on Maurice, "except that she's doing an outstanding all-around job in the department. So what's on your mind?"

"It's about a paper she wrote when she was in New York, Maurice, about three years ago. You probably know the article, a test for thrombolysins in frozen bank blood."

"I know she wrote it," said Maurice. "Not a paper of much importance, as I recall. I scanned it when she applied for the job here, but I can't say I've read it."

"Well, I was at a steering committee meeting in San Diego last week," said Abrams. "And a couple of people came up to me afterward and mentioned that the findings in that paper were incorrect. Nobody actually said the word *fraudulent*, but I could feel it hovering in the air."

"I've heard of no such thing." Maurice was angry. "But thanks for letting me know. I'll look into it."

"Good. And of course you're very welcome. I thought it was better to tell you now, Maurice, before you hear about it in some more official kind of way. I wanted you to be aware of this because I was thinking about that big problem they had at Yale, that started like nothing at all, then went on to become a major scandal that's affected every academic scientist in this country."

"Right. I'll check with Dr. Cairns and find out what this is all about. And I agree with you, Cliff," he went on, a warning in his voice. "We have to stop that kind of rumor at the source; I'm sure you understand me perfectly."

"Indeed, I won't breathe a word, of course. I'm surprised you'd even think I would, but as for stopping it at the source, it may be already too late for that."

The tone of offended concern in Abrams' voice made Maurice smile grimly.

"Anyway," went on Abrams, "just to clear the air, and because of course I want to help absolve our young colleague of any wrongdoing, I have instructed one of my people to reproduce the entire experiment. If he is able to reproduce it"—Abrams ran his tongue around his mouth before going on in an unctuous tone—"and of course I'm assuming at this point that he will. Once that's done we can lay the whole matter to rest."

Maurice pursed his lips as he hung up. What was that devious little man up to? What possible benefit could he get from smearing her? Maybe just his basic bitchiness, he thought, but probably not. Somebody must have tipped him off, Maurice figured, but knowing Abrams, there had to be something more in it for him than simple outrage about a sloppy piece of research. Without a substantial stimulus Abrams simply wouldn't bother.

Maurice made a couple of phone calls, one to NIH's

verification unit in Bethesda, Maryland. They refused to give him any information over the phone until he got Dr. Ira Lancaster, a friend of his and the head of the Institute for Metabolic Diseases, to call them. No, Maurice was eventually told, there had been no questions raised up to this time concerning any work or published papers written by Dr. Paula S. Cairns.

His next call was to a female researcher at Princeton who was making a career out of following up allegations of cheating or fraud in scientific research. Here Maurice drew a blank again, but the woman, a British biochemist by the name of Dr. Emily Fiske, whom Maurice had known when they both worked in Boston, cautioned him not to assume that the paper was free of errors simply because nobody had raised questions about it.

"We hear about maybe a tenth of the incorrect reporting that goes on in *major* scientific research, maybe less," she said. "In the general run, and of course in the soft sciences there's a lot more, but nobody bothers to report it, let alone try to duplicate it."

"Emily, if you had that kind of doubt about a colleague's work, what would you do?"

"First I'd have it checked by other people who worked in that field," Emily answered promptly. "And if they agreed it was flawed, I'd pass the info on to their granting agency. Nowadays most of the agencies have people to deal with that kind of problem."

Maurice didn't say anything for a moment, and Emily, sensing that she hadn't entirely answered his question, went on. "If you're seriously concerned about a particular *person*, the best bet is to get in touch with someone at the institution where the work was carried out. Coworkers, rival labs, technicians, former associates, they're the ones who really know, but of course most of them keep their lips tightly buttoned, as you ex-colonials are fond of saying, because nobody likes a tattletale. It ain't easy getting the truth, as I can tell you from experience, even if St. John was right and it does make you free. The best of luck to you, Maurice. Do let me know if anything interesting turns up."

Maurice sat looking at the phone, going through in his head the wide network of friends and acquaintances he'd built up through the years, but drew a blank. Bob. Bob Zimmerman, of course. He was a completely honest, umcompromising person. The only problem was whether he would remember that particular paper out of the dozens that came out every year from his department.

But when he phoned, he was told that Bob was presently in Tientsin with a team of physicians touring Chinese medical schools, and was not expected back for several weeks.

Maurice sighed, and did what he now figured he should have done in the first place, and that was call Paula.

She had just come into her office when the phone rang, and she set off down the corridor toward Maurice's office, thinking nothing of it, as a similar summons came for her on an average of three or four times a week. What she was thinking about was Steve, trying to figure a strategy to beat him when they played the next morning.

Maurice was looking pensive, and to Paula his smile did not seem quite as warm as usual. After asking how things were going with her, he sat back in his chair and stared at her, hesitating for a moment, tapping the eraser end of a pencil on the desk. "I received a phone call a little while back," he said. "Apparently there's been some concern about a piece of research that came out of Bob Zimmerman's lab three years ago." He paused, his eyes showing his worry. "Your name was on that paper as the lead author, and—"

"Was that the paper on thrombolysins?" Paula felt a sinking feeling in the pit of her stomach.

"Right. Apparently somebody's been tipped off that there were problems with that research, and I thought I'd ask you about it before it went any further."

Maurice watched her, interested to see how she would deal with this. He knew that under stress, or when accused of a potentially damaging action, many people reveal an unsuspected side of their personality, and it was important for him to see how Paula would react.

To his huge relief, she neither wept, got angry, or sulked, but answered his question frankly.

"This is what happened," she told him. "We'd developed this technique for measuring small quantities of thrombolysins in banked blood, and it seemed to work pretty well. I personally didn't think it was interesting enough to publish, but Dr. Zimmerman felt that any new procedure we came up with should be reported and at least submitted. He said the journal editors should be the ones to decide if it's interesting or not. He wanted to present the paper at a meeting, and we had to rush it because there was a deadline problem."

Paula could feel herself starting to make excuses and stopped. "Dr. Bennett," she said firmly, "I screwed up. Some of our reagents were outdated, and I didn't pick up on that until later. We sent the reagents we used to a commercial testing lab, and some of them were off by several percentage points. Later, I repeated the process over the full range with a fresh set of reagents, and found that the top end of the curve was off. Not a whole lot off, about six percent, but it was off."

"Do you feel you should have retracted the paper?"

"No, the technique was basically okay. I talked to Dr. Zimmerman about it, and we agreed to write a memo to the journal, pointing out the errors."

"Did you do that?"

There was a pause. Paula looked at her feet, then looked up squarely at Maurice. "No, I didn't"

Maurice seemed puzzled. "Why not?"

"At the time I was using every spare minute to start up the research I'm doing now," she said. "I was also in a pretty demanding residency program. I was always going to write that correction the next day, the next week, then finally I just put if off so long I forgot about it."

She looked so downcast and embarrassed that Maurice smiled. "Paula, this sounds to me like the kind of thing that could happen to just about any inexperienced researcher," he said. "Usually nobody pays attention and the whole thing passes into oblivion."

He paused, trying to figure it out in his own mind. "But in this instance it didn't pass into oblivion. It was your old friend Dr. Abrams who told me about this. Somebody, whether it's him of someone else, got suddenly interested, and my guess is that at some point you may have to defend yourself and your actions. So get ready. The first thing you need to do is write that correction and send it off to the editor of the journal. I know it's late, but do it anyway. Next, go over every other paper you've published, and check to see if there's anything inexact or that contains data that could be misinterpreted."

Paula was smiling at him and looking surprised.

"Don't take this lightly," he warned. "I have a feeling that right now, someone or some group is going over every single piece of your published work, every article you've written, every talk you've given. Someone is checking everything you've said and done with a fine-tooth comb. And you can be sure it's being done with hostile intent."

Paula shook her head. "Why? If somebody had a problem with the procedure and called me about it, I'd tell them. What's the purpose of making a big deal out of it?"

"I don't know," said Maurice, looking at his watch, "but I know the signs. I've been a target on occasion, so I know just how that feels. Somebody's trying to get at you, they've found a potential crack in your armor, and they're going to try to pry it open."

He sat still for a moment, looking at Paula with an odd, questioning expression. "Do you have any idea who it might be, aside from Cliff Abrams?"

Paula shook her head.

"I've been wondering where that information about your thrombolysins paper came from," went on Maurice. "Someone at Columbia-Presbyterian? What about your technician? I assume you've warned her not to talk to anyone about your work."

"Myra's okay," said Paula. "She's very loyal and in any case she keeps to herself. And she had a share of the responsibility, so I don't imagine she'd want to talk about it."

"What about the work you're doing now?" asked Maurice. "I'm sure a lot of people would like to have access to your data."

"Myra doesn't know that much about the enzyme sequence, or how it works, even if she wanted to tell someone."

"Isn't all that information in your computer? People have ways, you know. And industrial espionage has grown to involve university labs too. It's become quite an industry."

"I thought of that," replied Paula. "All my data is coded in such a way that even if somebody broke into the computer, they wouldn't be able to decipher the information."

"Does anyone know the code?" asked Maurice. "What would happen if you were in an accident, or you got seriously ill? Would all that work be lost?"

"It's taken care of," said Paula. "The university has the code. You know Mr. Susskind, the attorney in their legal section? Well, he has it. It's tucked away in a sealed envelope, sitting in his office safe with all the other lab computer codes."

"I hear that some of the pharmaceutical companies are reviving their research on intravascular clotting," said Maurice.

Paula pursed her lips and put her hands together. She had beautiful hands, thought Maurice, watching her. They were fine, long-fingered, strong; real surgeon's hands.

"I heard that too," she said. "Everybody wants to get there first."

"By the way," Maurice went on, "I heard from my friends at NIH and the Army. They can't bend the rules the way they used to, and we'll just have to send your applications through the usual funding channels. Sorry."

"How do you think Dr. Abrams manages?" she asked, after digesting that unwelcome piece of news. "There's a whole lot of really expensive equipment coming into his lab all of a sudden. I've seen the crates outside."

Maurice shook his head. "He must have got some outside support to try to catch up with your work," he said. "I've heard on the grapevine that Millway is about to cut him off at the knees."

"Do you think it could be Abrams doing this? asked Paula, interrupting his train of thought. "I mean, could he be digging up all that old stuff about the thrombolysins?"

Maurice looked up at the ceiling. He'd been asking himself the same question. "Why? What possible advantage would there be for him? Do you know of any reason for him to go against you?"

"Not that I know of," said Paula. "Unless he's still mad that I beat his candidate for this job."

Maurice shook his head. "He wouldn't waste his time for that. How about Charnley? He might want to cause a diversion, and get more time to catch up with your research."

"No way," said Paula, and her tone made Maurice look hard at her.

"While we're on the topic," he said, "do you think Steve Charnley can do the job?"

"I guess Abrams thinks so," said Paula. "I know Steve's written a few papers on clotting problems, but as far as I know, his main schtick is instrumentation."

Maurice tapped his fingertips together. "We'll soon find out, I suppose. Meanwhile," he said, "remember to write the retraction note to the editor of that journal and send it off today." He stood up. "Now, I have students in five minutes, so we'll have to discuss the rest of this another time."

Paula went over to her lab. Myra was sitting at the small computer, checking off lists of chemical and biological reagents and supplies. A small pile of supplier catalogs lay on the table next to her. She looked up when Paula came in, and there was a strange, appraising expression in her eyes. "I'd forgotten how *expensive* this stuff is," she said. "We need almost eight thousand dollars' worth just to get some of those tests going again."

"Wait till you see what the computerized analyzer's going to cost," replied Paula.

"Maybe Dr. Abrams would let us use his, when his people aren't using it, at night and on weekends," suggested Myra.

"I doubt it," said Paula.

"Oh, I'm sure he'd let us," said Myra, a sudden sparkle in her eye. "Dr. Abrams is one of the nicest people I've ever met."

She must have seen Paula's eyebrows rise, because she hurriedly went back to her list.

"Did the NIH application forms come in?" asked Paula.

"They're on your desk," replied Myra. "I'd guess the whole package weighs about four pounds. I looked at the instructions, and I think I'd need a law degree just to understand them. Oh, and there was a Mr. Susskind who called," she went on. "He left a number . . ." Myra turned back a page of her notebook. "Yes. He's from the legal department, and wants you to call him back on extension 4772."

Paula went into her office to call him, and when Geoffrey Susskind's tired voice came on the phone, Paula got such a sense of transmitted weariness from him that she had difficulty suppressing a yawn.

"We received a notification that you'd turned down the grant offer from Millway, Dr. Cairns," he said. "And I'd like to talk to you about it. Can you come over to the legal building tomorrow morning? About eight?"

"What's to talk about, Mr. Susskind? I turned it down. End of discussion, no?" The mere mention of Millway made her think of her last encounter with Seth, and she smiled grimly. His eye must have hurt for some time after.

"No," said Susskind. His voice was low, and Paula had to press the phone to her ear to hear him. "It's not the end of the discussion. Will eight o'clock be satisfactory?"

"No, it won't be," Paula replied. "Sorry, but I'm scheduled to do surgery with my resident team." And if he suggests an earlier time, she thought, tough. I'm playing racquetball with Steve.

Susskind's sigh was so faint that Paula might have imagined it. "Ten o'clock, then?" he asked. "Or would ten-thirty be more convenient?"

"Ten-thirty sounds about right, Mr. Susskind," replied Paula. "If I get held up in the O.R., I'll have someone call you."

Paula put the phone down thoughtfully. What was this

about? What did Susskind or the university or anyone care if she turned down a grant offer from Millway or anybody else?

She went back into the lab to work on her computer for a while before going over to the outpatient clinic, and a thought simmered quietly in the back of her mind. Could Seth possibly have been behind Susskind's call?

Chapter Nineteen

On the way to the outpatient clinic, where she was to see Nicky Millway in follow-up, Paula thought about Myra, and how her face had lit up when Cliff Abrams' name was mentioned, and by the time Nicky came in, Paula had come to a couple of conclusions.

"I've been playing tennis," said Nicky.

"What?" The cast was still on her lower leg, beaten up, the ends cracked and frayed but essentially intact, and Paula couldn't imagine how Nicky could get around a court fast enough to play.

Charlene Millway, who had brought Nicky in, flushed. "I told you Dr. Cairns would be furious," she said sternly to her granddaughter.

"Let's take a look," said Paula, smiling, and beginning to get an understanding of this undefeatable young woman. "I think we can take the cast off now. Everything's had time to heal."

The ankle was very stiff, as Paula had expected, and the skin was white and rough, in contrast to the smooth, healthy tan over the rest of Nicky's leg. The scar had healed beautifully, but, as she explained to Nicky, it would stay red for several months before fading.

"I've been winning too." Nicky stood up, put some pressure on her ankle, and winced, but that didn't stop her.

She walked across the floor and back. "It was easier with the cast on," she said.

'She's going to be a doctor," Charlene told Paula. "Like you. That's what she's telling everybody."

Paula outlined some exercises and movements for Nicky to strengthen her ankle, and told her what kind of sneaker would give her ankle the support it needed.

"We have inter-school tennis finals in six weeks," said Nicky. "Would you come?"

Paula gulped. This was insane; by that time Nicky should be barely walking slowly around, probably with a stick, but it didn't seem reasonable at this point to forbid her to play.

"I want you to know that you're taking the risk of pulling your tendons apart and doing permanent damage to your foot," she said as severely as she could.

"I've been telling her that since she got out of hospital," said Charlene, shrugging her shoulders in a bemused way.

"Please?" said Nicky, and her expression showed how much it meant to her.

"Okay, I'll come," said Paula to Nicky, giving her a big hug. "Take good care of that foot, and I'll be there rooting for you, I promise."

Ten minutes later, on her way over to the central medical library, Paula heard footsteps coming up behind her. It was Dr. Eagleton, the private-side surgeon.

"Nervous about something, Dr. Cairns?" he drawled when she turned around. "Work going slowly? I guess not," he went on without waiting for an answer. "By the way, we were all very, very proud to see that long article about you in the *Times* a month or so ago. Congratulations."

"Thanks," replied Paula, "but it wasn't any big deal. They save that kind of story for when there's no news." She felt momentarily amused at her own words; it was just the kind of reply a man would make, and appreciate: modest, without any arrogant overtones, but without giving up any ground either.

"Do you have time for a cup of coffee?" he asked suddenly as they came up to the cafeteria entrance.

"Sure." Paula felt uptight and anxious, and could use the break. Also she rather liked Walt, with his sharp, quirky cleverness, even though he usually seemed to get the best of any discussion with her.

They sat down at a small table under a window overlooking the parking lot. Walt didn't let his eyes wander from her; Paula had heard that he knew how to make women think they were something special and important to him.

"Are you married, Walt?" she asked rather abruptly.

"I was," he replied, then shrugged. He looked quizzically at her. "Cliff Abrams told me how pissed you got when he asked you the same question during your first interview."

"That was different," said Paula. She grinned, realizing she'd been caught. "I'm not interviewing you for a job."

"Then what *are* you interviewing me for?" Walt sat back, suddenly competitive, his eyes clearly saying to her, "Don't ever think you're going to get the better of me in a conversation, lady."

"Lighten up, sir," said Paula. "I was just asking you a simple question. Actually, somebody told me yesterday that every unattached female, and some attached ones, within a twenty-mile radius had their eye on you, and I wondered if it was your charm or simply because you'd become available."

Walt took a sip of coffee and stared at Paula over the top of it. "Both," he said in a tone that ended that conversation. "But that's not why I want to talk to you." He paused. "How's my friend Maurice?" he asked.

"Dr. Bennett? He's fine, as far as I know," answered Paula.

"Somebody saw him down in the X-ray department a couple of days ago," said Walt.

"So? We all spend time there, don't we?" Paula's tone was crisp.

"Maurice was in a hospital gown, being slid into a CAT scanner," replied Walt in a somber voice.

Paula was surprised. "I had no idea," she said.

"I hope he's all right," went on Walt. A curious expression came over his face as he spoke. "I'm sure you do too. He's been a very good friend to you, Dr. Cairns, a real champion, in the medieval sense."

"He certainly has," agreed Paula, wondering what could be the matter with Maurice. At the thought of his being ill, she felt a tightness across her heart. Maybe she'd never thought about it before, but now she realized how fond she was of Maurice, and how much she depended on him.

"Seeing as how you brought it up," said Walt, watching her with his sharp, all-seeing eyes, "let's talk about Maurice for a minute."

"I didn't bring him up," Paula pointed out. "You did."

"Well, let's talk about him anyway," said Walt. 'I'm sure you're aware that we all admire him greatly. He's one of the shining lights of our profession—"

" 'That to believing souls gives light in darkness, comfort in despair,' right?"said Paula, pleased that she still remembered some Shakespeare, and wondering what on earth Walt Eagleton was getting at with his not-quite-genuine admiration of Maurice Bennett.

Walt stared, then laughed. "I couldn't have put it better myself," he said. "We're certainly talking about the same guy. Anyway, the word is that he isn't going to be around here much longer."

Paula felt as if everything in the world had stopped. "Are you telling me he's really sick?" she asked, her voice sharp with tension.

"No, not at all," said Walt with an expression that made her want to slap him. "I hear he might be going to Washington in the near future."

"I certainly don't know anything about that," replied Paula, but her heart was still beating fast, whether it was out of annoyance at Walt or what, she didn't know.

"What about this great investigation he's supposed to be doing on the pharmaceutical industry?"

Paula shook her head.

"Somebody said he's going to blow the whole industry out of the water," went on Walt, playing idly with his spoon, twirling it, then catching it just before it fell. "He's going to expose all kinds of malfeasance, apparently. And his beady eye has been turning on certain companies in particular, maybe even one of own local employers, Millway Pharmaceuticals. Is that just idle chatter, do you know, or is it true?"

Paula wanted to tell him that if he was so interested, he should go and ask Maurice himself, but she thought better of it and said, "I've heard the same rumors. But Dr. Bennett doesn't tell me anything about the outside work he's doing."

Walt looked genuinely disappointed. Maurice and Paula were generally thought to have a very close professional relationship, but apparently it wasn't as close as all that.

"Then let's talk about you," he said.

Paula looked at her watch. "I was on my way to the library when you kidnapped me," she said. "I have to go."

"You know there was a lot of disagreement about your coming here," went on Walt as if she hadn't said anything. "Maurice used up a lot of points to get your appointment through the committees."

"You mean it wasn't only my ability that convinced them?"

"For a faculty job at a place like this," said Walt, "as you well know, there are plenty of qualified applicants. Aside from Steve Charnley, there were at least two with strong backing and who looked just as good as you." He grinned. "On paper, I mean. So the way it works out is that the person with the heaviest muscle behind him—or her—gets the job."

"What's all that to you?" asked Paula. The mere mention of Steve's name made her mind wander for a moment. "I thought the only thing you private guys were interested in was getting an early morning slot in the O.R."

"Look, Paula," said Walt, shaking his head. "I'm just telling you that there are people here who don't like you. Not personally, of course, on the contrary. What they don't like is that you're on the faculty. They think Maurice pulled rank to get you here, and that you shouldn't have got the job. And now, on top of everything, we're hearing all this stuff about some research paper you published a few years ago . . ." Walt's eyes scanned her lazily; they were the eyes of someone in complete control, a man who could afford to take his time. "So they'll get rid of you," he went on, nodding quite dispassionately, as if they were discussing some kind of rodent control. "Sooner or later. I've seen it happen before."

"Why are you telling me this?" asked Paula. "And whose side do you happen to be on?"

Walt grinned appreciatively. "Good point. I'm on *my* side. But I have no desire to see you crucified either. As I see it, you still have a number of options. You can try to tough it out. You can pick up your marbles and leave. But I have another option you might like to consider."

"Suicide maybe? You know, Walt, I'm getting sick of all this nonsense about my dubious research. I made a mistake. One single goddamn mistake. Tell me, Walt, have you ever made a mistake? In you whole professional life?"

"They used to say surgeons bury their mistakes," replied Walt, smiling tolerantly at her anger. "Now they say the lawyers bury the surgeons, but only after they've skinned them."

"That's not funny," snapped Paula. "And you didn't answer the question."

"I have a proposition for you, Paula," said Walt very seriously. "I believe it would kill a whole flock of birds with one stone. I've been watching you ever since you came to this center, and in my opinion you're one of the best young surgeons who's come down the pike. I'm tired of being a solo practitioner, I have more work than I can do, and I need an assistant"— Walt held up a hand—"who would become my partner in one year. I would prefer a female assistant, because more and more women want to be taken care of by women doctors. In your first year you'll make twice the money you're making now, and you'll be a part of the most prestigious practice in New Coventry."

Walt sat back, watching Paula.

"My research . . ." she started.

"I forgot to mention," said Walt, "that I'd arrange for you to have your own lab, with whatever equipment and technical help you need. The only limitation is that you don't neglect your clinical responsibilities for your research."

"Wow," said Paula, smiling, not certain if Walt was serious or just teasing. "That sounds like a very attractive proposition. Can I start today?"

Walt laughed. "Hold your horses, young lady. I'm thinking of starting you around the first of next year—that is, in, oh, about seven months." He settled comfortably back in his chair, looking very relaxed. "That would give you time to finish up the research projects you're involved in. Then you could start your new career as a *real* surgeon."

Paula thought quickly. It was a most attractive offer, but it was very unlikely that she could finish her research project before the end of the year, if ever.

"Let me think about it, Walt," she said. "I'm really flattered, but there are all kinds of things I have to add up before making a final decision. Could I let you know in, say, a week?"

Walt hesitated for a second. "Okay," he said, shrugging a little petulantly. "But I must tell you, you're the only surgeon in this town who wouldn't jump at the opportunity."

"I'm a slow jumper," said Paula, trying not to sound sad. She had a premonition that her research was going down the tube, or she wouldn't even be considering Walt's offer.

"That's okay," said Walt. "If you'd really jumped at it without taking time to consider, I'd have wondered if your research project was maybe in some kind of trouble."

Once again Paula didn't know what to say. Walt was watching her, his eyes gleaming with a kind of mocking awareness that made her uncomfortable.

"Thanks, I appreciate your confidence in me," said Paula, and a private demon must have seized her, because she followed that up by asking Walt if he'd like to assist her in surgery the next Tuesday. "I'm doing a carotid," she told him. "It shouldn't take too long."

For a second Walt stared openmouthed at her. It was unheard of for a junior attending such as Paula to ask somebody of his seniority and stature to assist in a routine case unless there was some particular difficulty expected, or some other imperative.

His eyes narrowed for a fraction of a second, then he laughed. "For a woman, you've got balls of steel," he said. "Sure, I'll assist you. What time are you doing the case?"

She told him. Just as they were leaving, Walt grinned

and said, "See you in the morning," and hurried off before Paula had a chance to ask him what he meant.

As she came in to the library, her pager buzzed briefly and she read the LCD message on the tiny screen. "Call Dr. Steven Charnley extension 3389."

She suppressed her desire to rush to a phone and decided, for no very obvious reason, to wait for ten minutes before calling him back. She walked up the wide, uncarpeted concrete steps to the new journals section and browsed there, but couldn't keep from looking at her watch, and she wasn't able to concentrate on what she was reading.

"Wanna go out to dinner tonight?" asked Steve when she called back. Paula was holding phone very tightly and didn't notice the nervousness in his voice.

"Sure," she replied instantly, although she'd planned to spend the evening in the lab.

"Can you pick me up?" he asked. "My car's having its brakes relined."

The image of Seth flew unexpectedly into Paula's mind; she couldn't imagine him asking her, or anyone else, for a ride. He probably had an identical Beamer waiting in his garage in case something happened to the first one.

"No problem," said Paula. "I'll be in front of the lab at seven-thirty okay?"

"How shall I know you?" asked Steve, delighted.

"I'll be holding a rose," she replied. "In my teeth."

Chapter Twenty

That evening promptly at seven-thirty, Paula drove her old faded green MGB around to the front of the research building and waited outside. At idling speed the entire vehicle shook, and she could smell the faint, acrid odor of exhaust fumes. She wound down the window and was about to switch the motor off when Steve appeared.

"You have to pull hard," she shouted as he tried to open the passenger side door. Finally it jerked open and Steve slid into the seat.

"Am I late?"

"I'm early."

They both felt a sudden discomfort at their physical closeness; Paula would have felt more able to concentrate if she'd been driving a school bus and Steve was in the back row of seats.

"Where are we going?" she asked.

"Metaphysically, hard to tell at this point," he replied, grinning at the opportunity to be smart, "but for dinner I thought we'd go to Rosselini's. A friend in L.A. told me you get the best Italian food in town there."

"Never heard of it," said Paula, but that wasn't surprising since she'd only been in New Coventry a few months, hardly long enough to have checked out all the various eateries in town.

"I looked it up," said Steve. "It's on Washington Street."

Paula hesitated, her foot on the clutch. "Washington Street? Not exactly the best part of town, is it?"

"I don't know," replied Steve. "Let's go take a look. If we don't like it, there's always Burger King. By the way, you need to check the brackets on your exhaust system. That's what's making the car shake like that, if you don't know already."

Five minutes later, Paula turned onto Washington Street, and she didn't like the look of it. A mangy calico cat strolled across the street in front of them, glowering as if it knew they didn't belong there. Several of the buildings on each side of the street were boarded up, and some had empty, fire-scarred windows. Rosselini's was halfway down the street on the left, and aside from a couple of cars parked outside it, the restaurant's red and green neon sign was the only sign of life. Paula parked behind the other cars, and they got out and walked along the sidewalk toward the restaurant. Grass grew between the cracks in the concrete, and the wires at the bases of the street lamps had been pulled out and were hanging loose. The surroundings made Paula tense; the area must have gone downhill a lot since Steve's friend was last there.

Inside the restaurant, they stood in the dimly lit foyer, waiting for someone to show them to a table. "We can go somewhere else if you like," said Steve in a subdued voice. They looked around. Only four tables were occupied. "I can't believe this," he went on. "Bob told me there were lines around the corner to get into this place."

"When was he last here?"

"It must have been a few years ago, I guess. And things have changed, from the looks of it."

The waitress came up, a large woman with straggly reddish hair. She looked tired, hot, and flat-footed.

"Two?" she asked "You wanna pick a table?"

Steve looked at Paula, and they simultaneously pointed at the same table, by the curtained window.

When the waitress came back, she looked at them curiously. "You folks been here before?"

"No," said Steve. "A friend of mine said this is where to get the best Italian food in New Coventry."

"The food's still good," said the waitress. "But we're closing at the end of the month. Today's special is *osso bucco*, and it's terrific. My name's Shirley."

"Why are you closing?" asked Paula.

"Look around," said Shirley. "The neighborhood gets all the time worse, and Mrs. Rosselini's tired of cooking, and she's going to retire in Pavia, Italy. You want wine?"

Steve ordered the *osso bucco*, Paula decided on *imbottini delizia*, mostly because she liked the name. It turned out to be a veal cutlet, pounded flat and rolled and tied around a sauce filling of cream cheese, ham, port wine, celery, white truffles, and spices.

Steve had spent an undergraduate term at the University of Milan, and told Paula about a great restaurant there, the Tantalo. "If you order *osso bucco* there," he told her, "to get the marrow out, they give you a big hollow needle. They call it the Tax Collector."

He asked for a bottle of Fontanafredda, his favorite Barolo, but all that was left from an extensive wine list was some Chianti and a half-dozen bottles of Valpolicella. Mrs. Rosselini came from the kitchen to apologize. A short, heavyset woman with dark rings around her eyes and no makeup, she wore black and had an air of resigned sadness about her.

Steve told her in Italian he was sorry the place was closing down.

"My poor husband," she said, wiping her hands down

the side of her long blue-and-white-striped butcher's apron, "this would have broken his heart if he was still alive. But I talk to him every night, and he agrees that it is best to close."

The Valpolicella was good, and while the coffee was being served, Steve told Paula about his brother Alan, who worked in Washington in the State Department, hosting foreign VIPs, fixing their parking tickets, and generally smoothing the strange American experience for them.

"Al had a client named Nikolavic from Bosnia who'd come looking for some emergency aid," said Steve. "Al went over to his hotel room with a list of private organizations for him to contact. Nikolavic was a small, unshaven guy in a big serge suit with wide lapels, and chain-smoked some kind of poisonous Balkan cigarette. He also had a black eye. Apparently he'd found a call girl, but afterward he didn't have enough money to pay her, so her pimp showed up, there was a fight, and the little guy lost. He didn't give a damn about the sources Al had spent hours finding—he just wanted to fuck American women, and asked Al for the phone numbers of any female friends he could spare because the Washington whores were too expensive."

"I hope Al was able to help him," murmured Paula, wondering if Steve was going on about his brother because he didn't want to talk about himself. But she was curious. "How about you? How's your work going? What are you doing? How do you like working with Cliff Abrams?"

Steve's eyes changed, and he seemed to withdraw. "Okay, I guess," he said, avoiding Paula's direct gaze.

"Well, excuse me for asking," she said. Paula didn't have much time for people who weren't totally involved and fascinated by what they were doing. "If it's only okay, if you don't really like it here, why don't you go somewhere else? When I came here for my first interview, they told me you were the smartest resident that ever came out of the L.A. Memorial program. I don't know if that's much of a recommendation, but that's what they said. So you should be able to go anywhere you want, right?"

"Well, it didn't work out that way," replied Steve, an acid tone to his voice. "I had that problem with the arterioscope, and all of a sudden my job at L.A. Memorial vanished."

"So? L.A. isn't the only place in the world." Paula's eyes flashed. "Are you being sorry for yourself or what?"

Steve took a deep breath. "You want to hear how it is? Really? Okay, I'm just wasting my time in New Coventry, and I'm getting out as soon as I can. Abrams is a politician, not a real researcher. He hired me to start up a clot-dissolving program to catch up with yours, but he has no idea where to start and neither do I."

Paula watched him, and listened, with an odd mixture of emotions.

Steve was launched now and went on. "You see, Paula, I was fucked over in L.A. I had a career that fell apart because I was trying something new and it didn't work." Boiling over with retrospective frustration, Steve slammed his fist on the table and the bottle of Valpolicella rocked. Paula caught and steadied it. Conversation at the next table stopped for a moment.

Paula was merciless. "So everybody's been mean and nasty to you and ruined your career. Poor baby! Maybe you should trot off home to mommy, and she can kiss it all better for you."

Steve half rose from his chair, his mouth a straight line of anger. Paula tensed, ready for a real explosion. Then something strange happened. He stared at her for a second, then sat back and laughed, a genuine, honest-to-God laugh, maybe the first since he'd left California.

"Thanks, Paula," he said. "I just saw myself, and I sure looked stupid." He leaned over the table, gazing with wry sincerity into Paula's eyes. "That's it. As of today I'll go back to being my old self, dynamic, enthusiastic, charismatic . . . well, all that stuff. And now I need another drink. How about you?"

He refilled their glasses.

"What about your arterioscope?" asked Paula, persisting. "It sounds like the most brilliant piece of equipment I've ever heard of. What's happened to it?"

Steve shrugged. "I've still got it. Why, do you need a doorstop?"

"Don't be silly. Why aren't you using it? When you did that case that went wrong at L.A. Memorial, the scope worked all right, didn't it?"

"Yes, it did. It worked perfectly, better than I could have hoped."

"So . . . ?" Paula stretched her hand across the table and put it on his wrist. They stared at each other.

"So?" she repeated, taking her hand away. "Why aren't you using it, improving it, developing it? Are you going to let all the work you did just go to waste? Shame on you, Steven Charnley."

"I tell you, Paula, I've been too disgusted even to look at it," said Steve. "And I don't have surgical privileges at the hospital yet, and I wouldn't get permission to use the scope, not after that last fiasco."

"So you're giving up?"

He sat straight up, and Paula could see him square his shoulders; her prodding seemed to be jostling some spirit back into him.

"Tomorrow I'll take it out of the box and check it out," he promised. "If you like, I'll show you how to use it. You have operating privileges, so you might get permission to use it clinically."

"No way," said Paula firmly. "It's your machine. Can't Abrams get you privileges? I'd have thought he'd have enough clout."

"Apparently not. But I don't think he's trying that hard either."

I'll talk to Maurice about it, thought Paula. If anyone can get things moving in this hospital, he can.

They were so involved with each other and with their discussion that when they looked up to see Mrs. Rosselini come up to give Steve the check, the other diners had left. He reached in his pocket for his wallet, and found that he'd left it at home. Paula paid with her Visa card.

"No sweat," she said, slyly enjoying his embarrassment. "You pay next time. Only we'll be going to a much more expensive place. I know how much Abrams is paying you."

Outside, it was dark, and the streetlight by the restaurant was out. Paula took his arm and they had started to walk toward the car, now the only ones on the street, when Steve noticed that the trunk of Paula's MGB was open and a shadowy figure was standing next to it.

"Go back in," he said quickly to Paula. "Call the cops."

Paula opened her mouth to protest, but he said, "Don't argue," and gave her a push back toward the restaurant, where the lights were already going out.

He waited for a few moments in the shadows, watching and thinking about what he should do. Then he walked slowly toward the car, stepping into the street so he'd have room to maneuver when he got closer. As he approached, he could see two men, barely visible in the dim light. The driver's seat door was open and the legs of one of them struck out as their owner leaned back into the car, no doubt trying to hot-wire it. The other man was tall, skinny, wore a black leather cap, and leaned over the top of the door, nonchalantly watching Steve approach.

All Steve's instincts told him to get out of this, to go back to the restaurant, call a taxi, and not risk his life for the sake of an ancient, clapped-out car. But there was something in his head, a kind of arrogance that wasn't going to let anybody intimidate him.

The man with the cap was on the far side of the open car door, and Steve made as if he was going to walk past them, slouching, hands hanging by his side. The man took a long step out to intercept him, exactly as Steve had hoped, and he saw the flash of a knife coming up and back. Steve, L.A. trained and no mean street fighter in his youth, had barely time to butt the man hard in the face, right where his nose met his forehead, hard enough to feel the crunch of breaking bone. The man grunted with pain and fell back, black blood pouring from his nose. Without a pause Steve caught hold of the open door and slammed it hard on the other man's legs. A muffled scream of pain came from inside the car, and Steve slammed the door again and held it.

A car turned into the street, roof lights flashing. The first man ran off down the street in the opposite direction, holding his hand to his crushed nose, leaving dark smears of blood on the sidewalk.

Later, when they got back to his apartment, Steve found he had a paralyzing bruise over his right forearm and could barely move it. "I don't even know how I got that," he said, wondering. "I didn't feel it until after the cops and the ambulance had gone."

"Did you hear what that cop said to me?" asked Paula indignantly. "He looked at my car and said, 'They were trying to steal *that*?'"

She helped him get his shirt off, then put a big glop of lotion she'd found in the bathroom into her hands, rubbed them together, and started to massage his arm very gently.

One thing led to another, and soon they both found themselves without any clothes on, with most of the contents of the lotion bottle spread in a thick, slippery film over both of them, and they slithered over and around, exploring every part, every nook and cranny of their bodies, and marveling at the excitingly different and erotic feel of their skins when they were completely covered in the fragrant, oily lotion.

And then a different passion began to replace the quiet search for the secrets of their bodies, and the exploratory lovingness ended. It started quietly at first, like the first whisper of a storm, detectable only by an increasing firmness, a tensing and resistance of their bodies. They stayed deliberately at that level for a long time, savoring it, enjoying their restraint. When they could resist no longer, and their movements became less gentle, less tentative, firmer, more directed, harder, faster, they could hear each other's breathing, and they didn't care how loud and raspy it became. Paula threw her head back, her mouth slightly open, showing her teeth, and growled and twisted her body and pushed her breasts aggressively up at him and ran her nails hard down the middle of his back. He bucked and thrust and put his hands under her and pulled her up to him, and tried to catch her breasts with his lips but wasn't able to do both things at once, and slid his hands all over her slippery breasts, feeling, absorbing their texture, then caught her nipples between his fingers and pointed them, and she started to say things to him that made him crazy and they both came, noisily, uninhibited, happy and finally exhausted, and fell back with their arms around each other. Steve's arm began to throb again, but he didn't care. They lay quietly pressed against each other, and it was that wonderful period of transition they both remembered long afterward, that luxurious time between wakefulness and sleep, when they were still conscious of each other's bodies and deeply aware of their profound and mutual contentment. Then, still enmeshed in each other, they fell into a sound and dreamless sleep.

Chapter Twenty-one

At breakfast with the residents next morning, Paula just managed to get down a couple of cups of coffee, some orange juice, and a piece of toast with grape jelly. She detested grape jelly, but she was feeling sore and otherworldly and didn't have the energy to get up and find something else.

"What's up, Paula?" asked Ken McKinley, who had been up most of the night and looked it. "You look sorta . . . out of it." Ken was a good doctor; even when he was bone tired, as now, he was still able to observe other people. And, of course, he liked Paula a lot.

"I have to talk to one of the university lawyers later this morning," she replied. "I guess I'm a bit nervous about it." What she had really been thinking about was how Steve had looked early this morning when he got out of bed and went into the shower, and she pulled the curtain aside and joined him. Later, after they'd decided to cancel their racquetball game, when they were taking her car to have the door fixed, he had to hang onto that door because it wouldn't close after being slammed on the car thief's leg. When she took a sharp left turn onto Salem Street, where the garage was, he almost fell out. The mechanic got the door to close, but then it wouldn't open.

She shook her head to clear it. "Anyway, how was your night?"

"There was a big mess-up on I-95," said Chris Engel, the junior resident, who had idolized Paula ever since the time she'd got him out of trouble in the operating room. He wasn't looking any more rested than Ken, but had enough energy to wolf down a great plateful of scrambled eggs and sausages. "You probably heard about it on the radio," he said, flicking a piece of egg off his cheek. "A tractor trailer jackknifed at the turnoff to I-91, crossed the median, and two cars ran into him. We got two DOAs, and one guy with a ruptured liver and spleen, another with a steering wheel in his chest. That one went to the cardiothoracic service and died on the table. Rick Mandel told us about it afterward. There was a tear right across his thoracic aorta, but it was just holding together, and didn't actually blow out until the moment they opened his chest."

"What happened to the guy with the ruptured liver?"

"We put him back together, sort of." Ken's red-rimmed eyes were fixed on Paula. "We had to take his spleen because it was in pieces. I've never seen one so smashed up, and there was no way we could save it."

"I had one of those at Presbyterian when I was a junior resident," said Paula. "He got a massive streptococcal infection ten days after we took his spleen out, and died."

"Did you remember to put our guy on an antibiotic?" Ken asked.

"Sure, of course," replied Chris, but he put down his fork and made a notation on one of his cards, and Ken managed a tired grin at Paula. Both of them had been junior residents not so very long ago, and they knew how things worked.

A few minutes after ten, Paula left the residents in the operating room, leaving Susskind's number to call if they got into trouble. She went to the changing room, pulled off her soiled O.R. greens, and dropped them in the bin, put her bra and panties in the top of her locker, and went for her second shower of the day. She came out feeling refreshed and confident, and as she dressed, she wondered why attorney Susskind wanted to talk about her refusal of the Millway offer. Leaving her white coat in the locker, Paula stepped briskly past the automatic doors of the operating room toward the elevators. The walk over to the building where the legal section was located took about five minutes. The weather had warmed up in the past few days, and spring was in full blast. Flowering cherry trees were in their short-lived moment of glory, and there was a feel of promise, of excitement, in the air as she walked across the green in front of the three old churches lined up in parallel. They were Methodist, Catholic, and Presbyterian, placed close enough to make a very esthetic grouping but, Paula lightheartedly supposed, far enough apart to avoid any risk of doctrinal cross-contamination.

The university's legal center had been built about fifteen years before, at the time when the lawyers were just beginning to take over the running of the hospital and the university. The architects, guided by the far-sighted legal luminaries of the day, had left plenty of room for expansion, but within four years it had been necessary to add three new floors, and a further major addition was now in the works, the plans again leaving ample room for future growth.

Paula checked her watch as she passed through the heavy glass doors at the front of the building. It was like the main offices of a big corporation, shiny, expensive, totally different from the elderly, plain, rather dingy buildings that made up the rest of the campus. For a second the setting made Paula think of George Orwell's *Animal Farm*, where all the animals were equal, but the pigs agreed that they were *more* equal than the others.

Susskind's office was on the seventh floor. It wasn't particularly palatial, in fact rather untidy, with a couple of diplomas, black-and-white framed photos on the walls of Susskind posing with various people in tuxedos or in front of a U.S. flag. Next to the telephone on the crowded desk was a wooden antique car model with a brass presentation plaque.

"Hi, Dr. Cairns," said Susskind, looking up after Paula had stood in the doorway for about a minute. "Let's go talk in the conference room. Would you care for a cup of coffee?" Paula shook her head. She'd already had two cups, enough for the morning. Susskind picked up a folder. He seemed just as tired and passive as ever, but a shade less friendly than last time Paula had met him.

There were footsteps in the corridor behind her, and she turned to see Walt Eagleton.

"Hi, Dr. Eagleton," said Susskind in the same weary, uninflected voice. "You two know each other, right? We were about to go across the corridor. You know where the coffee is if you want some."

Paula's eyebrows went up at Walt's unexpected arrival, but she said nothing.

The conference room was small, book-lined with eight high, square-backed leather chairs around a central rectangular table. There was an additional small table with a swivel chair at the end of the room opposite the door—for a stenographer, Paula guessed.

Susskind sat at one end, Paula sat on his right, and, in some surprise, watched Walt, who had followed them through, sit down opposite her.

Susskind opened the file in front of him. "We're here to discuss the Millway grant proposal," he said.

"What's Dr, Eagleton doing here?" Paula asked him.

Susskind looked over his half glasses at her. "Dr. Eagleton's on the university's grant coordinating committee," said Susskind, appearing mildly surprised that Paula didn't know. "And he's taking the time to give us his thoughts on what is now, I regret to say, becoming somewhat of a problem."

Walt grinned impishly at Paula and winked, but didn't say anything. Instead he sat back, his fingers linked in his lap, and assumed the serious expression that befitted a consultant.

"The Millway matter," said Susskind with a sign, ruffling some papers. "I have a formal notification here that you, Dr. Cairns, turned down an offer from the Millway Foundation that amounted to"—he turned over a page in the file—"one million, two hundred thousand dollars in the first year, with about the same amount for each of the three following years."

Susskind paused, took off his glasses, polished them with a large white handkerchief, and looked at Paula as if the enormity of such an refusal was clearly beyond his comprehension.

"Dr. Cairns, would you like to tell us the reason, or reasons, you had for turning down that grant?"

"I'm sorry," said Paula, "I'm not trying to be difficult, but why should I have to give you reasons? This was an offer made by a private foundation to me, and for me to accept or turn down. And as you noted, I turned it down."

There was a moment's silence around the table. Walt Eagleton spread his fingers out, inspected his nails with careful attention, and started to push back the cuticles with his thumbnail.

Susskind pursed his lips and replaced his half glasses halfway down his nose, which made him look like a Dickensian cartoon.

"I wish everything could be quite as simple as that," he said, putting both his hands on the file in front of him as if he were speaking to a junior high class. "For one thing"—he glanced at Walt, who was still occupied with his nails—"Dr. Cairns, do you think that Millway would have offered you that grant if you weren't working here, at this world-famous medical center? If they didn't know you had supporting facilities second to none in the world? No, of course not," he went on, answering his own question. "And that, of course, makes the university a participant in your work."

"Tell her about the money angle, Geoff," said Walt without looking up.

"I think what Dr. Eagleton is referring to is that the university takes a fee for administering grants," he said. "And on the basis of this . . ."

"A *fat* fee," said Walt reflectively, as if he'd like a good chunk of it. Paula couldn't figure his tone; he sounded as if he was trying to clarify things for her, but there was something else too, a slight derisiveness maybe, but she didn't have time to ponder who it was directed at.

"Fees are collected by the university from all grants to faculty members, and these usually amount to about twenty percent of the total amount of the grant," Susskind took up again in his pompous way. "In other words, the sum of fees collected in this way account for a substantial part of the university's income."

"Including paying for your salary, right, Geoff?" Walt was sounding bored now and fidgeted about in his seat. He'd taken a nail clipper out of his pocket and was playing with it, nibbling idly on the corners of his nails.

Susskind's tired smile was directed at Walt, but there was no humor in it. "No doubt," he said, "but that is not germane to the question we're addressing."

"Germane?" muttered Walt under his breath.

"Dr. Cairns, the point of this is that the university, which is your employer, needs the income from these grants. I assume that if you turned Millway down, you must have accepted another comparable grant from some other major agency?"

"No, I haven't," said Paula, after a brief pause to let Walt interrupt again if he wished to.

"Then perhaps you'd be kind enough to answer my original question, Dr. Cairns. Why did you turn down the grant?"

"The principal reason is that I read the small print in the contract," retorted Paula, who remembered Susskind's unsatisfactory explanation of that part of the contract. "It says that the patent rights to any process or invention developed under the grant would become the property of the Millway Foundation, which might, at its discretion, license it to Millway Pharmaceuticals or any other company. That would mean I'd lose the rights to my own work, and I'm not about to do that."

She could see Walt nodding approvingly at her ability to memorize this legal jargon, but Susskind seemed to puff up with a kind of lethargic annoyance.

"Now you look here, my dear young woman—" he started, but when Walt snorted with amusement, Susskind caught himself.

"Excuse me," he said, embarrassed. "Dr. Cairns, what I was going to say is that you are referring to the Millway Foundation's standard contract, which has been examined and approved by the university's legal department. As an employee of the university, therefore, you are not at liberty to reject a grant on such grounds."

Paula was tempted to tell him about the two other reasons she had to turn down the contract; Maurice had advised her not to accept it because Millway was under suspicion of illegal practices, and also because the new chairman of the foundation had tried to rape her.

Instead she told them mildly that she was applying for

major funding to the National Institutes of Health, the Army, and the Ford Foundation.

"Takes a long time going that route," said Walt.

"I know that," went on Paula with some asperity. "Meanwhile, just to get going, I'll be getting funds from a number of unassigned departmental sources."

Susskind's glasses had slid to the end of his nose, and he pushed them back with a sigh. "Is that definite?" he asked. "Papers signed and all that?"

"No, but I'm told that—"

"Won't happen," said Walt. "Right, Geoff?"

"What Dr. Eagleton is saying is that the university can't allow that to take place," said Susskind, talking once more in his usual regretful voice. "You can understand why, I'm sure. If a grant is offered, and these days that's a real triumph for any grantee, and it is turned down for no good reason, the university would obviously be very reluctant to give money out of its own pocket to replace it. It's bad enough losing once, and it simply wouldn't make any sense to lose money twice on the same deal. You do understand that, don't you?"

Paula stared at him. "Are you telling me that those 'unassigned funds' are under the university's control? I thought the department heads were in charge of them."

"In this case Dr. Bennett, of course," said Walt, nodding. "He's the one in full charge of the department of surgery." Again he flashed a disconcerting grin at Paula.

"In principle, yes," said Susskind, who now seemed to be picking his words with care. "The university likes to give department heads that kind of freedom. But of course if the university feels that allowing that privilege isn't going to be in its own best interests, it will withdraw it." Susskind paused and sat back, watching to see if she had understood.

"You're saying that if I don't take Millway's money, I won't be allowed to get any from other sources?"

"No, no, of course not. I'm just talking about internal funds, money that belongs to the university."

Paula sat thoughtfully, digesting that piece of news.

"You're putting pressure on me to accept that Millway grant, am I right? Is this the academic freedom I've heard so much about?"

Walt looked up and smiled at her. "Tell her the rest of it, Geoff," he said, not taking his eyes off Paula.

Susskind looked puzzled for a moment. "Yes, of course." He moved in his chair, like a sack of coal settling, then smiled. "You see, Dr. Cairns, I'm not just an employee of the university, but I'm also a sentient human being. I'm sincerely trying to look out for *your* interests, and I really want to help you avoid situations that could have serious repercussions on you and your career."

"I appreciate that, Mr. Susskind." If there was any irony in her voice, he missed it.

Susskind templed his hands. "When I'm discussing things of this nature with junior faculty members," he said, assuming a confidential, fatherly tone, "I always say this to them: 'Think about the impact on your careers.' Now in your case, Dr. Cairns, as I'm sure you know, your faculty appointment will be reviewed after six months, then on a yearly basis. And one of the things they look for these days in a junior researcher is, sadly but inevitably, how much money you're bringing in in grants."

Paula opened her mouth to interrupt, but he went on without a pause.

"And if in your evaluation records the committee saw that you were bringing nothing in, but had turned down a major grant, what do you think their reaction would be? What do you think their response with regard to promotion would be?"

It was a rhetorical question which Susskind went on to answer himself. "Negative," he said, "on both counts."

"Important point," said Walt, nodding. He looked out the window, obviously anxious to be out there, preferably on the golf course.

But Susskind hadn't finished. "I'm sure you also know that the policy at this university is that an assistant professor who isn't recommended for promotion within three years is, in the interests of maintenance of the institution's academic excellence, usually asked to leave."

"I see," said Paula. "Since I've turned down the Millway Foundation offer, you're not only going to prevent me from getting other research funds, but you're also going to get me fired."

Susskind put both hands up, palms facing outward, and shook his head. His face wore an expression that combined astonishment with shock, as if he'd been accused of plotting against the Constitution. "Not me, Dr. Cairns, my goodness, certainly not. All I'm doing, as I told you earlier, is to warn you of the implications of your actions. Any of the decisions I mentioned as possibilities would be taken only after careful deliberation, and by committees over which I have no control."

"Right," said Walt, looking at Paula. "In other words, don't shoot the messenger." He turned in his chair to face Susskind squarely. "Isn't there any way we can avert these . . . consequences?"

"Yes, there is, thank you, Dr. Eagleton." Susskind turned to address Paula. "The notice of refusal is still in my file, and I have—quite against the rules, I might add—not yet sent it on to the responsible authorities, thinking that after reviewing the matter, you might wish to change your mind."

"Don't say anything right now," warned Walt, seeing that Paula was about to come out with an angry rejoinder.

"Take it under advisement. But take it seriously." He turned to Susskind. "Geoff, how long can you give her?"

"One week," said Susskind in a lugubrious tone. "Please don't mention that we've had this meeting, Dr. Cairns. I'm sure you're aware that I'm putting my job on the line by doing this."

"Good man," said Walt, nodding to Paula, underlining the fact that Susskind had taken a major career risk to help a mere assistant professor. "Is that it, Geoff? Are we done?"

"I'll be in the office most of this week," Susskind said to Paula, collecting his papers and closing the file. "I'll be waiting for your call." He stood up, and the corners of his mouth turned up in a smile that was obviously costing him an effort. "Everyone says you have a great career ahead, Dr. Cairns," he went on. "We'd all be most distressed if you allowed a hasty decision to ruin it, isn't that so, Dr. Eagleton?"

"Absolutely," said Walt, getting up. "You got it, Geoff. On the nail."

Outside, Paula's hang-tough attitude collapsed like glass shattering around her. She turned toward the hospital, hurrying with long, desperate strides, crossed the street dangerously against the traffic, unable to fight off the tears of anger and frustration that came stinging into her eyes. Sometimes, she felt, she really hated men, with that superiority they assumed like a birthright, their patronizing attitudes, and their mealymouthed "I'm doing this all for you, dear," their hypocrisy.

She was just a couple of minutes from the hospital when she caught her heel in a grating and it came off. That was the last straw. She pulled off the shoe, flung it across the street, then hobbled into the doctors' parking lot and got into her car. She sat there with the top up and the doors closed, and screamed at the top of her lungs. Then, feeling shaky and sick, as if she were getting out of bed for the first time after the flu, she drove out of the lot and went home to get another pair of shoes.

Chapter Twenty-two

Her apartment felt slightly strange to Paula, as if it hadn't been expecting her to come back so early and wasn't quite ready for her arrival. Standing in the little hallway, her one good shoe in her hand, she resisted the temptation to crawl back into her unmade bed, pull the covers over her, and go to sleep. Instead she dropped the shoe in the garbage, regretting her earlier impulsiveness. She went to her clothes closet, pulled out an entirely different outfit, including a wonderful gray-green cashmere sweater that Sam and Charlene Millway had sent to thank her for taking such good care of Nicky. Then she slipped out of her clothes and stepped into the shower, and spent several minutes vigorously scrubbing Geoffrey Susskind, Walt Eagleton, and Cliff Abrams off her skin. And Seth too, although she was beginning to feel she'd maybe overreacted to his advances in the car; it wasn't the first time she'd been grabbed at, but she'd never felt that degree of panic before. Maybe because of the warmth of the stinging shower, of the feel of her hands sliding over her body, Steve came to her mind, and then she thought about the difficulties he'd had and was still dealing with. If he'd been a woman, Paula realized, he could have blamed his problems on discrimination, sexism, and the anti-female attitude of the male surgical establishment. But as it was, all he could blame was a tough and unforgiving system—and, of course, himself.

By the time she'd dried and dressed and put on her makeup and gone back to the hospital, she was feeling more like her old optimistic self. It wasn't as if she was really alone in her fight; Maurice was unequivocally on her side, and he was a force to be reckoned with.

Seth had been very busy since firing Desmond Connor. He had interviewed several applicants for the job, but they were mostly hacks who'd been fired from other jobs in the industry. So he hired a headhunting firm, but after he complained bitterly about the caliber of the applicants they sent him, the chief headhunter told him quite frankly that they couldn't get any top people interested. Millway Pharmaceuticals, he said, was not considered a good career move for those men and women who wanted to get to the top of their industry.

One of the reasons Seth was keeping himself busy was to keep his mind off Paula Cairns. Every time there was a moment between meetings or visits with accountants or his other executives, she appeared in his head. Again and again he replayed when she'd fought him off in the car, and made excuses to himself for the way he'd handled the situation. He'd been under a lot of strain at the time, and things had sort of got away from him. He hadn't done anything serious, he just wanted to kiss her good night . . . Well, whatever he'd done certainly hadn't deserved that savage gouging. And now, one minute he wanted to apologize to her, even grovel, if necessary, because he needed access to the work she was doing. The next minute he was balling up his fists, wanting revenge for his humiliation. In a lot of ways he didn't even like the woman; she was too quick and too smart for his comfort, and he couldn't think of any topic they'd be likely to agree on, or

anything else they had in common. But he wanted
her. . . . She was all he could think about, from the moment he got up in the morning until he went to sleep,
doing various things to her in his mind. Even asleep,
Seth's mind kept on exploring these electric fields of violence, and in some way that relieved his unbearable tension and gave him an acid-edged pleasure long after he'd
wakened.

When Paula got back to her lab, Myra told her, "Dr.
Bennett's secretary was looking for you." Myra's pale eyes
were fixed with a strange expression on Paula. "She says
you're to go over there as soon as possible."

"Over where?"

"To his office, I suppose. I don't know. I'm just telling
you what she said."

Paula reached for the phone, then changed her mind
and went out and along the corridor to the bank of elevators. The doors were opening as she arrived, and she
stepped in.

Clifford Abrams was standing in the elevator, looking
all pink and cherubic. He smiled at her, apparently fully
recovered from their last encounter. "How are things going, Dr. Cairns?" he asked. "I head the Millway people are
very interested in your work." The tone of his voice made
Paula wonder what exactly he meant. Abrams sounded almost benevolent, and his sarcastic overtones were clearly
more a matter of habit than aimed specifically at her.
Abrams asked her if she intended to present a paper at
the College of Surgeons meeting which would take place
in San Francisco later that year.

"No," she replied, omitting to point out that nowadays
her papers appeared in more prestigious surroundings.
"But I'm on a panel on coagulation problems. I believe
you're on it also."

"I'll be honored to appear with you," he replied dryly. "Although I expected the other panelists would be senior people whose opinions were worth listening to." His timing was perfect, and he got out of the elevator at the next stop without another glance at her. Paula felt sorry for Steve; if Abrams had the same attitude with him, working in his lab couldn't be much fun.

Maurice Bennett was in his office, sitting at his desk. "Come on in," he said, looking up from his papers. He smiled and pushed away the papers in front of him. "You look as if you've got a lot on your mind."

"So much I hardly know where to start," she said, then told him first about Walt's offer.

"Did you accept?" asked Maurice. Again there was that curious inflection in his voice, the same as when she'd told him about Seth and the Millway Foundation.

"I told him I'd think about it, and give him an answer in a week. Like he said, it's really an attractive proposal . . ." Paula's fists tightened. She might as well tell Maurice the truth now, since she would have to at some point anyway. "Especially as I don't honestly think that my system of breaking up clots in the body is ever going to work clinically. I'm sorry, Maurice," she went on, feeling close to tears, "I guess I'm just one of those hundreds of people who have a great idea but can't ever get it to work."

Maurice pursed his lips. "Don't despair just yet," he said. "Every researcher occasionally feels that what they're doing is a hopeless waste of time." He stood up and came around the desk. "And I'd like to remind you of a couple of things. How long did it take for Burnet and McFarlane to work out the structure of DNA? Or for Howard Florey and Ernst Chain to figure out how to mass-produce penicillin? Don't you think that if your process was easy, the pharmaceutical companies, with all the talent and money they have available, would have already done it?"

Maurice was standing beside her, his voice full of energy and passion. "Don't you even think of giving up," he went on, poking a finger at her. "I believe in you, I believe in your ability . . ." He grinned suddenly. "And more than all that, I believe in the correctness of the theory behind your process. It'll work eventually, I'm sure of it. You just have to keep on believing in yourself, and keep on working at it."

Paula wanted to hug him.

"Actually," she said, cheering up a bit, "I may have solved one of the problems. I think I know how to keep tne enzymes separate until they come in contact with the clot."

Maurice stared at her. "You've . . . And you were just telling me that it's all a complete waste of time." He shook his head. "I don't know if there's any hope for you, Cairns," he went on. "Maybe you're just too female ever to become a real researcher."

He grinned and went back behind his desk. "Another thing," he said, his voice all matter-of-fact again. "To come back to Walt, he's had half a dozen assistants in the last ten years, all up-and-coming young surgeons. None of them lasted six months. Walt is a brilliant and very talented surgeon, there's no question about that. But he's a one-man band. He's always right about everything, and he gets very mad if you don't agree. It has to be his way, exactly his way. That's okay with nurses and techs, of course, but somehow I don't think that with your personality you'd do any better with him than the others did."

"Oh, well, darn," said Paula, shaking her head. "There goes another career opportunity down the tube."

"That's the best place for that particular opportunity,"

said Maurice. "Now, tell me what happened at your meeting with Susskind."

Paula told him.

"Why was Walt there?" he asked, echoing Paula's own question.

"He's on a grants coordinating committee, something like that," replied Paula. "That's what Susskind said, anyway. I couldn't figure it out either."

Maurice thought for a moment, then seemed to put the question out of his mind. "Oh, by the way, the reason I called you was to discuss a patient with you."

He pointed at the bank of six X-ray viewing boxes on the wall to his left. "Take a look at those films."

Paula went over, flipped the switches, and waited until the lights flickered, then stayed on. Then she examined the X rays one by one. They were abdominal films, taken from different angles. After a minute, she asked, "Are there any more?"

"Right here." Maurice passed two large tan envelopes over to her. One was heavy with X-ray films and the other contained the films of a CAT scan on the same patient.

Five minutes later, after she'd finished examining all of them, Maurice turned on the lights, and Paula blinked in the glare.

"What do you think?" he asked, putting his hands together on the desk.

"This patient has an aortic aneurysm," said Paula. "You can see the line of calcification on both sides. It's not huge. I'd guess it's between four and five centimeters across."

Without a word Maurice handed her a ruler. She grinned and went back to the X rays to measure the width of the dilatation. A normal aorta measures between two and three centimeters, and this one was half again as big. The risk of such an aneurysm, as she well knew, was that as it grew inexorably wider, the day would come when it would rupture, usually with fatal consequences. The treatment was to replace the dilated aneurysm with a tubular graft made of a special grade of plastic. That added up to a very major surgical procedure.

"Four and one half centimeters exactly," she said, handing the ruler back.

"Correct. Now, Paula, would you like to take care of this patient?" he asked.

"Sure. Who is she or he?"

Maurice's voice was very quiet. "I'm the patient," he said.

Paula sat down rather abruptly in the visitor's chair. "Are you having symptoms?" she asked.

"Minor ones," replied Maurice. "A sense of fullness after meals, a few non-specific things like feeling tired occasionally. No big deal, though. Nothing that would make me think it's going to rupture any second."

He was being very matter-of-fact about this, thought Paula, and she felt a wave of real affection for him.

"Don't you think you should get somebody more senior to take care of you?" she asked, concerned about taking on such a responsibility. "Have you considered going up to the Mayo, or the Cleveland Clinic or Mass General?"

"Yes, I did," replied Maurice. He himself had operated on numerous colleagues from other prestigious medical centers. "But I want to have it done here, for a variety of reasons," he went on. "First, I know you'll do a first-class job. Second, I have a lot of things going on here, and I want to be able to keep in touch."

Paula took a deep breath. "I don't think you need surgery right now, do you?" she asked. "It isn't that big, and maybe it won't get any bigger. Maybe it's been there for years and just stopped getting any bigger—"

"Now, Paula," said Maurice gently. "That's just wishful

thinking. What were you taught about abdominal aneurysms? What has been your own experience with them?"

Paula said nothing; he was right.

"I'd better examine you," she said.

Fifteen minutes later, after Paula had done a very thorough physical exam, she said, "It feels just the way it looks on the X rays. You'll certainly need to have it fixed reasonably soon, but I don't think we're dealing with an emergency."

"I agree," he said, "but it won't do any harm to have things in place for when we need to do it, right?"

Paula felt a sudden sense of panic. She didn't want to be totally responsible for Maurice's care. What if she made a mistake? What if her judgment was warped because she was so close to him?

"I think we should get a second opinion, Maurice," she said. "And honestly, I'm not at all sure that I should be the one taking care of you."

"I've thought about that too," he said seriously. "But aside from my personal feelings, I don't think it would do you any harm professionally. You've been the target for a fair amount of criticism, and since I was the one who brought you here, I feel a certain degree of responsibility. I hope that my choosing you to take care of me will help to counteract such negative factors."

Paula smiled at Maurice's invariably courteous, formal way of speaking; he had clearly thought the whole problem over very carefully before saying anything to her.

"Who would you like for a second opinion?" she asked.

Maurice was thinking about something else. "This is coming at a bad time," he said. "We've been working hard on the pharmaceutical-industry investigation, and we're still a few weeks away from having an airtight case. The last thing I need is to have surgery or any other major distraction during this time."

"Second opinion? Please, Maurice?"

"Why don't we ask Walt Eagleton?" he replied. "He's very competent, and he'll give us a straightforward answer."

"Sure," she said. "Shall I call him, or would you rather talk to him yourself?"

"You're the doctor in charge," replied Maurice, determined to maintain correct medical etiquette. "I'm only the patient. You call him."

"Okay, I will. Now, how about the other stuff?" she asked, taking her notebook out of her pocket. "Do you have any medical conditions we need to consider? Diabetes? Cardiac problems? Hypertension?"

Maurice pushed a sheet of paper across the desk to her. "My full medical history is here," he said. "There's nothing in it of any major significance, I don't believe."

"Who do you want as your medical consultant?" she asked. "Do you have an internist?"

"I don't think I need one, Paula. I'd like Gabe Pinero to give the anesthetic, though, when we do the operation. I'm sure between the two of you, you can deal with any medical problems likely to arise."

Again Paula noticed his use of her first name, and something in his voice that hadn't always been there. Asking her to perform surgery of this magnitude, she realized, would bring about a special kind of intimacy between then, and for a second it occurred to her that although she knew herself to be a compassionate and caring doctor, she had no real notion of what it was like to be a patient. And Maurice was putting his life unrestrictedly in her hands. Paula shivered momentarily at the thought.

"Oh, Paula, there's one other thing. When you do it, I'd like to be operated on on a Tuesday, okay? Let's plan on about two months from now."

"Sure. You'll be our first case on a Tuesday morning." Paula grinned. Maurice knew how hospitals worked, and he knew that Tuesday was the best day to have major surgery. Monday operating schedules were always crowded, and if there were going to be any post-operative complications, it was best to have them early in the week when the hospital and intensive-care units were fully staffed. At weekends there were fewer people, often temps and parttimers, and the doctors were usually less available.

They talked about the lab for a while, and although his surgery was eight weeks away, Maurice rather formally assigned her to be in charge of the lab and the various research projects during the time he would be out of commission. "I won't saddle you with any extra work," he said, "and Helen knows about as much about running things here as I do. If you get stuck, she's the one who has the answers."

Maurice stood up and came around the desk. Paula put a sympathetic hand on his arm.

"How does it feel to be a patient?" she asked gently. She didn't know quite what to say to make Maurice understand how heartfelt her concern was for him.

"To tell you the truth, I'm feeling very shaken," he replied. He hesitated, and for a moment his face seemed to lose its normal firm control and showed an unexpected, and to Paula, a profoundly endearing glimpse of his vulnerability.

"You see, Paula," he said in a voice that showed how much he'd thought about what he was saying, "there are a lot of things we physicians don't really know much about." He smiled at Paula's raised eyebrows. "Particularly when it comes to feelings. Without meaning to, we isolate ourselves from our patients, the ones who are having the feelings of fear, fear of death, pain, economic hardship,

loss of love. That's one of the differences between the old-
time docs and ourselves. They used to be close to their
patients, but now we're insulated from them by everything
from our white coats and our incomes to the countless
laboratory tests we order for them. We hardly even need
to touch our patients anymore. . . ."

Maurice looked at Paula to see if she was with him.
She stood there quietly, watching him with a curious, at-
tentive expression, her hand still on his arm. He certainly did nothing to shake it off, and went on. "When
we deal with patients every day, an invisible wall grows
between them and us. We, the physicians, are by definition strong, healthy, and invincible, and they are sick,
frail, and vulnerable. However close we get to them as
their physicians, however kind and understanding and
compassionate we may be, we can never get inside their
souls, feel the fear of people who are facing death, the
loss of a limb, pain, disablement . . ."

Maurice stood there, his eyes fixed on some distant
point far beyond Paula. "But when a physician becomes a
patient, our perspective changes. We become one of
them, and it's a humbling experience. To paraphrase Sam-
uel Johnson," he went on, "I can tell you that the knowledge of impending surgery wonderfully concentrates the
mind."

Paula fought her instinct to retreat from him. Maurice's
transition from all-powerful doctor and mentor to vulnerable patient was taking place right there in front of her,
and seeing it happen made her want to turn around and
flee.

"We'll need to do a bunch of blood tests," she heard
herself saying. "And I'd like to get some more oblique
films of your abdomen."

Maurice smiled at her. "Whatever you say," he said, but

there was something in his eyes, a fixedness, maybe an anxiety about the prospect of handing control of his life to another person, any other person, that made Paula wonder if he would remain as amenable as he was now.

Chapter Twenty-three

When Paula got back to her lab, she was feeling very shaken. Maurice's aortic aneurysm was not very large, and in no immediate danger of rupturing, but she had operated on several similar cases and knew of the attendant dangers of pneumonia, gangrene of the legs, strokes. . . . Paula shook her head. There wasn't any use scaring herself with all the possible bad outcomes. Then she wondered about the advisability of operating on a man who was her boss. It wasn't a matter of ethics; the question was whether it was prudent for her to take on the case. If she ran into any complications, there were plenty of people ready to point the finger and say she should have given the case to a more experienced surgeon. And there were lots of those around New Coventry, and each one would feel that he should have been asked to operate on Maurice.

Myra was working at one of the analyzers when Paula came in, and was looking frustrated. Paula had rigged up a novel system whereby the different chemical formula diagrams showed up in three dimensions on the color monitor as part of the analysis routine. To identify an unknown enzyme, the program would narrow it down to a few possibilities, then it would be compared with the standards. "I can't get them to match," complained Myra. "I've been trying all afternoon."

Paula sat down and, with Myra watching over her shoulder, showed her how to match up the key enzyme factors in two dimensions first, then the tricky part, which was keeping the matched ones in position while manipulating the others until they too fell into place.

"This enzyme's chromium-based," she explained, using a tiny triangular pointer on the screen to show a single green dot on the display. "They're some of the hardest to fit." Using a computer mouse, Paula manipulated the chemical sequences, and they chased one another across the screen like brightly colored tropical fish until finally Paula was able to get two of them to merge precisely. That set the program in motion, and the computer hummed for a couple of seconds, then quieted. "That's it," she said, getting up. "When you print, it'll come out as a diagram but also with a complete numerical analysis. Can you do the others, or would you like me to do one more?"

"You sure made it look easy," said Myra. She pushed a stray lock of blond hair out of her eyes. "It's a bit like Nintendo, isn't it? I'll try again."

"I guess," said Paula. "Don't forget to make a copy on the backup tape, okay?"

"Right." Myra looked on her message pad. "Dr. Charnley came in looking for you. Nothing urgent, he said."

There was a little smile on Myra's lips, and Paula raised her eyebrows in an unspoken question.

"Oh," said Myra, stammering, caught unawares. Her smile faded into secrecy. "That Dr. Charnley, he's so good-looking, I wish it was me he'd come looking for."

Paula went into her little office, and Myra's eyes narrowed as she watched her boss close the door. She thought she was so smart, reflected Myra, with all these men prowling around her like tomcats, but things would be catching up with her soon enough. Myra was pretty smart herself, and had a pretty good idea of what her friend Dr. Abrams was up to. Not only that, but he'd promised that if anything went wrong with her job with Paula, he'd be happy to have her come to work with him. Well, Myra corrected herself, he hadn't actually promised, but that was what he meant, he'd left no doubt about that.

Paula picked up the phone and called Walt Eagleton to ask if he would see Maurice in consultation. Walt sounded surprised and cautious. "Sure, of course," he said slowly. "Thanks for asking me. Why don't I go over and take a look at him this afternoon? Would that be convenient for him?"

Paula suggested he call Helen Katz and set it up with her. "All Maurice's X rays and scans are in his office," she told him. "So don't bother looking for them in the X-ray department."

Who, aside from Walt, could she talk to about Maurice's aneurysm? Steve was the obvious person—and anyway she was aching to see him, so this was a good excuse. She stood up and walked through the lab, leaving Myra struggling with the intractable shapes on the computer screen. Paula hesitated for a second outside the double doors leading to Clifford Abrams' lab, thinking it would have been smarter to call first and see if Steve was in. A white-coated tech came out at that moment and, seeing Paula, smilingly held the door open, and that gave her the final little push to go on in. She'd been there before, once, for her interview with Dr. Abrams, but again she was astonished at the size and scope of the place. They even had a receptionist, an ample, heavily made-up woman with a great prow of jet-black hair. She was busy with a UPS delivery man, but while Paula stood waiting, the receptionist's eyes kept darting over the boxes to glance curiously at Paula.

There wasn't much Paula could see from the lobby, which had a thick ivory-colored carpet and potted palms that separated the receptionist's desk from a comfortable-looking waiting area with a glass-topped table, a cream-colored leather sofa, and two matching chairs around it. A second set of wide doors led into the main laboratory, and a small red light glowed on the numerical access-control panel on the wall next to the door. Paula turned to look at the lithographs on the wall, a Miró, rich in rounded red and yellow shapes, and next to it a dark, angled, and convoluted Kandinsky. Paula liked their placement, remembering that the two artists had been friends and worked together in Paris. She wondered if it had been Dr. Abrams or an interior decorator who'd thought to hang them together.

"Can I help you, Dr. Cairns?"

The UPS man was leaving, and the receptionist was standing in an almost protective way in front of the lab doors. She had a plastic tag with her photo and name, Dolores Devine.

"Is Dr. Charnley in? I'd like to see him for a moment, if he's free."

"Is he expecting you, Dr. Cairns?" The woman's expression was unsmiling.

"No. I was just passing by and thought I'd stop in. Is that a problem?" Paula's eyes flashed, and she could feel her temper rising. From the woman's attitude one would think she was guarding some kind of top-secret lab.

The woman didn't answer, but picked up a phone and dialed a three-digit number. When it was answered, the receptionist turned away and Paula couldn't hear what she said. A moment later, she turned back. "Dr. Charnley will be here in a moment," she said. "Would you care to have a seat?"

Already Paula was feeling that she'd made a mistake coming here; in her own lab, if anybody wanted to talk to her, she was there, no problem. Here it was like trying to get a private audience with the queen of England.

A quiet buzzer sounded, the receptionist pressed a button at the side of her desk, the door opened with a faint hiss, and Steve appeared, wearing a UCLA sweatshirt, faded blue jeans beginning to tear at one knee, and old gray-looking sneakers. His long, straight blond hair was hanging over one tired and droopy eye, and he didn't look as if he'd shaved that morning.

His face broke into a smile when he saw Paula. "Hi," he said. "Funny thing, I was just thinking about you."

"Just stopped in to say hello," said Paula briskly, aware of the receptionist's stare. "But if you're busy I can come back some other time."

"No problem," he said. "I came by your lab to see you a little while back, but you weren't there. Come on in." He turned to the receptionist. "Sign Dr. Cairns in, Dolores, please."

"You have quite a security system here," said Paula as she signed her name on the form. She was not entirely pleased at all this formality, and felt it was unnecessarily ostentatious. "Maybe it's time I got a barbed-wire fence and guard dogs around my lab."

Steve shrugged. "That's the way Dr. Abrams wants it," he said. "There used to be a fair amount of defense-related research going on in this lab, and I guess they still use the system the Army set up. Let's go down to my office." He held the door open, and as she went through, out of the corner of her eye she saw Dolores pick up the phone, and some instinct told her that she was calling Dr. Abrams to tell him of her visit.

The main part of the lab was white-walled, and Paula followed Steve between the long teak benches. Techs were working at different pieces of equipment, and although none of the white-coated workers looked up when she walked by, she knew that her presence had been noted and would be discussed later. On the benches Paula recognized the familiar analyzers, spectroscopes, and electron microscopes. But in this entire section of the lab everything was brand-new, state-of-the-art, and she wondered, with a touch of envy, how Abrams had managed to get hold of the hundreds of thousands of dollars that it all represented.

The first thing she noticed about Steve's office was how tidy it was. Unlike hers, she thought with a twinge of guilt. In her crowded office, full of filing cabinets, catalogues, research files, and papers, the desk covered with computer printouts and boxes of 3.5-inch floppy discs. In her mess, Paula thought wryly, a cat wouldn't be able to find its kittens.

Still, coming to her own defense, it crossed her mind that the research that came out of her untidy office had been pretty good, and that excused a lot.

Steve closed the door, and all of a sudden what they had felt that first time on the racquetball court, and after their dinner at Rosselini's, hit them, and they came together hard, standing in the middle of the floor. After a long moment, Steve detached himself, went behind his desk, and rather formally asked her to sit down in the single chair.

Paula collapsed into it.

Steve watched her and shook his head. "I don't know what it is you do to me," he said. "But it sure is some powerful ju-ju."

"Is that surfer talk?" she asked, forcing herself to take deep, regular breaths. Then she saw the reprint of her paper on thrombolysins lying on the desk, and picked it up. "This your bedtime reading, Steve?"

Steve went pink. "Damn, I forgot to tell you," he said. "Abrams wants me to repeat that set of experiments, down to the smallest details. He says he's going to use the technique, but I don't see that he has any kind of application for it."

"That technique won't work," said Paula, who had had to tell this story so often that she wasn't even embarrassed anymore. "We used outdated reagents. Abrams hopes you won't be able to reproduce those results, and his wish will come true. You won't."

"For some reason he's trying to nail you," said Steve. He took the reprint out of Paula's hands and flipped it open. "Well, I can take care of this very easily. The results he'll get on his desk will be identical to the ones you have in your paper."

"No, they won't," replied Paula sharply. He knows they're not correct. If you did that, and I thank you for thinking of it, he'd just get them repeated at some commercial lab and then you'd be in the soup too."

"So what do you suggest?" Steve seemed put out.

"Just tell him the truth. Tell him exactly what results you get. I've already sent off a correction to the journal, and that should defuse the whole situation."

"But that paper appeared three years ago, Paula. Do you really think they'll bother to print a correction?"

"We'll see. Anyway, that's not what I came to see you about." Paula's voice became serious. "Listen, Steve, I have a problem . . . "

Paula told him about Maurice's aneurysm. Watching her, Steve tried to keep his mind on what she was saying.

"How big did you say it was?"

"Four and a half centimeters across. Do we operate or leave it alone?"

Steve sucked air in through his teeth. "He's in good health otherwise?"

"Excellent. No medical problems. He takes real good care of himself."

Something about the tone of Paula's voice made Steve's eyebrows go up. "You really like the guy, don't you?"

"Yep. I surely do. Should we operate or wait?"

"I'd wait," said Steve after a moment's reflection. "It's not an emergency at this time. But I'd warn him not to do anything too strenuous or get into an accident, because that could cause it to rupture."

"I'll tell him," said Paula, straight-faced. "Just like you said, *Now, looky here, Moh-reeess, y'all take real good care, and don't you go gettin' yoself into no serious accidents, you heah me, doll?*"

Steve grinned, wanting to come around the desk and hold the length of her against him, but something in Paula's body language warned him not to, not now.

"How's the work going?" she asked.

"Okay," he replied. "It's not easy getting started up again, as I'm sure you've already found out."

"Well, at least you have all the equipment and stuff you need," she said. "I'm having a hell of a time just getting everything set up. By the way, Myra told me you'd stopped by the lab?"

"I did. Actually, I need a little help. I'm trying to get a paper together for the summer meeting of the Surgical Association." Steve indicated a thick folder on his desk, neatly closed with two elastic bands. "The closing date's in four days." He stroked his chin and felt the bristles, although because they were so blond they were hardly visible. "I was up most of last night," he said, shaking his head as if to clear it. "It's an important paper and I have to get it right, but I just can't seem to get the darn thing together."

"I know how that goes," said Paula sympathetically. "It gets so the numbers float around to where they make a kind of soup. What about Abrams?" she asked. "Can't he go over the data with you, and give you a hand with writing it up?"

"He's too busy," replied Steve briefly.

"I tell you what," she said. "If you let me take a look at it, I can get it back to you late this afternoon."

Paula held out her hand, and Steve thankfully put the folder into it.

The thought of his unused talent with instrumentation was still bothering her. "You know, Steve, I still can't believe you're not doing anything with your arterioscope. Do you have it here? I'd love to see it."

Steve stood up and went over to a closet. On the top shelf was a wooden box about two feet long. He looked up at it, reluctant even to touch the box.

"Come on, Steve, please!"

He took it down. It was heavy and the top was dusty, so he cleared it away with his sleeve. Inside the lined box was a long, slender, snakelike black tube, about as thick as a ballpoint pen refill, doubled back on itself. Several complicated-looking attachments were fastened down in different parts of the box. Steve took the tube out very carefully. "This is it, my baby," he said. "Most of what's inside this tube is fiberoptics, but there's also a carbon fiber drive for a drill, and a suction tube. See, here's the drill bit. It's made of iridium steel," He turned a knob at the side of the tube, and the tiny mushroom-shaped bit emerged from the tip.

"How could you make it so small?" asked Paula, fascinated.

"That was made for us by a West German company to our specs," he said. "You see these lenses?" He retracted the drill bit and pointed again at the tip of the instrument.

Paula squinted at it. Two tiny lenses winked back at her. Steve flipped a switch and a powerful beam of light came out of the smaller of the two lenses. "That's the illumination," went on Steve, his voice getting more enthusiastic. "The other lens is for viewing. At the other end there's an attachment for the TV camera. Here. I can't show you the saline jet working because it isn't loaded, but you can see the opening. . . . Here, use this magnifying glass."

"This is just amazing," said Paula. "I can't believe you packed so much into that tiny space." She put down the magnifying glass on the desk. "Steve you *must* get this scope working again. I'm sure we can get permission from the hospital to use it. Please, Steve?" She put her arms around his waist.

"Well, if you ask like that . . ." Steve leaned sideways and put the scope back in its box. The closeness and warmth of Paula's body made it difficult for him to think about anything else, even his scope, his beloved brain-child.

A minute later, Paula stepped back. "If we go on like this," she said rather breathlessly, "we'll finish up on the floor. I'm going to run. Thanks for your advice about Maurice. And stop by the lab again, any time." She grinned at him. "I'm sure I can get you a security clearance if you give me twenty-four hours' notice." She picked up the file with Steve's paper and was gone.

When she got back to the lab, the phone was ringing, and Myra was trying to heave herself out of her chair, but Paula got to it first. It was Steve.

"You want to go out for dinner this evening?"

"Anywhere but Rosselini's," she replied, pleased that

he'd called. "Why don't you come by the lab around six? We can talk about your paper, then go out. How about that?"

"Suits me," he said. "See you at six."

Chapter Twenty-four

Paula settled down to work, feeling very cheerful, not just because she was going to spend the evening with Steve, but because of the breakthrough she'd mentioned to Maurice. The technique she'd figured out was how to deliver the clot-destroying enzymes at the site of the clot where they were needed, without giving them a chance to dissipate in the bloodstream or destroy one another. Her new idea was to isolate each enzyme system in microscopically tiny capsules, whose ultrathin, chemically treated coatings would disintegrate on contact with the blood clot, liberating the enzymes. This was a very complex, specialized, and expensive procedure, and Rusty Hurwitz, the research director of a small local high-tech biochemicals company who'd taken the contract, was enthusiastic. They discussed various types of coating, making sure that the cascade effect wouldn't be lost. Paula had borrowed departmental funds through Maurice on the understanding that they would be repaid when her grant money came in. The first animal tests on a small batch of rats were scheduled to take place in a couple of weeks, and Myra and she were starting to get things ready, the anesthetics, the instruments, the IV microcannulas. Now Paula spent an hour making a checklist of everything they would need.

She looked at her watch. It was already five-thirty. She took a deep breath and picked up the phone and dialed

Geoffrey Susskind's number. He was about to leave, he told her, but she had a feeling that he'd been expecting her call.

"I most sincerely hope you're calling me with good news."

"I've made a final decision on the Millway Foundation grant," she said in a firm voice. "I've decided . . . not to accept it."

"You've considered the effects of that decision on your career?" Susskind's voice was abrupt, and he sounded surprised and angry. Paula wondered why it could possibly make that much difference to him. She had no illusions about his concern for her career.

"Yes, I have."

There was a moment's silence. "In that case, Dr. Cairns, I'll report your decision to my superiors. Good evening."

Paula put down the phone and tried to put Susskind, Seth, and the Millway Foundation out of her mind. Steve was coming back in a half hour, and she hadn't even looked at his paper. She sat down at the computer, placed his paper on the left side of the console. The topic wasn't particularly familiar to her, and she typed her comments on the keyboard as she went along.

She finished a few minutes before six and turned on the printer. She'd made several pages of notes; Steve's paper wasn't good, but it was salvageable. After the print run was finished, Paula sat back, waiting for him to appear, and a whole kaleidoscope of people and events in her life started to pass through her mind. This often happened about this time of day; she'd suddenly feel tired and reflective, and try to spend some time alone; then later in the evening things would rev up once more. She often did her best thinking work between ten at night and two in the morning.

Feeling overwhelmed by everything that was happening in her life, Paula's mind skidded into a different, familiar, more comfortable realm, and she found herself back in New Mexico, sitting out on her aunt Jackie's porch, narrowing her eyes against the bright sun and its painfully white reflections on the stucco walls, watching her aunt make pots. Her favorite recollection was one afternoon when Jackie had asked her if she'd like to throw her very first pot. At first Paula was too scared to try, but once she'd overcome her first fear, and Jackie had helped her center the ball of clay, what a sense of tension and excitement she'd felt, with that wet clay taking shape under her fingers. As it whirred around in its slippery motion, she put two fingers in the middle, her thumb on the outside, patting on the opposite side with her other hand, just as she'd watched her aunt do so many times, and the lump developed a hollow cavity and became a live and fragile thing that she herself was creating. As it grew, so did the fear that she'd make a clumsy move and the whole thing would collapse. But that first time it hadn't collapsed, and although it finished up rather thick and stubby, and with uneven walls, by the time she had applied some simple decorations and a coating of glaze and placed it in the oven with Jackie's batch of pottery, it had become an object that in a way contained the very essence of her own life, her own existence. Maybe that's what she should do, she thought, feeling nostalgic and a bit sad. Maybe she should go back there and join her aunt in her pottery business, and leave behind the anxieties and worries of her present life.

"Did you ever see that cartoon?" said a voice right behind her. Paula jumped and turned around very fast, remembering that for once she hadn't locked the door. It was Steve, and he put his hands on her shoulders. "Sorry, I didn't mean to scare you like that."

"You didn't scare me. What cartoon?"

"The one of Einstein, at his blackboard. He's looking puzzled and depressed. He's tried $E=Ma^2$, and that didn't work. He's also tried $E=Mb^2$, and that didn't work either. Now he's trying to figure out what to do next."

Paula laughed. "What made you think of that?"

"That's what you were looking like," he said. "Like Einstein trying to solve a problem. Now let's go and get ourselves a double cheeseburger with fries and a Coke."

"We're going over your paper first," said Paula firmly. "I've made some notes. Here, take a look." She passed him the typed papers and the pad with her comments. Paula had tried not to come across as authoritative or overcritical, but Steve's paper wasn't well put together. And she knew he was still very shaken from his experiences in Los Angeles, and might not react well to criticism, especially from her.

Steve read the comments without saying anything, but when he'd finished, he did not look exactly delighted. He tapped the notes. "Why didn't you summarize this and just say the paper is a piece of shit?"

"It isn't a piece of shit," replied Paula calmly. "It's a good paper, but it needs work. And like the IRS guy said to General Noriega, I'm here to help you."

Steve grinned, slightly mollified, and they sat down to review the paper in detail. The opening paragraph was vague, and he hadn't made the purpose of the report crystal-clear. Steve started to write down Paula's suggestions in the margin, but she decided that this method would be too time-consuming.

"Let's use the scanner," she said, picking up the sheets of paper and going over to her computer terminal. With a hand-held scanning device that looked like a small shovel with the handle attached to a black cable, she passed it quickly over each sheet, and like magic, the entire paper appeared on the screen. "Now we can edit it as we go along," she said, "then print it out when we're both happy with it."

She sat down at the console, he sat down beside her, and between them they figured out the clearest possible wording for the introduction, then reorganized some of the data and, using a 3-D computer program, made a couple of graphs that clarified some of the more difficult concepts in the paper. Finally, after an hour, they had between them rewritten the concluding paragraphs.

"Wow," said Steve when the entire paper had been printed. "That is spectacular. I can't believe you did all that. We should put your name down as a co-author."

They were about to tidy up and leave when they heard the door buzzer. They looked at each other, surprised, and Paula went to open it. In the doorway stood Seth, as big as ever, but looking very drawn and pale, and his one bloodshot eye gave him a look that made Paula step back involuntarily.

"May I come in?" he asked.

Silently Paula opened the door to let him in, and he stopped dead when he saw Steve.

"This is my colleague—and friend—Steve Charnley," she said, indicating Steve.

Seth, startled by his presence, stared at Steve, then nodded briefly before turning around to face Paula, excluding Steve from the conversation.

"First, I want to apologize," he said. His voice was low, pitched for her ears only, but suddenly he felt unsure of what he was going to say. "I mean for the ... incident when I was taking you home." He hesitated and glanced around at Steve, feeling a growing anger and jealousy at his unexpected and unwelcome presence. It hadn't even occurred to him that there might be another man in Paula's life, and that changed everything.

"If that was what made you turn down the Millway offer," he went on, clearing his throat, "I'd like you to reconsider it. That night I just got a bit carried away."

Steve, sitting by the computer, stood up without haste and came over to join them.

"I can assure you that nothing like that will ever happen again," Seth went on, ignoring Steve. "And my board is very anxious that our foundation should support your research. Please think about it," he went on when Paula started to speak. "It's a genuine, no-strings-attached offer, and you know as well as I do that these are hard to come by these days."

"Thank you," said Paula, embarrassed. She felt that she owed Seth an apology too, because in retrospect she'd jumped the gun that night, and she was the only one who'd actually inflicted any physical injury. If Steve hadn't been there, Paula would have said so, but right now she just wanted Seth to leave. "But that wasn't the reason I turned it down. It was because of . . . well, there were several reasons, and I pointed them all out in my letter. I'm sorry, Seth, but there's no point in going over them again. I'm not going to change my mind about it now."

There was such a finality in her words that Seth could feel his face sag with disappointment, and at the same time he felt a hot surge of energy, a desire to smash everything in sight, including her, and of course this son of a bitch intruder. He glanced at Steve, who was looking on curiously but saying nothing. He looks strong enough, thought Seth, but he was sure he could take the guy in no time. His fists unconsciously clenched and unclenched. Boy, would he like to do that. But his attention was diverted from Paula only for a second. She was filling his sights right now, she was the one he was concentrating all his furious energies on. And she had suddenly become utterly remote, untouchable, hateful.

"Let me know if you change your mind," he said, making a huge effort not to show his seething frustration and anger. Then he left without another word, knowing that if he stayed there a minute longer something really violent would happen.

Chapter Twenty-five

"Hi, Dr. Bennett?" said the voice. "My name is Freda Bunce, and I'm in charge of public relations with the Pharmaceutical Council."

Maurice smiled grimly to himself. He'd been expecting a call like this. They must have chosen this woman for her voice; it was soft, educated, with a hint of an English accept, and very sultry.

"Yes, Ms. Bunce," he said crisply. "What can I do for you?"

"The council is aware of the wonderful work you've been doing," she replied. "And we were particularly interested in the great write-up they gave you yesterday in the *Washington Post*."

"Thank you," said Maurice, glancing at the copy of the *Post* open on his desk. He nodded to Walt Eagleton, who had just come in the door. He put his hand over the mouthpiece. "Have a seat, Walt," he said. "This won't take long."

"We're very anxious that you get a balanced view of the industry as a whole," she went on. "We know there are problems, and we want to recognize and correct them, but we do want to be certain that you understand what an ethical and caring industry we are."

Walt picked up the paper. There was a two-column article about Maurice, with a photograph, and he sat down to read it.

"That's most kind of you, Ms. Bunce," said Maurice, keeping a straight face and the irony out of his voice. He was aware that this conversation was in all probability being recorded. "And how do you propose to do that?"

"I'm coming up to New Coventry next week," she said. "And I'd love an opportunity to talk to you."

"I'm going to be very busy," he replied, "so that won't be very convenient." Maurice was being careful; if he refused to see her, they could use that to show he was completely biased and wouldn't listen to the industry's arguments.

"How about next Wednesday evening?" she persisted. "I'll be staying at the New Coventry Marriott. May I take you to dinner?"

"That's most kind," replied Maurice with his usual courtesy, "but under the circumstances I'm sure you can see that I can neither take nor break bread with you. In any case," he went on, "quite honestly, I don't think it would be a very useful experience for either of us."

"Dr. Bennett," she said in her purring voice, "I'm quite sure it *would*, but perhaps we can meet the next day, that would be Thursday?"

Maurice found a time for her late in the afternoon, and Ms. Bunce promised to be exactly punctual, because she knew how valuable a doctor's time was.

Walt looked up from the paper when Maurice replaced the phone. "Wow!" he said. "This is some write-up. I didn't know you were going to be appointed the next U.S. surgeon general."

Maurice shook his head. "Walt," he said, "you know how the system works as well as I do. It all depends on a whole lot of political and other factors over which nobody has any control." He grinned. "So don't count on my leaving just yet."

"And you committee has the pharmaceutical industry 'in your sights'?" Walt tapped the page and watched Maurice's eyes.

"Well, you know how the press is," Maurice replied easily. "They make things sound dramatic, and they like to turn a little story into a big one."

"They say here that you're preparing a big exposé of the industry, and it should be out in a month or so. That sounds like a pretty big story. I'm really surprised," he went on, smiling his wily cat smile at Maurice. "I always thought our pharmaceutical colleagues were just like us, selfless, dedicated, concerned about the suffering masses of humanity."

"Yeah, right," said Maurice, not wanting to go into any details. "Aside from a few minor peccadillos like milking the public, price fixing, false advertising . . ." He smiled at Walt. "And then of course, there are also a few really bad apples in that barrel."

"Any names?" asked Walt. "Any particular company you have in mind?"

"Yes, of course." Maurice nodded amiably, but he wasn't giving anything away.

Walt stared at him for a moment, but realized that he wasn't going to get any further on that topic. He changed the subject abruptly. "So what's this our enchanting Paula Cairns has been telling me? You've developed an aortic aneurysm?"

"Just a little one," murmured Maurice in a diffident tone. "I don't think it's big enough to bother you with, but both Paula and I thought we'd ask for your opinion about it."

Walt was very thorough. After examining the X rays and CAT scans and every page of his past medical history, he took Maurice over to the outpatient area and into an examining room.

Fifteen minutes later, back in Maurice's office, Walt sat down.

"Maurice," he said, looking at Maurice with the utmost seriousness, "there's absolutely no question. You need to have that aneurysm operated on, and it should be done as soon as possible."

Maurice's eyebrows went up, and Walt went on. "I know the statistics," he said. "You have only a one-in-twenty chance of that aneurysm rupturing in the next six months. But if you were my patient, I wouldn't dream of letting you take that risk."

Maurice sighed to himself. Walt had made up his mind, and once that happened, he never listened to any opposing views. More that that, anyone who disagreed with him became an enemy.

Desmond Connor, former head of research at the Millway Pharmaceutical laboratories, had been impossible to live with since his firing. He had come home that night, leaving black skid marks in the driveway for the ten yards up to the garage and almost smashed right through the closed doors. That night and the next day he stamped about, shouted, and worse than anything, started to drink heavily again, a habit his wife thought he'd got rid of forever ten years before.

That lasted only a few days, fortunately. Then he settled down into a morose, angry state, made a lot of phone calls, and started to go through the reams of papers that were piled untidily in cardboard boxes in his study.

"Who are you talking to?" Nora asked as she came into the airy, well-lit room with yet another cup of coffee. It was amazing, she thought, how that man could use his sober business voice for minutes on end, sounding so interested and affable, even occasionally laughing with the person he was talking to, then turn around and scream at her like a demented person.

"Calling in some debts," he said.

A different kind of mail started to come in for him, some in large manila envelopes, others in packages, mostly with handwritten addresses, others typed. Nora, who always picked up the mail as soon as the little white Jeep had gone further down the road, noticed that the letters and parcels rarely bore return addresses.

And the telephone rang a lot.

"Read today's *Washington Post*," said one of his unnamed phone pals. Many of his calls were only a few seconds long, without identification, but nearly always he knew the voices. They all belonged to present or former employees of Millway Pharmaceuticals, and many of them had worked for him.

Connor had to make a decision; either accept his firing graciously, or go ahead and blow the whistle on Millway. It wasn't easy; if he accepted his firing, he would probably be able to get another job in the industry, although not at the same level. On the other hand, if he blew the whistle on Millway, he'd never get back into the pharmaceutical business. In addition, he knew enough about Seth Millway's methods to realize that he might be putting himself in personal danger.

But after reading that article in the *Post*, Connor decided to discuss the problem with Nora. Until now all she knew was that he'd been fired. Feeling a strange sense of freedom, Connor clumped downstairs to find Nora in the kitchen, and to her astonishment he kissed her hard on the mouth.

"What happened?" she asked, stepping back from the sink, where she'd been scraping carrots. She wiped her mouth with the back of her sleeve.

Connor reached up to the closet above her, brought

down two small glasses, and took them over to the sideboard and filled them with dry sherry. Nora preferred sweet, but she didn't say anything. She did notice that his hand was shaking a little.

"Come and sit down," he said. "I need to talk to you."

Nora looked at the pile of unscraped carrots, shrugged, and came out into the adjoining dining room. Connor had put one glass on her side of the immaculately polished table, and she sat down, hoping that the bottom of the glass was dry, and wondering if he was going to tell her he was about to leave her forever.

"All my working life," said Connor, twirling the stem of his glass, "I've done my very best for Sam Millway and the company."

Nora sighed, hoping she wasn't in for a lecture. The chicken was in the oven already, and carrots took a long time to cook.

"In old Sam's day," Connor went on, "things were good. Everybody in the department got along together, we were increasing our market share every year. Well, most years."

"Could you not tell me this in the kitchen?" asked Nora. "I'm in the middle of making dinner."

"I'll just be a minute," replied Connor. "This is what the problem is, Nora. Seth Millway is a crook, and I've got proof. He's keeping the company going with a huge chunk of money from the drug cartels, and before that with money stolen from the employees' pension fund, and I can prove that too."

Connor took a swig of sherry, which tasted like water after what he'd been drinking for the last week.

"You see, Nora, I know exactly what'll happen if I go to the police, or even the FBI. Seth Millway will hear about it within minutes, and I'm a dead duck. There'd be an accident inside a couple of weeks, and suddenly you're a widow."

Connor stopped and looked at Nora to see her reaction, and was not entirely happy about the calm way she accepted the prospect of widowhood.

"I have life insurance, you know that," he said, feeling his throat tighten. "The policy's in the second drawer on the left in my desk."

"I know," said Nora. "So what's the problem?"

"There's this doc," said Connor. "He's at NCMC, a really important physician. It said in the paper that he was going to be the next surgeon general, so that tells you. Anyway, he's been finding out about all the dirty tricks the pharmaceutical industry's been up to, and he's going to spill the beans in a couple of weeks. Apparently he's singled out Millway. I have info that he couldn't possibly have, and the question is should I give it to him."

Nora got up and went into the kitchen, leaving her sherry untouched. Connor, one eye on her retreating back, picked it up and drained it.

"How do you know he'd keep your name a secret?" The sound of scraping started again, and Nora's back quivered with the activity.

"If he didn't, he'd never get anybody to talk to him ever again," said Connor reasonably.

"I think you should just keep your mouth shut and go find yourself a job," said Nora. "If you talk to anybody, whether it's the police or that doctor or whoever, it'll be the worse for you. You've nothing to gain by it."

"Thank you, Nora," said Connor, standing up. "You always help me to make up my mind."

He went upstairs, picked up the phone, managed to reach Maurice Bennett after a couple of tries, and made an appointment to meet him at a roadside McDonald's on I-95, halfway between exits 38 and 39. Then he spent a half hour sitting in the chair by the window with his head in his hands, wondering if his sense of outrage, his hatred of Seth Millway and all he stood for, was really enough reason to be sticking his head in a noose. Then he sat up and thought, here I am, fifty-seven years old. I've never done anything truly worthwhile in my whole life, which, by the law of averages, doesn't have a whole lot more to offer me at this point. I've spent my life compromising, doing dull, basically useless stuff because that was my job and that was all there was to do. Yes, he said out loud. He stood up and pounded on his desk. Yes, goddamn it, I'll do it.

Chapter Twenty-six

About the time that Desmond Connor was making up his mind, Vince Coletti, Seth Millway, Clifford Abrams, and Geoff Susskind were meeting in Seth's office, with Mike Petras as usual sitting by the door. An open copy of the *Washington Post* lay on the desk. They had all read the article about Maurice Bennett.

"No wonder Dr. Cairns won't accept our grant," said Seth through tight lips. He tapped the paper, but he was thinking about the expression on Paula's face the night before. "Her boss is trying to destroy us, and scuttle our whole fucking industry."

"Don't exaggerate," said Vince. He was sitting in one of the easy chairs and had both feet up on the edge of the glass desk. He looked relaxed enough, but there was an aura of impatience that hung around him like a mantle. When he had put the syndicate's money into this project, he hadn't planned on being involved in the day-to-day operations, and he didn't like it. "And don't be so simplistic. The industry's far too big to scuttle, and far too powerful. It has enough lobbyists and money to buy as much of Washington as it needs." He looked at Seth. "Not that Bennett can't do a lot of damage to individual corporations."

"What do you mean by that?" Seth's voice was truculent. He was feeling under a great deal of pressure, and also didn't like people putting their feet on his desk, not even Vincent Coletti.

Coletti replied, looking at the ceiling above Seth. "Aside from that article," he said, "the scuttlebutt I hear says Bennett and his committee are going to make an all-out attack on Millway Pharmaceuticals."

"Because Millway's the weak member of the pack and doesn't have the finances to defend itself?" Susskind's cynical, heavy-lidded eyes moved from Vince to Seth and back.

"Maybe. I don't think they'd know about the refinancing, not yet," said Vince, examining the tips of his Guccis.

"I'm not going to waste that money defending ourselves against attacks from people like Bennett," said Seth aggressively. "We need it right here. For manufacturing, production, and to position ourselves in the international markets when the anti-clot process is ready."

"You're missing the point," said Vince. He held out his hand to Mike, who was ready with a cigar. Vince checked the rounded end before holding it up to his ear and rolling the center between his fingers.

Seth, the health nut, winced at the thought of cigar smoke about to pervade his sanctum.

"Bennett can ruin you, Seth," said Coletti. "I personally don't give a rat's ass about that, except that it would damage me too." He bit off the end of the cigar and delicately blew the pieces of tobacco onto the carpet. "No lawyers, no public relations consultants can undo the damage he can do to you. To us. We have to approach it differently. Like the doctors say, prevention is better than cure."

"Prevention?" asked Seth.

"You got it. But like I said about Dr. Cairns, we'll take care of that piece of prevention too. We got the expertise."

Susskind stood up. "Look," he said, his voice sharp. "If

you're saying what I think you're saying, I have to completely dissociate myself from that. I'm a lawyer, and I
can't possibly participate or condone any such matters."

"That goes for me too," said Abrams, rising also. He
was visibly sweating. "In any case, it's not just Bennett.
He's just speaking for his committee."

"Shut up and sit down, both of you," said Vince without
moving. "Bennett's committee is just a bunch of yes-men.
There ain't one of them with the guts or the ability to do
what he'd doing, so if he goes, our problem's over. As for
the prevention bit, accidents happen. That's tough, but it
ain't your problem, okay?"

Something had appeared in Vince's voice, and in the
way that he looked at them, that made Abrams and
Susskind sit down abruptly.

"We're wasting time here," said Vince. He took his feet
off the desk and turned to Abrams. "What's happening
with the Cairns woman?" he asked abruptly. "Your job was
to take care of her credibility. How's it going?"

"Good," replied Abrams. He told Vince about the faulty
research paper and how he was planning to use it as a
weapon against her.

"Okay, back to Bennett," said Coletti. "You know how
guys like him work. They get hold of a disgruntled employee, as senior as they can find, and that's where they
get their most damaging information from."

He looked over at Seth again. "You have any of those,
Seth? Disgruntled employees?"

Seth thought for a moment and told him about Connor.

"A prime target for Dr. Bennett," said Coletti. "Tell
Mike here the details, where he lives and everything.
We'll keep a close eye on Connor, right, Mike?"

Later that day, Steve and Abrams traveled to St. Louis
to the Surgical Association meeting. Steve was to present

the paper Paula had helped him put together. Abrams was going mainly to do some politicking, have dinner with other academic surgeons, and be the moderator of a couple of discussion panels.

For a couple of days before they left, Abrams had not been pleased with Steve. His assignment to redo the experiments in Paula's paper had for some reason been going very slowly, and finally Abrams gave it to his chief technician with orders to get it done even if they had to stay up all night.

Now Abrams was much more affable and, after reading Steve's paper on the plane, complimented him on it.

"I got help with writing it," said Steve, but didn't elaborate.

Abrams was feeling good, especially since he'd consumed two Bloody Marys in quick succession, and didn't pursue the matter.

The lobby of the Marriott was crowded with surgeons registering for the meeting, young, worried-looking surgeons who were presenting papers, and older, relaxed men who were there mainly to have a good time and do a little business with their buddies. Steve found a couple of friends from California, and Abrams went off in the other direction, glad-handing his way through the lobby, greeting one doctor after another by name, slapping backs and generally acting like the patron saint of surgery, with his beaming smile and halo of white hair.

Next morning, at the session on intravascular coagulation, Steve presented his paper. It was well received and earned him a round of discreet applause.

At the end of the session, the moderator, a Professor Earl Macklerod from Baltimore, who Steve knew was a friend of Abrams', stood up and addressed the crowded room. Macklerod was an important man, a candidate for president of the College of Surgeons, and very active in medical politics. His face was grave. "I have a most serious question for all of you," he said. The chatting stopped and everyone paid attention. "Have any of you in the audience had occasion to measure thrombolysin levels in banked blood?"

Half a dozen hands went up.

"A colleague of mine came to me yesterday with some very disturbing news," went on Macklerod. "Attempting to do this test using a technique described in the *Journal of Hematology*, the June 1991 issue, he was unable to get the results he expected. He then reviewed the entire technique and found it to be misleading and incorrect. Have any of you had the same experience?"

Apparently no one had suffered such a trauma, because no hands went up.

"Who wrote the paper?" asked a voice.

Macklerod put on his glasses and picked up a reprint in front of him. "The lead author was a Paula S. Cairns, M.D.," he read, "together with a small group of other collaborators."

He surveyed the audience, most of whom looked puzzled. "The implication here," went on Macklerod, and Steve, appalled at what he was hearing, could almost hear Abrams' voice speaking, "is that this work was either fraudulent or merely careless, but I personally believe that the former case is correct. I shall be reporting this matter to the various interested authorities, and I'd be grateful if any one here has any pertinent comments to add to my report."

Nobody had.

On the way out, Steve heard one of the other attendees mutter to his neighbor, "That old bastard Macklerod, if there's one thing he really enjoys, it's crucifying people. He'll go all the way with this one, especially since it's a woman."

On the plane going back, Abrams seemed very pleased with himself. He'd met up with a lot of his old friends, eaten and drank a lot, and, of course, had accomplished his main goal, getting Earl Macklerod involved.

"By the way," he said to Steve as he anxiously watched the drink cart coming down the aisle, "it's come to my attention that you've been seeing Dr. Cairns socially. I would strongly advise you against that. You know how news travels, and Earl Macklerod was telling me that her reputation in surgical circles around the country will be in tatters within a week. My advice to you is to stay away from her. You know what they say—dirt sticks."

Chapter Twenty-seven

Seth sat at his desk, looking gloomily at nothing in particular. He had just come back from a meeting with his senior executives, and it hadn't been an easy session. He'd told Carl Dornier, his new head of research, to figure out how to develop an oral preparation of enzymes to prevent blood clotting inside the body, supposing someone, somehow, were to unlock the secret combination. Dornier had been less than enthusiastic, and talked more about why it wouldn't work than how to go about it. And the other execs were acting so nervous and conservative that he was losing his patience with them. Nolan Hostak, his director of finance, had told him privately that the sudden firing of Desmond Connor had sent shock waves through the entire organization, and the survivors were scared for their own jobs, and were hunkering down, just anxious to survive.

And the whole frightening business with Vince Coletti was making him nervous. Vince was taking a larger and larger part in the running of the company, and there wasn't much Seth could do about it. And if his methods were rough, Vince's were more so. The good thing about it was that Vince had a plan, and seemed to know what he was doing.

Seth got up and went to the window, stared over at the blue and white research tower, and thought about Paula.

He couldn't get her out of his mind, and a feeling of embarrassment and fury swept over him at the thought of the night before when he'd come, hat in hand, to apologize to her, only to see her there with that big blond guy. And on top of that, she'd rejected his olive branch without even a discussion. He would have to punish her for that in a way she wouldn't forget. Even the knowledge that Abrams was working hard to discredit her among her own peers didn't make him feel any better.

With his mind packed tight to bursting with incessant thoughts about her, he took the elevator down to the basement health club, where he worked out for an hour, lifting weights, running on the treadmill, doing push-ups until every muscle in his body ached, but it didn't help. Paula Cairns had taken over his thoughts, his life, and he hated her for it. In a way he was relieved by Coletti's plan to "take care of her," but as he told himself, he was by nature a participant, and didn't like other people to carry out projects in which he had a personal interest.

Seth was learning how to get inside his obsession and dress it up with fantasies. But he wasn't able to control his thoughts and plans for her, which grew and spread like a fast-growing, poisonous fungus in the dark corners of his mind.

The day had arrived when Paula and Rusty Hurwitz's biotech team were going to do the first in vivo testing of the new microcapsules, Paula's brainstorm that would allow each enzyme to react with clot inside the blood vessels without destroying the other enzymes in the sequence.

Rusty's group arrived at 7:00 A.M., a half hour early. "I couldn't wait," he told Paula. "This is the most exciting day of my life."

He'd brought a supply of the microcapsules in a sealed

container, heavily insulated, packed inside a spring-loaded box to absorb any shocks on the way. In the container was a series of twelve sealed bottles filled with a cloudy-looking solution of microscopic capsules, each containing a minute quantity of enzyme.

"They're just perfect," said Rusty, "and, I'm here to tell you, I do not exaggerate. The capsules have exactly, precisely the stability you need, Doctor. Separation is 99.929 percent, way above the critical limit. If I'd thought of it sooner, I'd have brought a bottle of champagne to celebrate."

Paula and Myra had prepared a series of experiments using rats to test the system; clots would be injected into their bloodstream and would come to rest in the lungs, plugging the blood vessels. That would cause the circulation in the lungs to come to a virtual standstill, so the transfer of oxygen and carbon dioxide gases would be severely slowed. The effectiveness of the microcapsules would be measured by the speed of restoration of normal gas exchange. Everything was ready, and using correct sterile procedures, Paula stuck the needle into the first container and started to draw up the first batch of the ultrathin-wall capsules into a syringe. She had to do it very delicately to avoid rupturing the capsules.

"It's really stiff," said Paula after pulling gently on the plunger for a few moments.

"Oh, that's just the oil they're suspended in," said Rusty, watching her every move, his eyes gleaming with excitement. "Take your time, it'll come up all right."

Paula slowly put down the bottle and the syringe and turned to him. "Did you say *oil*?"

"Sure. Linseed oil. That's the only way to keep the capsules from touching each other. In water or saline, they break up in a few seconds."

Paula wanted to scream, throw the bottles at him, then

run out of the lab and jump over a cliff. Instead she explained to him that if she injected linseed oil into the veins of any animal, rat or human, it would be fatal within moments.

After discussing the problem for over an hour, Paula, Rusty, and his dejected assistants concluded that at the present time it was impossible to manufacture what she needed. They were using state-of-the-art technology, and nobody in the entire world knew how to suspend that type of microsphere in a non-oily solution.

After they had gone, Paula went down the corridor to the staff toilets, locked herself in a booth, and wept.

The pressure was really on. Paula had run out of ideas, and once she admitted that there was no way to deliver the enzymes into the bloodstream in an effective way, her entire research project would be doomed.

She went back to her lab, settled down, and worked steadily, concentrating as hard as she could on the task. But nothing was happening, everything seemed to be going around in circles when, just as she was about to throw in the towel for the day, an entirely new possibility came into her mind. With growing excitement she started to work out a whole series of chemical reactions and interactions, but soon it became too complicated to work out without a special software program. It was late, but there was no thought in Paula's mind of going home and starting again the next day. So using several manuals and preexisting programs already in her computer's hard drive, she toiled, corrected, swore at uncooperative formulae, corrected some more, got up to make black coffee, yelled with frustration when an entire sequence vanished from the screen for no apparent reason, then when it was all ready, ran the program. It worked. Exhausted, Paula wanted to set up the actual enzymes and run them, but that would have taken her an additional twelve hours, and she knew she couldn't function effectively that long. So she curled up on the easy chair and fell asleep within moments. When Myra came into the lab the next morning, Paula woke up, stretched her cramped muscles, and got up, with a bad taste in her mouth and feeling as if she'd been to one party too many.

"I got a method for sequencing the enzymes and keeping them separate, finally," she told Myra. "In theory, anyway." Then she told her assistant how to set up the actual enzyme tests. "I'm going home to shower and change," she said finally. "I'll be back in about an hour."

Paula shut down the computer after coding and copying all the work she'd done, then left the lab. Myra's hostile little eyes followed her to the door.

On her return, Paula's first stop was to go up to tell Maurice the good news. He was sitting in his office. Outside, the rain was coming down in torrents and beating like winter against the windowpanes.

First he had some news for her. "A few days ago I resigned as chairman of this department," he said when she sat down. "It's not because of my aneurysm," he went on, smiling at Paula's astonishment. "I'm going to be traveling a lot to Washington, and right now I'm spending a lot of time on this pharmaceutical investigation, so I can't really devote the time I should to the committees and the other responsibilities of a chairman."

"That should be really good for you," said Paula, thinking that for her it wouldn't be so good. Maurice as chairman had vast clout. "You'll have more time to spend in the lab too, and that'll be a shot in the arm for everybody."

"I've thought about the effects of this decision on your career, Paula," he said with typical thoughtfulness. "And I don't think it'll make much difference. This very morning I obtained some interim financing for you from an outside philanthropic source, a kind of private donation. It should be enough to keep you going up to a year. And he might be willing to renew it." Maurice smiled. "The thing is, Paula, that as soon as your work is completed, you won't need any help from me or from anyone else. You'll be launched."

"That's wonderful, I mean about the financing." Paula's voice went up at the end of the sentence, indicating a question.

"Your philanthropist is a retired stockbroker," said Maurice. "I've known him a long time. I operated on him for a duodenal ulcer years ago, when we were still doing surgery for that condition. And, you'll be happy to know, there are no strings attached."

Paula shook her head and laughed. Maurice always seemed to know exactly what she was thinking.

"When will your resignation take effect?" she asked.

"At the end of this month," replied Maurice, enjoying the thought of being rid of all those irksome responsibilities. "And that's in three days."

"Do you know yet who's going to replace you?" asked Paula cautiously.

"No, and it's not up to me. I asked the dean this morning, and he's already appointed a committee, so it shouldn't take too long for them to come to a decision. A long hiatus would be bad for the department."

"Do you think the new chairman will come from inside the department?" persisted Paula. It had suddenly occurred to her that Clifford Abrams would be a strong contender unless they decided to appoint someone from another university.

Maurice smiled and shrugged. "I really don't know. By the way, did Walt Eagleton ever get back to you after he saw me?" he asked.

Paula sucked air through her teeth. "Yes, he did. Boy,

was he emphatic! I'm sure he told you already, he's convinced that you should have that surgery immediately."

"He did tell me. I told him I didn't want it done now, and that you agreed. He said that at this point I was a patient, and shouldn't have any say at all about what was best for me. My, our friend Walt is old-fashioned, isn't he?"

"That's more or less what he told me too," said Paula. "Except that he also said that if I didn't operate on you within a week or hand over responsibility for your care to another surgeon, I was recklessly endangering your life and basically committing the worst kind of malpractice."

"This kind of thing happens all the time," said Maurice. "It's just a matter of interpreting statistics. He thinks waiting is unacceptably risky, whereas you and I feel that it isn't quite so urgent."

"Should we get a third opinion?" asked Paula. "I mean about your aneurysm? Then take a vote?"

"No," said Maurice firmly. "We have quite enough problems with only two opinions. I'm going to take it very easy, not play tennis or do anything else to put my blood pressure up. And as soon as I've finished with that pharmaceutical business we'll do the surgery, okay? I want to be in good shape for the fall; apparently they're going to start the confirmation hearings then."

Paula jumped up. "Confirmation? For surgeon general?" She put her arms around him and gave him a big kiss on the side of the cheek. "Maurice, I'm so glad! That's just wonderful!"

Maurice blushed, the first time Paula had ever seen him so taken aback. "Well," he murmured, touching his cheek, "I must say, Paula, that was a great incentive. Maybe I'll go on to have a shot at the presidency."

It was Paula's turn to blush, but Maurice went on as if he hadn't noticed. "How's the work going?"

"I think I finally have the sequence and a method of keeping the enzymes separate," she said. "But I still don't have a way of delivering them to a clot deep inside the body."

"My God," said Maurice, astonished. "Congratulations! That's a huge step forward. If you've really accomplished that, Paula, you've just about won the battle."

Paula shook her head. "For months I've been knocking my brains out trying to figure a delivery system, and I'm no further forward than the day I started. It's driving me nuts."

She told him about the experience with the tiny spheres suspended in oil, and just talking about the fiasco sent shivers down her back.

Maurice was sympathetic but firm. "Sure, it may take a long time," he said. "So you'd better hunker down, get your mind prepared for a long siege. I expect it'll take years to try out all the various methods and techniques you'll come up with before you find one that works. That's why we've been thinking about long-term financing for you. Nobody's expecting you to do it in a couple of months."

He paused and smiled at her. "You know, Paula, you're running into one of the problems that surgeons often experience when they're doing research."

"What's that?"

"Well, surgeons' minds are geared for quick results. The cycle is over in a few days or weeks at most."

"What cycle?"

"From the time you first see the patient until they go home. The tests, the diagnosis, the operation, then the recovery period, all that takes anything from five to ten days, with exceptions, of course. At that point the cycle is completed. Then you start all over again with another patient, again with that short-term cycle fixed in your mind.

But with this kind of research, your sights have to be set much further into the future. The cycle of any worthwhile piece of research takes months at the very least, years in most cases."

"You know, Dr. Bennett, you've been getting a lot more philosophical since we found out about your aneurysm," said Paula, smiling.

The phone on Maurice's desk rang, and he seemed almost relieved at the interruption. He listened for several minutes, with barely a word from him. He didn't take his eyes off Paula, and his expression got grimmer and grimmer. When he got off the phone, he sat back and said nothing for a few moments. Then his voice was as grim as his expression. "I thought this might happen," he said. "That was Earl Macklerod from Baltimore on the phone. He tells me that the Surgical Association people are mounting a full-scale investigation of that paper you published on thrombolysins. Apparently they've asked him to chair the inquiry, and he says that because of the present awareness and reaction to medical fraud, he's going to make the hearings public."

They talked about that for a while; both of them were shaken, but Maurice was more interested in figuring out why Macklerod was taking the time to start up what looked like a witch-hunt. "He's up for president of the College of Surgeons," he told Paula after thinking about it a while. "I guess he wants to make like he's a forceful defender of scientific integrity."

"Do you think Macklerod is doing this on his own, or did somebody put him up to it?" asked Paula, feeling as if she were being pursued by a posse of mindless avengers.

"I've no idea," replied Maurice. "But I can find out. I know Earl pretty well. He's one of those humorless, ambitious people who try to raise themselves by bringing other people down, because he doesn't have the ability to bring himself up."

"I'd just *love* to meet him," murmured Paula, trying to sound lighthearted.

"You probably will," replied Maurice.

As Paula was leaving his office, Maurice put his hand lightly on her shoulder. "I'll be in the office as usual tomorrow," he said, "but after that I won't be in for about ten days," he told her. "I'll be in Washington part of that time, and in Europe for a few days. If something really urgent comes up, ask Helen. She'll be able to track me down."

Chapter Twenty-eight

Maurice Bennett had some experience with industry public relations people and knew that they could be dangerous, especially if there was anything to be gained by discrediting their target. So that afternoon when the predictably gorgeous Freda Bunce appeared at his office for her appointment, dressed in a stunning red outfit with a very short skirt, and the sheerest of sheer stockings covering her elegant legs, Maurice took a leaf out of the industry's book.

In preparation he had made Helen Katz, his secretary, give up her comfortable wheeled swivel chair, which they spun until it was at its highest position, then placed it in front of his desk where the normal visitor's chair would be.

When Freda was ushered into Maurice's office, she was a little surprised by the swivel chair, but when invited to, she sat down on it, tucking her heels inside the steel ring above the wheels. She had long legs, and her knees stuck up a little, but not uncomfortably so. She had just sat down when Helen opened the door and said, "Oh, Freda!" so urgently that Freda spun around in her chair, her knees a few inches apart, just in time for the flashbulb.

"Thank you, Miss Bunce," said Helen in her normal voice, putting the camera down. "Dr. Bennett always likes to get a shot of his guests for his records," she explained. She smiled down at Freda, who was looking at her open-mouthed. "Love those lace panties," Helen whispered to her before leaving the room.

"That was a dirty trick," said Freda indignantly to Maurice, who had stood beside her, deliberately grim-faced, while the photo was being taken.

"Not at all," said Maurice, smiling at her in his best ambassadorial style. "We always send our guests a nice five-by-eight print as a memento of their visit, and I'll personally make sure you get yours. I'm sure you'll love it. Now," he said, sitting down behind his desk and speaking in a much less agreeable tone of voice, "what exactly did you want to tell me about the pharmaceutical industry?"

By this time Freda was completely unnerved, and her message was shorter and less persuasive than Maurice had expected. In fact she was almost incoherent, although she did pass on the message that the Pharmaceutical Council was very impressed with his findings and would be honored to award him a large grant to continue his work. That made Maurice mad, and he gave Freda a very uncomfortable ten minutes during which he quizzed her about the council's position on bribery, then challenged her on a few of the more recently uncovered misdemeanors by the pharmaceutical industry. Freda was completely outclassed, and finally she stood up, pulled down the hem of her dress with a furious wiggle, and left.

On the way out, Helen sweetly asked her where the print should be sent, and Freda pulled a business card from her pocketbook, slapped it down on the desk, and was gone in a pouting flurry of high heels, sheer stockings, and Opium.

Maurice spent the next hour taking phone calls from various people in and out of his department. Everybody was concerned about his aneurysm and also about his leaving the chairmanship of the department. Maurice had run the affairs of the department in a fair and even-handed way, and a number of people expressed their lack of confidence in his just-announced successor.

"I had nothing to do with his appointment," Maurice replied, "but I'm sure Cliff will do a very competent job."

The chairman of the department of medicine, an old friend who had sat on many a committee with Maurice, called. "Maurice, I hear you've resigned, and that you're going into the hospital right away? You have a big aneurysm? How come this information is all over the hospital before it gets to me? And how come I have to hear about it in the staff toilets?"

"You shouldn't spend so much time in there, Claude," replied Maurice calmly. "Then you wouldn't hear so many rumors."

All afternoon he patiently tried to correct the various stories that were flying around, even one that had Walt Eagleton forcibly taking over his case because of Paula Cairns' inept handling.

At the back of his mind was the thought of his scheduled meeting later that evening with Desmond Connor. Hopefully he'd learn a whole lot more than he already knew about Millway Pharmaceuticals; Connor had been high up in the Millway management, and he certainly wouldn't have bothered to set up such a clandestine appointment unless he had a lot of information to divulge.

But again, caution was in the forefront of Maurice's mind. He'd recently had several telephone warnings to lay off his investigations, and these had been followed up with a number of threatening calls, usually around three in the morning. He didn't pay too much attention, although he had alerted the police and now kept a watchful eye when he was outside the hospital. Also, because the police had told him to, he didn't always leave the hospital at the same time, and took a slightly different route home every day.

"We can't give you a bodyguard," said the police sergeant, although Maurice hadn't asked for one, "because nothing's happened yet."

"So if I get shot dead here in my office, then you'll give me one?"

"Yes, sir." The sergeant grinned. "Actually, it would be an honor guard rather than a bodyguard, wouldn't it, sir?" The sergeant was still chuckling over his quip when he got back to the station house.

Steve had spent a good part of the afternoon in the library, and when he got to the lab, Dr. Abrams was waiting for him, looking very cheerful and Santa Claus-like. He told Steve that he'd heard from other people how well his paper had been received at the Surgical Association meeting, that it looked as if his star was in the ascendant again, and that his career hadn't been permanently affected by the problems he'd had in Los Angeles.

"And by the way," he said, "we're having a little champagne party in the lab at five this afternoon. There was a dean's committee meeting this morning, and they appointed me the new chairman of the surgery department."

"Congratulations," said Steve, surprised. "Why did Dr. Bennett resign?"

"There's been a lot of pressure on him recently," said Abrams in a confidential voice. "And also you may have heard that he's sick and will need surgery."

"Will you be doing it?" Steve couldn't resist asking, although of course he knew that Paula was in charge of Maurice's case. He also knew that Abrams had the repu-

tation of being an "occasional" surgeon, neither technically very competent or up-to-date.

"I imagine so," Abrams replied airily. "Who else would
he ask?"

Chapter Twenty-nine

Maurice parked his car in the crowded lot behind the restaurant. The McDonald's restaurant was only a small part of the truck stop; beyond was a giant filling station with six rows of pumps and four diesel lanes for the eighteen-wheelers. Dozens of these behemoths were already parked for the night behind the restaurant and the filling station.

Maurice had changed from his business suit to an unobtrusive sweater and chinos. Connor had described himself with some accuracy, but to make sure they didn't miss each other, he said he'd be standing at one of the phone booths outside the entrance, with a black leather briefcase between his feet.

And there he was, a phone in his hand, watching the people coming in and out. Maurice nodded to him and went in. He turned right, past the crowded video game room, and stood in one of the lines, not at all hungry although he hadn't eaten anything since he gulped down a cup of soup at lunchtime. In any case, he couldn't bring himself to ask for a Chicken McNugget or anything with such a ridiculous name.

He settled for a cup of coffee—medium, with milk, no sugar—found a table by the window, and sat down.

When Connor came in, he seemed very nervous. He passed Maurice once, walked down between the tables, did a complete circle, then came back and stopped at his table.

"Dr. Bennett?" he asked very quietly. When Maurice nodded, Connor said, "Get a table away from the window, please," then went off to join the food line. Maurice obediently picked up his paper cup and two empty milk containers and found another table, this time near the door, thinking that Connor must have been reading too much John le Carré.

Connor came back, holding his tray in one hand and the briefcase in the other, and sat down with a grunt. He wanted to be sure of Maurice's identity before saying anything, and insisted on checking his driver's licence. Then he opened the cardboard container in front of him and pulled out a double-decker hamburger, opened it, emptied three small packs of ketchup over the meat, and started to eat, glancing at Maurice all the while. Maurice said nothing and sipped his coffee, slowly becoming aware that Connor was very afraid, and was resisting a very powerful urge to get up and get the hell out of there.

"*If* I have information for you," said Connor, "what are you going to do with it?"

"Depends on what the information is," replied Maurice, watching him steadily. "It could all be stuff I know already, or material I couldn't use."

"I doubt it. It's specifically financial info about Millway Pharmaceuticals and also the foundation." Connor's hands were as tense as his face as he sat there, his half-eaten cheeseburger grasped tightly in his hand. Red blobs of ketchup dripped unheeded onto the tabletop.

Maurice said nothing. He took a sip of coffee and waited.

"Everything was okay while old Sam was in charge," Connor blurted out suddenly. A shred of lettuce appeared on his chin, and Maurice suppressed the urge to pick it off. Instead he nodded encouragingly.

"We did our job the best we could," went on Connor. "We didn't get any Nobel nominations, but that's not what we were hired to do. Sam Millway was honest and fair. That man never did a dishonest thing in his entire life."

There was a pause while Connor put the remains of his cheeseburger in the container and went back to the counter for more ketchup. Maurice looked around and, catching the mood from Connor, checked to see if anyone was watching their table, There were a few families with small children, half a dozen dusty workers from a nearby cement factory, but most of the customers appeared to be truckers, none of whom looked even faintly suspicious.

When Connor came back and started to talk in a low voice, Maurice very quickly knew that he had struck gold. Connor had a wealth of information about the money that had suddenly appeared from nowhere, the conferences, the setting up of new facilities to take care of large-scale production of a so-far unnamed product.

"About this money," said Maurice, leaning forward so he could keep his voice down, "there's nothing wrong with getting additional financing, is there? Hadn't Seth been trying to get money from Wall Street and the investment banks for months?"

"According to my contact in the accounting department," replied Connor, "this is dirty money. Some of it's been laundered, some of it hasn't. How does my contact know?" he went on, anticipating Maurice's next question. "A number of reasons. First, the money didn't come in one giant check. It came in two big Post Office sacks, literally thousands of checks for much smaller amounts. That tells you a whole lot for a start, but the real tip-off was where these checks were drawn. United Mutual Bank of Miami and a couple other Miami banks, the Federated

Bank of Geneva, the Bahama Central Trust . . . According to my source, every one of these banks is notorious in the banking and money business. For God's sake, she says, even the feds know about them, although they're all still open and flourishing."

"Those checks, they've been cashed and returned to the people who sent them, I suppose?"

"We have Xeroxes of every one, and I brought a whole bunch of samples right here," said Connor, tapping the briefcase.

"Great. That was good thinking. Now," he said, going off on another tack, "Millway Pharmaceuticals is a public company, right? How did they account for all this new cash to the stockholders?"

"They didn't. It all went into a special fund, not on the official books, and apparently they've used some of that money to buy back their own stock, which is at a low point right now, and lots of people are only too happy to sell. Mary said they're doing it very quietly, using stockbrokers who don't attract attention."

"Hoping to resell it, I suppose, when the price goes rocketing up again."

Connor didn't answer. He was attacking the barklike coating of some kind of apple pastry in a way that made Maurice wonder when the man had last eaten a square meal.

"Isn't Seth Millway worried about the SEC?" asked Maurice. "This is exactly the kind of thing they're looking for, and if they come down on him, he's out of business."

"The *Wall Street Journal*'s estimate," said Connor, his mouth full of apple pie, "is that the SEC can't take on a tenth of the cases that are crying out for investigation. Seth's a smart cookie. He's taking a calculated risk, and he'll most likely get away with it. And if his enzyme process ever actually works, then he'll have all the money he needs to pay off whoever he has to."

"Do you have any documents?" asked Maurice. "To back up all you've been telling me?"

Connor patted his briefcase. "It's all here. I don't want to take the stuff out now. I'll give you the case, but I'll need it back, okay?"

"That'll be just fine," said Maurice. "Would you kindly open the case for me? Just unlock it, both sides, then open it as far as it'll go, then close it and lock it again."

Connor frowned. "Why?" Then he laughed. "I guess you've been around the block a few times more than I have," he said. He put the briefcase on his lap, took a small key out of his pocket, unlocked both sides, opened it fully, then closed it.

"Thanks," said Maurice. "I really appreciate what you're doing. And I'll get the briefcase back to you."

"No disclosure of sources, right?" said Connor, passing the tiny key across the table to Maurice. He was sweating, a string of tiny droplets along his hairline. You know that if anybody even suspects I gave you this stuff, I'm dead. You don't know the guys who are behind Millway now. They're lethal."

"Not a word," Maurice assured him. "Who are *they*?"

"They are a guy by the name of Coletti, who's fronting for a whole bunch of other people, all in the drug business, and I don't mean aspirin. They're cleaning up their money by investing in legal corporations. I tell you, if I was Seth Millway, I'd rather jump into a pond full of starving sharks than do business with Coletti or any of these guys."

Both men left together soon after. They had not noticed the sturdy-looking man in a black leather jacket and aviator glasses who had come in soon after Connor and sat down on the other side of the crowded restaurant. But neither of them had ever met Mike Petras, so there was no danger of recognition.

But Mike had studied newspaper photos of Maurice, and was pretty sure that was the man who'd been talking to Connor. To make certain, he left the restaurant behind them, and while Maurice was getting into his BMW, he slipped behind the car and got the license number.

Chapter Thirty

When Paula came into the lab next morning, she called Walt Eagleton, thanked him for his offer to take her on as his assistant, and politely turned him down. At first he sounded shocked, then made a couple of flip comments, and Paula, thinking back about her entire experience with him, wondered uncomfortably whether this man, this very accomplished surgeon, this chameleonlike man, had any sincerity in him at all. He seemed to say one thing, feel another, and his actions appeared unrelated to both. But there was something about the tone of his voice that made her wonder if he was taking her refusal as calmly as he made out.

In the days following, Paula noted that the atmosphere in the hospital had subtly changed. People stopped talking when she came by, and there was a coolness from people who had until then always been friendly to her. At first she thought it was her imagination, but she put together scraps of conversations and muttered comments here and there, and figured that Walt, in spite of his apparent friendliness to her, had been bad-mouthing her because he felt that she was not taking proper care of Maurice. Eva Karno, one of the surgical pathologists and a good friend of Paula's, confirmed this. "Walt always *knows* he's right," said Eva. "And if you disagree, he'll attack you. As you're finding out." Not only that, Eva told her, but Cliff

Abrams was going around dropping hints that "a female member of the faculty," had been caught doing fraudulent research, and leaving little doubt about who he was referring to. Eva was very concerned and wondered how Paula had managed to make such a pair of powerful enemies in such a short time.

Who knows? Paula answered angrily. And who cares?

Eva told her that a few days before, Abrams had got himself into trouble again in the operating room and, as usual, had taken it out on someone else. This time it had been Chris Engel, the junior resident. "Abrams is really a lousy surgeon," Eva said. "In the pathology department we get the pieces he cuts out, so we know."

Maurice was away, and Paula felt a strong sense of loss, because he was always somebody she could turn to, and he usually knew how to deal with difficult situations.

The first hint of more serious trouble came in a registered letter on the university's headed notepaper from the dean's office. "Dear Dr. Cairns," she read, "It has come to our notice that doubts have been expressed concerning certain aspects of research performed by you in the past, and that an investigation into this matter has been started by the Surgical Association, a leadership body in your field.

"Please consider this letter a formal notice that a separate investigation will be carried out within the Department of Surgery at NCMC. A preliminary hearing will be held at eleven a.m. on the 5th of June in the main conference room in building five, under the chairmanship of Dr. Clifford Abrams in his capacity as Chairman of the Department. Your attendance will be required at this hearing. If you wish to be represented by legal counsel, please inform this office no later than June 1." The letter was signed by the dean.

Reading the letter, Paula could feel herself starting to

sweat. She stared at the typed page, a weird sense of unreality coming over her. How could this possibly be happening to her? And of course, Earl Macklerod's investigation was also gearing up. She sat at her desk and put her head in her hands. The letter lay open on the desk in front of her like a death warrant, and for a while she couldn't bear to look at it or touch it again.

Then she sat up, filled with a resolve that she wasn't going to let these people get her down or interfere with her work. She would go to their hearing and make it clear to Abrams and his committee that this had been a minor error committed at the beginning of her career, that she had admitted her mistake, and that since then her work had been irreproachable.

Feeling suddenly better, she went to the lab and spent most of the day making revisions to the enzyme-sequencing program, for the tests with actual enzymes had showed a few minor anomalies.

Paula noticed that Myra was acting differently; she did her work as efficiently as ever, but now was very quiet, and a couple of times when Paula looked up she found Myra staring at her with a really strange, almost triumphant expression. Some alarm bells started to go off in Paula's head, and she put a few little incidents together, things that individually would have been meaningless.

After Myra left, Paula sat at her computer, pensive, feeling that she had become some kind of community target. Everybody was having a shot or two at her. Why? That, she could not figure. She was doing her job well, teaching her students and the residents, working hard at her research, and, to her knowledge, not doing anything that deserved retribution or attack. But there was no doubt that she was under attack, and from several directions.

Her feelings about Myra also made her uncomfortable;

the woman was competent, but had never been a particularly forthcoming person. Back in New York, when Bob Zimmerman had first suggested that Myra come to work for her, Paula had tried to get to know her, had taken her to lunch a couple of times, but her interest had got her nowhere. Myra clammed up tight about her private life, her family, her likes and dislikes, and didn't seem to be enthused or excited about anything. Except the second time Paula took her to lunch, she suddenly seemed to come to life, but that was about dessert, a trifle with cherries and whipped cream on top.

Paula had never thought about Myra's professional loyalty to her; it was something she had always taken for granted. But now she felt its absence, from the way that Myra acted, the way she looked at her, and from something—Paula couldn't find the exact work in her mind, but *evasive* came close enough—about the way she acted.

Pursing her lips, Paula went back to work on the computer.

Late that afternoon, Paula went to the scheduled staff meeting in the small surgical conference room, the first such meeting to be run by Cliff Abrams. Every week the doctors discussed their more interesting cases, and the research doctors would bring their colleagues up to date on their various projects. From time to time private-side surgeons would attend, and on this occasion Walt Eagleton came.

As people were about to leave, Walt turned in his seat to face Paula, who was sitting in the back. "Dr. Cairns, can you give us an update on our former leader's health? Have you operated on Maurice Bennett yet?"

Surprised, Paula briefly replied that no, she hadn't.

"Is it true that he's going to the Mayo to be operated on?" asked someone else. Paula had heard that rumor too. Now every eye was fixed on Paula.

"I don't know for sure," replied Paula calmly, "but I don't think so."

Walt bored in. "Dr. Cairns, why didn't you operate on him as soon as you found he had an aneurysm? You were obviously unsure enough of your own judgment to get a second opinion. That second opinion, mine, was that he should be operated on immediately before he developed complications." Walt stood up and pushed back his chair. "We here are all very fond of Maurice," he went on. "Many of us have known him for years, and we're most concerned about the way you're dealing with him. In fact," Walt's voice rose a little, "since this is a departmental meeting, and we've always had the privilege of saying exactly what we thought, I am saying here and now that in my opinion, your handling of Maurice's case is negligent and verging on malpractice."

All of a sudden everyone was talking at once, voices were raised, and it was clear to Paula from the comments that were made that most of them agreed with Walt.

Abrams' voice rose above the hubbub. "If you wish to continue this discussion, please do it outside. This meeting is adjourned. We'll meet again next week, gentlemen, same time, same place."

He walked out, studiously avoiding Paula's gaze.

Vince Coletti had virtually taken up residence in the Millway Building. He had moved into an office in the penthouse suite, installed Mike Petras there too, and when Seth came in to express his discomfort with the new arrangement, Coletti told him what he had in his mind. Some of it, anyway.

"As soon as this show's on the road," he said, "me and

Mike are outa here. I don't like this company and I don't much like you either, but I'm not leaving until this whole business is settled. That will be when we have that process in the bag and the woman's been taken care of. From that point you're on your own." He looked at Seth contemptuously. "Not that it'll be any better for you, with your fancy ideas. You putz around this place like a monkey playing with his dick, but you're not actually getting anything done."

When Seth protested that things were happening, that he was getting a lot done, and explained that Paula was being put in a position where she would be forced to work for them, Coletti said whatever they were doing, results weren't coming in fast enough.

"You and Abrams, you're just playing games," he went on. "How do you know that she won't just go ahead and publish her work in some journal? If she does that, then we're all screwed."

"For one thing, she's not ready yet, not by a long way, and she's not going to publish anything until she's damn sure about every step and then double-checked it," said Seth, smiling. "She's been burned once, and she's no fool."

"You don't have anything going on the side with her, do you?" said Coletti, staring at him.

"Of course not." Seth stared back. "Why?"

"You just look funny when anyone mentions her name," replied Coletti. "But of course you'd have too much sense to get involved with a chick who's not going to be around that long."

"Right."

"Listen, Seth. Like I said, things aren't moving fast enough, and my friends are beginning to ask questions. They check the *Wall Street Journal* every day for the big story, and they are very disappointed it ain't showed up yet."

"They get the *Wall Street Journal* in Medellín?" asked Seth sarcastically.

There was a long pause while Coletti stared coldly at Seth, who had a sudden queasy feeling that maybe he shouldn't have said that.

"You better believe it. How long will it take before she's worked out that enzyme process?"

Seth shook his head. "I don't know. She doesn't keep me informed about her progress."

Coletti pushed his face forward suddenly, and Seth, startled, backed off. In spite of his size and strength, he was afraid of Coletti.

"You get that info right now," he said in a voice that chilled Seth. "I want to hear how near they are to completion. I need a closing date I can tell my associates. And I want the answer by tomorrow morning. Now beat it."

Activated by an urgent call from Seth, Abrams called through to Paula's lab, hoping she wouldn't be there, and was lucky. Myra answered. Abrams hadn't called or stopped by for almost a week, and she sounded sulky, but brightened up when he invited her over.

"So what's happening over in your neck of the woods, Myra?" he asked, pushing the plate of cookies over toward her. They were Sandwich Creams, one of her favorites. "It's been ages since we talked, how have you been?"

"You were right about that thrombolysin paper, Dr. Abrams," said Myra, looking at the cookies. She decided to tantalize herself and not even touch them for a little while. "Everybody seems to be getting on her case about it."

"Well, I sincerely hope that'll all blow over," he said, waving a pudgy hand. "How is her enzyme work going?"

"Great. She finally got the computerized sequence

right. She's very excited about it, and we've reproduced those results using actual enzymes."

"That's wonderful," said Abrams. For once his enthusiasm was genuine. "What's the next step?"

"Animal tests," replied Myra; the urge to grab a cookie was becoming unbearable. "Although the last time was a real fiasco." She told Abrams about the microspherules.

"Yes, animal tests, of course," agreed Abrams. "But now she's got the theoretical part of it right, the actual practical part should be a piece of cake, right?"

The mention of cake did it, and Myra picked up two cookies at once and put them into her mouth.

Unable to speak, she nodded.

"Isn't she worried about security? Some unscrupulous person might want to tamper with or steal that valuable information."

"Uhn-uhn," mumbled Myra. "It's all coded. In fact, it's encrypted, which is even more difficult. No way can anybody steal that material. Even I don't have the code, in case you were going to ask."

Abrams looked at Myra's puffy face with its malicious little eyes looking out at him from between folds of fat, and realized that Myra was no fool. She'd figured out why she was getting all those cookies and doughnuts.

There was a silence for a few moments while each of them watched and wondered how much they could get out of the other.

"I'm not doing this for cookies anymore," said Myra. "I'm risking my job telling you all this stuff, and anyway I don't like doing it."

"Good. I'm glad we understand each other," said Abrams briskly. "And I entirely agree. Of course I was going to get you a really nice present as soon as this business was over. . . ."

"Yeah," said Myra. She licked her finger and went

around the plate with it, picking up the crumbs. "I know who does have the code," she went on. "I mean, aside from Dr. Cairns."

Abrams pursed his lips and came to a decision. "Okay, then," he said. "Let's talk money."

Fifteen minutes later, Myra had gone, well pleased, having divulged the information that a copy of the access code to Paula's computer system lay in Geoffrey Susskind's safe.

As soon as Myra's ample figure had squeezed out of his office, Abrams took an air-freshening canister from his desk drawer and sprayed all over the room. The nerve endings in his nose were peculiarly sensitive to body odors.

Steve happened to see Myra come out of Abrams' lab, and it occurred to him that there was something guilty about the way she glanced at him and waddled off in the opposite direction. Why was she there anyway? He made a mental note to mention it to Paula.

Abrams sat in his high-backed leather chair, thought for a few minutes, then picked up the phone and told Seth what he had learned. In turn, Seth went over to inform Vince Coletti.

"Tell Susskind to pull that code out of his safe," ordered Coletti. "Make sure Cairns isn't in her lab on Friday night, and get the lab keys from her tech. Give her a big bonus to keep her quiet. As soon as we have the code, I have a whiz kid who can extract every last scrap of information out of that computer."

A half hour later, a friendly and affable Clifford Abrams called Steve to find out how things were going. "By the way," he said as an afterthought, "I have a couple of tickets to the symphony for Friday. I can't use them, and if you've got nothing better to do, you're most welcome to have them. They're orchestra stalls, so you should enjoy it."

Steve said that if he could use them, he'd come over and pick them up in a half hour. He called Paula, who was delighted. She hadn't been to a concert for months, she was exhausted with everything that was going on, and now that one phase of her work had been completed, she felt she deserved a break.

Paula had been able to get Seth successfully out of her mind, to the point that she rarely thought about him anymore, but Seth's obsession with her was not only as strong as ever, but its content had taken a very dangerous turn.

Late one afternoon, as he was driving home in his car, he felt his mood change again to a tense, visceral excitement. Something really weird was happening to him, and he knew it. It was as if he were consciously handing himself over to another self, a controller who showed him the mysteries and excitements of sensations and instincts he didn't know he possessed.

Once, as a boy traveling with his parents, he had visited the communal museum at Bruges, in Belgium, and had been enthralled by a sixteenth-century painting by Gérard David which depicted the flaying alive of a corrupt judge. There had been a reason for that visit, he realized now, and for his having stopped so long in front of that painting.

He picked up his mail on the way in to his home, and was gratified to see an eighteen-inch cardboard shipping box. He hefted it and smiled. After closing the door, he put the box on the kitchen table, opened it, and took out a skinning knife he'd ordered through a mail-order catalogue that catered exclusively to hunters and fishermen. "Razor-sharp high carbon-vanadium steel," the ad had read. "Skin your deer faster than the pros." And it *was* sharp. Seth tested the blade gingerly against his thumb. Again he saw one of the villainous bearded executioners pulling the skin back on the corrupt judge's leg, while holding his bloody knife between his teeth.

It was a warm evening, and Seth was feeling restless. He wasn't hungry and decided to give dinner a miss. While he was putting his new knife away with the others, he had an idea, went through to his bedroom, changed into jeans and a dark sweater, slipped on a pair of blue sneakers, put both sheathed knives and a tightly rolled plastic bag in his trouser pockets, and was about to leave when the phone rang. It was Fleur, making a collect call from Cannes. Seth hung up on the operator, then reached into the top of the hall closet for a pair of fur-lined gloves.

Outside, it was a warm evening, and Seth felt like a predator, a cat silently hunting for rodents in the long grass. A cat, a cat, a feline cat. Humming softly between his teeth, he went to the back of his cluster of luxurious condos onto a raised path that ran along the river's edge. To his left was a wide, shallow pond, mostly overgrown with reeds, a wetlands area that so far had resisted the onslaught of home builders. It was dark. A few streetlights shone dimly a couple of hundred yards beyond the pond, and their reflected light made long, wiggly yellow lines toward him in the gently moving water. To his right, almost a mile up the river, he could just distinguish the lights on the I-95 bridge, strung out like pearls in a graceful curve above the dark water.

There isn't any such thing as real silence, Seth thought, it's just different levels of sound. Now he could hear the leaves in the bushes rustling in the night breeze, the far-off roaring of traffic on the bridge, with the occasional explosive crackle of a distant eighteen-wheeler changing gears, and then that sound receded as the path turned momentarily away from the river and out of sight of the bridge. Now Seth had to strain to hear anything. He found himself holding his breath, and heard the beating of his heart.

There was a sudden scurry in the undergrowth just ahead of him, and he stepped forward and waited. There was just enough light for him to see a small black and white cat, obviously domestic because it had a collar and a round silver tag that glistened in the faint light. Without any fear it stepped onto the path with a little squeaky purr and trotted up to him, rubbing against his leg and swishing its tail.

Seth reached down and stroked it for a moment with his gloved hand, and it arched its back contentedly. Then Seth's fingers reached forward and very gently slipped around the cat's neck.

Chapter Thirty-one

As soon as Coletti heard that Abrams' bait to Steve and Paula had been taken, he made a phone call to Boston, and an hour later a car set off down the Mass Turnpike, heading for New Coventry. Driving the car was Rafael Borra, a distant relative of Vince's, and as Vince had proudly said, a computer whiz. The first time Rafael had got his name in the papers was at the age of fourteen, when he'd managed to hack his way into the computer of the Central Bank of Boston, but the trespass was discovered before he had time to open an account and transfer funds into it. Rafael learned a number of things from the experience: not to be greedy, not to tell anyone what he was doing, and most important, to seek and rely on his more experienced elders when considering a scam.

In fact, after an unsuccessful two years during which the banks, law enforcement, and private agencies were getting more sophisticated and tougher on this kind of crime, Rafael stopped planning his own scams altogether, and only did work for members of his family. That meant specialized intrusions into computer systems, sometimes for surveillance purposes, sometimes for retribution, occasionally for larceny. The operations were always carefully planned by somebody else, and so Rafael made no more appearances in the headlines or in court.

He did very well by accepting the limitations of the system; he earned much respect from the family for the brainy kind of work he did, and made enough money to have a nice apartment, a year-old Pontiac Grand Am, and give his various girlfriends an occasional major good time. Rafael was a good-looking young man, with long blond hair, a single gold earring, and a confident and aggressive attitude blended with physical gentleness. Women raved about Rafael, lost sleep over him, but after a few narrow escapes he had learned how to dance around the altar without actually going up to it. For some reason that nobody understood, not even Rafael, this evasiveness rarely lost him any of his admirers.

As a result of the change in his M.O., Rafael Borra's name showed up in the Boston City Police stats as one of the small number of young offenders who had no arrests for over four years, and his former probation officer took a modest pride in Rafael's rescue from the world of crime.

Rafael didn't know anything about the job that Vince wanted him to do in New Coventry, except that it was to get into a scientific computer whose access code they already possessed. Rafael wondered why Vince or any of his people couldn't do it themselves, but he'd found a strange inability, in his family and in everyone else over the age of thirty-five or forty, to do the simplest computer procedures beyond employing the ready-made spreadsheets and word-processing programs they used in their everyday business.

Over the years Rafael had assembled a toolbox like no other. Made of high-impact plastic and lined with thick foam rubber, it contained a high-speed modem of advanced design which also included a custom-made piece of electronic wizardry that obliterated the usual identifying signal sent through the wires every time a phone was used to dial a number. That signal allowed the telephone company or others to trace the call, and had been his undoing the time he infiltrated the Central Bank of Boston's computer.

In his toolbox Rafael also had a microammeter with an audio output for locating the faintest of electronic signals, a specially altered laptop computer with a gigantic memory of nine hundred and sixty megabytes, and all the hardware and software needed to download even the most complex and sophisticated programs and data bases. A stack of three and a half inch discs, held together with a rubber band, contained a set of sophisticated statistic-based programs that could input an incredible number of variables when code breaking was part of the job, although when the user was employing the latest encryption techniques, none of his programs stood a chance.

Rafael's answer to that kind of situation lay in the top left-hand corner of his toolbox. It was a miniature video camera which could be hand-held but also had various jointed mounting attachments, a short collapsible tripod, and a remote radio controller that could not only switch the camera on and off, but move it silently in any direction, and vary the focus and zoom. Packed snugly in the toolbox next to the video camera was a high-speed Leica with a special shutter and optics, including an eighteen-inch telephoto lens, and nestled below that was a portable printer/copier with a small supply of paper. He rarely needed that, since usually there was plenty of paper available on site. Completing the inventory was a shovel-shaped hand-held scanner, and last, as a protection against surprises, a pressurized canister of formic acid, the material that makes ant bites so painful and which, when squirted in concentrated form into the face and eyes of an intruder, causes intolerable pain and totally immobilizes the victim.

From time to time Rafael had added minor items to this inventory, such as a complete set of interface adaptors and a system for getting inside CD-ROM programs, and he felt confident that he could extract just about any information that any state-of-the-art computer contained.

Rafael sang along with the radio rock group until the station faded a few miles south of Route 128, and he made the rest of the trip in silence. It took him just over three hours to drive to New Coventry, and another twenty minutes to find the address that Mike Petras had given him.

Vince had thought that getting Rafael past the security guards might present a problem, but it was solved by Myra. She warned the security office that a technician was coming to work on her computer, and when he presented himself at the front door, she came down to get him, and had them issue him a temporary ID. Myra wasn't concerned about secrecy, because she'd been assured that no one would be able to detect that the computer had been broken into.

So at six-thirty, with Paula safely out of the way, Rafael followed Myra along the curving corridor toward the lab, carrying his heavy suitcase and watching her wobbly, both-arms-extended waddle with hypnotized interest.

Myra opened the door, switched on the lights, closed and locked the door again, and showed Rafael the computer. She was interested to find out how he would access the data; although she had a copy of the code in her pocket, she didn't know how to use it.

Myra and Rafael didn't get along too well at first.

"I need another table," he said. "That one." He pointed at a plain square metal table at the far end of the room. It bore a coffee machine, a stack of Styrofoam cups, and a box with sugar and milk substitute.

"Get it yourself," said Myra, who would have got it for him if he'd been more polite.

He got it himself, but accidentally dropped the glass

coffee jug on the floor, where it broke. Rafael had a short temper, and in any case had no patience with people like her.

He put the table next to the computer and the printer, and installed his equipment on it. Myra hung around behind him, watching.

"Get the fuck out of here," he said to her in a pleasant enough tone of voice. "I don't like people watching me work."

Furious, Myra retreated to Paula's little office and watched him from there. Why didn't anybody treat her with consideration or politeness, or even just like a human being? And she'd taken a liking to him, with his long blond hair and muscles and everything. She knew that with most people, when they liked a person, that person usually liked them back, but it never seemed to work for her. Myra had been fat long enough so she already knew the answer, but she was honest enough to admit that things hadn't been much better when she was thinner.

Rafael looked up. "Where's the code?"

Myra took the envelope out of her pocket, heaved herself to her feet, and walked toward him. She took the sheet of paper out and dropped it on the computer keyboard, and without so much as a glance at him, she went back to Paula's office and sat down again.

Rafael wrinkled his nose for a second, then got on with it. For ten minutes there was no sound except for occasional bursts of clicking as Rafael typed a set of instructions on the keyboard, usually followed by a single beep from the computer.

Watching him carefully, Myra noticed that his hand and head movements were changing in a subtle way. His smooth and confident actions were getting jerky and fast, and there was a feeling of tension and annoyance that spread right over into the office. She could see that things weren't going the way he'd expected them to, and she felt glad, because he was such a pig and deserved it.

Rafael suddenly got up from his chair and came toward her, holding the piece of paper in his hand. Myra watched his expression and felt a tingling, anticipatory fear that he was going to hit her.

"What the fuck is this?" he asked quietly, pushing the paper in her face. "This isn't the code that's in use now. Somebody changed it yesterday evening. There's a date and time stamp. Eight twenty-three p.m. Where's the new code?"

Staring at his face a few inches from hers, and too frightened to say anything, Myra shook her head. She didn't know what the new code was, but she did know that Paula had been working on the computer when she left the evening before.

Rafael stood back and looked at her with disgust. "You stinking fat cunt," he said, then went back to the computer.

Ten minutes later, Rafael had already put most of his equipment away in the padded case, and had taken out the video camera and the mounting bars with their joints and clamps. He looked around the ceiling for several minutes, spending most of his time in the part of the room in front of the computer. He took a chair and checked out different locations, then finally found a place that seemed right, about six feet behind and to the left side of the computer. He raised the white ceiling panel and found what he needed among the wires, conduits, and lighting fixtures above. It was an eighteen-inch black metal support strut, holding the framework of the hanging false ceiling to the concrete slabs above.

"Pass me up those mounting units, please," he said in a conciliatory voice, and Myra hurried over to help him. "Yeah, all three."

Myra picked up the black and chrome metal tubes with their jointed ends and passed them up to him. Most of Rafael's head was inside the false ceiling, and his voice was muffled by the sound-absorbing panels.

It took him only five minutes to cut a four-inch diameter round hole in the panel he'd removed, and cover it with a piece of transparent plastic. Then he mounted the video camera so that its lens was almost but not quite touching the plastic film when the panel was back in position. Rafael found an electric socket somewhere in at the back of the false ceiling, and running an orange-colored extension cord up to where he was working, plugged the camera in. From where Myra was standing, with the panel in position, neither the camera nor any of its attachments were visible.

"Ever heard of shoulder surfing?" he asked.

Myra shook her head, but she was now feeling much better about Rafael. He'd actually spoken to her, and in an almost kind tone of voice.

"That's what this is, sort of," he said. He smiled at her. "When you need an access code, or something like that, you photograph the operator while he's at the keyboard starting up the program and inputting the code. You usually do it from outside, from somewhere that looks down on the office or lab through a window, with somebody holding a minicam on his shoulder. This, what we're doing here, is a bit more sophisticated. That's a high-resolution cam up there"—he pointed at the ceiling. "It can see the screen and the keyboard, so you can film everything the operator's doing, the keys they're pressing. The data's digitized and transmitted out to a receiver that's up to two hundred yards away, then reconverted onto tape and then onto a screen. When you analyze the pictures, then you have the code right in front of you."

"That's brilliant," Myra managed to say. "But where would you put the receiver?"

"In a car," said Rafael. "Out in the street. Now we're going to test the system. Sit down at the keyboard and be ready to go through the start-up procedure. I'll tell you when to start."

While Myra was getting herself positioned, Rafael attached the radio-controller with a cable to a miniature videotape deck which in turn was joined by a larger cable to his laptop computer. He opened the laptop, tiny lights flickered, a subdued whirring lasting a couple of seconds came from inside it, then the LCD screen flickered on.

"Start," said Rafael.

As Myra's fingers touched the keys and the monitor screen lit up, Rafael worked the focusing and zoom controls until the monitor and the keyboard completely filled the screen. After a few adjustments Rafael switched his equipment off. "Everything's working just right," he said. "You can shut down now."

Rafael was much more cheerful now that things seemed to be under control. "Hey, thanks," he said to Myra, quickly packing all his stuff back into the case. "You were a great help. By the way, what's your name?"

"Myra," she said, blinking rapidly and wondering why he couldn't have read it off her name tag.

"One thing, Myra," he said as he was leaving. "Tomorrow, when your doc lady is here working in the lab, don't look up at the ceiling, okay? Nobody notices what's up there unless somebody draws their attention to it."

Myra sat in the chair for a few moments, wondering why Paula had decided to change the computer access code, and why now. Did she suspect that Myra was giving out information about her? Was there any conceivable way that she could know that she was spying for Abrams?

Feeling sure that if she'd known anything, Paula would

have confronted her, Myra got up, switched off the lights, and locked the door after her. She thought about Rafael, and how beautiful he looked. Suddenly she felt hungry. It wasn't the pleasant, anticipatory hunger of a normal appetite, but an imperative, ravenous, utterly self-engrossed, famished-wolf feeling. At times like this Myra felt that she would kill anyone who got between her and her food. And not just kill, but hack and stab and smash until she was exhausted. As soon as she left the building, she headed for the corner of Elm and Stanford, where a new Burger King had just opened.

Chapter Thirty-two

After the concert Paula and Steve went back to his apartment, and although it was late, they decided it would be more fun to make a pizza rather than send out.

"By the time we got Domino's to deliver," explained Steve, "we'll have already made ours, and it'll be in the oven cooking. Not only that, but it'll taste *incomparably* better." He stressed the word *incomparably* and said it with an exaggerated Italian accent, and Paula laughed.

Steve was a good cook, as she knew from past experience, and he also liked to show off a bit. Paula had never made pizza before, and wanted to learn the technique.

"It's easy," said Steve. "You open the bag, empty out the floury mix into a bowl . . ."

Paula stood behind him and watched while he did it, trying to keep her hands off him and let him work.

"We've pre-heated the oven to 425 degrees," he went on. "Then you take half a cup of hot water, add it to the flour, and stir it up with a fork for a few minutes."

Steve, following his own instructions, beat the mixture furiously until he finished up with a sticky ball of dough. "Then you put a bit of olive oil over the dough, like this, covering the entire surface. Then you put a plate or something over the top and put it in a warm place for five minutes. I like to put it in hot water." He put a black rubber plug in the sink's drain hole, put the covered bowl in, and ran hot water until it came high enough to make the bowl start to float.

"What can I do?" asked Paula, standing very close behind Steve. Although she enjoyed standing there, feeling the muscles of his body moving against her, her fingers were itching to do something. She enjoyed cooking too, and wasn't used to being cooked for.

"Okay . . . You can slice the pepperoni, please, cut up the red pepper, open the can of mushrooms, and grate the cheese. You like olives? Good, there's a jar already open. There's two kinds of cheese, Romano and Swiss. Equal amounts of each."

"Yes, sir."

"Do you really have to move, Paula? Can't you do it standing right there?"

"No, sorry. I might get carried away, slicing that pepperoni."

Five minutes later, Steve took the ball of warm, raised dough, and stretched it all over the rectangular pan, turning it up at the edges. Then Paula poured the red pizza sauce, spread it out with the back of a soup spoon, then added the Parmesan that had come in the packet, followed by sliced pepperoni, mushrooms, cut-up olives, red pepper slices, and finally distributed the Romano and Swiss cheese over the top.

"Looks good enough to eat," said Paula, watching him put it in the oven.

"Twenty minutes max," said Steve, looking at the clock. "Let's go watch the news while it cooks."

They caught the end of the newscast, which showed some footage on a mini-epidemic of plague in northern Arizona, then a brief piece about a new museum that had been opened in honor of Richard Jordan Gatling, who had invented numerous agricultural devices and of course the famous Gatling gun. This gun, the announcer told them, standing next to the weapon and patting the top of the barrel, had been manufactured continuously from its invention in 1861 until 1911, and had seen service in the Civil War. There were close-ups, and the curator demonstrated the hand crank that spun the multiple barrels around.

Steve was about to change the channel when he saw Paula's expression. Utterly engrossed, her mouth slightly open, she was staring at the screen as if it held the answer to all her prayers.

"My God," she whispered. "That's it! That's really it!"

The program changed and Steve turned the set off, watching her with astonishment, aware that something dramatic was going on inside her head. Wisely he said nothing.

Suddenly Paula jumped up. Her voice was tight with excitement. "Steve, I think I know how we're going to deliver these enzymes. We have to make a kind of Gatling gun attachment to your arterioscope, with each barrel containing one specific enzyme. Then each one can be injected in the correct order without mixing with the others. Steve, do you realize what's just happened?"

Paula was dancing with delight. Steve didn't have the faintest idea of what she was talking about, so she filled him in quickly. "Can you do it?" she asked. "Could you make something like that? Do you think it could possibly work?"

Caught up in her excitement, Steve grabbed a pencil and paper and started to sketch out the possibilities. "One of the problems is size," he told her. "In a really thin tube there's a lot of resistance to flow. . . ." Steve took a calculator from his worktable and spent several minutes calculating flow rates, viscosities, Reynolds numbers, all things that Paula had little or no knowledge about.

"I think we can do it," he said finally. "It's really an engineering problem, but these numbers say it's at least theoretically possible."

Delighted beyond words, Paula hugged him, and at that moment an odor of burning and a curl of smoke came around the door from the kitchen.

"We're going out," said Paula, after they had examined the charred remains of the pizza. "I'm sure we can find some place that's still open. And it's my treat."

The next day, Steve woke up early, his head full of Paula's "Gatling concept" of pumping the enzymes through the arterioscope, one at a time, giving them no chance to mix and inactivate one another. The idea had totally caught his imagination, and while he shaved, his mind was already working on the various engineering and mechanical problems that would have to be solved before the Gatling concept could become a reality.

Rather than using a whole bunch of fine plastic tubes, he thought, it would be better to take a block of Lucite and drill a dozen tiny channels in it, in the shape of a ring; the size could be better controlled, and the channels wouldn't expand under pressure. Each little cavity would then be filled with the enzyme solution, and the whole thing could then be rotated under computer control, applying pressure sequentially to pump each solution out into the scope. Then there was the problem of how to get the enzyme solution to pass through a thread-thin tube in the scope.

His mind still buzzing with these questions and their possible answers, Steve put on a track suit and headed for the racquetball court. Paula's game was improving, and she'd beaten him twice in the past couple of weeks.

After a drawn game, they went back to the hospital together and he headed for the lab. Paula had told him about her research windfall from Maurice Bennett's old stockbroker patient, and that meant money would be available to pay for the design engineering, machining, and all the other materials and expertise he would need. Even so, he knew it would take time and a lot of effort before they had a working prototype in their hands. As soon as his other lab work was finished, Steve made some phone calls and went back to his design work on the Gatling device.

He calculated the required size of the channels in the Lucite block, and found that even the finest available steel drill would be too bulky to do the job. If he reduced the length of the block, then he could use a wider channel, he found, but even then the actual making of the channels would present a huge technical problem. Steve scratched his head, trying to figure a feasible method. He called a local firm that specialized in plastic moldings, thinking that the channels could be molded into the block, but the man laughed when Steve gave him the dimensions.

"*Micrometers?*" the engineer on the other end said incredulously. "No, sir, we can't handle little tiny measurements like that."

It wasn't until lunchtime, and Steve was working on something else, when it came to him. Lasers. Laser beams could cut or drill most materials to any size with wonderful accuracy. Another few phone calls and Steve found a guy who said he could do it, and it wouldn't even cost that much.

Chapter Thirty-three

Rafael Borra spent a cramped and uncomfortable day in his car. It had dark windows that prevented anyone looking in, but these windows also seemed to absorb heat, and it was an unseasonably hot day outside, which made it almost unbearable inside. The passenger-side seat folded forward and gave him access to the back, where the monitoring equipment was, but even then, every so often his right leg would cramp up and it was agony for a few moments while he tried to stretch in the restricted space.

Myra had told him that Paula sometimes came in to the lab as early as seven o'clock, so Rafael was there in the public parking lot at six, testing and checking his equipment. Everything worked perfectly, as usual, and he settled down to wait. Although he had two fully charged heavy-duty industrial batteries in the trunk, hooked up to a DC/AC converter, the monitoring and control equipment took a whole lot of power. About noon he turned the black-and-white monitor down to minimum brightness to cut down on the power drain, but even so, by four in the afternoon, Rafael was getting anxious. The woman hadn't shown up in the lab, or at least hadn't sat down at the computer. He'd backed off several times with the camera, but it had a relatively narrow angle for high definition, and he could never be sure whether or not she was in the lab. He saw the screen-filling Myra several

times; a couple of times she waved up at the camera, and
he'd waved a single-digit salute back at her, although of
course she couldn't see it.

By five o'clock, the monitor was dimming, and he'd
stopped using the radio controls for the camera. At a few
minutes past five, he jumped up from his reclining position in the backseat and turned up the brightness to max.
Sure enough, it was the Cairns woman, in a white coat,
and she sat down on the console. Rafael turned the knob
that controlled the zoom to bring the keyboard and her
monitor to fill the screen. Nothing happened. Rafael, already hot, felt sweat suddenly pour down his face and
back. Furiously he twisted the knob back and forth, but
still nothing happened. Then, just as Paula started to
touch the keys, his monitor slowly faded away as it drew
the last drops of current from the dying batteries.

Rafael slammed the hand-held controller to the floor of
the car. Normally he would have rather cut his wrists than
damage his precious equipment.

"Fuck!" he shouted at the top of his voice inside the
closed car. "Double fuck!"

Paula spent only a couple of hours in the lab that evening, and as she drove home, she thought about the problems that were coming in on her from all sides. Maurice's
replacement as department chairman by Cliff Abrams had
been a disaster for her, and since he was away, she
couldn't get his advice about how to handle Abrams' upcoming inquiry. Her stomach tightened painfully when
her thoughts turned to Professor Macklerod and his investigation. A public hearing! She knew what that would do
to her reputation as a researcher; right or wrong, guilty or
not, her research papers would be returned unpublished
by the scientific journals, and there would be no more in-
vitations to talk at meetings or to be on panel discussions.

In her frustration Paula slammed both fists on the steering wheel. The worst of it was that she had been wrong in allowing the paper to be published, and the fact that her boss, Bob Zimmerman, had put pressure on her to send it in didn't reduce her responsibility.

It had been raining again, intermittently but heavily, and the sky was as gray as her spirit when she pulled into the parking area opposite her apartment building. The driver's-side door still wasn't closing properly, even though it had been repaired, and the thought that she would soon have to send her beloved MGB into honorable retirement really upset her, but the engine was starting to burn oil, and replacement parts were expensive and hard to find. Also she didn't have much money, and after her rent was paid, there wasn't much left for monthly payments on another car.

Paula wasn't paying attention and stepped out of her car into a puddle, and said some words out loud that most people wouldn't have thought she even knew.

Still, things could be worse, she thought, balancing on the other foot and emptying water out of her shoe. She remembered a story her mother had told her about Mrs. Solomon who meets Mrs. Katz on the Grand Concourse. Mrs. Solomon unthinkingly asks Mrs. Katz how she is, and Mrs. Katz tells her about all the troubles she's having, headaches, an inflamed gallbladder, female problems, stomach trouble, hemorrhoids, arthritis, etc., etc. Finally Mrs. Solomon cuts her off with "I'm sorry to hear all that, Mrs. Katz, but as long as you've got your health . . ." For some reason that story had always made Paula laugh, although when she told it to others, they didn't always seem to appreciate the humor of it as much as she did.

Paula picked up her mail in the foyer, and started to open it in the elevator. The lights in the corridor on the fourth floor were out, and, annoyed, Paula felt her way in the gloom along to the sixth door on the right where she lived. She took the key out of her purse, and when she reached the door, reached around to find the keyhole. While she was doing this, she felt something cold and sticky, apparently attached to the door. Startled, unable to see, Paula jumped back and screamed. A couple of seconds later, the door opposite opened and lit up that part of the hallway. Other doors opened and people came out, concerned and fearful.

"What happened?" asked the tremulous old lady from the apartment opposite.

Speechless, Paula pointed at her door. A stick-on picture hook was attached to the top of the door, and hanging by the neck from a foot-long cord was a dead black and white cat. The creature had been disemboweled, its stiff gray entrails hanging out of its belly cavity, and it had been partially flayed, the skin hanging off each side of its thin red carcass.

The police seemed to take their time, although the police station was just around the corner; the old lady had dialed 911 and the dispatcher said it wasn't an emergency because nobody'd been killed or was in serious danger. Finally two large cops in dark blue uniforms arrived and advanced down the corridor, both with the irritatingly slow, rolling swaggers that seemed inseparable from guns and nightsticks, lighting up the dark corridor with their flashlights.

When they saw what was the problem was, they took it seriously. One of them asked her for a bag to put the cat in, and the old lady dived back into her apartment and came out holding two Safeway bags out at them. The senior cop took a pair of rubber gloves from an inside pocket, gently picked up the cord and dropped the remains of the cat in one of the bags. It leaked, so he put the first bag in the second bag, and it stopped dripping.

The policemen insisted on opening Paula's apartment door themselves, and they both went in, telling Paula to stay outside. The old lady retreated inside her apartment, but left the door open enough to see what was going on, and kept up a monotonous mumbling meanwhile. *She* wouldn't have got that kind of kid-glove treatment from the police, she said. Oh no, but then of course she wasn't young and beautiful or a *doctor*, either.

"We don't think he got inside your apartment, ma'am," said the younger of the two cops as they came back to the door.

"How do you know it's a 'he'?" asked Paula sharply.

The two cops glanced at each other. They knew that this kind of thing always shattered women's nerves.

"Experience, ma'am," said the crew-cut older cop. He had some kind of bronze citation or medal for bravery over the left upper pocket of his uniform. "It's always men that do this kind of thing. Always."

Thinking of the movie *Fatal Attraction*, Paula said nothing. She went into the kitchen, took some paper towels from under the sink, and mopped up the fluid on the door and where it had dripped down onto the floor.

For the next half hour, the two cops quizzed her about her present and past boyfriends, ex-lovers, men who might be jealous of her. Most of her relationships had ended more or less amicably, and none of the men she'd known well lived in New Coventry or anywhere near. She told them about Steve, explaining that her relationship with him was just fine. Seth's name had occurred to her immediately, of course, but she kept him for last. Her instincts told her he was capable of it, but she didn't want to accuse anyone without proof. They wrote down everything she said without comment.

"Maybe the guy had the wrong address," suggested the younger cop.

"Call us if anything like that happens again," said the other. "The NCPD has a new stalking unit. Just started. Here, this is their number." He laboriously wrote out a number on a piece of paper that Paula gave him. "Keep your eyes open for anybody who might be following you," he went on in a monotone, as if he'd learned these instructions by rote. "Make sure you lock all the doors and windows, whether you're at home or not. Don't open the front door to anyone unless you know the person, and it's somebody you can absolutely trust."

"Like your mother," said the young cop.

"You have a phone with automatic dial?" went on the older one.

"Ten numbers," said Paula. To her annoyance, she found that her whole body was shaking.

"Reprogram it so that when you press 1, it dials 911, okay?"

"Yes. Thanks, that's a good idea, I'll do it. Would you guys like a cup of coffee?"

"No thanks, ma'am, I guess we're on our way."

Something occurred to Paula as they were leaving. "Did you notice that cat's fur?" she asked. "It was all matted and wet. It's raining outside right now. Do you think it had just been killed?"

"No, ma'am," said the crew-cut cop. "That cat had been in a freezer."

"We'll keep an eye on this place," said the younger one. "We're going off duty soon, but we'll tell the next unit to check every hour or so."

As soon as they had gone, Paula called Steve. "I'm coming over right now," she said. "And I'm spending the night." She hung up before he had time to ask any questions.

She packed a few essentials in an overnight bag, locked up, and left. The lights were still out in the corridor, and she was a wreck by the time she got down to the parking lot.

Her car was where she'd left it, and she got in and drove off. She hadn't gone half a mile before she realized that there had been a big, dark-colored BMW parked in the far corner of the lot. She shrugged, thinking she was really getting paranoid. In New Coventry there were BMWs all over the place.

Steve was watching from the bedroom window of his second-floor apartment, and ran down to meet her when he saw the MGB pull into the parking lot. He helped her out of the car. She was shaking.

"Don't say a word," he said, picking her bag off the seat and taking her arm. He could feel her trembling. As soon as they were in his apartment, he got her a whiskey sour, her favorite drink; then when she sat down and told him what had happened, he got her another one.

"Who could have done that?" he asked. She shook her head and didn't reply. Steve held her until she stopped shaking, then helped her undress and tucked her into bed. He was about to go back to his study, but she didn't want to be alone. He sat on the bed, held her hand, and talked to her, then got undressed too, climbed into bed, and held her until she fell asleep.

Several times during the night, Paula woke up, thinking there was someone in the apartment. Rigid with fear, she hung onto Steve, who was sleeping the sleep of the just and resisted her panicky desire to wake him. The night seemed to last forever, and she got up about six, dressed, and tiptoed out. It was daylight, and Paula felt quite safe going back to her apartment. There were still some smudges on the door, and she scrubbed it until the paint shone. She made herself a cup of coffee and a slice of toast with marmalade, then had a shower, dressed, and went off to work.

There were no BMWs in the parking area, but then at least half the spaces were now empty.

The sound of the front door closing woke Steve, and he sat up, immediately awake. The recollection of the evening before, of Paula's presence in his bed, came back to him in a rush, and he wondered why she'd left him without even saying goodbye.

While he brushed his teeth and shaved, he thought about the cat left on the door of her apartment, and felt a rising anger at whoever could have done that gruesome act. It certainly didn't sound like a prank, but of course, as the policeman had thought, it could be a case of the wrong address. Meanwhile there wasn't much he could do except give Paula as much support as he could.

That morning, the Lucite disc was delivered complete with its laser-made channels, and Steve went back to his work on the modifications to his arterioscope with renewed vigor. It was coming together nicely, and unless a major problem surfaced, he would soon have a functioning instrument. Steve had been through the excitement of making new equipment before, and the memory of his first clinical trial haunted him. But his enthusiasm was building again, and he knew the stakes were dizzingly high. If the system lived up to even a tenth of what he and Paula thought it was capable of, it could eventually save hundreds, maybe thousands of lives. And once the entire system was perfected, he would license the manufacturing rights to Olympus or one of the other big instrument makers, run seminars to train surgeons in the use of his scope, and that would be the start of a whole new medical technology.

All this time, at the back of this head he was thinking

and worrying about Paula. He called her at the hospital to make sure she was all right.

"Thanks, Steve," she answered in a subdued tone. "I'm really glad you called. Everything's okay."

Steve went back to work. The next logical development would be a method of *preventing* the formation of blood clots inside the body, and he knew that the potential for that was equally vast. An oral preparation would have to be devised, one that people could take as easily as Tylenol. Figuring out a way of administering the enzymes orally would not be easy, but with the esoteric micropackaging systems that were already available, it would happen, for sure. It's easier to find a mailman than it is to write the letter, he thought happily. And he and Paula between them were surely writing one hell of a letter. An hour later, Steve was so engrossed that he jumped when the phone rang. It was Bill Wilson, his old boss at L.A. General.

"I've been hearing about that paper you presented at the Surgical Association, Steve," he said. "Congratulations. Our medical technology people are still talking about it. Aside from that, I wanted you to know that we have a job opening here that you might be interested in. It's a bio-technology lab we're opening as soon as we have somebody to run it."

"Well, thanks for thinking of me, Dr. Wilson," replied Steve, thinking about Paula across the street in the hospital, and about how his attitude had changed since getting to know her. "But I'm actually very happy right here in New Coventry."

"Really?" Wilson sounded surprised. "Anyway, we won't be making that appointment for another six weeks or so, so if you change your mind, call me."

Even though Steve didn't want the job, the call cheered him considerably. All that depressing stuff they'd told him only a few months before, that in the medical field, once they get you down, you never could get up again, was apparently not so.

He went back to his scope, now lying dismantled in a dust-free chamber, isolated from the outer world by a double barrier of Plexiglas. The chamber had come with the standard rubber gloves for manipulating materials inside it, but these were too thick for the kind of work that Steve had to do, so he'd replaced them with surgical latex gloves.

The biggest problem he had to solve was that there simply wasn't room within the slender instrument for the additional tube needed to transmit the enzyme solutions, although it wasn't much thicker than a toothbrush bristle. After many frustrating trials and errors, Steve reduced the number of fiberoptic filaments by a third, and compensated for that by increasing the light input. It worked. It wasn't perfect, and the light source overheated after a few minutes of activation, but it worked. Using a tiny hand-held syringe as an injector, he could see minute drops of the special low-viscosity test fluid appear at the tip of the probe. He then carefully measured the time/volume ratio so that he could set the tiny pump to the correct output, then flushed and dried the inside of the tube by blowing pure oxygen through it.

Back with the Gatling injection system, lying in pieces on another bench, he set up the pressure hose, lubricated the surfaces with a graphite-based lubricant developed for NASA, and started to check that the holes matched exactly, using an optical interferometer he'd designed himself a couple of years before. By the time he'd finished working, it was two o'clock in the morning, he hadn't eaten, and was exhausted.

He called Paula at home to tell her that all systems

were go, and he was ready for final testing with the enzyme carrier fluids.

Paula, awake instantly, was ecstatic. "Steve, you're just
wonderful. And you have a great sense of timing. Just tonight we finished the compatibility studies, and they're
'go' too, so we're all set."

Steve put down the phone, and, too tired to go home,
rolled up a bunch of towels to make a pillow, and lay
down fully dressed on the orange plastic couch at the far
end of the main lab, where the techs usually sat when
they having their coffee breaks, and fell asleep instantly.

Paula was so excited that she didn't go back to sleep for
an hour, and even then she was so restless that she finally
got up at five-thirty, put on a sweatsuit, and ran around
the block, holding a small black cylinder of Mace in her
right hand. The earliest lines of pink were appearing over
the horizon, the trees were green and still, and the beauty
and the quiet of the scene made her glad again that she
was living here. But she hadn't forgotten about the cat,
and there was an alertness, an underlying fear that made
every tree a place for an assailant to hide behind, every
bush a cover for a lurking strangler. The shock from seeing that dreadful disemboweled cat had passed, but it had
been replaced by a hard, unforgiving anger, mostly because she had lost her peace of mind, the peace she
thought she'd found again in New Coventry after those
unpeaceful years in New York City.

Although it was still early, Paula was about to leave for
work when the phone rang. It was a Lieutenant Olive
McKenzie, who introduced herself as the head of the
NCPD's new stalking unit and asked if she could come
over and talk about the recent incident with the cat. She
had an educated voice with a faint accent which Paula
thought was either Australian or from New Zealand. As

soon as possible, said Olive, because she felt the matter was urgent.

"Come on over now," said Paula.

"I'm at the station just around the corner from you," said Olive. "I'll be there in a couple of minutes."

By the time she arrived, Paula had put on a fresh pot of coffee.

"I hope this isn't too early," said Olive, and Paula grinned at her.

"I was on my way to work," she said. "Would you like some coffee?"

"Yes, please. The stuff the boys make at the station house is really poisonous."

Olive was very neatly dressed in a dark blue uniform, pretty in an austere way, with hardly any makeup. Her blond hair was tied up in a bun at the back of her head. There was an air of competence about her, and the two women took to each other immediately.

"The officers who answered your nine-eleven turned in their report to us," she said. "They were both very concerned about the incident."

The coffee machine perked.

"How do you like it?" asked Paula.

"Black, please. No sugar, no milk." Paula noticed that Olive was unobtrusively taking in everything she could see of the apartment—windows, doors, where the light switches were.

"This is great," said Olive appreciatively, tasting the coffee. "You know, you even look a bit like that Taster's Choice lady, except with more class."

Paula was about to ask her why she had come, but Olive got there first. "We're worried about the implications of that cat," she said, leaning back against a white counter. "My team feels that it's important to find out who did it, because that isn't going to be the end of it. Something's going to happen again, and we want to abort it, or at worst, be prepared for it."

"What implications?" asked Paula.

"That cat was strangled before it was cut up, partly skinned, and had its insides pulled out," said Olive. "We're all concerned that this is some kind of a warning, a dry run, so to speak."

Paula put her hand up to her mouth. "Are you saying that he or she is planning to do the same thing to me?"

"More or less. And it's a *he*. This has all the characteristics of a male crime."

"How can you tell?" asked Paula curiously.

"Strangling a cat. Cutting it open. Skinning it. This is a pure male aggression-substitution pattern, and the FBI forensic people at Quantico I talked to yesterday agreed. They also agreed that he was thinking about you while he was knocking off that cat."

Paula exhaled a long breath; she didn't know whether Olive's matter-of-fact approach was reassuring or scary. "Okay," she said, "let's get started."

They went quickly through the possibilities, again finishing up with Seth.

"How well do you know him?" asked Olive.

Paula told her, including their dinner together, their second date, and what had happened outside her apartment building.

Olive didn't say anything for a moment. "We know about him," she said after the pause. "Seth Millway. Not officially, because he's never been charged, and that's because nobody's ever pressed charges against him. But we know that at least two women have been hospitalized after encounters with him, one in Hartford, one here."

"That must have cost him, to pay them off," said Paula, thinking that on her two dates with him she'd had narrower escapes than she realized.

"He has plenty," replied Olive. "At least he had at the time. The last one was about two years ago. Anyway, we don't know that he had anything to do with this cat thing. We worked up a profile, and again we got a lot of help on this from the FBI's data base. The perpetrator's a male, probably in his late twenties or thirties, very sexually oriented, high on testosterone—"

"How can you tell that?"

"Let me finish. He's also into symbols. The cat was a symbol. He's probably successful at his work, and certainly successful with women. For some reason you are unattainable to him and he can't stand it. He can't stand anything being out of his reach when he really wants it, and would rather destroy it than be forced to admit a failure. He's in love with you. . . ."

Paula felt cold hands crawling over her heart as she listened. It was Seth, without a doubt. He was the one person she knew who fitted this description.

They talked some more about him, and Olive felt there was a high probability that the perpetrator would return with more lethal things in mind that hanging a dead cat on the door. They also discussed various kinds of burglar alarms and other preventive measures.

"You know, Olive," said Paula, "I'm sure I knew all the time who it was. Why didn't I recognize it?"

"You used a perfectly normal defense mechanism. You didn't want to admit that anyone could hate you that much, because the normal reaction to that is 'What terrible thing did I do to make him feel that way?' And that would be valid if you were dealing with a normal person. But not for this Seth guy."

Olive went over an emergency system that Paula could use to get in touch with her, and suggested that she get a cellular phone for her car. "You never know when you might need it," she said. "Anyway, I'm surprised that, as a doctor, you don't have one already."

After Olive left, Paula sat down and thought about the situation, and a wave of pure anger came over her that Seth or anyone else could have the gall to intrude into her life and terrify her in this way. Okay, she thought, I can use psychology too. She delayed going to the hospital for almost an hour while she thought about Seth and tried to use what little she knew about him to figure out what his next step would be, and how best to deal with it.

Then, with a sinking heart, she went out to her car. Dr. Abrams' hearing was scheduled for eleven that morning.

Chapter Thirty-four

The university committee put together to investigate Paula's alleged research misdemeanors was carefully selected by Clifford Abrams, and consisted of Walt Eagleton and three other surgeons he felt certain would go along with him. Knowing that Maurice was away, Abrams called his office the day before the meeting to invite him to be on the committee, and was suitably distressed when Helen Katz told him Dr. Bennett would not be available.

Paula had thought about getting an attorney to represent her, but decided not to, partly out of stubbornness, partly because she felt she could defend herself as well as any hired gun, but mainly because she felt that a committee of her peers would surely understand what had happened. Steve, who had had some experience with this kind of committee, didn't agree, and urged her to get the best attorney she could find. She did call the American College of Surgeons headquarters in Chicago for advice, but was told rather briskly that they didn't interfere with local disciplinary problems and couldn't help her. Similarly, the legal counsel for the New Coventry Medical Society was overloaded with problems concerning late insurance payments to the society's members, and could not offer any advice. Her old boss in New York, Bob Zimmerman, was still abroad, and according to Helen

Katz, Maurice was in Europe also, so she prepared her case as best she could on her own.

The meeting was held in the surgical conference room, and Paula appeared with a file of papers under her arm, looking purposeful and grim. Abrams noted with satisfaction that she had come alone, and very courteously asked her to sit at the end of the table. As Paula sat down, she noticed that Geoffrey Susskind was sitting on Abrams' right side.

"What's he doing here?" she asked Abrams rather brusquely.

"He's here representing the university," replied Abrams. "And, to a certain extent, you as an employee. We want to be sure that we don't do anything to compromise your rights in any way, isn't that correct, Mr. Susskind?"

Susskind's heavy-lidded eyes drooped for a second, indicating his agreement. He didn't look at Paula, who figured he was still upset with her over the Millway business.

The proceedings started quickly enough. Abrams, at the head of the table, harrumphed for silence, then started to read a prepared statement. "Ten days ago," he said, "I received a phone call from Dr. Earl Macklerod, who, as you probably all know, is an internationally renowned senior surgeon from Baltimore. And that call . . ." Abrams paused for dramatic effect, "concerned Dr. Paula S. Cairns, from our department."

Abrams looked over his glasses at Paula, as if to make quite sure she was there. The whole tenor of his voice showed his dismay at that conversation, which had apparently thrown doubt on the integrity of the entire New Coventry Medical Center. It reminded Paula of the first time she'd ever seen Abrams, when he'd told her about the woman doctor who had disgraced the department.

"Dr. Macklerod told me that he had been requested by the Surgical Association to open an inquiry concerning

Dr. Cairns' previous research, because allegations of misrepresentation and fraud had been made."

Abrams shook his head sadly. "Obviously, we couldn't allow one of our own people to be investigated by an outside body without finding out the facts ourselves. So my first unhappy task as chairman of this department," went on Abrams, looking reproachfully at Paula, "has been to convene this committee."

Walt Eagleton, sitting on Abrams' left, with his hands flat together in an attitude of prayer, looked at the ceiling as if for divine guidance and nodded slowly. The others continued to look uncomfortable. Nobody looked at Paula. Susskind pursed his lips and wrote notes on a legal pad.

"Now, Dr. Cairns," said Abrams, "we're here as your colleagues simply to find the facts of this matter. This is not a disciplinary hearing, and you shouldn't feel threatened in any way. Now, please tell us what happened concerning your paper, entitled 'A simplified technique for measuring thrombolysins in banked blood,' which was published in June 1991 in the *Journal of Hematology*."

Paula explained. She told them about the new test she had developed, how although she didn't feel it was of major importance and might be of some use as an in-house technique, she'd discussed it with her boss, Dr. Bob Zimmerman. There was a big medical meeting coming up and he didn't have anything to present, so he told her to write it up for the journal. It was done in a hurry because of the rush for publication, and afterward she developed doubts about the reagents, and at her request tests were carried out by an independent lab. She knew she'd been in error, she told the committee, sincerely regretted it, and had subsequently written to the journal to modify the findings she had reported.

"Thank you, Dr. Cairns," said Abrams, "for your account of what happened. Now, I'm sure the committee members have some questions for you. I'd like to start off by asking one. Would you please give us the date of your retraction letter to the *Journal of Hematology*."

Paula told him.

"But that was just a few weeks ago," said Walt, sounding surprised. "How come you didn't write to them sooner? You had the information, didn't you?"

"Yes, I did," replied Paula. "But what with all the other work I was doing, it had simply slipped my mind."

"What happened to unslip it, Dr. Cairns?" Walt was still staring at the ceiling. "I mean, what persuaded you so suddenly to write to them? Did you get religion? Born again, maybe?"

"I discussed the matter with Dr. Bennett," replied Paula. "We agreed that such a letter was needed. To clear the air, I suppose."

"Good thinking, by Dr. Bennett." Walt turned abruptly to Abrams. "And where is our distinguished colleague? Wasn't he supposed to be on this committee?"

"Dr. Bennett was formally invited to be a member," replied Abrams. "Unfortunately, at this time he is on a leave of absence, and could not join us."

"Pity about that," murmured Walt. Slowly his gaze dropped until he was looking at Paula. "A good man, Dr. Bennett." He spoke as if Paula had already killed him.

"Let's get back to our discussion, please, gentlemen," said Abrams. "Dr. Cairns was telling us why she suddenly decided to confess her sins in a letter to the editor of that journal."

"Case of closing the stable door, wasn't it?" said Dr. Wesley Bishop, an elderly, semi-retired ENT doctor with thinning but immaculately coiffed white hair, who until then had sat quietly on Susskind's right.

"You could say that, yes, indeed, Wesley, well put," said Abrams in an ingratiating tone. "Now, Dr. Cairns . . ." He turned a page in the folder in front of him. "What do you consider is the responsibility of any researcher to the public, who in the final analysis is paying for the work that's being undertaken?"

Paula, realizing that this was a heavily loaded question, tried to sidestep it. "The researcher's responsibility is to do the very best he or she can," she replied. "But in research, as in every other human activity, errors can be made. They're not crimes, they're just mistakes, the kind that everyone makes from time to time, and hopefully the researcher is able to learn from them."

Susskind was writing furiously, and Paula wondered why they hadn't used a tape recorder. It then occurred to her that maybe she should have brought one for her own protection.

"Thank you, Dr. Cairns," said Abrams, one eye on Susskind. Abrams seemed to be waiting for him to catch up, and toyed with the file, turning pages, then turning them back. When Susskind put his pen down and leaned back, Abrams asked another question.

"Dr. Cairns," he said in an unctuous tone that showed how committed he was to give Paula every possible chance to exonerate herself. He glanced out of the corner of his eye at Walt Eagleton, and Paula wondered if Walt had suggested the question. "Dr. Cairns, would you care to tell us your thoughts about the importance of integrity in surgical and other researchers?"

Paula saw the direction in which Abrams was taking the inquiry, and she was getting angry. "Dr. Abrams," she replied in a crisp voice, "I thought I was here to answer questions about my early research, not about philosophy."

Abrams looked at her with well-simulated astonishment, then his expression hardened. "Dr. Cairns," he said, "I'm sorry that you don't feel able to cooperate with this committee. I believe we now have all the facts in this case, so we will now have a ten-minute recess while the committee deliberates on the questions before it. If you would kindly wait outside, Dr. Cairns, we'll call you back as soon as we have come to a conclusion."

Paula stood up and went out, closing the door after her, cursing silently and wishing that Maurice was there to advise her.

Exactly ten minutes later, the door opened, and Susskind motioned to her to come in.

"Please sit down, Dr. Cairns," said Abrams in a dignified tone. "It is my task to report to you the *informal* findings of this committee." He took a deep, audible breath. He wanted everyone there to know how unpleasant that task was for him. "This committee finds that you have been guilty of gross carelessness and negligence in the performance of your past research. It also finds that even when you became aware of the full extent of your carelessness and negligence, you cynically refused to correct it until forced to by the threat of imminent disclosure. Third, that you caused this error-ridden research to be published, without consideration for the responsibility that a scientific author has to the public, which has to rely on the integrity of the individual researcher."

His voice rose. "Dr. Cairns, I hope you are aware of the seriousness of these charges, and of the inevitable results of this investigation. We will have to report our findings to the dean, and certainly to Dr. Earl Macklerod, to assist him in his own investigations into this matter."

Paula looked up, trying to hide the panic that was tightening her chest, but she didn't say anything. She knew that her lips would tremble and her voice would crack, and if there was one thing she didn't want to happen, that was to look afraid or defeated in front of this bunch of assembled executioners.

"Inevitable results, I said," went on Abrams. "These are as follows. After presentation of this adverse report, it is our opinion that the university will decide to terminate your employment here. If that happens, the hospital will certainly rescind your staff privileges. The chances of your finding comparable employment will be nil. None of the public or private agencies will ever even consider you for a research grant. Your career as a researcher and probably as a surgeon will be over."

Paula clasped her hands tightly together, trying to keep them from shaking. A feeling of total unreality was spreading over her, as if she were watching these proceedings from somewhere high above, watching this woman being crucified.

Abrams watched her, judging his moment. "Now, Dr. Cairns," he said in an entirely different, almost affectionate tone, "my colleagues and I have discussed this most difficult situation, and we believe there is a way around it."

Abrams was fully aware of the irony of the situation, and remembered the similar discussion with Seth Millway and his group, when he had been on the receiving end of the ultimatum, and he restrained an urge to shriek with wild laughter.

"If you were to come and work under the umbrella of my laboratory," he said, "I believe that we could cancel out most of the difficulties I referred to. My lab is well established and, without any false modesty on my part, very highly regarded. With this level of backing and influence, I believe we could get you back in the mainstream of research—"

"Rehabilitated, so to speak," interrupted Walt, nodding in agreement.

"As you probably know," went on Abrams, "I have a fair amount of influence in this field, and I do believe that under these circumstances, when your work would be under our strict but helpful monitoring, the university could be made to see matters in a different light."

Abrams was watching Paula carefully, gauging her reaction. "So what do you say?" he asked.

"Can I have some time to consider this?" asked Paula in a quite composed voice, because she was suddenly feeling that the clouds had parted and sunlight was streaming into her life again.

"Regretfully, no," said Abrams, his voice almost a purr. "Due to the pressures that are being applied on us, we have to have an answer now."

"You haven't left me any option," said Paula, trying to look utterly defeated but thinking that now the Gatling project was completed and ready for clinical trial, even if she did join Abrams' lab, he wouldn't have the rights to her work. If she went along with him, he would obviously back off on his threats to pass on an adverse report to the university, and Paula felt that in the short term it would be a prudent thing for her to do.

"When do you want me to start? Do you want me to move to your lab?" she asked Abrams, thinking what a damn fool he was, making all this fuss for a poke that didn't even have a pig in it anymore.

Abrams had a triumphant smile on his round pink face. "Yes," he said. "I want you to move in at the end of the month. Dr. Charnley will be leaving us at that time, although he isn't aware of that yet. You can take the space he's occupying now."

"Okay. I'll do it. Whatever you say, Dr. Abrams."

But as Paula left the room, she realized that even

though this problem had been defused, there was no guarantee that Dr. Earl Macklerod's investigation would be stopped, and she had absolutely no idea what to do about that.

Chapter Thirty-five

"You think you got a good education at that business school up in Boston, don't you?" said Vince Coletti to Seth. They were sitting in the office Coletti had appropriated and were reviewing the policy changes Seth had pushed through his advisory committee.

"What d'you mean?" asked Seth, who was trying to visualize Paula's expression when she found the cat.

"You don't know shit about business, that's what I mean. Not about real business. Maybe you know about profit ratios, price/earning multipliers, and give a great lunch talk on business problems to the Rotary Club. That's not what I'm talking about."

Mike Petras, there as always, lit a cigarette, his eyes moving constantly from Vince to Seth and back.

"For instance, there's a whole important field in business that you don't know a goddamn thing about," went on Vince. "And that's personal injury, and I don't mean insurance."

"Not on my curriculum, as I recall," said Seth.

Vince shook his head at Seth's innocence. "Personal injury. You're just a new boy, but d'you think the biggies in the pharmaceutical business don't know about it? Son, personal injury's like a staple. You gotta have it."

"If you're suggesting that we start beating up our

competitors . . ." Seth grinned. "I'd like to remind you we're not in the garbage or trucking industries."

Vince sighed. In a way he was getting to like Seth, and knew that he didn't have quite as many scruples as he made out. And if Millway was to make the kind of profits his investment group was expecting, Seth would have to learn a few things about the real world.

"If you think it's just done in trucking and garbage," he said, grinning, "you're even more naïve than I thought. Personal injury's a technique, a way of dealing with people. It has to do with your image, and the image of your corporation. For instance, suppose your competitor wants to increase his market share, and drops his price on something you're both selling. *You* would play a game of golf with their CEO, tell him he's giving you a problem, threaten to do the same or more if he doesn't back down. Very nice, but it doesn't work. Whatever happens, you lose. If you're forced to drop your prices, your profit goes down the tube. If you have to increase your advertising to keep your market share, that hits your profits too."

"So what would you do?"

"I'll tell you what did happen in exactly that situation just a few months ago. The marketing chief of the company that dropped its prices suddenly disappeared. He'd told his wife he was taking a trip, but when he didn't call home, she got upset and called the head office."

Vince pulled out a cigar and lit it. "That's step one in the personal injury business," he went on. "The opposition has to know you're doing something about the problem, otherwise you can't expect them to respond. Anyway, nothing happened for two days; the CEO hung tough, kept his prices down. Then he got a present in the mail. It looked like a cigar"—Vince looked at the glowing end of his own cigar—"packed in one of those silvery metal cigar tubes. But when he opened it he found a finger, and he didn't have to be told who it was from or what to do about it. The prices went back up that same day. The marketing chief went home, a bit dazed but okay. He was a piano player, and they say that now he misses every tenth note. . . . But you see, that's real business, where everybody finishes up happy and nobody loses money. And the real advantage is that you only need to do that once. They never fuck with you again. Never."

"That happened in America?"

"If you call Cincinnati America. It was one of the Fortune 500's too."

"Okay," said Seth, beginning to see the possibilities. "But with this situation with Dr. Cairns and Dr. Bennett, you're talking about killing people. That seems, like, well, different from just fingers."

Coletti shook his head. "Matter of scale, that's all. It's the same people doing the same kind of work, they're just using different techniques and skills. You save that solution for certain extreme situations."

"What kind of situations?" Seth leaned forward, interested. He felt that his postgraduate education was just starting, and he had a lot to learn. He liked action, and this sounded a lot more interesting than committees. And more effective.

Vince moved in his chair and puffed hard on his cigar. "Like the Cairns woman, for instance. If she tells *anyone* her research secrets, your whole entire plan is blown, so you can't afford to keep her around. That's one. Another is if somebody betrays you. That's another thing you can't afford, because if they get away with it, *you're* dead."

Seth wasn't satisfied with that explanation. "What about their wives, kids, employers? Don't they kick up a fuss? And what do you do with the bodies? Don't the police or the FBI ever figure it out and track down the guys who did it?"

"First, we don't do it a lot. For obvious reasons." Vince's cigar had gone out, and he flipped it into the wastebasket before turning his attention back to Seth. "Now, if you had a needle you wanted to hide, where would you hide it?"

Seth shrugged. He didn't like rhetorical questions. "In a haystack, I suppose."

"Wrong." Vince's voice was loud, insistent, and Seth sat up a little straighter. Vince liked people to pay attention when he spoke to them. "With a metal detector or X rays the needle's found in no time. No, not a haystack. The intelligent place to hide it is in with a whole lot of other needles."

"So?"

Vince's voice took on the tone of a professor burdened with a slow learner. "What's the leading cause of death in this country for people under the age of sixty?"

"I dunno. Cancer?"

"Motor vehicle accidents. They cause about forty-five thousand deaths every year. That's over five every hour. And five times that number die a few weeks later or are left crippled for life. So if you want to kill somebody without anyone knowing, that's the smart way of doing it. No guns, knives, poisons, nothing detectable. And with a car it's easy. You can mess with an auto in ways you could never detect, like you can cut almost through a steering link, or put a new card in the computer that controls the steering or the brakes in new cars. Nobody'll ever know. The cars all look the same when they're smashed up, and anyway, nobody'd even think of it. Even if they did, by the time they've thought of it the next wreck victim's on the slab and his auto's been pulled into the pound. Life goes on. That's how it's done."

"So why are you telling me all this stuff?"

Vince shrugged. "Because, aside from your Dr. Cairns,

we have a couple of candidates, Dr. Bennett, and your old research chief, whatsisname, who turns out to be Bennett's informer."

"Connor? How did you find that out?"

"My people tell me Bennett's scheduling a national press and TV conference for the middle of next week," said Vince, ignoring Seth's question. "And we can assume Connor spilled his guts to him. What's he got on Millway that I don't know about?

"A lot." Seth started to sweat, thinking about it. "Details of a lot of financial transactions, including yours, some stuff about the employees' pension fund, an untaxed incentive system for docs who prescribe our drugs, things like that."

Vince hadn't moved, but there was no mistaking the anger emanating from him. "Where did Connor get all this info? How did he, as a research director, have access to that kind of financial stuff?"

"I know where he got some of it. Connor had a friend in the accounts department who's been collecting the info and giving it to him. She's been fired already."

"Yeah, well, Mike here followed Connor. He met Bennett in a McDonald's on I-95, and gave him a briefcase full of papers. If we'd known what was in that briefcase, Bennett would never have made it home."

Coletti reached for the phone, and while he was dialing a long-distance number with a 617 prefix, he said, "My guys already know all they need to about Cairns, but they'll want a lot of info on Bennett and Connor, so be back here in two hours, okay? We can take care of these two business problems for you, and there'll be no extra charge."

Seth got up and left without saying anything more, but he wasn't happy about Coletti's plans for Paula. He already had his own plans for her.

Chapter Thirty-six

When Maurice returned to New Coventry after his leave, he went up to Paula's lab. She was there, and so happy to see him she would have hugged him but didn't because Myra was there. Maurice was looking very fit and altogether seemed in very good shape. He nodded to Myra, who was repeating the final set of compatibility experiments, and sat on the corner of the bench to talk to Paula.

Maurice's work on the pharmaceutical industry was close to completion, he told Paula, and it had turned even more explosive than he'd thought. He'd spent two days in Basel, Switzerland, the European capital of the industry, and had also been able to get some very interesting information right here in New Coventry. He didn't mention Connor.

"Now that I'm back," he said, "we should schedule my surgery. You know, I think that aneurysm started a couple of years ago, when I was kicked in the back by a horse once when I was out riding in New Mexico, near Albuquerque."

"You know Albuquerque?" asked Paula, surprised. "I didn't know that. Did you live there?"

"Just on vacation," smiled Maurice.

Paula took her appointment book out of her pocket. "Let's set a date for your surgery."

"Let's see, I'm giving that press and media conference a week from today, up in Hartford. The governor's going to be there"—Maurice laughed—"only because he's having some argument with the governor of New Jersey, where most of the American pharmaceutical companies are based. Anyway, I'll have to be around for a lot of questions, maybe even hearings after that. Let's do the surgery a couple of weeks after that conference, if that fits in with your schedule."

"Fine." Paula made a notation.

"About that press conference," said Maurice, a thought coming into his mind, "would you like to come up with me? It's scheduled for four in the afternoon, so we'd leave here just after lunch. It's a dull drive up to Hartford, and I'd enjoy your company."

"Great," said Paula enthusiastically, turning some pages and writing the date down in her notebook. "I'd really love to. Now," she went on, "about your aneurysm. Walt Eagleton has been giving me a very hard time on that subject. He attacked me at the staff meeting, practically said I was murdering you by not dragging you immediately to the operating room and putting in a graft as soon as I'd seen your X rays."

Maurice shrugged. "And how's your research coming along?" he asked.

Paula told him about the way Abrams had forced her to transfer to his lab, and Maurice's face settled into a look of serious anger.

"It's actually okay," she said, grinning. "We've made a lot of progress on the enzymes, I've worked out the sequence, and we've got a system to deliver them, so Abrams has wasted a lot of time and energy *por nada*."

"Ah, yes," said Maurice, "Cliff Abrams." He glanced over at Myra. "Let's go into your office," he said to Paula. Once the door was closed, he turned to her. "Abrams. I'm going to tell you something I learned about him, in complete confidence, okay?"

Paula nodded.

"He's recently been appointed as Millway's medical consultant," said Maurice quietly. "He's on their non-public payroll, gets forty thousand a year, plus expenses. He's also the recipient of a sizable stock transfer made only a couple of weeks ago."

"That bastard," said Paula angrily. "How about Susskind, the university attorney? Is he on their payroll too?"

"I'm not sure. There's nothing about him on any of their accounts."

"He's a lawyer," said Paula. "I bet he knows all the tricks. If he does work for them, he probably gets his money once a month in a paper bag, in used ten-dollar bills, passed to him in a taxi."

Maurice laughed. "You're probably right. Maybe they pay him in pesetas . . ." He glanced at Paula. "To change the subject, another thing we have to deal with is that situation with Earl Macklerod down in Baltimore. He's a pompous pain in the ass, but I know him pretty well. I can take care of him, I'm pretty sure."

Maurice smiled reassuringly at her, and Paula felt a huge sense of relief that he was back. Nothing seemed as difficult, nothing seemed impossible, when he was around.

"What are you going to say about the pharmaceutical industry?" Paula asked curiously. "They don't seem like a specially evil bunch to me. And is it true you're going after Millway in particular?"

Maurice's face took on an expression of quiet outrage. "They *are* an evil bunch," he said, "and I've known it a long time. The first thing that got to me about them was their hypocrisy," he said. "In their advertising, in their public relations. I know that's hardly an indictable offence, and it's common enough in other industries too, but when you're dealing with the health of a gullible population, it really sticks in your craw."

"Like what?"

"They boast that they're an *ethical* industry, and pretend that their main interest is the health of the people of the world." Maurice's lips came together and Paula could feel his anger suddenly swell. "Let me tell you a little story," he said. "A few years ago I spent a couple of months in Afghanistan, in a town called Jalalabad, working with the doctors there. There was an epidemic of diphtheria, and a lot of small children were affected. You know how diphtheria develops, with a membrane in the throat that grows until it chokes them. We were doing tracheostomies all day long, sometimes on really tiny babies. . . . Anyway, of course we started giving antibiotics to the other kids, the ones at risk, but it didn't even slow the epidemic, let alone stop it, which it should have done, and I couldn't figure it out."

Paula watched him as he talked, feeling a strong sense of admiration for Maurice. "Then I looked at the antibiotic vials we were using on those children," he was saying. "They were all outdated, some by over a year."

"Sounds like my reagents," said Paula, but Maurice was back in Afghanistan watching the babies die, and he didn't even hear her.

"I made a few inquiries and found that the drug companies had a policy of 'donating' antibiotics and other medications to third world countries, and used that fact prominently in their public relations. It was true, that antibiotics *had* been donated, but they shipped them out just before their expiration date so that they could get a tax rebate for their full value. The fact that inactive drugs were then being used in Afghanistan and other poor countries didn't matter to them. Their lawyers had cleared it;

they couldn't be sued because it was a gift, and the expiration date was clearly marked. God damn it, Paula, even now the memory of that makes me so angry."

Paula put a hand gently on his arm. "Don't get your pressure up, Maurice," she said. "Remember your aneurysm."

Maurice detached her hand. He was more worked up than she'd ever seen him. "I reported that whole story to UNESCO, to the State Department, even to the Secretariat of the United Nations. I didn't even get a reply, except from the State Department, who thanked me for my interest and noted my comments. None of them, or anyone in Congress either, dared to take on the pharmaceutical industry. Paula, you have no conception of the size and power of their lobby. They're one of the most profitable industries in this country, for a variety of reasons, many of which are totally unethical, and they want to stay profitable. The cheapest way to do that is to spend a chunk of that cash in Washington, on lobbyists to guard their interests, on donations to reelection campaigns, as cash gifts, vacations, holiday homes, you name it."

"Isn't that common enough?" asked Paula. "Don't a lot of industries do that? Like the tobacco industry, or defense, even the AMA? Don't they all have lobbyists who spend a whole lot of money in Washington?"

"Sure. But we can't get them all at once. And in my opinion it's always best to start at the top." He grinned at her, a confident, youthful grin.

"What else?"

"What else what?"

"What else are you going to say about them? The pharmaceutical people?"

"Things like pricing. When you buy a car, you buy one you can afford. If the makers don't keep their prices down, they go out of business. But now most people don't buy their medicines, their insurance companies buy them, so there's no incentive to keep prices down. The beauty is that everybody makes money with it, so why change? The pharmaceutical people charge outrageous prices, the retailers get a bigger cut, the insurance people pay without complaint, because they just put up their rates and that too makes more money for them. The only folks it doesn't work too well for is the poor old consumer, but who cares about her?"

"Do you have details? Can you really make a case?"

"Trust me," said Maurice. "I'm a doctor."

"So what about Millway?"

"Oh, I've really got *them*. I've got them *nailed*. But enough about all that stuff. I want to hear more about how you're going to deliver the enzymes in a clinical situation."

"One more thing," said Paula, who was thinking about Seth, and shivered at the thought of the cat. "How about your safety? I mean your personal safety? With all this stuff coming up, and they must know about it by now. Aren't you worried at all?"

"I've taken certain precautions," he said. "Now, tell me about your delivery system."

Paula told him about the Gatling project, and Maurice was amazed. "How ever did you think of such a solution?" he asked. "I remember Bob Zimmerman told me that as well as being smart, you were one of the most imaginative people he'd come across. But I figured he was talking you up so he could get rid of you."

"Yeah," said Paula. "He couldn't afford to keep me. Actually, I thought of the idea while I was watching a TV show on Richard Gatling, the guy who invented the gun. Steve's pizza got burned as a result."

"Steve . . ." said Maurice. "You mean Steve Charnley?"

"Yes. He's made the entire delivery system. When it comes to instrumentation, he's a genius."

Maurice left the lab a few minutes later, and after making a couple of phone calls Paula followed him over to the hospital. On the way it occurred to her that she hadn't told Maurice about Seth and the cat, but then, she thought, it would just unnecessarily concern him, and he had plenty of other worries to take care of.

The moment the lab door closed behind Paula, Myra picked up the phone and called her friend Dr. Abrams. "Cliff," she said, "I have some interesting news. Can I come over?"

Chapter Thirty-seven

Quite independently of Coletti's plans for Paula, Seth had developed his own design for her destruction. He knew that he would probably never get a chance to put it into action, because Coletti's people were very efficient, but he had carefully assembled the equipment he would need. Ever since he was a child, Seth had known that there was something inside women that made them different, desirable. Now that he had experienced the full force of this power, he wanted to find its anatomical source, take it out, and examine it. His other principal goal was to reduce Paula to pieces small enough so that his memory of her as a whole, living person would be obliterated, and then, he hoped, he would be free.

Having made a preliminary decision to flay her, and unable to find any modern references to guide him, he started to spend time in the university's medieval library, where he found what he needed in modern reproductions of fourteenth- and fifteenth-century texts by authors such as Congreve and Caxton.

At that time, flaying was a not uncommon form of punishment, and according to these and other writers, such as the Monk of Evesham, survival time was dictated by several factors: the proportion of the total area of skin removed, the age and health of the victim, and, possibly most important, the skill of the flayer. The most crucial consideration was bleeding; always fairly copious, he read, it could usually be stanched by hot compresses, which were removed once their job was done. But if an unskilled or careless flayer happened to cut into a large vein or artery in the course of his dissection, that invariably hastened the demise of the victim.

A philosophical question troubled him; at what point would Paula Cairns cease to be herself, a person? At what point would she actually cease to exist? Certainly not merely by dying, because afterward he'd remember her as he last saw her; even dead, she'd always be in his memory as a human being. But if torso, legs, arms, face, skull, hands, and feet were to be cut up into parts, small enough to be unrecognizable, would she then be truly destroyed? How about his memory of her? Would staring at the dismembered pieces really replace his recollections of the vital way she walked, her smile, that funny, enthused way she had of talking about things that fascinated her? And that was what Seth really wanted, what he felt compelled to do, to be truly rid of her, to expel and obliterate her from his mind. He knew that some killers he'd read about liked to keep locks of pubic hair tied in a ribbon, driver's licenses, photos, all tucked away in a drawer, to be taken out from time to time to relive the experience. Well, there would be none of that kind of stuff. Nor would he go to any memorial service or funeral, even assuming they had one. She would be *gone*.

The problem was that right now he couldn't get her out of his mind. Walking down the street, he'd see someone that for a second looked just like her, and his heart would leap, but of course it always was someone else. Even if it had been Paula, he'd have crossed the road to avoid her, although he still spent time watching her apartment at night, hoping to see her come in or out. Once he saw a severe-looking blond young woman with a bun come out of the building. He didn't recognize her, but had an intuitive feeling that she'd been visiting Paula. It was all very strange, and he knew it. All the time he wondered how she had reacted to the cat. He played that over too in his mind. He'd imagined how she'd looked and felt when she touched the raw, cold body of the cat in that darkened hallway, and wondered if she'd thought he might have done it.

Now Seth seemed to be passing through a relatively quiescent phase, insofar as he had no immediate desire to do anything but watch her. But he did know that at some point his lethal impulses would light up again. It had even crossed his mind to turn himself in, to tell a psychiatrist or the police or someone what was going on inside his head, tell them what he'd already done, and, more important, what he was planning to do. Sometimes he felt like a huge tank outside a small village. The motor was idling, there was nobody at the controls, but at some point it was going to rev up on its own volition, get itself into gear, and start to rumble forward and flatten and destroy everything in its path.

There was one other thing he needed to do. One morning around eleven he drove to Paula's apartment complex, rang the service bell, and went down the steps to the basement office, next to the concierge's apartment.

"I need an apartment," he said to Mr. Parker, the concierge. "Two bedrooms."

"We don't have much vacant space available." Mr. Parker took a large file out of his desk and consulted it. Seth looked around. On the wall behind the desk was a large, old-fashioned wooden key locker for the building. At the side of the locker was a hook with two keys on it, labeled MASTER KEY.

Seth started to cough. Then he sat down. The coughing got worse, and he was red in the face and gasping.

Concerned, Mr. Parker asked if he'd like a glass of water, and Seth, unable to speak, nodded. When Parker came back a moment later with a brimming glass, only one master key was still hanging on the hook. It turned out that the only vacant apartment was on the first floor, and Seth didn't want that, so he thanked Mr. Parker for his time and left.

A few days before, Seth had met with Coletti and a couple of men who worked for him and who had apparently come down from Boston. One was a short, cheerful, tubby, friendly wisecracker of about forty whose name was Chip. The other was about average height, about the same age, but thin, dark-complexioned, with black, slicked-back hair which came forward to a point in the center of his forehead in a prominent widow's peak. His eyes were cold and watchful, and he neither smiled nor said a single word during Seth's visit, but his presence made Seth feel uncomfortable. Nobody named him, or said anything to him, but his presence seemed to cast a chill over everybody there.

Chip sat down in one of the big chairs, his knees apart. "Two guys we need to know about," he said in a Boston accent so strong it smelled of garlic. "Let's take them one at a time. First, the doc; Maurice Bennett, is that right?" He glanced at Coletti.

"Right, but I don't know much about him," said Seth. "I've only meet him once."

"Works at the medical center, right?"

"Yes."

"Regular hours?"

"I have no idea. You're going to have to ask someone else about him."

"Drives a large blue 1994 BMW 740i sedan?"

Seth shrugged.

Chip smiled. "Okay . . . Now, we do know the date of

his press conference. He's doing it in Hartford, the state capital, right, so he'll be driving up there, in that nice automobile of his?"

"So I believe. Dr. Cairns will be going up with him," said Seth. Abrams had passed on every scrap of information he'd been able to get out of Myra.

"Sounds nice and cozy," said the tubby Chip, and raised his eyebrows for a second when Seth glowered at him.

"I guess you're going to have to do your own research on Bennett, Chip," Coletti said to him. "Ask him about Connor."

"Sure thing. He comes first, anyway, right? Or should I say goes first?" Chip grinned contentedly at his own wit.

Seth was able to give Desmond Connor's address, the kind of house he lived in, and yes, it was a quiet residential street, several blocks from a main street that led to I-95 a couple of miles farther.

"Perfect," said Chip. "That fits with what Mike told us. Does Connor go to work?"

"I don't think so," said Seth. "Not since he worked here. The personnel people haven't had any requests for information about him, not so far."

"Married? Children who live with them?"

"Yes, he's married. No, no children."

"Does he go on trips a lot?"

"I don't know. I doubt it, though. They probably don't have a lot of money, his company pension's been held up, so they're probably trying to keep their expenses down."

"D'you know all that, or is that guesswork?" asked Coletti, putting his feet up again on Seth's desk.

"Mostly guesswork, but I've known him for some years, went to dinner there a couple of times when my father was in charge, so I have some knowledge of him."

"Night bird, is he, Mr Connor?" went on Chip. "Takes his dog for a walk down the road, maybe, late at night?"

"Yes," said Seth. "Probably. They had a small collie a couple of years ago. I don't know if they still have it."

"Athletic, would you say? Does the health club bit, all that sweaty stuff?" The tubby man's questions seemed inexhaustible, but after another half hour he was done, but not at all happy.

"We'll need to do a whole lot more checking," he said to Coletti with a reproachful glance at Seth. "Connor was a talker, a snitch, wasn't he, sir?" to Coletti, who nodded. With his elbow the tubby man nudged his silent companion, sitting in the chair next to him.

"The two of us, we like to make the 'punishment fit the crime,' you know, Mr. Millway," he said, smiling. "That's a line from *The Mikado*," he added as an aside. "Wonderful lyrics that W. S. Gilbert wrote, don't you think, Mr. Millway, even if today they're considered maybe a little bit dated?"

Seth stared at him and said nothing.

The two men got up, Chip said goodbye for both of them, and they left, leaving Seth alone with Coletti.

"Great guys," said Coletti. "Chip used to run a garage and repair shop for the Boston Police Department. He's a Gilbert and Sullivan nut, knows all those comic operas backward and forward."

"How about the other guy? Doesn't he have a name, or a tongue in his head? He didn't say a single word."

"Oh yes, he has a name." Coletti grinned. "And a tongue. It's funny you should ask that."

Chapter Thirty-eight

There had been so much anticipation of Maurice's conference that it was now scheduled to be broadcast on national TV, and the media was buzzing, although the conference date was about ten days away. His office phone was ringing all the time, reporters from the wire services, the press, the talk shows—everybody wanted some advance information, tidbits the competition didn't know, any insights that the others didn't have. Helen Katz even had to evict a reporter and cameraman from CBS News who had managed to get past the security desk and set up their equipment in the corridor outside his office, waiting for Maurice to appear.

"It's a hot topic," said Helen to Paula. "And of course people know he's going to be the next surgeon general, so they pay a lot more attention."

For a second Paula tried to imagine what it would be like working in the hospital and the lab without Maurice around, and it didn't feel good.

She was too busy to dwell on it. They were almost ready for the first clinical tests of the anti-clot enzymes. She and Steve had worked hard and long to get the bugs out of the Gatling system, the animal tests had been successful, and they had sent a request to Charles Kingston, the hospital administrator, for permission to use it when a suitable candidate appeared. Kingston, Paula knew, had

had a long conversation with his friend Maurice Bennett about it, but so far there had been no official reply.

Other things were happening too, and Paula laughed out loud when she recalled Maurice's telephone conversation with Earl Macklerod.

Maurice had first called Dr. Bob Zimmerman, Paula's old boss, who was back in New York after his trip abroad, and told him about Earl Macklerod's plan to set up an inquiry into Paula's research paper.

Bob, who had a quick temper, was absolutely furious, quite beside himself with rage. He had shouted all kinds of unprintable comments about Macklerod, but eventually settled down.

"That asshole," he said in a more moderate tone. "Doesn't he realize *my* name's also on that paper, as head of the lab? So if he thinks he's flinging shit at Paula Cairns, that stupid son of a bitch is really flinging it at me?"

"Precisely," said Maurice. "I suggest we make a conference call to good old Earl right now."

When they got Macklerod on the phone, Zimmerman crisply told him what his problem was.

"I'm really sorry, Bob," replied Earl, sounding very pompous, "but I can't allow friendship or this kind of pressure to change the course of events. I'm sorry if you feel implicated in this mess, but you know as well as I do that we have to restore a public sense of faith in our researchers, and to do that we have to expose and get rid of the bad apples in the barrel."

Zimmerman raved and ranted, but Earl Macklerod held on to his high moral ground and remained implacable. It would cause a dangerous precedent, he boomed. If it became public knowledge that such an inquiry had been pushed underground, any kind of credibility he had as a defender of the public welfare would be destroyed.

Maurice listened to all these sparks flying to and fro for several minutes; then when they had reached a stalemate, he quietly interposed. "Earl, you're up for president of the College of Surgeons, aren't you?"

There was a surprised pause, during which both Macklerod and Zimmerman changed gears, wondering why Maurice was introducing that topic at that moment. "Yes, I am, Maurice," said Macklerod. "But I don't see why you're bringing that up at this point, in the middle of a discussion about an entirely different matter."

"Well, Earl, you're right, of course," said Maurice in an apologetic tone, "but I wonder if you've thought about the college's electoral process. There is a committee of five regents, all influential senior members. I'm sure you know that these are the five men who ultimately decide who the new president is going to be."

"Yes, Maurice, I'm well aware of that. But if you're trying to sidetrack me into talking about something else, it won't work. At this point in time, we're talking about a problem that has nothing whatever to do with the college, and I wanted to emphasize to Bob in particular that my stance on the Dr. Cairns matter cannot under any circumstance be changed, because—"

"Earl," interrupted Maurice patiently. "Bob and I are both on that regents' committee."

There was a long, shocked silence, and Maurice could feel an ecstatic high-five coming from Bob Zimmerman through the wires.

"Ahhhh," said Earl in a long exhalation. "Yes." Another silence. "Well, Maurice," he said in a completely altered voice, "thank you for reminding me of that fact." This time the pause lasted so long that both Maurice and Bob thought Earl had hung up. Then his voice came back on, quiet, and shorn of all the pomposity that had characterized it for the past ten minutes.

"Gentlemen," he said, "thank you again. I trust that I can count on your support at the college elections."

After Macklerod had hung up and Maurice and Zimmerman were still on the line, Bob said, "Maurice, that was so fucking brilliant I don't know what to say to you. But Earl is such a damned fool, do you think he really understood?"

"That was the last we'll hear about his inquiry, I'm quite certain," said Maurice. "Unless, of course, we decide to vote for someone else. And now I have to do a little work on Cliff Abrams, and at some point I may need your help with that. Bob, I'll be seeing you at the association banquet, okay? Yes, it was good talking to you too. . . ."

Excitement was building in the Millway Building too, in large part because the problem of access to Paula's computer data had been solved, almost accidentally.

Seth told Coletti about it, smiling broadly. "We have a printout of her entire process. According to Myra, the technician, Dr. Cairns closed down the computer system in the normal way when she finished with it last night, only she forgot to shut down the last encryption stage, which is a separate operation. Myra happened to come in early this morning, and when she started the computer, she found she was actually inside the encrypted program, and was able to get all the data out. She printed out the entire file, and it's on a forty-page printout that's at this moment in my safe."

"Forty pages? Surely the sequence isn't that long?"

"She printed the whole file, which Myra says has a whole lot of other data in it, earlier attempts, simulations, stuff like that. The sequence is tucked away somewhere in there, she's quite sure."

"What now?"

"I've already given it to my research people to figure

out. That's one thing they are good at. They're already working on a way of packaging the enzymes in pill form, and as soon as we have the exact sequence, we're in business."

Seth's top research people, including the new head of the research laboratories, Carl Dornier, labored night and day to work out the sequence of enzymes hidden in the huge mass of data contained in the forty-page printout that Myra had obtained for them. Six days after the printout was made available, late one night, after transcribing the data into their own computer and applying some very sophisticated analysis techniques, they finally solved the problem.

"The entire sequence, you're telling me it's only seven units long?" asked Carl disbelievingly when they brought him the final worksheets.

"That's it," replied Iztakh Mayer, his Israeli second-in-command, red-eyed with fatigue and long hours of staring at a color monitor. "We worked it out a dozen ways, Carl. Fourier analysis, every technique and method you could think of, and that's what it comes down to every time. I must tell you it's not at all what I expected. I don't recognize most of those components."

Dornier took the papers and scanned them. Several complex analytical formulae had been used, and he couldn't find fault with any of the techniques, but as Iztakh had told him, the results on each run were identical, and the list of enzymes, together with their stereoisomeric chemical formulae, was clearly the same on each page, without the slightest variation.

"It must be correct," Dornier said. "Otherwise it wouldn't come out as a list of anything, let alone enzymes. It would just come out as a lot of gibberish."

He sat down at the desk, a frown of concentration on his face. The listed compounds certainly had the chemical properties of enzymes, and the accompanying formulae supported that, but he was surprised that none of the enzymes he'd expected to see appeared on the list, enzymes known to be effective in various phases of blood coagulation, such as variants of the thrombokinases, thromboplastin, or proconvertin.

Maybe this Cairns woman had hit on to something totally unexpected, he thought, and a wave of interest and excitement seeped into his tired brain. Maybe she *had* found a completely new method of destroying blood clots by the interaction of a series of apparently unrelated enzymes. If that was so, no wonder the big commercial labs had never been able to figure it out.

He shook his head, feeling dizzy with the strain of long hours spent on this tantalizing puzzle.

"Okay," he said finally, "let's look each of these up in the International Enzyme Index, and we'll try to figure how they all interrelate."

"Could we do that tomorrow?" pleaded Iztakh. "It'll take hours, and it's almost three in the morning, and I've been here since seven yesterday morning."

They worked at it for two more days, and the scientific staff of the laboratory who were working on the project found themselves in increasing confusion. None of the enzymes in the list seemed to have any known effect on blood coagulation; nor were they chemically related in any way that would allow them to have the cascade effect that they had been expecting.

Carl Dornier sat at his desk, his frustration reaching a peak. He stared at his copy of the list, trying to make some kind of sense out of it all. He read the list of enzymes out loud. "Formaldehyde dehydrogenase, Undecylenic acid oxidase, Cyclophenolic urease, Ketosteroic arginase, Yohimbine benzoic esterase, Oligocyclic deaminase, Ursodeoxycholic polyaminase . . ."

Then it hit him. His face went an apoplectic red and he picked up the intercom. "Get Mayer in here. Right away," he said.

Iztakh came in a few moments later, and Dornier slammed the paper down on the desk in front of him. "Look at this," he said. "Read that list!"

Iztakh, exhausted, leaned against the desk and looked dully at the paper. It was just the same old incomprehensible sequence of chemical names.

"Read the first letter of each enzyme, you imbecile," said Dornier, "and put them together."

Coletti was coldly angry when he heard Dornier's toned-down version of what had happened. "Could that have been the technician playing some kind of a joke?" he asked Abrams, who had been urgently summoned to his office.

White-faced, Abrams shook his head. "I'm sure it wasn't Myra," he said. "I'm sure such a thing wouldn't even occur to her. . . . Dr. Cairns must have figured that someone wanted to get into her computer data bank and constructed that . . . offensive message."

"Brilliant," said Coletti sarcastically. "The problem now is how to get the correct information. After all this, we're back at square one." He smashed his fist down on the desk.

"How about the camera in the ceiling?" asked Abrams. "I thought that was going to give you all the information you needed about how to get into the program."

"She moved her computer," replied Coletti curtly. "It's now in her office, and the only thing the camera picks up is that fat beast of a technician."

But Myra, on her own, had figured out the correct sequence, because the enzymes had to be arranged in the proper order for the clinical tests, and she was able to work back from the manufacturers' invoice codes. This information was passed to Abrams, then to Seth, and finally to Coletti, just a couple of days before Maurice's scheduled conference.

"That's great," said Coletti, after Dornier had confirmed that the sequence made sense and in all probability was correct. "Now we can take care of the final details."

Chapter Thirty-nine

Around twenty minutes before ten on the day that Maurice was scheduled to go up to Hartford for his press conference, an old but rugged-looking auto wrecker truck drove along I-95 from Bridgeport. The driver, a tubby, middle-aged man in faded blue coveralls, was talking to his silent partner.

"There's a whole lot of different ways of fixing them," he said. "Everything changed with all the computer controls you have in today's cars, but in some ways that makes it easier. A couple of times we put in new computer cards, once in a Jag and another time in a Town Car, so that the timing got worse and worse until the engine was knocking so bad the guy had to pull over. Unfortunately for them, we were coming right behind him, ready and able to help."

They turned off the highway at the exit with a big, square white-on-blue *H*, and chugged along the connector.

"But the best way hasn't changed much, though," he went on. "In a BMW 740i the brake fluid reservoir holds exactly eight and one quarter fluid ounces. So if you make a hole in the hydraulic line going to one of the brakes, some of the fluid'll squirt out every time he puts on the brakes. Now, depending on the size of the hole, you can figure how many times the brakes will work before the fluid's all gone. The front one's easier to get at . . ." Chip glanced over at his companion; he hadn't actually said anything, but there was a questioning look on his face.

"You mean why just one of the lines, and not all of them?" asked Chip.

His companion nodded.

"Because they're all connected, that's why. If you make a hole and the fluid leaks out, that line'll refill until the reservoir is empty, and then all the brakes fail at once."

Chip glanced at him out of the corner of his eye. His companion didn't like being looked at, it made him nervous, and Chip was very careful about that. "I know what you're thinking," he said. "You're thinking, how about the brake fluid warning light when the level gets low? You're right, that's a good point, and it could mess you up if you don't take care of it. That light's connected by just a single wire from a sensor in the reservoir, and I'll show you how to unhook it. It's easy."

There was a brief silence while Chip negotiated the sharp turn onto Elm Street. The research tower of the NCMC was visible, looming high over the lower building in the foreground.

"You're thinking, what about the emergency brake, right?" He grinned, looking straight ahead. "You're right again. On the Beamer there's a mechanical link that works on the rear wheels so that you can stop the car if the hydraulics fail. This is where a bit of artistic judgment comes in. For years I used to just cut both links to the back wheels, but one time about eighteen months ago I almost got caught and had to get the hell out real quick after I'd only done one side. It turned out better, would you believe?"

Chip paused to give his companion time to visualize the scene. "Well, what happened was this guy and his wife were in his Jaguar, going fast in a lot of traffic. The brakes failed just about where we figured they would because the fluid was gone, so he grabbed the emergency brake handle and pulled hard, thinking it would work on the back wheels. It did, but only on one side, and that put the car out of control and it swerved right in the path of a Wal-Mart truck." Chip thought about the scene for a moment and shook his head. "What a mess that was. She'd been right pretty, and him, well, there was no way you could tell."

When he reached the employees' parking lot beyond the hospital buildings, Chip turned right, up the ramp and stopped at the barrier. He put Myra's card in the slot and drove in. As he had found on a previous reconnaissance, the doctors' lot was adjacent to the employees' lot, separated only by a brick ledge about a foot high. Chip pulled up next to the ledge. Maurice's car was visible in the reserved parking area, only a few yards away.

Chip looked quickly around the lot from his elevated position in the truck cab. As he had figured, there was nobody around. The doctors were either in the hospital for the morning, or would be arriving later, after lunch.

They both got out. Chip reached back into the cab for a hand-held drill, already loaded with an eighth-inch chrome-moly steel bit. His companion brought out a lantern, a heavy, long-handled bolt cutter, and a flexible telescopic tool for reaching and grasping remote, hard-to-reach objects.

Within seconds they were both on their backs under the front of the big BMW. "If only he'd left the wheel turned a bit," grumbled Chip, "it would made this a lot easier. Shine the light over here," he said. "See, this is the best place to drill the hole, in the flexible line just before it enters the caliper, because that's where it's braced. Farther up, you can't drill because the line's flexible and just skids out of the way." The drill whined, and the bit cut

through the metal sheathing and the hydraulic line inside
it, all in the space of a few seconds. Two drops of golden
brake fluid dripped onto the concrete when Chip pulled
the drill out, with the bit still turning.

"Okay," said Chip, "now the fluid warning light." He
took the lantern and aimed it up, picking out the cast alu-
minum fluid reservoir in a second. "There," he said, giving
the lantern to his companion. "Hold it, right there, keep
it on that yellow wire. Pass me the grasper." He put his
hand out for the telescopic tool, and felt it being placed
in his hand. Even now Chip felt a quiver of distaste mixed
with fear when his companion touched him. In a moment
he had passed the long tool up to the left of the engine
block, slipping it between all the wires and other equipment in the tightly packed engine compartment. He
turned the knurled end of the tool, grabbed the end of the
yellow wire with the jaws, then pulled. Nothing happened. Chip grasped the wire nearer the terminal and
tried again. This time it came out easily.

Then the two men scrambled out and went under the
back of the car, and in a moment the half-inch thick mechanical emergency link to the left rear brake was cut
with the bolt cutters, offering not much more resistance
than a piece of spaghetti, and they quickly gathered their
tools and hopped back in their vehicle, their mission accomplished. The whole operation had taken just under six
minutes.

As they rumbled out of the parking lot, Chip, cheerful
as always, was half singing, half humming " '. . . a victim
must be found, I've got a little list . . . who never would
be missed . . .' " He paused. "You know," he said reflectively, "of all of them, I think *The Mikado* is my favorite."

While Chip and his colleague was trundling back along
I-95, Paula was in the operating room, having finished a

small private case of her own, and about to start helping the residents do a colon resection. She was excited about Maurice's upcoming press conference, and looking forward to seeing how he handled a big-time public occasion, how he'd deal with loaded questions from the media, and hostile comments from the industry people who would certainly be there in force, interspersed among the media. They would do their best to discredit him, ridicule his findings, and at least try to minimize whatever damage he might cause.

After finishing the case with the residents, Paula changed into her street clothes and ran over to Maurice's office. He was sitting at his desk, talking on the phone. He looked up when she came in, and pointed at a newspaper clipping on his desk. She picked it up and sat down to read the brief article.

DRUG SLAYING SUSPECTED, she read. "The body of Desmond Connor, former head of research for a local pharmaceutical company, was found yesterday in a deserted wetlands area some miles from New Coventry, after the police received an anonymous tip-off. Mr. Connor had been depressed because of his recent firing, said his wife, Nora, who was contacted by telephone. However, a member of the public relations department of Millway Pharmaceuticals, who refused to be named, stated in a police interview that Mr. Connor had been let go because there was a question of drug use on the job. A spokesman for the New Coventry police department confirmed that the slaying was thought to be drug-related, and are pursuing the investigation. Mr. Connor was fifty-seven."

Maurice put down the phone at the same time Paula finished reading.

"Who was he?" asked Paula. Then she remembered and put her hand up to her mouth. "Oh, my God," she said, horrified. "I met him. He was at that meeting I had with the Millway people. Oh, my God . . ."

"Connor gave me a lot of crucial information about Millway," said Maurice in a somber voice. "Not for any kind of gain either, and I'm sure he knew the risk he was taking."

Maurice saw Connor's face again, staring at him across the table, and felt his fear, the fear he had been unsuccessfully trying to smother with great mouthfuls of cheeseburger and tomato ketchup.

"I was talking to the detective in charge of the case," went on Maurice. "He's convinced that it was done by out-of-state drug enforcers. . . . Paula, do you know what a Colombian necktie is?"

Paula shook her head.

"This is a specialty of the drug people," said Maurice. He put his hands flat on the desk, trying not to picture it too clearly on Desmond Connor. "They make a cut in the neck, up and down, from the chin to the top of the breastbone. They usually do it after their victim is dead, but not always. Then they reach up through the opening in the neck, catch the tongue, and pull it down through the opening."

Paula shuddered. "They did that to him? Oh, God, Maurice, his poor wife."

"Poor him, I'd have thought," said Maurice, wondering, as he occasionally did, at the strange workings of women's minds.

"Why did they do that, do you think? Was he selling drugs?"

"I doubt it. Paula, this is the way I'm looking at it. It was a punishment to him, but also a very strong warning to me. The Colombian necktie is usually reserved for informers, and one of their people must have seen him talking to me, unless he also told someone else, the police, maybe. . . ." Maurice thought about that. "No, it was me, because he gave me all the papers."

"Do you think they timed it to come just before your press conference this afternoon?"

"Yes," said Maurice. "Without a shadow of a doubt."

Chapter Forty

"Are you ready?" Maurice was dressed formally in a dark suit, black shoes and socks; the only touch of color was his tie, dark red, as he said, for the television. He picked up his briefcase and headed for the door.

Paula too was dressed up, not as dark or as formal, but in a stunning gray cashmere suit she'd bought a few days before for the occasion, a silk blouse with a man's bolo tie with five big turquoises set in a silver circle, and a matching lapel pin and earrings.

They had just reached the door that led out to the parking lot when Paula's beeper went off. Maurice looked at his watch, then they went back to find the nearest phone. It was the O.R. They needed Paula to check the patient they'd been operating on.

"Go on, take care of it," said Maurice. "I'll wait for you in the car for five minutes. If you're not back, I'll go on and you can follow. Do you think that old heap of yours can make it up to Hartford? The conference is at the City Auditorium."

It didn't take Paula long to take care of the problem; the patient was already in the recovery room, and had a temporary fall in blood pressure, easily fixed with medication, after consultation with the anesthetist.

Paula ran back down, taking the emergency stairs because it was faster that way, and hurried out, hoping that

Maurice hadn't gone off without her. But his parking space was empty. Upset that she'd missed him, Paula looked at her watch. She'd been away no longer than seven minutes. She ran to the corner where she could see the exit, but he was gone. When Maurice said five minutes, that was precisely what he meant.

She went over to her own car and climbed in. It started first time around, and Paula patted the steering wheel encouragingly. This was going to be a long ride, and the old four-cylinder motor tended to heat up and burn a bit of oil on long trips.

On the way along the connector of I-91, the road that went straight up to Hartford, she looked over at the tall Millway Building and thought about the man Connor. She tried to remember what he looked like: not very tall, a lot of gray hair . . . When Paula wanted to remember, she had the ability to concentrate very hard. Now Desmond Connor was coming back, with his rakish look, the way his eyes narrowed when he'd smiled at her. He'd been wearing a green tie. Paula shivered, thinking about the dreadful Colombian necktie he'd died with.

What did his wife think? She would have known if he was into drug dealing, and he'd have to be in it very heavily to get killed for it. But of course, Maurice was sure that he'd been killed because he'd passed on all that damaging information and documents. Maurice . . .

On I-91, she bowled along merrily in her little car, going at the regulation maximum of fifty-five mph, nursing the engine for the long run. Then, unexpectedly for this time of day, the traffic started to slow down. The MG sat lower than most other cars on the road, so she couldn't see ahead, but when she came to a stop, she was next to a high, khaki-painted military truck. Caught with a sudden anxiety, she looked up and shouted to the soldier who was driving. He wound down the window and grinned appreciatively at her.

"What's the holdup?" she cried.

"I dunno," said the soldier, not taking his eyes off her.

"What's holding *her* up?" said his mate, laughing and leaning over and looking down at Paula.

"Is it an accident?" she persisted.

The driver finally looked ahead. "Yes," he said. "There's a car off the road. It's not far up. We should be moving in a few minutes."

"What kind of car is it?" Paula's heart was beating at twice its normal speed.

"Who knows, lady?" He peered again. "I dunno," he said. "It's like a dark blue or black."

That was enough for Paula; she was certain that something had happened to Maurice. There was just room to pass in front of the army truck, so she backed as far as she could, then cut in front of the truck and got onto the shoulder and went as fast as possible, keeping an eye open for anyone who might have the same idea.

Right behind her came a rescue vehicle, lights flashing, horn blaring angrily at her. She ignored it and kept going until she reached the scene. It was a BMW, all right, she knew from the blue and white medallion on the back of the trunk. On what was left of the trunk. The car had apparently hit the central divider, bounced back, and been hit again by an eighteen-wheeler which had stopped fifty yards farther up, tilted at a precarious angle on the edge of the shoulder.

She jumped out and ran toward the car. Two state police cars were there already, parked, lights on, doors open, radios on full gain, occasionally crackling out an incomprehensible message.

"Get back to your vehicle, lady," shouted one of the

cops, moving to cut her off. The other had managed to open the driver's side door and was leaning inside.

Paula slowed down, trying to get some semblance of control over herself, and walked up. The cop was angry, but Paula didn't give him a chance to say anything. "I'm a doctor at NCMC," she said. "And I think the driver of that car is my boss."

The cop's expression turned to relief. He turned to his colleague and shouted, "Let this lady take a look at him. She's a doc."

Paula could dimly hear the emergency crew coming up behind her, but her attention was totally focused on the smashed car, and she felt herself beginning to shake. She couldn't see how anyone could have survived inside the crushed shell.

Maurice had not only survived but was conscious. The air bag was deployed, and had almost certainly saved his life.

A small trickle of blood ran down from one nostril. He tried to smile at her, and only then did Paula see how pale he was. Oh, God, she thought, his aneurysm. Sometimes all it took to rupture the weakened wall of an aneurysm was a blow.

"We'll have you out in no time, Maurice," she said, putting a comforting hand on his shoulder. "You're going to be all right."

She backed away to let the emergency crew in. "Don't move him until everything is free," she warned them. "And be as gentle as you possibly can. He has an aortic aneurysm."

The crew punctured the airbag and it collapsed out of the way. Then they cut the seat belts at the shoulder and waist with a massive pair of scissors. The biggest medic, tall, crew-cut, and with muscles of a football tackle, put one hand gently under Maurice's legs and the other behind his back and lifted him out like a baby, while Paula held his head, and they placed him on the stretcher they'd brought with them.

While they were busy with transferring Maurice, an ancient-looking tow vehicle with flaking red paint was moving into position to pull the car out and lift it onto its platform.

"I'm going back with you," said Paula to the ambulance people.

"Gimme your car keys, then, Doc," said the cop, looking up from his notebook. He held out one hand, and she gave him the keys with a strange momentary feeling of reluctance.

The ambulance was like a square box, and she could just stand up inside it. They put Maurice in the berth on the right and strapped him in. Now he really wasn't looking good. His face was pale and sweaty, but Paula couldn't do anything until the ambulance had finished jolting over the wide grassy median and was back on the road, racing back toward New Coventry.

She checked his pulse and blood pressure. The first was high, and the second was low, and with growing apprehension she undid one of the retaining straps, undid his jacket, unbuttoned his shirt and pants, and put a hand on his belly. On the left, deep inside his abdomen, there was a pulsating mass the size of a grapefruit. His aneurysm had enlarged hugely, and Paula had no doubt at all that it was about to rupture. If that happened before they got him to the operating room, Maurice would die.

The ambulance men watched her, recognizing that she knew more than they ever would, and also knew exactly what needed to be done.

Paula cut the sleeves of his beautiful suit up to the elbows, and started two IVs, one in each arm. "Set up two bags of Ringer's lactate," she told the crew as she worked.

Maurice was staring up at the roof, and she wasn't sure how conscious he was, so she kept up a chatter about unimportant things, watching for his responses. The veins in his arm were collapsed, and it wasn't easy, but she managed to put in the biggest cannulas they had on board.

Once the IVs were running, Paula went to the front and opened the square communicating window. "Call the hospital," she told the driver's mate. When he got through on the direct line to the E.R., she told them what had happened. "Tell the O.R. we're coming straight up," she said. "Tell them to get eight units of blood ready. You'll find his blood type in his medical records, and we can cross-match them up there. He has an abdominal aortic aneurysm . . ." Paula looked back for a second at Maurice lying silently on his stretcher, and, in a gesture she had retained from her childhood, unconsciously crossed her fingers. "Which is in the process of rupturing."

Before hanging up she asked the E.R. supervisor to contact Charles Kingston, the hospital administrator, and tell him what had happened. Paula figured they'd be back in New Coventry in about ten minutes. Out of the corner of her eye she saw the driver, who was listening to her conversation, nod in agreement.

Paula closed her eyes for a second. "Please, God," she whispered silently, "don't let it burst before we get him to the O.R. . . ."

Chapter Forty-one

Seth and Vince Coletti, together with the ever-present Mike Petras, were in Seth's office waiting when the news came through on Chip's cellular phone from the scene of the wreck. The fact that Maurice hadn't been killed on the spot made Coletti very angry, but Seth was relieved that nobody else was involved, because from the beginning he really had wanted to take care of Paula himself. He knew now that it was written in the stars, that he was destined to be the one to destroy her, and that had she died some other way, he could never have got rid of her; she would have haunted his every moment until he too was dead.

The telephone rang again a little later. Chip was at a wrecker's yard near Bridgeport, where Maurice's BMW was now submerged under other anonymous masses of twisted metal. It would be going into the crusher within a hour. And yes, he had recovered the guy's briefcase. It had been jammed inside the trunk, and it hadn't been easy to get it out. They'd needed some special tools, but the briefcase itself seemed to be intact.

"Get it up here pronto," said Coletti. "Put the briefcase in a cardboard box first. What did you do with the wrecker truck?"

Seth, listening, was reminded of Jimmy Carter, who

had also liked to know the minute details of paramilitary operations he had approved.

"It's here too. We've got the new plates on already. They're going to paint it up a bit." He laughed. "Those state cops are going to have a stroke," he said. "I got them to sign the release papers for the Beamer, no problem. They didn't even look."

When Coletti replaced the phone, the irrepressible Chip was humming, "The policeman's life is not a happy one," from Gilbert and Sullivan's *Pirates of Penzance*.

Soon after, Chip came in with a large cardboard box tied up with twine, and a makeshift handle made from a coat hanger.

"Okay," said Coletti after the box and the briefcase has been opened and emptied, and they had gone over and classified all the papers and documents. "Let's get busy."

It didn't take long for them to find the originals, although these were located in different departments, and soon two large boxes of potentially damaging records were taken up to Seth's office.

"Chip's taking them back to Bridgeport," said Coletti in response to Seth's question. "There's a furnace in that wrecker's yard that's hot enough to melt steel. Those papers'll last about two seconds in there."

Chip took the boxes down on a dolly, and within minutes the shipment was on its way to Bridgeport.

"Well, that takes care of that," said Seth. "Now they can search all they like, suspect all they want, but half an hour from now, the proofs will be all gone up in smoke."

"Yeah," said Vince, "but we still haven't taken care of the Cairns woman. It makes me nervous to think of her out there with all that valuable knowledge inside her head."

"I'm going to take care of her."

For once Coletti was caught off guard.

"*You're* going to?" He stepped back and looked at Seth as if he'd never seen him before. "What are you talking about? This isn't a job for amateurs. My guys are professionals." He clicked his tongue like a disapproving schoolteacher. "They've been doing personal injury work for years; it's not something you can just take up, like needlepoint."

"I'm doing it," repeated Seth. "Your guys can take care of Bennett if he survives. But I'm going to take care of Dr. Cairns."

Coletti shook his head. "Look," he said, "there's one thing the personal injury pros never do, and that's hit anybody they have a personal relationship with. When your emotions are involved, you don't see as straight as when it's just a job, and if you're involved, other people are going to know it, and that makes it a whole lot easier to track you down."

Coletti was giving excellent advice, but in the back of his mind it occurred to him that if Seth were to take on that responsibility, it might work out better for everyone, with the possible exception of Seth.

The ambulance journey took only about fifteen minutes, but to Paula it seemed to last forever. Although she wanted to get Maurice to the hospital as fast as possible, she had to tell the driver to slow down on the turns because Maurice was getting pushed hard against his retaining straps.

Sitting on the empty stretcher opposite, she talked quietly to him, held his cold hand, and watched him intently, took his blood pressure every few minutes, and kept up a silent prayer that nothing dreadful would happen there, although she knew that at this point he was staying alive by the grace of God, from moment to moment. She could visualize the already-thin aneurysm wall pulsating inside his abdomen, tight, distended, poised to tear all the way, needing only a slight increase in his blood pressure, the sort of rise that could occur from something as minor as sitting up in bed or even having an angry thought.

This is where the man's character shows, she thought, watching his face. He was in severe pain, there was no question, but he didn't yell or move or even groan. His eyes were open, and he was aware of what was going on. Although he didn't look at her, Paula was sure he knew that she was there and was glad of it. Maurice seemed to be accepting what had happened. He didn't seem angry, or resentful, or even scared. He seemed quite content at this point to leave everything else aside, and put his faith in her competence and judgment.

Everybody was ready when the ambulance pulled up outside the hospital's emergency entrance. Hands reached up and opened the doors almost before the vehicle had come to a halt, and in no time Maurice was carefully taken out of the ambulance. The transport techs were about to transfer him to a hospital stretcher, but Paula vetoed that.

"No unnecessary movement," she said. "We'll take him up on the ambulance stretcher."

In the space of the few minutes since Paula had called in from the ambulance, everybody in the hospital seemed to have learned that Dr. Maurice Bennett had been in a serious automobile accident, and the E.R. was crowded with colleagues and other bystanders. Paula waved them all off, and the techs hustled the stretcher along the corridor toward the elevator. One of the stretcher's wheels was out of balance, and made a continuous clickety-clack noise as they went along, but nobody paid any attention. One of the lab techs had come to meet them at the door of the E.R., and she hurried along, following the stretcher, knowing that the only time it would stop long enough for her to draw blood for tests and cross-matching blood for transfusion would be while it was inside the elevator.

She was fast. In the time it took to get from the ground floor to the twelfth, she had tied a tourniquet around Maurice's arm, found a vein, stuck in her needle, filled four rubber-capped tubes with blood, and finally put a Band-Aid over the puncture hole.

Maurice's eyes were closed, but his breathing was regular, and again she had the feeling that he was very aware of her presence, and wasn't interested in very much else at this moment. Paula had supervised his transportation and transfers with an eagle eye, and now walked quickly alongside the stretcher.

When they reached the operating suite, a nurse ran ahead to push the wall plate, and the doors opened.

Just inside the door stood Dr. Abrams, in O.R. greens, something that that didn't happen very often. Standing next to him was Charles Kingston, the hospital administrator, in his usual dark business suit. He was looking very anxious and concerned. Behind both of them was the figure of Walt Eagleton, also dressed in greens.

As soon as the stretcher was inside the suite and the doors had closed, Abrams marched up to the stretcher and spoke in an unnaturally loud voice to Paula, who had her hand on Maurice's shoulder.

"Dr. Cairns," he said. "I'm sorry, but as chairman of the department, and in Dr. Bennett's best interests, I have decided to take over this case. Dr. Eagleton will be assisting me."

Chapter Forty-two

Meanwhile, Seth had gone home to collect his equipment; it was ready in a small case, packed in the inverse order he would need them, the .38-caliber Smith & Wesson at the bottom because he didn't expect to use it, then the hospital greens he would change into when he got there, the knives, latex gloves, a spare pair of rubber gloves, and finally a hard rubber club, a South African police model he'd bought through a mail order catalog. As he drove Fleur's gray Escort toward Paula's apartment building, he went over the protocol he'd finally decided on. He had briefly thought about removing the pieces of Paula afterward and disposing of them some other place, but decided against it as being too dangerous.

He felt sad and excited at the same time. Sad because this was it, the end of the road with Paula, and she'd been with him every day, every waking moment for a long time now. Excited because he was finally about to find out the secret of women, what they had inside them that was different, voluptuous, and whatever secret component it was that drove men mad.

He had studied the apartment complex from the point of view of activity, the comings and goings of tradesmen, the people who lived there, and of course, Paula herself. Postal deliveries were usually around eleven but varied a good deal. Most of the people who lived there were either young professionals or older people, some retired. Most of the young ones were out by seven-thirty in the morning, and the older ones went out to do their shopping between ten and noon.

When Seth got there it was jut before three, the quietest part of the day, when the old ones were having their naps and the others weren't home yet. He parked the Escort near the door, pulled on his thin latex gloves, took his case, and let himself in with the stolen master key. There wasn't a soul in sight, not in the lobby, the elevator, or the fourth-floor corridor, which he well remembered. The apartment door opened easily and he went in quietly but fast, and put his case down on the floor before looking around, finally, at the place where the woman lived, this woman who had invaded his life. Seth felt a jolt of discomfort, because now his fantasy had run head-on into reality. This was how her apartment was, not how it should be, not the way he thought it would be.

There was a small hallway inside the door, with a dark closet that held a couple of winter coats, a white summery woolen one, a metallic silver raincoat, and a transparent, folded umbrella. The paint work in the apartment was ivory; that was okay, but the kitchen was to the left of the door, where the dining room should have been.

Leaving his bag by the door, he went into the bedroom, the site of most of his fantasies. Seth was delighted—it was different, and the reality almost instantly displaced his own imaginings, just as he hoped the reality of Paula's dismembered body would destroy his otherwise inescapable visions of her.

The bed was unmade, and he approached it cautiously. There was a white nightie dropped carelessly by the bed, not a long one but a short, utilitarian model. He picked it up and held it for a moment, then dropped it before going into the other room, which was apparently the place she used to work and study. There was a large set of book-shelves on one side, a filing cabinet, a floor lamp. Her worktable stood in the center of the room, loaded with papers, a telephone, and a computer on the far side, facing away from him. There was only one chair, opposite the computer, facing the door.

Seth glanced at the pictures on the wall, and walked up to one, a large sepia photo of a thickset, jovial-looking man with whiskers, standing possessively in front of a large building, which Seth thought might be in New York. His name, Augustus D. Juilliard, was signed below in a bold scribble, and Seth idly wondered if he might have something to do with the music school.

He was about to turn and leave the room when he noticed that the computer was on, and there was a glow from the screen reflected on the wall. Mildly curious, he went and sat down in the chair, but almost leaped out again when he saw the message on the screen.

WELCOME TO MY HOME, SETH.

He stood up and looked around, suddenly feeling afraid. Was she here? He checked all the rooms, the bathroom, peered inside the closets.

Nothing. Nobody.

He checked the door, double-locked it, and went back to the computer. He sat down, very slowly, staring at the screen. At the bottom of the screen in small letters was a further message: *Please press* ENTER. Seth thought about it for a second, thinking about bombs and self-destructing devices, then took a chance and pressed ENTER. A new message appeared. "When you came in, a silent alarm went off. Within a few minutes the police will be here. If you hurry, you just have time to get away. Now press EN-TER again."

Seth leaped up again, almost knocking the chair over. He walked swiftly to the door and examined it. There was no sign of a burglar alarm, no wires, no contacts between the door and the jamb. He ran to the bedroom and looked out over the parking lot. Nothing. It was almost empty, and silent. He opened the window to listen. No sirens, nothing except the vague traffic noises of the city.

He went to the door, unlocked it, picked up his bag, and stood there, indecisive. Still there was no noise. He put the bag down, wondering what would happen if he pressed ENTER again.

He went back and did it, and the message faded slowly, replaced by the images of tropical fish, in full color, traveling lazily back and forth across the screen. Seth waited for about a minute, then was about to press ENTER again when a message appeared, again at the bottom. "Please hold . . . another message will appear in two minutes exactly. Meanwhile, relax, enjoy the fish."

Intrigued, Seth decided to wait the two minutes, after which he would get out.

The exotic, brightly colored fish meandered quietly across the screen, trailing long semi-transparent fins through the languorous blue water. It was hypnotic, and Seth found himself almost forgetting where he was, caught up in the slow, sensuous movements of the fish. Then, very slowly, the fish disappeared. Seth got up, ready to go as soon as he'd read the message.

It appeared very, very slowly, in barely decipherable letters that to Seth seemed to take an age to appear. He strained at the screen, turned up the brightness level, but it didn't make the letters light up any faster. Gradually, gradually, then came up on the screen, until he could make out a letter here and there. Then the letters brightened up suddenly.

IT'S TOO LATE, SETH. THEY'RE HERE.

At that moment he heard heavy steps coming along the corridor, and he started to sweat, but he couldn't believe that it was really the cops, that he was caught.

The steps came to a halt outside, and someone banged on the door. "Open up. Police!"

Seth opened the door.

"Yes?" he said.

Both policemen had their guns drawn. "Put your hands up and step back," said the older one of the two. "Don't move quickly, keep your hands up where I can see them. Step back slowly, then get down on the floor. On your face, hands behind your back."

Seth did as he was told, saying in a quiet, reasonable voice, "You're making a big mistake. I'm a friend of Dr. Cairns, and I'm waiting for her to come home. We're going out to dinner. . . ."

"On the floor," repeated the senior cop. He didn't take his eyes off Seth. "Switch off the alarm," he told his partner, who reached up into the closet near the door. He obviously knew exactly where the switch was.

"So how did you get in, sir?"

"She gave me her key . . ."

"Where is it?"

"On the side table, by the door."

The younger cop went over, picked up the key, and looked at it. "That's it," he told his buddy. "The master key that got stolen."

"Now take a look in that bag," said the older cop, pointing with his foot at Seth's case.

"That is my private property," said Seth in a louder voice. "Do you have a warrant?"

"We sure do, sir," drawled the older cop, leaning back against the front door until it closed with a click. "And that allows us to search anything and everything in this apartment. Now get back down on the floor like I told you, before I get mad."

The other cop opened the case. At the top was the South African police club, lying on a pair of latex gloves.

The cop put the things out neatly in order, the knives and the gun last. Seth, pale with rage, watched them from his prone position.

"So you were going out to dinner with Dr. Cairns, huh?" said the older cop, picking up the club and examining it. "Going down to the ghetto first, sir, to knock a few heads in? Wearing rubber gloves? And what were you going to do with this staple gun, sir? And this here . . . now that's a skinning knife, isn't it?"

Suddenly Seth was on his feet, a roaring bull of a man, charging at the two cops. The older one, quick as lightning, picked up the club, sidestepped Seth, and hit him hard on the back of the head as he hurtled past.

"I was hoping he would do that," he said.

Chapter Forty-three

Paula stood looking at Abrams, her mouth open, and then it snapped shut, but only for a moment. "Taking over the case?" she said. "You'll do nothing of the sort, neither you nor Dr. Eagleton. Now get out of our way, we're in a hurry."

Abrams stood firm, his little eyes gleaming with the light of battle. "If you refuse to cooperate, Dr. Cairns, I will suspend your operating room privileges on an emergency basis, as I am entitled to do as chairman of the department." Abrams glanced over at Charles Kingston for confirmation. Walt, still in the background, watched. His eyes, even in this crisis, were amused, cynical.

Everybody looked at Paula—the nurses, the transportation techs, the doctors. Everything seemed to stop, just for a moment.

Then to everyone's surprise, Maurice spoke, the first words he'd uttered since arriving in the hospital. "Dr. Cairns is my doctor," he said, quietly but in a tone that nobody there was about to argue with. "She's going to do whatever needs to be done."

It wasn't so much what he said, but Maurice's tone struck Abrams like a slap in the face.

"Get out of the way," said Paula again to Abrams, hissing at him. She started forward with the stretcher, and Abrams had to move quickly to avoid being run down.

"I'll give you a hand," said Walt to Paula as she passed.

Paula didn't hesitate. Maurice's survival was the prime consideration at this time, and she knew that Walt was a first-class and very experienced surgeon. She would be crazy to refuse his offer of help.

"Thanks," she said.

In the operating room, Gabe Pinero, the anesthetist, was already getting his syringes and other equipment together. Paula was glad he was there; his competence and calmness would be a huge help, and she knew she would need all the help she could get.

Maurice said one more thing before going in. "My briefcase," he said. His voice was only a whisper now. "All the papers . . ."

Paula felt as if her heart had stopped. "I'm sure the police must have got it," she said, but she felt unforgivably careless not to have thought of it or brought it back with her.

She handed Maurice over to Gabe Pinero, reluctant to leave him even for the short time it took to change and scrub.

Charles Kingston, made by the supervisor to put on bootees, a paper cap, and a mask, poked his head into the scrub room, looking slightly comical in his mixed attire. "Good luck, Dr. Cairns," he said to Paula. "We all know he's in the very best of hands." His tone was encouraging and respectful, and his words gave her morale a great boost. Her heart was still beating fast from her encounter with Abrams. She gritted her teeth in silent fury thinking about him.

Ken McKinley, the senior resident, came in with Joan Pringle, the intern, and went up to the scrub sinks. "Thought you might need a couple of extra pairs of hands, Dr. Cairns," said Ken, smiling his tired smile. "I sent

Chris over to the blood bank. They always work faster when there's a doc waiting."

"Thanks, Ken." She told him briefly what had happened, and that Maurice's previously small aneurysm had swollen as a result of the crash, and was about to burst.

Ken looked apprehensive but said nothing. Joan glanced at him, then at Paula, not fully appreciating the situation. She turned the water on with her knee. Walt stared straight in front of him and, to his credit, didn't say that Paula should have operated on him when she first found out about his aneurysm. With all the water running, there was too much noise to talk, and nothing was said until they were inside the operating room.

"He's asleep," said Gabe in his usual unflappable voice. This might have been a routine appendectomy, judging from his tone, but Paula knew how careful Gabe was. He sounded casual but never missed a trick, and had a wonderful knack of catching disasters before they happened.

"How's his pressure?" Paula looked over her mask at him while the scrub nurse pulled on her gloves.

"Good. No problem. 122 over 74."

The nurses had placed the drapes over Maurice's abdomen, and the transparent yellow betadine film glowed in the overhead lights. The bulge of the aneurysm showed now that his abdominal muscles were relaxed.

"I'd guess we have maybe ten minutes to fix this before it bursts," said Walt quietly to Paula. He had taken up his position opposite her on the left side of the table. Joan, as the junior assistant, was on his left, in a good position to hold retractors, and Ken was on Paula's left, so as not to get in the way of the scrub nurse, who had to be next to Paula.

"Skin knife," said Paula, and there was a slight tremor in her voice that infuriated her. Walt's eyes flickered.

Paula felt the incision as clearly as if someone were actually doing it to her. Cutting into Maurice ... She couldn't imagine it. But there she was.

"Right-angle retractor."

Joan put a long, wet sponge over the edge of the wound, and Paula placed the retractor. "Lean with it," she advised Joan. "You're going to be here for a while."

Within a few minutes, they had the abdominal contents packed out of the way, and the great pulsating, reddish bulge of the aneurysm projected forward from the back wall of the abdomen.

"Long scissors." Very carefully Paula started to dissect around the aorta, above the aneurysm. Yes, there were the artery and vein to the kidneys, and they were clear. But she and Walt knew how critical that was; if the kidney arteries were involved in the aneurysm, it made the whole operation hugely more difficult.

"Long right-angle clamp." The scrub tech passed the instrument, and Walt picked up a long, wet tape and held it while Paula, ever so gently, passed the clamp behind the aorta.

"Got it." She pulled the tape through and clipped the two ends with a hemostat.

That was a relief to both of them. Now, at least, the aorta was under control, and if a catastrophe occurred, if the aneurysm ruptured, they could stop the hemorrhage by tightening up on the tape around the aorta.

Walt was doing a superb job, and once again Paula was made aware of the importance of the first assistant. An incompetent or careless one could turn a routine operation into a disaster, but an excellent one made everything go more easily.

"Gabe, we're going to clamp the aorta in about three minutes," she told him, while she turned her attention to the lower end of the aneurysm and started to clear the tissues around it.

"We'll be ready." Gabe turned to his assistant, and up went two more units of blood on the stand, ready to go.

Walt was unobtrusively doing a little work from his own side, and it took him only a few moments to clear the inferior vena cava, a vein the thickness of a cigar, off the aorta, a particularly hazardous part of the procedure.

"Thanks, Walt," said Paula, who was clearing the tissues on the other side of the aorta. Then very quietly she said, "I'm really glad you're here."

Now the aneurysm was isolated, pulsating away like a malignant thing, a bomb with only time as its fuse. They all looked at it for a moment, staring at the enemy.

"Crafoord clamp," said Paula, and when the instrument was in her hand, she looked at Gabe over the ether screen that separated him from the operative area. "Thirty seconds," she said.

Gabe nodded and opened the stopcocks wide. The blood started to pour into Maurice's veins.

Twenty seconds of total silence. Paula braced herself. Walt stood there, cool as ever. "You're doing good," he said very quietly. Then a moment later, he said, just as quietly, "That job offer's still open, you know."

"Yeah, thanks, Walt," said Paula, but she smiled in spite of herself at the nerve of the man.

She took a deep breath. "Now," she said, and closed the clamp around the aorta, above the aneurysm. Now there was no arterial blood passing to the lower part of Maurice's body, and she had to work fast and very accurately. At the same time Walt placed another clamp below the aneurysm, and the clock was ticking.

She opened the aneurysm down the middle. It was full of blood clot, and only a narrow channel had remained open. Now she could see the wall of the aorta—it was paper-thin, and as they both knew, they had got there in the nick of time.

It didn't take Paula long to sew in the graft, a plastic tube that replaced the aorta where the aneurysm had been. Walt picked up the curved needle after each stitch, and they worked together in utter silence, concentrating totally on what they were doing.

With only a couple of stitches to put in, Paula said, "I'm going to check the backflow and get the air out of the graft."

Walt gently released the lower clamp for a second, and the blood welled up, just the way it was supposed to.

"Great."

When the last stitch was in and had been tied securely, Paula straightened up, and the rest of the world came back into her consciousness: the other people around the table, the sighing sound of the anesthesia machine blowing air in and out of Maurice's lungs. It still wasn't time to relax, not yet.

"Bottom clamp is off," she said, releasing it completely. The graft filled, swelled. No leaks.

Paula felt her whole body tightening up. "Top clamp coming off," she said. "I'm going to open it slowly."

"His pressure's good and steady," said Gabe. He seemed to be trying hard to encourage Paula by his tone, and she noticed and appreciated it.

Paula bit her lip with anxiety when the full force of Maurice's blood pressure hit the inside of the graft. It tightened, bulged, strained, distended . . . and held.

It wasn't a sigh, but a palpable sense of relief spread all through the operating room, reverberated on the glossy white walls, and leaked out into the hallways and instrument rooms, all the way to the reception area, where a small crowd of doctors and administrators was anxiously waiting.

Paula nodded to the circulator, who turned on the intercom to the reception area. "The graft's in and functioning," said Paula in as matter-of-fact a voice as she could muster, and as soon as she'd spoken the words, a lump rose in her throat and she wasn't able to say anything for several moments.

"Well done," said Walt.

Paula put her head down, hoping that the tears that had formed in her eyes wouldn't roll down her cheeks and embarrass her. A moment later, she had completely recovered herself.

"Check the pulses in his ankles," she told the circulator, and her voice was calm, without a trace of a tremor.

A minute later, the circulator reported back. "Both are strong," she said. "Anterior and posterior tibials both."

Satisfied that blood was now circulating normally below the graft, Paula was about to start closing.

"Let's just make sure he didn't get any other internal injuries in the accident," Walt reminded her, and they took a few moments to check the liver and other organs for damage.

"He's clear," said Paula. "No other injuries. Now let's close up."

Twenty minutes later, Maurice, still asleep, was trundled to the recovery room, a beaming Gabe Pinero leading the way along the short corridor. It had been a perfect case, no complications, no alarms. But Gabe was very aware of the old surgical dictum that was a warning to surgeons who operated on their peers. *If anything can possibly go wrong, it will, and even when nothing can possibly go wrong, it still will.*

But with Maurice Bennett, so far, anyway, they seemed to have got home free. But Gabe's vigilance didn't let up, not for a single second. He'd been caught out before, and like everyone else, he had a great admiration for Maurice, and a fierce desire to do his best for him.

Paula was so exhausted by the strain of the operation

that she stayed in the operating room for a minute after the others had left. She sat down on one of the high stools, and felt all the weight of tiredness and responsibility crowd in on her.

Then she stood up, thanked the nurses and aides, who were checking and cleaning the instruments, wiping the table and mopping the floor, and walked slowly toward the reception area, pulling off her sweat-soaked latex gloves. Walt was already there, telling the little crowd of doctors and administrators what had happened. He turned when Paula appeared and clapped his hands, discreetly, just three times. It was a nice compliment that was not lost on the others.

"How did it go, Dr. Cairns?" asked Charles Kingston.

"Better than average," replied Paula with a smile. Everybody seemed to be there, gathered around her, with the notable exception of Dr. Clifford Abrams.

"She did a superb job," said Walt. "If I'm ever brought in with a rupturing aneurysm, call Dr. Cairns, even if she is an academic."

The crowd had dispersed, and Paula was writing a brief operative note in the chart before going back to check her patient when the intercom crackled.

"Dr. Cairns?" It was high-pitched, barely recognizable as Gabe Pinero's voice, and a cold shiver went down Paula's spine when she heard it.

"Please come to the recovery room," he said, his words stumbling over one another. "We have a really major problem here."

Chapter Forty-four

Paula dropped the chart and ran. There was a small crowd of nurses around one of the beds, and in a second she was there, her heart in her mouth.

"Look," said Gabe. The sheet was pulled up over Maurice's legs, both of which had turned a mottled blue color.

"Oh, my God," said Paula, unwilling to believe what she was seeing. She tried to feel the groin pulses, and went from one side to the other with increasing desperation.

"There's nothing there," said Gabe. "I tried already. His pressure's down too. I'm giving him a fluid load . . ." He glanced up at the two IVs, now running wide open.

"We'll have to take him back in," said Paula dully. "He's clotted his graft. There's nothing getting through."

Gabe hesitated. Paula saw that he was sweating with anxiety, Gabe, of all people, and it didn't make her feel any more confident.

"Honestly, Paula," he said, glancing up at the monitor, "I don't know that he would survive it. I know he's a very fit man, but he's already undergone one very major surgery, and to start all over again . . ."

Paula looked at him and then back at Maurice. He was not conscious, and oh, how she wished she could have asked for his advice at this time.

She took a deep breath, picked up the wall phone next

to her, and dialed a number. "Steve? Is the arterioscope functional? Good. Can you bring it up to the recovery room right away? And pick up the enzyme package from my lab on the way? Yes, it's all ready, Myra knows where it it. We have to use it. I know that, Steve, but I just told you, *we have to use it.*"

Gabe was watching her with disbelief, and his eyes were almost popping out of his head as she spoke. Paula hadn't put the phone down before he was yelling at her, "You can't use that thing! You know the administration refused to allow you to use it only a few days ago. Are you crazy? It's still experimental, and you think you're going to be allowed to use it on Maurice, of all people?"

"I'm not asking permission," said Paula. "There isn't time. Gabe, that scope will work. It was tried in California and worked then. You know about our system to destroy blood clots, and that works too, and we've developed a system to deliver the enzymes through that scope. Please, Gabe, there's no other way, you know that. Look at him, Gabe. If we don't, Maurice is going to die, and we can't let that happen. Will you help me?"

Gabe took a deep breath. Then he turned to the nurses. "Get Dr. Cairns whatever she needs. And let's get this show on the road."

Steve arrived a few minutes later, carrying the box containing the scope, wondering what was going on. Paula told him tersely what was happening.

"You're lucky," he said. "I had the scope gas sterilized two days ago so we'd be ready for the tests." He looked over at Maurice's face, then at his legs. "When did you get permission to use the scope clinically? I thought . . ."

"I didn't," replied Paula, a stubborn look coming over her face. "But we're going to use it anyway. But it won't be your responsibility, it'll be mine."

"Yeah." He hesitated for a moment, thinking about the

implications of what Paula was proposing to do, but it didn't take long for him to make up his mind. "I think we should go in through the left femoral artery and work up to the graft from there," he said. "If you'd like to prepare his leg, I'll get the scope ready." He turned to the head nurse. "Now, I'll need four liters of saline for the infusion, a TV monitor, and if you could show me where the nearest shielded electric outlets are . . ."

While Paula and Steve were getting everything ready, Charles Kingston appeared at the door, and Gabe went over to talk to him. When he came back, he was smiling. "You've got emergency permission to use the scope, this one time only," he said. "And Mr. Kingston says good luck."

Within ten minutes, everything was ready. A TV monitor had been borrowed from the orthopedic room, where it was normally used for arthroscopies, and trundled through to the recovery room, where they had decided to do the procedure rather than move Maurice again. By a stroke of good fortune the connector plugs were standard and matched, so Steve was able to attach the scope.

The tension in the room was so intense it seemed to crackle. People had gathered again outside, and Paula felt all the eyes watching her through the windows in the double doors.

Paula, still in her O.R. greens, prepped both Maurice's groins, put on a pair of latex gloves, and picked up a scalpel from the tray of emergency instruments. She looked at Gabe, who was sitting on a stool behind Maurice's head, holding an oxygen mask over his face. He nodded. Paula made a very short incision in the groin over the femoral artery, hoping that Maurice wouldn't feel it. He didn't; Gabe had given Maurice a short-acting dose of anesthetic, and he didn't move.

It took Paula only a few minutes of frantic work to expose the artery. It was soft, with no pulsation. All the blood that would normally be passing through it was obstructed by the clot that had formed above it.

"We're ready," she said after passing two tapes underneath it.

Steve, standing opposite her, picked up the front end of the scope. "We won't need clamps," he said. "Make a quarter-inch longitudinal incision in the artery. That'll be just enough to let this sucker in."

The TV monitor screen, which had been white, went red. While Steve was manipulating the scope, Paula checked the Gatling cylinder. It was loaded and ready, each numbered channel containing its measured enzyme dose. Paula didn't allow herself to think of the consequences of failure, but the thought that Maurice could die from all this made her hands shake uncontrollably for a moment. Then she forced herself back under control. Maurice's life depended on her; she had to remain able to function accurately and exercise good judgment.

The screen cleared as Steve injected a dose of saline, and a sigh of astonishment arose from the watchers. He had passed the scope up to the place where the clot had blocked the new graft, and it showed up now on the screen like a blob of red gelatin filling the inside of a white tunnel.

"There it is," he breathed. "Paula, we'll be ready to inject in about ten seconds. I'm going to put the tip right up against the clot . . . *now!*"

Paula pushed the button that activated the Gatling equipment. A faint hum came from the electric motors, and the green numbers on the digital pressure gauge flicked up so fast she couldn't read them, then they settled. "Eighty-two psi," she said, her knuckles white inside her gloves from the strain. "We're off and running." She pressed the activate button, and the Gatling cylinder made a thirty-degree rotation. Then there was a faint hiss, the pressure gauge went crazy for a couple of seconds, then came back to exactly eighty-two psi.

"Number two."

Paula pressed the button again, and quickly looked at Maurice's other leg. Of course, nothing had happened yet, and anyway it would have been difficult to see any change under the yellow betadine film. Paula had assigned two nurses to take his ankle pulses, one to each leg.

"Number three." At this point Paula let the automatic timer take over, and with each injection taking exactly four seconds, the entire sequence was over within a minute.

"It's all in." The silence in the room was absolute.

They waited. Nothing happened. Steve looked at Paula questioningly, and she looked at the nurses checking the pulses. Both of them shook their heads.

Paula felt her knees shaking, and for a moment she thought she might faint. Gabe Pinero looked first at her face, then back at the blood-pressure monitor, his own heart sinking.

"Can we take a look inside?" Paula asked Steve.

"Negative," he replied. "I don't want to squirt saline up there if there's a clot breaking up."

"It should have broken up by now," said Paula. Tears were pricking her eyes, and a horrible feeling of helplessness started to take over.

Steve stared at the all-red monitor, then at his arterioscope. It was sinking into his mind that this was the last time he'd ever use it. After two consecutive failures, no hospital anywhere would give permission for it to be used again.

Now the nurses were looking at her, waiting for Paula to tell them officially that the attempt was over.

Gabe Pinero said nothing; his eyes were moist, and he

just gazed sadly at Paula over his mask, waiting too, not making a move until she said the word.

Steve went and sat down on a chair, and put his head between his gloved hands.

"I got a pulse," said the nurse assigned to the left leg. Almost at the same moment the other nurse announced that she too had felt a pulse.

"Getting stronger," said the first one excitedly.

Paula looked at the artery where the scope had been inserted. "We got it," she said, her voice high with emotion. The artery had filled suddenly and was pulsating again.

"I'm going to take the scope out," she told Steve.

"Don't you want to take a look inside the graft?" he asked.

"I don't need to," she said, beaming under her mask. "Just look at his legs!"

Within a few seconds Maurice's legs had gone from a cold, mottled blue to a warm pink.

"Let's close up and get outa here," said Paula happily to the nurse who was acting as scrub tech. "Give me a 6×0 proline suture for the artery, then Dexons for the fascia. We'll close the incision with clips."

Epilogue

Nicky Millway called Paula as she had promised. "The finals are next Saturday," she said in a voice that lacked her usual confidence. "Do you think you'll be able to come?"

"Sure," replied Paula. "I've been looking forward to it. Can I bring my boyfriend?"

She had seen Nicky in follow-up several times, but had met with stubborn resistance when she suggested that her tendons weren't well enough healed for her to play in a tournament.

"I've been playing every day," protested Nicky. "And I'm not straining it, I swear."

Paula saw Sam and Charlene Millway sitting near the end of one of the benches, and, followed by Steve, she came and sat next to them. Paula introduced Steve.

Sam, looking pathetically sad and frailer than ever, leaned over and shook Steve's hand. "Congratulations," he said. "I read about your appointment in the paper."

The day after Seth's arrest, Myra Jennings had gone to the dean of the School of Medicine and told him what had happened with Dr. Clifford Abrams, even how much he'd paid her for her services. Within twenty-four hours, under the threat of prosecution, Clifford Abrams had sent in his resignation, and Steve had been appointed chief of the lab pro tem.

"I'm so sorry about Seth," said Paula in a low voice to Charlene.

"They don't think he'll stand trial," she whispered back, looking stricken. "He's really gone crazy. He didn't recognize me when I went to see him. He keeps shouting about somebody called Vince. The doctor said he means Coletti, that man who disappeared."

"Where's Nicky?" asked Steve, anxious to meet Paula's young patient.

"With her team," replied Charlene, happy to change the subject. "She'll be here in a minute." She smiled at Paula. "She's so excited that you're coming."

Paula reached for Steve's hand and looked around. There was a crowd of about a hundred people, about half of them from the visiting team; it was a beautiful day, neither too hot nor too humid.

Charlene pushed a strand of gray hair out of her face. "We saw Dr. Bennett on TV last evening," she said. "We didn't agree with everything he said, but he sure looked wonderful."

"We discharged him from the hospital this morning," said Paula. "He's an amazing man. He wanted to go back to work on Monday, but we talked him out of it."

Paula watched the kids running around excitedly between matches, and smiled to herself. These kids didn't seem so different from her at that age.

Nicky came up, looking radiant.

"How's your foot?" asked Paula after giving her a big hug. She was still very concerned about what this strenuous activity could do to the tendons.

"Fine. I've been doing everything you said." Nicky glanced at Steve, then whispered in Paula's ear, "He's just *gorgeous!*"

Sam, who had seemed in a daze, said suddenly to

Paula, "Did you hear they caught the two men who tried to kill him?"

Paula nodded. She'd actually been in the hospital when Chip and his friend got past the security desk with fake IDs. They had got as far as his room, and only the alertness of a detective guarding Maurice had saved his life. "Yes," she replied. "And I hope that will be the end of it."

A whole bunch of Nicky's friends were sitting close by; Paula had met some of them in Nicky's hospital room, and several of them came by rather shyly to say hello. Nicky went off to get ready for her match, the last one of the afternoon. So far the two teams were neck and neck.

"Nicky's is the deciding match," Charlene told Paula. "She's playing that girl over there."

Her opponent was a long-legged, tall, skinny young woman of about the same age, but about six inches taller than Nicky. She had freckles, short red hair, a rather sullen expression, and was sitting with her parents a few seats away from Paula. The mother was a thin, redheaded older version of her daughter, wearing a long-brimmed white cap. The father, in a similar cap, was chubby and restless, and they were both talking earnestly to their daughter.

"Remember she has a bad foot," Paula could hear the mother saying "Keep her running. Jerk her from one side to the other. Sandra, are you listening to me?"

Sandra said she had to go now, and left for the changing rooms.

When Nicky and Sandra reappeared together in their tennis outfits and carrying their racquets, there was a ragged round of applause from the audience.

It was to be a three-set match, and as soon as they got started, it was clear they were well matched. Sandra was strong and fast, with a hard, accurate serve and a powerful return that just skimmed the net; Nicky had more

shots in her repertoire, played for position, and had a better technique, with a sophisticated top spin that astonished Paula.

Nicky won the first set, but Sandra wiped her out on
the second, and to Paula's severe concern, Nicky developed a limp she couldn't disguise. "Make her run!" Sandra's mother kept crying, until Paula wanted to go over
and throttle her.

Nicky seemed to collect herself while they were resting
after the second set, and ran out when the umpire called
them, just to show Sandra her foot wasn't going to lose
her the match.

Nicky won the first game, breaking Sandra's serve, and
after that each girl managed to hold serve. At five-four, it
was Nicky's serve for the match, but Paula was now very
anxious about her foot. Nicky was tiring fast, her limp was
severe, and she was half hopping on the other foot when
she ran. Paula thought that the coach would stop the
match, and mentioned it to Charlene. "He's scared of
her," replied Charlene. "If he stopped the match now, he
knows she'd kill him."

Nicky took a little longer to come out this time, and
walked slowly to her position behind the service line. Sandra, crouched, waiting, looking tired too but very confident.

Nicky's first ball hit the net and stuck in the mesh, and
there was a nervous titter from the crowd. Paula found
herself biting a knuckle and holding tightly onto Steve
with her other hand. Nicky's second ball was wide, and
Sandra trotted happily over to the other side of the court.
There hadn't been many double faults so far, but this one
had come at an opportune moment for her. All she had to
do was win this game; in Nicky's weakened state, she
knew the final one would be a pushover.

Love-thirty. Nicky's friends were silent. Two more points to Sandra, and the match was over.

But Nicky wasn't dead yet. She put in two great serves, both down the middle, winning the point each time.

At deuce, the atmosphere in the court was so tense that even Sandra's mother was quiet, her bony knuckles gripping the rail in front of her.

Nicky was looking desperate; her blond hair was straggly and soaked with sweat, and although she was still trying to run down every ball, it was costing her a great effort and obvious pain. Paula couldn't stand it; she could see those repaired tendons, overextended and overworked, finally giving way. . . .

Nicky stood, foot just behind the service line, near the middle line. She'd served all her down-the-middle serves from that position, and Sandra edged over to be ready for it. But Nicky's ball went fast into the outer corner, and Sandra had to leap to get to it. Her return was high, and Nicky got into position, waited for the ball to come down, Sandra ran the wrong way, and Nicky smashed it into the opposite court.

Advantage Nicky.

Paula closed her eyes, feeling she couldn't look any more. Something terrible was going to happen, she was sure of it. She'd hear the snap of those tendons parting. . . . She forced herself to watch.

Nicky's first serve was out, and her second serve was weak, and Sandra jumped all over it, rocketing the ball back to land at Nicky's feet. But Nicky just managed to scoop it up, and got it back over the net. But now she was in a bad position and knew it. All Sandra needed to do was drop the ball over the net, and there was simply no way Nicky could get to it in time. Finally resigned to her fate, Nicky lowered her racquet and a little sob of sheer frustration escaped her. With all the will in the world, she couldn't make her legs run. But Sandra, poised for the shot, overhit the ball and it sailed out of the court and the match was over.

The kids cheered and ran out onto the court to surround Nicky, and somebody gave her a bunch of flowers wrapped in cellophane.

Nicky hobbled over, kissed Sam and Charlene, then came and gave the flowers to Paula.

Paula, laughing and crying at the same time, hugged her until they were both breathless, and at that moment Paula realized that the generation gap wasn't that wide after all.

OFFICIAL **MUSIC TO YOUR EARS** COUPON

Enclosed please find _____ proof-of-purchase coupons from my Penguin USA purchase.

I would like to apply these coupons towards the purchase of the following Mercury artist(s): (Please write in artist selection and title)

_____   _____

_____   _____

_____   _____

I understand that my coupons will be applied towards my purchase at these discounted prices. *

Two book coupons	CD $13.99	CT $8.99
Four book coupons	CD $12.99	CT $7.99
Six book coupons	CD $11.99	CT $6.99

(* Once coupons are sent, there is no limit to the titles ordered at this reduced rate)

Please check one:

___Enclosed is my check/money order made out to: **Sound Delivery**

___Please charge my purchases to:

Amex#	_____	exp. date_____
MC#	_____	exp. date_____
Visa#	_____	exp. date_____
Discover#	_____	exp. date_____
Diners#	_____	exp. date_____

Please send coupons to: **Sound Delivery**
                            P.O. Box 2213
                            Davis, CA 95617-2213

NAME_____

ADDRESS_____

CITY_____STATE_____ZIP_____

All orders shipped 2-Day UPS mail from time of receipt.
Offer expires December 31, 1994 • Printed in the USA

And everyone who redeems a coupon is automatically entered into the **MUSIC TO YOUR EARS SWEEPSTAKES!** The Grand Prize Winner will win a trip to see a Mercury Records artist in concert anywhere in the continental United States.

For complete sweepstakes rules, send a stamped, self-addressed envelope to: Rules, MUSIC TO YOUR EARS SWEEPSTAKES, Penguin USA/Mass Market, Department KB, 375 Hudson St., New York, NY 10014.
Offer good in U.S., its territories and Canada (if sending check or money order, Canadian residents must convert to U.S. currency).